Rise

of the

Alchemist

by

Craig Gallant

ZMOK
BOOKS

The Rise of the Alchemist
Cover from De Chemia Senioris, 1566
This edition published in 2020

Zmok Books is an imprint of

Winged Hussar Publishing, LLC
1525 Hulse Rd, Unit 1
Point Pleasant, NJ 08742

Copyright © Zmok Books
ISBN 978-1-945430-87-9
LCN 2021932617

Bibliographical References and Index
1. Fantasy. 2. Alternate History. 3. Dystopian

Winged Hussar Publishing, LLC All rights reserved
For more information
visit us at www.wingedhussarpublishing.com

Twitter: WingHusPubLLC
Facebook: Winged Hussar Publishing LLC

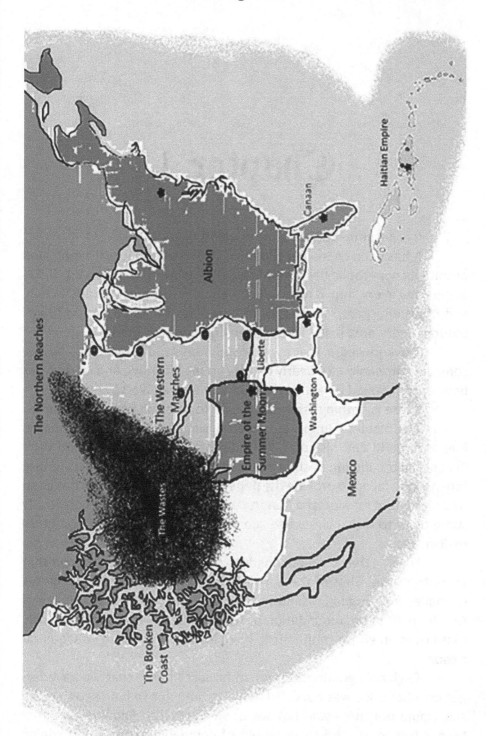

Chapter 1

It is autumn, 1860 and my England is dying.

It has been over a decade since I first made that realization, and despite its hyperbolic flair, the phrase haunts my every thought. It has dogged my every step, it has skulked behind me in sunshine and in rain, and it has whispered tauntingly in my ear for hours on end as I have scoured every dust-laden library from Edinburgh to Cardiff.

The knowledge that my beloved homeland is dying has been a constant companion for nearly half my young life, now. And lately it has been accompanied by a thought, if possible, even worse.

There is nothing any of us can do to forestall England's demise.

The blame, I suppose, could be placed upon the unlamented King George III and his coterie of advisors and confidantes and their ill-conceived handling of the troubles in the American colonies. Entire forests have fallen to provide the paper upon-which that story has been told and retold for almost a hundred years. Although there is obviously some truth to that, I choose to see our plight in far harsher and more realistic terms.

For it is the so-called Kingdom of Albion, the hated nation that arose from the ashes of the uprisings in the colonies, that now closes its mailed fist around England's throat. It is the thrice cursed House of Arnold, built upon a foundation of two-fold betrayal and infernal luck, that drives an entire continent to howl for the death of my once-great nation.

England's greatness is not so far lost in time that we have forgotten what once was ours. There was a time not so long ago that the sun would not, no, *could* not set upon the British Empire. Alas, that time is lost to us. The stranglehold of damnable Albion's burgeoning fleets has sent too many brave English sailors to the bottom of the sea. We have lost our far-flung holdings and now cower upon our few, small islands like a beaten cur, waiting only for the ageless demon, King Benjamin of the House of Arnold, to decide the time has come to crush us once and for all.

I had decided that I, for one, would not stand idly by and await that day's coming. There must be something that could be done. My early studies at Oxford and Cambridge gained me some small modicum of fame in academic circles for my work with the strange energy fields that surround living organisms and interact with their environment. In those early, heady days of my work I had dreams of taking my place beside the great natural philosophers such as Charles Darwin, whose work, before the English captains could no longer support his journeys, opened up entire conceptual worlds.

But Darwin languishes now in Down House, barely able to rouse himself to intellectual discourse, so disheartened as he become. And so many of his generation have followed him. Having been cut off from the wider world, they either turn their minds inward, ignoring the realities of England's plight, or they founder, unable to come to grips with a world in which they are nothing more than shades, their ideas and theories no more esteemed than a lunatic uncle kept in the upstairs flat.

I will not be so easily silenced, however. I have tracked tantalizing snippets of folklore and legend from out of the esteemed libraries of our greatest universities and symposia and into the overgrown back trails of England, into the dark and forest-covered hinterlands and beyond, into the very mists of her earliest days.

I have poured through the ancient English tales. I have gone farther still, to Rome, Greece, and even Mesopotamia and Egypt, finding tantalizing similarities, parallel structures, and hidden scraps of hope in those primeval accounts. Coupled with my own researches, I can only conclude that there is more to these stories than has been assumed for hundreds of years. In these tales of heroes and legends, could it be that some of the more fantastical elements, dismissed as metaphor and hyperbole for all the history of modern academic study, actually contain some grain of truth?

And if such truth might exist, if there is some veracity to these legends, might there not be some hope, as well, for England's current plight? Might there not be some sling stone hidden in the mists of time with which our fiendish Goliath might be felled?

As ever, when my thoughts raced along these familiar paths, my hand slipped into my pocket to touch the cloth-wrapped object I always kept there. Ever since I plucked it unceremoniously from that dusty old museum cottage in Britany, having skulked through half of the Kingdom of France and out again, I have never allowed it to leave my person. The French had no interest in it, certainly, and as I first gazed upon it, opaque with dust and grime on its spider-infested shelf, I despaired. There was no sense of power or awe about the stone, and certainly nothing that cried out to me concerning one of the most powerful legendary figures of our shared history.

The object my papers referred to as Merlin's stone.

But after I got the stone home to Bromley St. Peter and St. Paul and cleaned it up, I will admit that its beauty captivated me. There is still no sense of power or majesty about it. It is inert in every way I could conceive to test. But there is an undeniable beauty to the thing's dark inner core and the almost oil-like sheen of blue over that onyx heart. Even in my pocket, I can feel the unnatural weight of the thing. It defies explanation, but the drive it set in my heart was enough to push me from my comfortable position at Cambridge, from the arms of my loving fiancé Felicity, and onto this God forsaken monstrosity of a steamship, the *Ett Hjerte* out of Oslo.

As if the constant looming shadow of England's fall was not enough, the very boards beneath my feet, vibrating to the thrum of the ancient steam engines deep below, were a constant reminder that I was forced to seek passage on a Norwegian ship to cross the Atlantic. What English captains remain categorically refuse to brave the cold expanse, knowing that the huge behemoths of the Albian fleet scour it night and day for the fading hope of adding another British ship to the list of the dead.

Captain Larsen had been polite during the crossing, as I would expect, given how much gold weighed down his own pocket on my behalf. His crew has been another story, however. There is little respect remaining among the common folk of Europe for the shade that England has become. And in few places is this most obvious as among those who make their living on the sea.

Only one man, Jan, a young sailor from Oksval, had given me any attention at all. Jan was fascinated with his people's folklore and was homesick on his first voyage onto the ocean. Many of the fears that plagued my own sleep troubled him as well, and we would often talk, sometimes for hours when he was off duty, about our homes, and the tales of our people, to avoid thinking about the Albians, the Haitians, and the myriad other dangers of the Atlantic.

A certain amount of trepidation would be expected in any case as we plied the Atlantic, making ready to thread the needle between the string of islands that make up the Haitian Empire and the peninsular Papal State of Canaan thrusting southward from the bulk of the continent. If the threat of Albion warships was not enough, the reputation of the Haitian pirate fleet carried with it an entirely deeper level of dread, especially for crews whose flesh carries the pallor of Europe.

But I needed to continue my research, and I had exhausted the resources of the more 'advanced' cultures of the Old World. I needed to find a people more closely allied to their mythic past, a nation that still walked with their gods and spirits, so to speak, and beg them to take me along. I had researched the manifold native tribes and clans of the Americas, and believed they were my best hope for unlocking the mysteries of my ancient stone, and perhaps guiding me towards the weapon I seek. And even I, locked in my ivory tower half a world away, was able to glean from what word leaked back to England from our former holdings, that the Empire of the Summer Moon, deep in the heart of that strange and alien continent, held my best, indeed quite possibly my only hope.

Most European travelers seeking to venture to the vast prairie nation might take a comfortable ship from any of a number of ports on a short crossing to the Albian port cities of Dare, Portsmouth, or Boston, and thence overland threw the kingdom to their Western Marches and beyond.

But that path was closed to an Englishman. The very crime of English blood was enough to cost a man his life in Albion. Nearly a century of fomented resentment and demagoguery had riled the subjects of the House of Arnold into a froth of fury and indignation that might well see an Englishman hanged from the nearest tree before a constable was even called.

And so, if an Englishman were to seek to meet with the Five Bands of the Comanche who rule the Empire of the Summer Moon, he needed to seek a ship carrying the flag of one of the neutral nations, hold his breath as he crosses the chopping Atlantic, thread the Caribbean needle, and cross the Gulf of Mexico to New Orleans, the capital of the free French republic of Liberté. From there, one might hope to travel overland by steamship, horse, foot, or even airship north to the Comanche territories.

All of which went a long way to explain the crew's ambivalence toward me, without my having to look too deeply at the fallen nature of England's name on the world stage.

But it did little to ease my own resentment and feelings of inadequacy.

The *Ett Hjerte* had been at sea for almost a week, traveling south by south west across the Atlantic, and we had blessedly seen no sign of Albion or the Haitians. Truth to tell, we in England knew little of the power of Albion, as most English who face their ships never come home to tell of it. And as for the Haitians, we know almost nothing. They still use sailing ships, but other than that? We have only vague rumor and tall tales.

What that says about their own efficacy, I didn't like to think about with a deck pitching beneath my feet.

Captain Larsen had been polite at meals, and would occasionally approach me for conversation on deck, but his responses were often perfunctory, and I had the feeling he wasn't really listening. As the sun began to touch the waves off to our right on our seventh night at sea, I watched an answering darkness that had been building to our south all day; I could only reflect, again, on the loneliness of my chosen path.

"Mr. Hawke, I trust your day has been pleasant?" Anders Larsen was an older man, probably in his 50s at least. He kept his blue uniform pristine despite the cramped quarters aboard the snarling *Ett Hjerte,* and I had to admire the man for his commitment to regular shaving aboard a ship that lacked any internal plumbing to speak of. I wondered, not for the first time, how many of his men contributed to the morning ablutions that resulted in such well-kept sideburns.

"Captain." I nodded, easing one elbow onto the railing and looking out over the bow of the ship to the building darkness. "Looks like the good weather is abandoning us."

Larsen cast a glance toward the lowering clouds and shrugged. "We've had more than we should expect, this time of year. We were bound to hit weather sooner or later." He peered longer at the distant clouds with a frown. "Although, I'd have to tell you, it does look to to get interesting for us."

As was his usual wont, he asked a few vague questions about my research, quirking one white eyebrow up, as always when I tried to explain to him the connection, I theorized between the energy field I could easily prove to him surrounded each man on the ship, and the ancient stories that attributed fantastical powers to the heroes of the distant past.

Eventually, as he often did, he simply shook his head. "I often forget how close to madness Albion has driven you English, Mr. Hawke. I should travel with your countrymen more often, as a reminder."

That stung as much as it had the first time, he'd said it, with that half-smile nestled between his muttonchops, the dark twinkle in his eyes. This time, I didn't try to hide my annoyance.

It only added to my frustration when he smiled even wider.

"Mr. Hawke, you'll have to forgive me if it's a little hard to hear a man of science, as you describe yourself, talking about magic and fairies."

The familiar anger flared, my vision tinged a dangerous red, but I did everything I could to temper my breathing. "Captain, I speak of neither magic nor fairies, but of possible flaws in our own understanding of—"

He put up one gnarled hand. "I meant no disrespect, sir. But I don't understand it, and if you'll forgive me a little observation of my own, you often seem more than a little confused yourself. I have seen more than one man turned from the light of day by anger or jealousy or resentment. It's all well and good to question current understanding, of course. It is how we push every boundary mankind has ever faced. But would you not admit, at least, that the vast majority of challenges to current understand prove, eventually, that current understanding is understood for a reason?"

The anger continued to build, despite my best efforts, and I am honest enough with myself to admit, this usually means it's because I've heard a grain of unpalatable truth.

"And yet, push we must, yes?" I looked out over the ocean again, knowing that somewhere off to the right was the enormous kingdom that has sought to bring England low for so long. "Even if it makes no sense, surely there is a nobility in struggling for the sake of the fight?"

Larsen looked at me for a moment, and I had no idea what he was thinking. Then he nodded and looked away. "There is always nobility in a righteous battle, Mr. Hawke. I won't deny you that."

The silence between us stretched into uncomfortable minutes before, with a grunt about duties, he pushed himself away from the railing and made his way toward the forward wheelhouse.

For a very long time I stayed there, staring out to sea, my eyes shifting from the darkening horizon to the impenetrable wall of cloud to the south. It was dark enough now; I thought I could make out flashes of lightning flaring from within the churning storm. It was going to be a rough night.

Chapter 2

I was in the cramped little hold the captain graciously called a cabin, going over the small collection of books that represented nearly all my research from the last few years, when the shouting on deck took on a higher, more jagged tone. Over the constant creaking of the hull and the distant chugging of the steam engines, I thought I could also detect a strange, deep, buzzing sound that put me ill at ease, although I could not have said why.

I made my way, as hastily as I could, given the constant lurching motion of the floor beneath my feet, above decks, meaning to seek out Captain Anders in the forward wheelhouse. But as I came out of the small stair-shed into a warm, biting rain, I could see Anders was already out on deck, standing at the *Ett Hjerte's* bow, staring back, up over the wheelhouse.

I turned without thinking, shielding my upturned eyes from the rain with one hand, and felt a chill race down my spine despite the thick, tepid water running over my skin.

A light was stabbing out of the sky, down toward the ship. It swept from the bow, where Anders was standing with several of his officers, aft, passed over me without pausing, and then illuminated a small clump of sailors standing at the stern, all frozen as they looked straight up into the light.

The buzzing I had half-heard belowdecks was much more pronounced here, and although I had never encountered anything like this before, that spear of light could only mean one thing: An Albian airship was approaching.

I looked back into the darkness of the stairwell. The desire to dive back down into the murk was almost overwhelming. According to the dictates of the Albian throne, it was a capital crime for an Englishman to be found crossing either ocean to the New World.

Suddenly, my decision to run off after these last threads of my research seemed the utter height of foolishness. Was I going to die here, in the middle of the ocean, never to see England, or Felicity, or my parents or friends again? Would they just dump my body into the water and that would be that?

But hiding belowdecks was hardly the action of an innocent man. And I had been instructed on how to dress by Captain Larsen. I was wearing drab work clothes, the same muted blues of the rest of the crew. If I could make my way into a huddled group, and trust them not to give me away, I might be okay. This could be nothing more than a routine customs inspection, in which case we might even be headed south again soon enough.

I kept repeating this to myself as I eased my way aft toward a knot of seamen who had been working with a pump and hose snaking down through a drain in the deck.

I was nearly into the group, most looking up, but one or two casting odd glances in my direction, when a sharp crack echoed across the deck.

It was just bad luck on my part that I was staring at the man . I was looking directly into his blue eyes when his head was flung violently downward, the rest of his body clumsily following. My little group shattered like thin glass, the men running in all directions.

"No! No! We are a licensed vessel out of Oslo!" Larsen had a speaking tube to his mouth and was screaming himself hoarse, but it didn't seem to matter. More cracks, gunshots, I realized now, were ringing out. As I cowered behind a gray cowling, watching the men around me die, I experienced a thought I had never entertained before.

I was going to die.

Maybe not in that moment, although that seemed likely; but this realization was more profound. Even if I escaped the massacre aboard the *Ett Hjerte* there would come a day, soon or late, when my life would end. And I had voluntarily placed myself upon a path that would see that day, in all likelihood, would come more soon than late.

More shots rang out, and more men died. There were also additional spears of light slashing down now, and I could see the weapons fire, brief snaps of brilliant white like lightning in the darkness behind the beams. They seemed to be coming from several firing positions hovering above us. Judging by the dispersion of the muzzle flashes, I thought the airship's gondola might be about half the size of the *Ett Hjerte*. That would make it a large airship indeed.

My curious mathematics were cut short when the constant snap of rifle fire was drowned out by a deep-throated roar. The forward wheelhouse shattered in a bright orange fireball that sent splinters of wood and jagged bits of metal spinning in an expanding ball of heat and light.

Larsen and his officers, huddled now by a winch in the bow, shielded themselves with upraised arms. At least one man was down, I saw, his body still and lifeless on the pitching deck. The wood there, already slick with rain, was running pink with the blood of the dying crew.

"Please, stop!" Larsen had fumbled the speaking tube to his lips again, but in his position, huddled against the painted steal of the winch housing, shoulders hunched against the destruction of his dying ship, his words were incoherent.

It didn't seem to matter in any case, as another roar boomed out overhead. This time I caught the muzzle flash from the corner of my eye. There was a cannon up there somewhere, as of course there would be. And the momentary flash of weapon fire illuminated a dark, boxy shape suspended beneath an enormous silvery shadow like a whale. The gondola was studded with firing ports and vision slits, with two large fins extending from the back, holding what looked like massive engines. Propellers were spinning slowly behind these, helping the ungainly-looking creation keep its station.

I felt a moment's anger. England owned nothing remotely like this monstrous war machine. The most advanced lighter-than-air ships the United Kingdom could boast were the small two-man vessels that occasionally rose over London, more to prove a point than for any practical effect. But then, no one else on the planet really had anything like this terror either. Albion, alone, had managed to make weapons of the Montgolfier's' dream. Their mastery of ceramics and metallurgy were said to be at the heart of these warbirds, and they guarded their secrets most carefully.

The second cannon shot had torn out the aft of the *Ett Hjerte*, the deck bucking and breaking apart beneath my fingers. I heard another roar, thinking that the thing overhead was firing again, but this sound just went on and on, accompanied with a worrying gurgling sound. The ship was taking on water, probably through the wound that had just been torn into her stern, and the world began to tilt towards the terrible, splintered hole.

Several more rifle shots rang out, and then everything was silent save the buzzing of the airship's engines, the soft sounds of the building rain, and the rushing of the ocean making its way deeper and deeper into the *Ett Hjerte's* hull.

"Unidentified vessel." The voice was peremptory, unconcerned with the death and carnage reigning below. "Gather by the bow of your ship, hands raised over your heads, or I will finish this here and now."

I saw, at once, most of the crew were making their slow, stunned way toward the captain. Larsen was pulling himself to his feet, hands already over his head. Every eye was bent skyward, none of them giving me the slightest glance. But I knew it was only a matter of time. Albion was not at odds with Norway. There was no reason for this ship to have been attacked without provocation. I knew, even if the crew had not made the realization yet, that whatever had convinced the captain of the airship to attack, he wouldn't be able to leave any survivors. They would come up with a pretense, and I thought I could guess what that pretense would be.

But the crew was too shocked to follow that tangled line of logic now, and as I made my way forward with all the rest, it looked as if none of them were giving me a second thought.

When the survivors of the attack were all gathered in the bow, the voice overhead spoke again.

"Now, lest you think to make some ill-conceived move once we've come aboard—"

Another gunshot rang out, and a sailor, seemingly chosen at random, spun onto the wet, canted deck in a sodden, bleeding heap.

The men around him moaned and whined as they pressed closer together. We all watched, half in horror half in awe, as ropes dropped out of the darkness. Several soldiers in dark uniforms slid down, immediately swinging short carbines around to point in our direction. The men wore black scarves bound around their lower faces against the wind and rain, their eyes shadowed by the brims of black knit caps. It made the event seem even more surreal. I noticed several men disappear belowdecks and figured they must have been sent to search for anything of value; something, perhaps, that might be used to justify their attack.

Or maybe they were just curious.

We were surrounded, tightly bunched up, with killers every-where. and surrounded by killers. After what seemed like an eternity, the men who had disappeared below were back, gathered amidships behind the shattered wheelhouse, their plunder collected in a large, waxed canvas bag. I wondered if my books were in that bag or if they were already lost below, soaked in salt water, ink dissolving into clouds of useless color.

Another line was dropped, and I expected to watch them secure the bag to that, but instead, another figure dropped down from above. Two more landed lightly behind the newcomer, taking up positions off either shoulder in an unmistakable guarding posture.

Surely the captain of the beast above us wouldn't come down in person?

The figure came closer, collar raised against the approaching storm, cap pulled low, and I was shocked to see that it was a woman. It was not unusual to find women in the military in England either, up and down the chain of command; but it had never crossed my mind that the architect of our bloody, unprovoked destruction might be a member of the fairer sex.

She looked us over with disdain, then singled Larsen out of the crowd. She tilted her head to the side and spoke, her eyes never leaving the captain's pale face, and one of her bodyguards moved forward, grabbing Larsen by his lapel and dragging him out of our huddled group.

"Captain?" Her voice was crisp and low, carrying over the sounds of storm and fire like a pistol shot.

Larsen tried to nod but it was as if had lost control of his neck; his head just wobbled aimlessly for a moment before he gave up trying.

Again, the woman leaned over to one side and said something to her companions. The man who had fetched Larsen from the bosom of his crew reached out lazily and slapped the man, almost idly, across the face.

Larsen shook himself, as a man coming out of a nightmare, and tried to stand a little straighter.

"Captain, would you like to declare what contraband you were carrying, to expedite this process so my people and I can get on with our evening before that storm begins in earnest?"

The woman's accent was not entirely unfamiliar. She did not sound British, but neither did she sound strange to my Anglophilic ear. She tapped one booted foot, waiting for a reply, while Larsen's mouth opened and closely foolishly.

This time she didn't speak: she just nodded, and this time the guard's blow was not a slap, but a sharp strike that sent the captain to the tilting deck.

"You might want to think about answering my questions before your ship sinks beneath you." She looked down at the inoffensive little man, and I was struck by the sheer hatred in her eyes.

"Captain Peyton." Another soldier stepped forward, pulling a dark bandana away from his mouth and pointing upward. "Lieutenant Alistair is signaling. We need to get off the ship. The wall of the storm is very nearly upon us."

The woman nodded; eyes still locked on the sniveling Norwegian that had been kind to me. "I will ask one last time, Captain, and if you are unable to answer, I will consign this wreck and your surviving crew to the depths without a second thought."

But you're going to kill us all, anyway. I very nearly said the words, knowing they would be the end of me as my accent would have given me away. But my jaw was so clenched with fury and fear that I barely made a whimper, thank God.

"Please..." Larsen pushed himself up to his hands and knees. "We have nothing."

I knew what she was looking for: an excuse. Any excuse to kill us all that would fit onto a brief report so she could go on her way. Could the airship rise above the bad weather? Could those enormous propellers push the ship fast enough to escape?

Again, I was reminded of the vast gulf between my home and this realm I had set out to destroy.

And how soon was that ridiculous dream crushed by the juggernaut of reality?

"We have nothing. Please." Larsen shook his head again, trying to rise without success.

Peyton nodded, and this time her guard slid a long, heavy-looking revolver from a holster under his coat, raised it, cocked it, and fired in one fluid motion. Larsen was thrown down to the deck again, this time still as a stone, contributing his own blood to the pink foam sloshing across the splintered wood.

"We've got an English!" The words were harshly accented, but I turned, and I couldn't even conjure a look of hurt. These men were grasping at straws in a whirlwind. They had no idea what was about to happen to us all. I understood completely what had led to this new betrayal, and I could not condemn the man for it. Even if we had spent countless hours during the voyage talking about the folklore of Norway. Jan's terrified, round eyes now had nothing of the soft nostalgia of homesickness they had carried throughout those pleasant conversations.

Captain Peyton's head turned sharply at the words; one dark eyebrow raised almost to the brim of her peaked cap. "Excuse me?"

And the damn burst. They might have been willing to let me stay amongst them; many may have even forgotten I was there. But between Larsen's murder and the young man's sudden declaration, there was no other way things could have gone. I found myself pushed out of the group, toward the Albian captain and her cohort. Every gun on the ship swung around to cover me, and I stopped as soon as I could on the slick deck, my hands straight up over my head.

"No." The woman sounded amused. She took two steps toward me, her guards maintaining station off her shoulders, and tilted her head just a little to get a better glimpse of my face. "An *Englishman*?"

I had had several moments to acclimate myself to the idea of death, and perhaps that gave me a little courage. I had known death was inevitable the moment they shattered the ship. Now I was just going to die a little sooner than the rest, was all.

"I am." I stood tall; the example of the late Captain Larsen's cringing form still fresh in my mind."

Her smile widened. "Let me guess. London?"

It wasn't, actually. Bromley, or Bromley St. Peter and St. Paul, is a small suburb just south of London, but I didn't think that was the moment for a casual conversation concerning the capitol of England and its surrounding municipalities.

I just nodded.

She stopped smiling.

"It's been a while since we captured our last spy, Beau, has it not?"

One of her bodyguards nodded but said nothing.

"I've been hoping to meet another one of you bastards. The Admiralty always rewards those who bring them such little toys." Her eyes were narrow slits, shadowed by the brim of her hat. "By the time I get you back to port, you'll be singing like a songbird."

I wanted to say something. I wanted to protest my innocence, or spit defiance. But the blatant hopelessness of any of that was clear to me, even in my state of advanced panic and rising anger. I wanted to ask her what she thought of her own nation's crimes, considerably bloodier and long-reaching than anything England had even been capable of in over a century. The anger and injustice closed my throat, choking out my voice. I could hear the blood pounding in my ears as I stared at her sneering face.

The pounding continued, rising in tone and pitch, pain rising up behind my eyes to match its hellish pulsing beat. I was lost in my own hell, carrying the music of my own destruction in my mind.

And then I saw Captain Peyton flinch, most minutely, in time with the latest strike on the drum in my head.

She had heard it.

And then she turned, looking up and over my head, brows drawn down, rain streaming over her cheeks like tears.

Against my will, I turned as well, terrified at what fresh horror might be so revealed.

The storm wall was almost upon us, the wind picking up in violent gusts, the rain starting to pour down all around. The beams of light connecting the airship to the slowly listing *Ett Hjerte* were more solid, somehow, with the sheer volume of water they pushed through.

For a moment, it seemed like an enormous shadow welled up within the dark barrier of the approaching storm. I felt almost as if I could reach out and part the wall like a curtain.

And then the curtain of darkness *did* part. An enormous figure came gliding out of the wall of rain and wind, white teeth gleaming in an ebon face; the cruelest smile I had ever seen. It was a man but towering above the wreckage like a giant from the old stories, a length of chain dangling from either outstretched hand, their broken ends swinging wildly with the force of the wind.

Above us the Albian airship exploded.

Chapter 3

The survivors of the *Ett Hjerte* fell screaming to their faces as the air above the shattered vessel flared with light. I shielded my eyes, both from the whipping rain and from the searing heat of the airship's death, and watched, my mouth open, as I caught my first unimpeded glimpse of an Albian airship in all its transient glory.

Only a glimpse. Even as I watched, the thing disintegrated before my astonished eyes.

The elongated balloon from which the ship hung was enormous, easily fifty yards from one rounded end to the other. The fabric of the vessel was blazing, flashing away in the building winds in ribbons of yellow and orange fire. It looked as if a sleek black ship's hull was attached beneath the bag, where the basket of a Montgolfier balloon would hang. Except that the many ports and windows looking out from the structure would have meant its instant sinking should it ever attempt to float as a conventional ship.

And even as that thought occurred to me, I realized that this theory was about to be tested.

The hull was plummeting, the short wings containing the propeller housings folding up and flying away as it fell. Shreds of fabric and fire trailed after it even as the remains of the balloon flashed upward into the storm. The fires were quenched by the deluge as they scrambled to eat up the few remaining scraps of silvered material.

But the dangling hull was not left to fall in peace, but seemed, to my untrained eye, to be struck several times by brutal, hellish hammer blows in rapid counterpoint to rumbling detonations coming from behind the enormous approaching figure.

Before the hull could even touch the roiling, storm-tossed waves, it exploded in a blast so violent that it flattened the water beneath it, sending wreckage spinning madly off into the sheeting rain.

When I looked back at the Albian captain I was in a daze, entirely out of my depth, now, but certain of one thing: I couldn't be in any worse a situation than I had been moments before.

Captain Peyton's eyes were huge in the fitful light of my burning ship. The solid beams of brightness from the airship's lamps were gone, of course, having gone dark after swinging wildly out into the storm for one fitful moment. The Albian officer turned back to stare at the enormous man approaching, and only then did my battered intellect fill in the necessary details to bring me into line with what I was seeing.

It was a huge figurehead crashing over the waves toward us. The huge man's waist emerged from the graceful lines of a ship's prow, and over his burly shoulders I could now see reefed sails above thick, straight masts. The massive ship came about smartly, broadside weapon ports peering blindly down upon us as, high up on her deck, what looked like a squat wooden fort spun slowly around, bringing two enormous cannon barrels in line with the dying Norwegian ship.

It could only be a Haitian pirate.

I had never seen such an enormous sailing ship. This vessel dwarfed even the balloon of the airship it had just killed, although looking up from the low deck of the *Ett Hjerte*, it's possible my vantage point was exaggerating its size somewhat.

The rigging above the giant warship was swarming with sailors bringing in her already shortened sails, and she seemed to slow her headlong approach, coming up beside the *Ett Hjerte's* corpse and the Norwegian and Albian sailors now huddled on her deck.

"Do not move." The booming words were in heavily accented English, but easy to understand even over the rising fury of the storm.

One of the Albian soldiers, more brave or foolish than the rest, took several steps towards the railing, dropping his weapon as he ran.

"No!" Captain Peyton reached out, but it was too late.

I was expecting a single cracking rifle, as Peyton had used to silence the crew of my own ship. I would have given anything for it to have been a single rifle shot.

Somewhere overhead was the sound of tearing canvas and a strobing flare of flashing lights. A torrent of blazing red bars washed over where the Albian sailor had stood, chewing apart the man and the deck beneath him with equal ease. It had to be guns, or a gun, of some kind, possibly firing a sort of phosphorescent ammunition?

I didn't know the particulars, and I knew that my mind was grasping onto these trivial thoughts as a drowning man might cling to flotsam in a raging sea.

The sound overhead cut off as abruptly as it had begun, and there was no movement at all on the tilting deck save from the guttering flames.

"Do not move." The deep voice from the darkness repeated the words, and this time, no one was inclined to disobey.

Dark figures leapt down from the high deck of the warship with lines, securing them to cleats and protruding bits of equipment along the steamship's deck. As each sailor secured their rope, they turned towards us, pistols and cutlasses appearing in their hands, gleaming in the skittish light. Soon, we were all surrounded; the crew of the *Ett Hjerte* huddled up now with their attackers of only moments ago.

"I demand to speak to your captain." Peyton stood tall despite the reversal of fortune; her chin high as she hooked thumbs into the belt of her heavy coat. "I am an officer of the Albian navy, and this—"

"Enough." The voice, still deep, was louder now, coming from the railing high overhead.

The sailors around us, each grinning brightly from dark faces, did not take their eyes from us even as, behind them, a new figure jumped down onto the dying steamship's deck.

"Enough." The word came again, but without the hollow tones of a speaking trumpet. The figure was smaller than Peyton, but more solidly built. As it swaggered into the light of the dying fires, I was shocked, despite myself, to find it was another woman. This woman had a wild mane of thick braids splaying out from beneath an enormous hat, complete with a somewhat bedraggled feather streaming water.

The short woman stopped when she saw Peyton, her fists resting on her hips as she whistled silently into the storm.

"Alisha Peyton." The woman smiled grimly, teeth flashing, and shook her head.

"Christiane Bisset." Peyton spat the name out with contempt. Clearly, there was some history here. I found myself, despite the fear screaming through my mind, curious as to what that might be.

"You can call me admiral, if you'd like." The squat woman flicked one finger along the gold braid dangling from her epaulets, then jerked one thumb over her shoulder, her grin even wider. "He gave me *La Arbi-*

tre; flagship of the Northern Fleet, after our last encounter." She looked out over the railing at the scattered, burning wreckage of Peyton's own command. "That wasn't *Winglocke*, was it?"

Peyton twitched at the name, and then nodded with a silent, grim jerk of her head.

"Ah, well, damn." The dark-skinned woman with the wild hair spun about on one heel and rested her hands on the railing, the very picture of relaxation. "That's too bad. She stunk like a burning mule, and was louder than a flatulent cow, but she was a fantastic piece of engineering all the same." I know I was not entirely in the best frame of mind to judge, but the woman actually seemed sincere in her regret.

Peyton grunted, but did not otherwise respond.

"Fortunes of war, I guess." She stood and turned to face us. "Had our situations been reversed, I doubt I would have received any more mercy from you."

That seemed to reach Peyton where none of the other words had. "Why would I have attacked you?" She yelled the words, and I wasn't sure if it was to be heard over the rising roar of the storm, now fully engulfing both ships, or if her anger was getting the better of her. "I never would have done what you have done!"

Bisset looked wounded at this, even putting one hand to her chest. "Alisha, you wrong me. I would never attack a fellow sailor unawares in time of peace. You know me better than that."

Peyton's anger burned even hotter. "There is no war between Albion and the Empire!" She spat. "There wasn't. There will be now! Do you think King Benedict will stand by and see you go unpunished for what you just did?"

It was an admirable display of bravery and anger; I'm certain the woman was lost in her own nightmare of misery and loss or she might have noticed that the Haitians surrounding us showed nothing but amused contempt for her courage.

"Surely, captain, you have heard the tale of the *Dame Sombre*?" The name meant nothing to me. I assumed it was another Haitian ship, from the French, but I'm afraid I was finding my years of study had been more than a bit narrow for my current experience.

But Peyton was familiar with the name, I was certain, as her outrage faltered slightly and her eyes skipped to the side for just a moment. "That was an accident. Our governments came to an understanding. Reparations were offered and accepted."

The deep, throaty laugh from the short admiral might have been infectious in another place or time, but now I found it only chilling. As chilly as the whipping rain that had lost all of its tropical warmth.

"Reparations." The word was a curse. "Gold, for the hundreds of lives destroyed without a thought? Words, to replace the husbands and wives, sons and daughters that will never return to the Empire? His Majesty Jacques-Victor is generous and forgiving, but there is always a price to be paid for crossing the Haitian throne, captain. Your King Benjamin knew this, even as he bowed his head and signed over all that gold. He knew there would be another price; a blood price."

My neck hurt, swiveling back and forth, trying to follow the interplay. It was fascinating, after a lifetime in the staid and stagnant halls of England. "The subjects of Albion will not let this stand, Admiral." Even in her sorry situation, Peyton managed to make the title sound like an insult. "And my gracious king will hear their pleas. Make no mistake, this is war. And there is no way your little string of islands will be able to stand against the might of Albion. When word of this night's dark deeds reaches Tintagel Castle, your little realm will shake."

Bisset was nodding, her face somber beneath the wide brim of her elaborate hat, setting the long feather to bobbing in the wind. "Certainly, certainly." She seemed thoughtful for a moment, then shrugged. "On the other hand, since *Winglocke* is no more," she gestured with one vague hand over the side, to where even the wreckage of the airship had faded into the darkness. "And since no one is ever going to hear of what happened here tonight, I think we can all admit that Benedict will have the fig leaf he needs to cover his honor, despite all the world knowing what really happened to you, your crew, and your ship."

Despite her anger, Peyton was brought up short at this, confusion clear in her eyes. "I will never allow—"

"Oh, captain. You will never allow?" It was almost pity, now, shining from the Haitian woman's dark eyes. "This is a true Caribbean hurricano that surrounds us now. You know the *Winglocke* and her kin are terribly vulnerable to such weather. This particular storm is only getting into its stride. It will most likely smash into Albion along the Brocelann coast, maybe striking the port of Dare itself. No one will wonder, when your ship does not return home. Just another sad airship disaster, lost with all hands, to the whims of weather and fate. Too bad her captain wasn't more wary of the dangers posed by those terrible Caribbean winds."

Peyton's eyes widened at this last, and only continued to widen as Bisset's hand emerged from her coat with a heavy, ornate revolver. There was a single crack, the Albian captain's head jerked back, and then she fell to the deck, not far from where poor Captain Larsen lay.

Bisset looked down sadly at her fallen foe, then looked up to her sailors and nodded one sharp signal. Before any of us knew what might possibly happen next, pistols snapped out, a wave of light and noise washed over our huddled little group, and every Albian sailor jerked once and fell.

Several of the Norwegian sailors, spattered blood running in rivulets with the rain down their faces and chests, screamed, falling down a moment later, but I was almost certain none of them had been hit. It was terror that drove them to their knees, not Haitian lead.

"Now, my friends." Bisset turned to us as she slid her pistol back into its holster. "Who among you speaks English?"

I moved to raise my hand when a voice behind me; Jan, my one-time friend, then accuser.

"I spea—"

A pistol barked once, and Jan fell to join the Albians, dead and cold on the deck.

"Does anyone else speak English?" The smile on the woman's dark face was pleasant, and all the more terrifying because of it.

I kept my hand down.

She spun on one heel and moved toward the railing, wrapping a line around one hand. Over her shoulder she muttered, "Take the whites. Even if they talk, who will believe them? Who will care, in Haiti? I'd rather not come away from this with nothing to show for it but Jacques-Victor's signature on a piece of sheepskin."

I couldn't move. I had no idea what that meant, or what might happen next. Before that night, the closest I had ever come to death was the passing of my sainted grandfather who had passed peacefully in his sleep when I was still a young man. Now, with blood and seawater sloshing at my feet, corpses staring up accusingly from the skewed deck, I was quite certain my mind was shutting down, refusing to take anything else in for fear of breaking completely.

I thrust my hand into my pocket, trying to take some comfort in the firm weight of Merlin's stone, but it was just a cold lump of rock in a soaked linen bag. I looked back at the Albian kit bag that might or might not contain my books. Everything that had driven me to this moment seemed trivial now, and certainly nothing that could protect me from a world hell-bent on bringing death and ruin down around me.

I heard something behind me, a grunt, and then a heavy thud, as if someone had dropped a sandbag onto the sodden deck, and I turned, but too slowly..

Something tremendously heavy came crashing down on the base of my skull, driving me to my hands and knees. I couldn't think. The knot of excruciating pain flaring out from the point of impact drove all other thoughts away. I tried to push myself back to my feet, but I was struck again. I felt the wet wood of the deck pressing against my cheek. I feared drowning, remembering that the ship was sinking, the planks awash with rising water, rain, and blood.

Blood. I could taste blood in my mouth and panicked. Was I tasting the blood of the dead and dying? Was it my own blood?

There was another blow, bouncing my screaming skull against the deck, and I knew nothing more.

Chapter 4

My memories of the journey south are unreliable to say the least. I am not entirely certain what fragments are true and what are figments of my overwrought imagination. The hold in which I awoke, the remaining crew of the *Ett Hjerte* beside me, was dark and stale. From the gentle swaying motion, I knew *La Arbitre* was still at sea, but we had either outpaced the hurricane, or we were heading south, and it had left us behind as it rampaged north toward the Albian coast.

Of course, we were heading south. I should have guessed that without any further evidence. But my mind, held as it was now in a skull that throbbed with pain and unrelieved trauma both physical and mental, was hardly at its best. In fact, my chief memory of that fateful journey was that I could not string more than two or three minutes of conscious recollection together. There was the clink of chains, the swaying beams of diffuse sunlight that made it down to us below; the quiet, hopeless moans of my fellow prisoners. I would emerge from the cocoon of my pained slumber only to experience these things for a moment, or two, or thee, and then I would sink back beneath the waves of agony and loss once again.

I believe, even absent the repeated sharp blows to the back of my head, that my mind would have been behaving thus. I was being protected from the full impact of my plight. We were being dragged into the hellish barbarian kingdom of the Haitians, to be sold into slavery, I knew now, where I would spend the rest of my life working off a debt my own family had never incurred.

I would have been grateful to my mind if I had been capable of rational thought at all.

If nothing else, it made the miserable journey pass more quickly.

Eventually, the sounds outside our little world of misery and humiliation changed. The calls of sailors on deck were now being answered by returning hails coming from farther away. The creaking of the ship around us took on a gentler tone as she heeled slightly over onto her left flank. There was a deafening rattle just over our heads, which I took to mean we were being kept somewhere not far from the winch room for the great anchor, and soon the ship was rocking gently back and forth, all other sense of motion faded away.

Admiral Bisset and her crew were apparently in no hurry to fetch us from the hold, and I quickly lost track of time again as I sat in the fetid semi-darkness, awaiting the next phase in the hell my life had so swiftly become.

I had journeyed west knowing that the greatest threats to my mission and my freedom were the hated Albians and the mysterious Haitians. And then, in the span of less than an hour, I had encountered both; and they had both more than lived up to my terrified expectations.

When eventually the plank trap at the top of the steep ladder opened, letting in a flood of diffused light, I was ready to do almost anything to get out of the sweltering hold. The temperature had been rising steadily since I came back to myself, and we were not graced with an abundance of water by our handlers. In fact, several of my Norwegian compatriots had succumbed to heat and thirst and had not moved for what felt like hours.

I shielded my sensitive eyes from the light, waiting for the next injustice to descend upon us. I did not have long to wait.

A sailor, skin the color of teak, came halfway down the ladder and ducked so that his head came down below the ceiling.

"*Komme. Du Kommer.*" The words were halting, but the men around me rose at once and began to move toward the ladder.

Something within my chest rebelled at this sign of surrender, meekly following the orders of our captors. But the hold was like a dim, roasting hell, and I would have done almost anything to escape its close confines. I followed the last survivors of the *Ett Hjerte* up the ladder and into the chamber above the hold. We were in a narrow passage with a low ceiling, small doorways scattered down its length, staggered to either side. We were led down the hall by the same sailor, repeating his calls of *'du kommer'* over and over in his lilting accent.

Up another steep, narrow stair and we were on a gun deck, enormous breach-loading cannons on either side, snouts pressed to closed gun ports locked against the gentle roll of the ship. I am no expert with naval weapons, heaven knows. I have been aboard an English warship a time or two, as they rest at anchor in Plymouth or the Thames, too afraid to nose their way past sight of the home island. But I will tell you true: Nowhere in the Royal Navy are their weapons to compare to those cannons I saw on *La Arbitre*.

But then we were free of the oppressive heat of the hold and blinking, blind and scared, in the furnace heat of midday. But as I rubbed the darkness out of my eyes, trying desperately to see around the floating globes of white that marred my vision, I could barely make out a large structure directly forward of where we emerged. It was the assembly I had seen from the deck of the sinking *Ett Hjerte*, the wooden cabin housing two enormous cannons.

One of the sailors noticed my look and smiled. *"Tourél la."* He saw my confusion and stammered on. *"Zam tourél la? Ahh..."* He frowned. *"Ah, innhegning? Um, borg?"*

I almost asked him aloud what he was saying. I had been told most Haitians spoke at least a little English; there was an excellent chance the sailor would be able to tell me what I was looking at without all this difficulty. Why was he stammering out these nonsense words?

Then I stopped. Norwegian. Of course. The sailor, along with everyone else aboard the massive warship, believed there were no English speakers left among the prisoners. Bisset believed she had killed any witnesses to her final conversation with Captain Peyton. If I asked my simple question, there's every chance I would be shot out of hand. I would have to wait, I suppose, hoping for my curiosities to be addressed some other time. For his part, the sailor grew bored, waved me away with one brown hand, and went back to whatever it was he was doing, with a large pile of thick rope against the polished railing.

And that was when the reality of my situation came crashing back upon me. I was a prisoner of war, for all intents and purposes, and I was to be sold into slavery, I believed, at some time in the not-so-distant future.

My situation was infinitely better than when I was in the clutches of Captain Peyton and her sadistic crew, but the improvement was one of degree, not of overall condition. Looking at sweating my way through decades of hard labor in this sweltering tropical hell before I passed on, unremarked and unremarkable to any who had known me here, my family and my friends back in England, especially my parents and sweet Felicity having mourned me and move on years and years before.

That future held no great attraction for me, either. And what of Albion and England? I knew of no efforts toward freeing my home from the tyrannical yoke of the Arnolds and their poisoned subjects. If not me, then who?

And with thoughts of my foolish quest rising to my addled mind once more, my hand of its own volition slipped into my pocket, now stiff with dried salt and sweat, and for a moment the significance of the supreme lack of contents therein escaped me. I merely searched my other pocket, but that, too, was empty.

And then I knew true despair. Merlin's stone, the only concrete evidence I had that this entire affair was more than a mere fantasy, was gone. And with that, I realized my books were probably gone as well. I might know success without the books. I remembered enough, at least, to muddle along and hope for the best if I could get myself to New Orleans. But without the stone? I had no proof the trail even existed, other than the stone. I had nothing to show any initiates into these secrets that I might find among the Comanche, or any of the other tribes I might be able to find. I had nothing to tie me to the legacy I knew, in my bowels, was the only hope for my home.

My despair only deepened as I realized that, although all that was true enough, even if I *had* the stone, it wouldn't matter. Chained to this burning island for the rest of my mortal days, what would it matter if I had such an artifact or not?

I was barely aware as a sailor pushed me toward a rope ladder hanging over the side, and down into a waiting longboat. The entire surviving compliment of my little steamship was in the boat as well, with Haitian sailors laughing and joking among us, seated at the oars and pulling hard for the long stone quay rising up behind them. Above us swept majestic hills covered in vibrant green, jungle canopy swaying gently in a breeze I could not feel. Behind the quay were stands of palms, and beyond those, the tan buildings of Port Au Prince rippled slightly in the terrible heat.

I had eyes for none of it. At the quay we were pushed and prodded out of the boat and onto a low stone walkway, then up a set of stairs and onto a broad courtyard. The heat radiating off the stones was biblical, I could feel sweat running down my back, into my eyes, and prickling across my chest. But I didn't care.

I had left home for one reason and one reason only. I had come to save my home. I had joined the countless heroes of the past who had left everything behind to sacrifice themselves upon the altar of the greater good, and my foolishness had only led me here; to a slave market in the middle of the sweltering Caribbean Sea, to be traded for like a cow or pig, and then used as my new masters saw fit until this new life wore me down to nothing. It was worse than a death along the journey, in a way, as I would now die, alone and unmourned among strangers who hated me for the perceived crimes of my race alone.

I didn't care.

I went where I was directed. I kept my eyes downcast; no curiosity moved my heart or my mind. I ate when I was given food, drank when I was given water, and slept when I was left alone, which was almost always. I know several days passed in this way, but I could not have told you how many. It might have been two, it might have been ten. For all I know it may well have been a hundred or more. Each day was like the day before. We were fed twice, given water three times, we relieved ourselves in filthy buckets that were removed each morning, and the unrelenting heat, probably more even than our current situation, kept us down.

The crew of the *Ett Hjerte* spoke only Norwegian now, as only made sense. Even if anyone spoke English, which logic would have dictated must have been the case, the sad example of seaman Jan was never far from anyone's mind. No one was going to speak English this close to the port, where the sounds of the ships and the cries of the gulls were a constant reminder of what had happened to us far to the north. And so, having very little Norwegian to speak of, I was even more isolated and alone than any of my fellows.

Which suited me perfectly, as I had nothing to say, and no great desire to say it.

When they finally came for us, there was almost a sense of relief among the sailors. I didn't know why, entirely, until we found ourselves guided gently up onto a newly erected platform in the center of a great plaza. It may have been the same courtyard we had walked through upon our arrival. I did not know, and I did not care. In fact, I paid very little attention at all, until the proceedings began.

A large crowd was forming, their faces a monochromatic mélange of dark skin, ranging from tea and cream to blackest night. Bright teeth shown in brilliant smiles, children rode their parents' shoulders to better see the oddities now stumbling across the stage. Off to one side I saw the squat form of Admiral Bisset standing with a man whose black clothes carried more brocade and lace than any three garden party dresses I could remember. The man was wearing a hat similar to the admirals, except in that its feather was even grander, longer, and more ridiculous than hers.

I have far more French than I have Norwegian, and so as the auction began, I had little problem following along. I had no great desire to, however, so can hardly convey much of what went on. The sailors, one by one, were showcased, their specialties listed for the buying public, and it soon became clear that even the wind-powered navy of the Empire of Haiti could find a use for seasoned steamship sailors like these.

I noticed that with each sale, money would change hands with a fat, sweaty factor with bushy mustachios, and then a runner would skitter through the crowd to the man in black standing with Admiral Bisset. The man would take a handful of scrip, passing a portion of it to the short woman beside him, and the runner would return for the next auction.

There were not many of the men of the *Ett Hjerte* left, and soon it was my turn on the block.

I was gently prodded to the center of the rough wooden stage. The sun overhead beat down, pressing on everything around me with a bright weight. The overseer began his little speech, but I paid no attention to his words. I cared nothing for whatever these men and women might see in me, or what spurious claims to seamanship the barker might make in my name. I could not escape the dark thought that, no matter how I might hope to turn this new situation to my advantage and escape, this might actually be the end.

My only confident memory of that moment was the silence stretching on and on after the man ended his speech. There were no shouted bids; the crowd just stared up at me, bemused.

"*Allons!*" The overseer seemed exasperated. "*Allons!*"

And then the crowd of curious faces parted. Someone pushed through from the back, a man in a nondescript dun-colored suit, taller than anyone he moved past. It was clear the people recognized him, quick as they were to move out of his way. There seemed to be a mix of fear and anticipation as they watched him pass.

I felt a dull stirring in my chest for a moment, but then the heat, and the sun, and the exhaustion pressed it back down, and my shoulders slumped within the stiff, sweat-drenched confines of my shirt.

The man jumped up onto the stage and crossed briskly to the overseer. They spoke quickly together, and I would swear that no money exchanged hands. The overseer's eyes were wide in his dark face, he turned to look at me, then back to the newcomer, nodding the entire time.

I looked out over the harbor, at the impressive fleet of massive warships rocking gently there amidst the scattered diamonds of sunlight sparkling on the waves. Closer by, I noticed Admiral Bisset watching with a bitter twist to her full lips. Whatever was happening behind me, she was not pleased. I almost turned, vaguely curious as to what it might be.

When the bag dropped over my head, I wish I could say I was hardly surprised.

But I was.

Chapter 5

I was roughly forced down the crude stairs of the auction platform, the sun shining brightly through the coarse burlap covering my face making for a strange, hazy, sight without sight that somehow still managed to blind with the tropical sun's fierce light. I could sense the crowd all around me, parting once more to make way for this strange white specimen being bundled off to God alone knew what fate.

I felt the vague stirrings of curiosity in my chest. Who was this man? Why had they bothered to throw a bag over the head of a man who was already condemned to servitude for his remaining days? What were they afraid I was going to see?

Who were they afraid I was going to tell?

After our hurried trek, my companion pushing me not ungently the entire while, I was hoisted unceremoniously up onto a rough, splintery surface. Wood, obviously, and also obviously exposed to the sun, as the heat rising off it was radiating an almost physical pressure.

A bit farther ahead I heard the whicker of a horse, and the quick "Tut, tut" of a drover. No matter the language, it seemed the same sounds calmed a skittish horse the world over.

The boards beneath me rocked slightly, but with a more grounded, regular cadence, somehow, than the free, directionless movement I had come to associate with the sea. I was on a cart or wagon, I realized. How far was I going to be transported? Was this going to be a short trip to one of the hillside forts above the harbor, or was I to be taken somewhere farther away?

I had no real value as a prisoner, as far as I knew. England and the Empire were not overly friendly, but they were not at war. It was more a case of 'the man who drives my enemy insane is not quite my enemy' than anything else, but it was enough to maintain regular diplomatic contacts.

Likewise, I had no skills that might recommend me for any particularly important trade or occupation. I very much doubted that anyone in the Empire of Haiti needed any emergency research into energy fields, the development of higher reasoning in ancient primitive cultures, or British folklore anytime soon.

So why had they seen fit to bundle me away from the auction and toss me into a cart? Was it embarrassing for the slavers to have brought such an inadequate fellow onto their stage? What had Admiral Bisset been angry about? Was she not going to get her cut of the profits from this new stranger?

And if not, what did that say about him?

The wagon began to move beneath me, and I scuttled away from the back edge, where my feet still dangled out into the air. I pressed my back against the wagon's rough side and settled in, resigned to wait as long as I must for these questions to be answered.

As we rocked our way through Port Au Prince, the smells and the sounds of the city made themselves known to me in a way I doubt would have been the case had I not been robbed of my vision. With each sway of the surface beneath me, everything seemed to change. I caught the scent of strange spices and roasting meats, and then almost gagged as the foulest stench imaginable rose up to take their place. I heard merchants calling out their wares, buyers crying in mock indignation in the midst of some heated negotiation. I heard children laughing, people talking all around, and somewhere in the distance, I even heard a woman's crystal voice rising in a sad, slow song.

I lost myself in these observations, occasionally holding my breath as a stink wafted by, but then breathing deeply of cooking, flowers, or incense. I turned my blind face away from the cries of an angry woman, but then peered in the direction of a laughing gaggle of men and women rushing through the streets in some wild air of celebration.

If it had not been for the heat and the blindfold, and that all the rambunctious humanity around me was communicating solely in French, I might have been convinced I was back in London, or maybe Plymouth or Bath.

But sooner than I would have wished, the sounds and smells of the city faded away. There were fewer people around us, and their conversation was lower, and drifted quickly off into the heat of midday. Not long after, the echoing of our horse's hooves on cobbles came back at me from nearby to either side and overhead. We had passed through a tunnel of some kind, or perhaps a gate in the squat city wall. And then we were back out in the fresh, if humid, tropical air, moving steadily upward, leaving the city behind.

Eventually, I slept. Before the *Winglocke* met the *Ett Hjerte* I never would have believed sleep was possible in the face of such adversity, fear, and uncertainty. But the weaknesses of the human body had been made apparent to me, and what pride might have kept me from sinking into slumber had long been burned away in the hold of *La Arbitre*.

The rocking that had lulled me into unconsciousness stopped, and I came to myself suddenly, all at once, without the gradual rising that I had experienced most of my life. It was dark within my hood, and the air was cool. There was a fitful breeze that set a loud susurrus all around me, and I assumed I was surrounded by foliage of some kind.

Off to the side two voices spoke quietly, too low for me to make out any meaning from their clipped French. Then, footsteps, as someone approached the cart.

My foot was pulled toward the open back, and a gruff voice said, *"Vous venez avec moi."* And then repeated it again, punctuated with a firmer pull on my pant leg. *"Venez!"*

I raised my hands, trying to indicate my lack of resistance while sliding over the rough wood, dropping to the ground. Beneath my bare feet I felt stones, smoother and more regular than cobblestones, I thought, still radiating the warmth of the day.

Someone took me lightly by the elbow and led me forward.

"Faites attention. Escaliers." And sure enough, as I tentatively moved forward, raising my foot higher than was natural, I found myself moving up a gentle flight of stairs. The stone was smooth, but with more texture than I would expect from marble or polished granite.

Again, I found myself more curious than I would have thought. I had half-expected to be brought to a farm or plantation. That should have meant being shoved into a ratty cabin or holding pen waiting for the morning and my first workday as a slave to begin. I realized I knew precious little about how the agriculture and other industries of Haiti were arranged.

What I had not anticipated was that I would be brought to a stout stone structure somewhere far from the capital's harbor. I did not know how long we had been wending our way up into the mountains, but it had been hours, for sure. There was certainly no hint of salt in the air.

The sounds around me became dull. I guessed we had entered a building, and soon my companion's footsteps clicked out, echoes now returning with a ringing, hollow snap. I couldn't be sure, but it felt like we had entered a large chamber. My imagination filled in all sorts of wild details, envisioning a receiving hall with soaring columns and polished floors. Beneath my sore feet, the stone was smooth and cool. So different from anything I had encountered since boarding the *Ett Hjerte* in what seemed now like another life.

I was led through several rooms that must have varied in size and shape, based upon the returning echoes. We went up two flights of stairs, along what I would have sworn was a gallery of some kind, with a sense of a vast empty space off to one side. Eventually, I was taken to a small room, pushed slowly down onto a low pallet bed, and left to my own devices. A door closed with a solid sound, followed by the mechanical click of a key in a lock.

I wanted to ask what I was supposed to do. I wanted to beg for more information. Where was I? What was to become of me? Was I going to be left overnight? Longer?

But I remembered again Jan's empty eyes staring up at me from the blood-soaked deck, and I held my tongue.

I was too afraid even to remove the hood, although eventually I came to believe I was alone. I had been given no instructions, and over the past harrowing weeks, I had been conditioned out of a lifetime of inquisitiveness and questioning authority. None of that fire remained, I realized.

I was mildly ashamed.

But I still didn't remove the hood.

I settled back on the bed, easily the most comfortable I had experienced since Oslo. There was even a pillow. I'm embarrassed to admit it, but I very nearly cried.

Had someone asked, I would not have believed myself capable of further sleep. But after only a moment with my head blissfully resting on the soft, cool pillow, rough cloth still tight across my face, everything slowly, quietly, gently faded into darkness.

*****

I awoke to a gentle prodding of my shoulder.

"Monsieur, vous devez vous réveiller." Again, a hand shook my shoulder, urging me toward the side of the bed. *"Vous êtes convoqué."*

That it was time for me to wake up I didn't doubt. But I was being summoned? Did one summon slaves so graciously? It had been a veritable gulf of time since William Wilburforce and his collegues had rid England of slavery. Still, it felt more than a bit formal, somehow, to so summon a slave.

"Je vous remercie." I just remembered to respond in French and not English, and wondered, for a moment, why no one had been gabbling Norwegian at me since leaving the waterfront. These men might not know I had been brought off a Norwegian ship, but it was equally plausible that they didn't speak the language. While French was the language of diplomacy throughout the civilized world, and English was still the language of choice in the far-flung holdings of the former Empire, the tongue of Norway had been on the decline since the Vikings had been forced back into their icy home waters more than a thousand years ago.

I wondered what it meant, that the hood was being left in place. Perhaps I had been right not to remove it the night before.

I was led out of my little cell, down what sounded like a long, wide hall with smooth stone floors, and into a small, closed chamber that seemed to press in from my personal darkness on all sides. I stumbled on the first step, and my guide muttered an absent apology before leading me further upward. We continued for a long time, the light fading to a dusky twilight for several minutes before brightening again, bright flashes moving steadily past us on our left as we climbed. Eventually, we arrived in another small chamber, the light here steady and warm. But, although the light was much brighter, and the heat of the tropical sun was making itself felt more here than my night's accommodations, there was no sense of the sun's direct impact, and the floor here was still cool despite the bright light.

We entered a vast new room, sunlight now coming from every direction. I moved hesitantly, not wanting to run headlong into any grand furniture; not wanting to entirely trust my guide despite my gratitude for his help, knowing he was complicit in my blinding and imprisonment. The fact that I still wore my hood didn't help his case any, either.

That might have been the strangest part of the entire ordeal: I was a prisoner, wearing a hood over my face, being pushed from one place to another, treated like an animal, and yet at any perceived kindness, an appreciation welled up in my chest that far outstripped the actual act that had engendered it. It added an anger and a shame to the storm of emotions that roiled beneath my hopeless despair.

"Please remove the hood, if you would be so kind, Maurice?" The voice was cultured, calm, quiet. It had the same lilting, singsong undertones that had marked Admiral Bisset's speech.

And it had spoken in English.

I jerked back from the hand drawing the hood away from my eyes, cringing from first the contact, then a brilliant light that nearly blinded me. My hood had allowed light through, but it was nothing compared to the flood of sunshine striking my face as the fabric was pulled away.

The voice had spoken in English. And that, for poor Jan, had meant death. Was this all a ruse? Could they be trying to trick me into speaking English? It seemed far too elaborate, considering I was a slave already, and subject to my captor's every whim and fancy. A ruse justifying my death struck me as being far too cruel, even for slavers such as these.

"You have nothing to fear here, Mr. Hawke." The voice sounded amused, which was all I had time to process before I realized what I had heard. My name. The man had called me by my name.

I rubbed at my eyes, cursing the blindness, wanting desperately, suddenly, to see this man and my surroundings. As vision slowly returned, I was rewarded with a sight much like the chamber I had imagined in my mind, save for the urbane figure standing in the middle of all the rugged splendor. I was momentarily startled to see leaving the room the man who had ascended the stage of the slave auction just the day before, still in his dun-colored suit. He backed out of the room with a brief bow, his brown face expressionless. As the door closed behind him in an ornate wooden frame, I saw that this was the only section of the chamber's walls that did not blaze with light.

We were in a wide, round room with paneled walls. Along these walls were rows of tall windows set in ornate stone sills. And the views beyond those windows were not to be believed.

One half of the view was comprised of low, rolling mountains covered in jungle. It looked like some barbaric Eden, teeming with life. And opposite this verdant scene was the sea far below us, with an arm of green-shrouded land stretching out to encompass the water to either side.

It was a glorious view, and under other circumstances, I might have been able to appreciate it more. As it was, however, I could hardly focus, between the lingering light-induced pain in my eyes and the man staring at me with a slight smile, hands hooked into his uniform belt, standing not ten feet away. He had a dark, refined face with an aquiline, aristocratic nose.

"I am glad to see you are well, Mr. Hawke. When I was finally able to ascertain your whereabouts, I was worried that someone might have done something ... irreversible, before I was able to spirit you away."

The man's voice was deep and rumbling. I thought I detected genuine concern. I was at an utter loss for words.

"I apologize for how you have been treated. Are you hungry? I have had several breakfasts prepared, in the hopes that one might suit you?"

And either at the verbal suggestion of his words, or just pure chance, I was suddenly aware of the mouth-watering scent of bacon and tea.

I didn't want to eat. I wanted to rant and rave; I wanted to demand to know where I was, who this man was, and most important, where my belongings might have gone.

But I was starving, and I fell upon the elegantly prepared food like a beast. Shame nearly drove me back from the table, but it simply could not overcome my hunger, not merely for food, but for the comfortable foods of England.

Truly, it was an Irish breakfast, not, strictly speaking, an English one. There was bacon, and ham and eggs and toast, and even a roasted tomato. But there were other platters as well, and I began to sample from those also. I didn't stop until my stomach rebelled, my gorge rising, and I remembered that I hadn't eaten well in a very long time. My body was going to exact its vengeance for the sudden rich feast, but in that moment, I didn't care.

When I had slowed my eating at last, my host approached, his hands raised above his head. "I knew you would be hungry, perhaps I misjudged just how hungry you would be." He smiled, looking at the wreckage I had made of the table's offerings.

I felt like an animal, and took up a napkin, patting my lips and trying to recover my dignity.

"I'm sorry."

He smiled and waved my apology away, his eyes warm. "It is I who should say that, Mr. Hawke. It was truly an unfortunate series of events that has brought you to Haiti. I believe that we might be of great benefit to each other, and I hope that we can move beyond the moment."

My eyes narrowed. "I'm not certain what I can do for you, Mr..."

It felt presumptuous, considering my position, but it seemed far past time for him to have introduced himself, if he truly believed we might help each other.

He smiled again and looked away. "You may call me Mr. Black."

That could not have been the case; it had to be some kind of joke. But among the many questions arising in my mind now, I thought I could let this pass.

"Alright, Mr. Black." From the slight widening of his smile, I knew I had guessed correctly. "I don't want to seem ungrateful ... although the circumstances of my capture do complicate that gratitude some-what ... but I am having a hard time fathoming what possible assistance I might be to you, given our relative differences in circumstance."

The man shook his head, moving toward a large desk I hadn't noticed. "Mr. Hawke, I honestly have no idea." His voice grew soft, dis-tracted. "But I think I'm willing to make an investment in you, given, as you say, our relative differences in circumstance."

I saw, as he sat down, a small pile of books on the desk.

Books I recognized.

My books.

I took a step toward them, and the man reached out and placed one graceful, long-fingered hand over the pile. "Recovered from the *Ett Hjerte*, Mr. Hawke." He pushed them gently across the desk. "I trust they are all there? We had no way of knowing how thorough Captain Peyton's people were before they were...interrupted."

With shaking hands, I picked the books up, holding them in my left and drawing my right fingers over their spines. It was a small collec-tion, I reflected. Pathetic, really, given they represented the sum total of my life's work to that point. A small survey of ancient British myths and legends, a travelogue of North America more than twenty years out of date, and three tattered notebooks filled with my own crabbed writing. Every salient fact regarding my initial findings on energy fields and living organisms, and then the trail of my research through England, Europe, and beyond; tracking the connective tissues of the various stories and the more tenuous connections between those tales and my own theories.

Five volumes. My life.

And then the surge of warmth and hope that rose up within my chest subsided. I put the books down quickly and swept the desk with my eyes. It was bare.

Without Merlin's stone my search ended here, no matter what this strange, regal man might intend.

I looked up at him, the nascent hope dying in my eyes, only to see a sly, boyish grin creep across the other man's face.

He withdrew a silver chain from his pocket, pulling with slow, deliberate drama, as his hand rose, until the stone was swinging over the desk between us, my host's teeth now bared in a gleaming smile.

"And then there's this, of course."

I lurched forward and snatched the stone away, inspecting it with care in the palm of one hand. The stone's linen bag was gone, replaced with a beautifully-crafted silver setting, the long supple chain passing through a hoop situated at one end of the slightly oval gem.

The stone itself was unchanged, and as I touched its smooth surface with a fingertip, I felt a thrill of energy leap from the object to my flesh. I knew that it was only a figment of my imagination, but I could not be entirely sure, and even the illusion, if that is what it was, was comforting.

The man had settled down behind the desk and gestured for me to take a seat on the other side.

"Mr. Hawke," the man began speaking before I had even moved, and I felt myself lowering into the comfortable chair almost despite myself. "I find your researches, to date, intriguing. I have no idea if your planned next step has any hope at all. The tribesmen of the northern plains, no matter their imperial pretensions, are utterly alien to me. I do not know if they possess the information you seek, nor can I even begin to guess if they would deign to so much as speak with you, never mind impart to you the keys to the knowledge that has driven you from your home."

I wanted to speak, I wanted to tell him I knew all that, but that Albion had left me no choice. In fact, as I listened to him, I could feel my curiosity and concerns fall away, replaced once again by the old, driving rage. But whether it was that very rage, my own fear of the truths he spoke, or something buried even deeper in my mind I could not say. Whatever the reason, I remained silent.

"I have a problem, Mr. Hawke. A problem that defies solving nearly as certainly as your Albian dilemma." He looked straight at me; his dark eyes intense on either side of that blade-like nose. "I have despaired for many years of ever freeing myself of this problem, with no visible hope." He placed one hand on my books. "Until today."

I shook my head. My theories might be foolish, they might be hopeless, but they were mine. A small voice within my mind asked the eternal question, was it intractable hopelessness that kept me clinging to this mad dream, or was there real merit in the concept? And as always, the lack of answer drove me away before I could look too closely at my own motivations. I was not about to let this stranger, no matter our circumstances, move me to even deeper introspection.

"There is theoretical merit—" I began, feeling my voice grate in my throat as it so often did when my anger was aroused.

But before I could continue, the man held up one hand. He drew one small volume, one of my journals, to him, flipping it open to a bookmark I had not placed.

"Do you truly believe what you have written here, Mr. Hawke? 'The power of gods and demons, sorcerers and saints.' It seems rather grandiose." He flipped forward a page or two, and I knew precisely what he was looking at. "The ability to part the seas, tear down mountains, level cities?"

I shrugged. "They are most likely exaggerations, distortions from hundreds of years of retellings. But I believe they may well be based upon real events." I felt my energy draining from me under his steady gaze. "They offer hope, at any rate, where, elsewise, no hope remains."

He nodded. "I can see some merit in your theories, Mr. Hawke. Truly I can, or we would not be having this conversation. I just wish to be honest with you, and with myself. I do not know if that merit is valid, or merely a figment of my overwrought imagination given my current predicament."

It occurred to me, not for the first time, that I had no idea what this man's predicament might be, but I was past such polite concerns.

"There are too many similarities in these old tales—"

This time the man's voice was firm, his gesture sharp as he brought his hand down between us like a knife. "Mr. Hawke, you have no need to tell me about old tales." Now, his eyes took on a haunted look, and he rose, moving toward the nearer window, looking out over the verdant interior of the island. "I have lived those tales all my life."

And that, where none of his other words, penetrated my rising cloud of anger. There was a poignant truth in the man's tone that called out to the part of me that had spent countless thousands of hours poring over ancient texts and transcriptions of stories hundreds and thousands of years old.

"What—"

He silenced me with a raised hand without turning around. "Do you know anything of my own land's mythology, Mr. Hawke?" He shook his head, still looking away. "There is no need. Such knowledge will not help you, and indeed, may harm your own chances for success, further down the path you have chosen."

He turned, and his face was now rigid with resolve. "I am going to release you back onto that path. I am going to give you back your books, and even allow you to keep your stone. It is not the first I have seen, and I know that it will prove essential if your mad scheme is to have any chance of success."

That comment, almost made in passing, brought me up short, but before I could ask anything more, he had moved on.

"You will be provided with supplies and gold and silver, everything you might need to get you into the Comanche lands. I will see you delivered to New Orleans safely as well." He withdrew something from his pocket and turned to hand it to me, although I thought I sensed some vague unease in his eyes. "If you find yourself in particular difficulty, you might show this to any Haitian official you might meet along the way, it may secure for you additional assistance."

I closed my fingers over the object but locked my gaze on his. "Why are you doing this?"

He smiled briefly through that haunted look. "Hope." Then he shrugged, turning away. "Call it enlightened self-interest, if you want. I will be aware of your progress, Mr. Hawke. Please believe I have people more than capable of getting me word of what transpires on the mainland. I will know if you succeed or if you fail." He glanced over his shoulder. "If you succeed, you will hear from me again. I will expect you to return today's favors on that day, should it ever come to pass."

Again, a righteous anger threatened to darken my vision. Favors? Returning my things and setting me back on the path the Haitians had derailed; these were favors? But then I remembered the shape of the *Winglocke* hovering over my head and the anger sputtered into a dark, growling background noise.

I looked down to see a small ring, an intricate symbol painstakingly wrought on one widened face. I peered closer to see the symbol of the Empire of Haiti in fantastic, minute detail, its miniscule lions clutching a shield embossed with a palm tree so small as to be almost invisible.

My gaze rose back to the man, but he was looking out the window again. I was about to ask him what the ring could possibly mean when his back stiffened and he moved closer to the window, looking down toward the base of the building.

I moved to the man's side and followed his gaze. By the light of the rising sun, I saw an enormous carriage working its way up a switchback road toward us. It looked like something out of a fairy tale: black and gold, ornately carved with gargoyles crouched upon miniature towers creating the look of a moving castle or cathedral. Flags snapped out in the tropical winds coming up from the shore far below, and I saw that they incorporated the seal of the Empire, but the fields of the flags themselves were deep sable rather than the azure over crimson of the official Haitian banner.

When my strange host whipped back to look at me, his face was contorted in a strange combination of fear and anger that resonated uncomfortably in my own chest. "I'm afraid you'll need to leave sooner than I had intended, Mr. Hawke."

Before he finished the words, the man in the light brown suit pushed the door to the big chamber open after a quick, perfunctory double knock.

"He comes." The man's liquid tones were soft but carried an urgency all the same.

"Thank you, Maurice. I noticed." His smile was forced, and I wondered who it might be riding in that ridiculously baroque conveyance. Could it be Emperor Jacques-Victor himself?

My host took me by the elbow and guided me toward the door. "Go with Maurice, please, Mr. Hawke. I had hoped to speak more about your theories and your findings in Europe and abroad, but alas, time has nearly caught us out, I'm afraid."

The man in brown, Maurice, was holding the door as we moved through. "There is a fast carriage in the basement, with fresh horses and everything you will need on your journey. Please follow Maurice's instructions precisely, as if your life depended on it."

I had so many questions, but at the same time, I was being ushered out of this castle, or fort, or whatever it was, a free man seemingly, and my curiosity, once again aroused by this strange change in events, was easier to tamp down, given that one salient fact.

I was free.

Maurice and I fled down a narrow stairwell, windows descending with us on our right. We left my strange benefactor above, watching us descend. Eventually, we left the windows behind, and the stairwell grew murky and close. There was still a glow far above us, and I thought I could see some faint illumination below, but as we made our dizzying way, round and round down the seemingly endless flight of sandstone steps, I wondered if I had just fallen from one strange dream into the next.

Eventually, we emerged into a dimly lit chamber, gas lights lining the distant walls, rows of carriages of all shapes and sizes arrayed stretching forward toward a low, wide doorway on the far wall. In the center the hall several groomsmen in ornate uniforms stood by one tall carriage, a pair of sleek horses already in the traces.

"You will find clothing within, Mr. Hawke." Maurice's voice was low, as if afraid whoever was in the approaching coach might hear through the immense pile of stone between us and the front courtyard. "Please change as soon as we are on our way. I will ride with the coachmen atop the carriage for the first leg of our journey, to afford you some privacy."

It was a dark, nondescript post carriage, I saw, with just enough room inside for two passengers. Changing would be difficult, but I thought I could manage it.

"I'm afraid for the duration of the journey you will need to keep the curtains drawn, as well. Your skin is too light for you to pass unremarked, and we need to slip you out of the Empire without anyone knowing you are gone. As far as the authorities in Haiti are concerned, you were just another sailor, less gifted than most, taken in action up north and disappeared into the dark mysteries of Haiti." He grimaced as he turned away. "It happens often enough."

Within the carriage I found a bundle of clothes and Maurice past me my books, which I had forgotten about in the rush upstairs. I nodded my thanks and climbed within.

As I was changing, the carriage began to rock, the groomsmen all speaking in harsh whispers as we pulled away and into the blazing light and heat of the tropical morning. Even through the curtains, the light was painfully bright. Soon, however, dappled shadows began to flicker against the fabric, and the green gloom of the jungle fell across the windows. The carriage was bouncing erratically as we gained speed, and I assumed we were on some sort of secondary road leading away from the rear of the keep.

And with that thought, my curiosity truly got the better of me, and I slid across the narrow seat, opening the window to look back.

We were deep in the jungle already, plunging down a steep, sloping road. The enormous pile of stone behind us was nearly eclipsed by the canopy of palm and pine trees rising up between us, but I could still make out the soaring towers of a fortress larger than any I had ever seen before. It dwarfed nearly every castle I had ever seen in Europe, that was certain. It's dark stone strangely out of place rising above the thick, luxuriant jungle.

While researching my prospective journey I had not spent a great deal of time on the realms I had not intended to visit, but even so I knew about the largest fortress in the Americas: *La Citadelle*. It stood upon a mountain overlooking Port Au Prince and the harbors of the capital of the Empire of Haiti and was said to be the private refuge of the Emperor himself.

Once more I found myself wondering who my mysterious benefactor could have been, and who might have scared him so much as to drive me quickly away.

I closed the window and rested back against the seat. The rocking of the carriage was violent, and several times I feared we might careen right off the roadway and into the jungle. But the driver knew his business, or was inordinately lucky, and we eventually made it to a smoother, wider thoroughfare. And as the brutal, jerking motion of the vehicle settled into a gentler swaying, once again I found my traumatized mind drifting off into a surreal slumber.

Chapter 6

I quickly came back to myself as the tenor of the carriage's wheels changed.

It was dark outside the veiled windows. Even as I shook off the last tattered remnants of slumber, I could feel the iron-rimmed wheels clattering over cobles rather than the packed earth that had marked most of our journey. Maurice was not in the carriage with me, but a wooden bottle of water flavored with a bright juice was on the seat beside me, as well as a small bag of hard bread and cheese.

I wolfed down the food and guzzled the drink, realizing, as soon as I saw it, how hot and close the confines of the carriage had become. My new clothing stuck to me with sweat; my throat screamed for the water.

I heard footsteps outside, and not wanting to be passive any longer, I opened the door and stepped out rather than wait for Maurice or one of the drivers to summon me.

We were in a small fishing village; I could tell by the smell. I had traveled across half the world, and yet the smells of this place were immediately recognizable to me from the countless similar towns I had visited in England, France, and beyond. The buildings were mainly small huts of lashed upright tree trunks and thatched roofs. Most of the windows were dark, although I could see curious eyes peering from one or two where the soft light of a candle flickered in the dimness.

Maurice came around the back of the carriage holding a heavy pack that he handed to me without comment. I took it, thought about checking through it, and then decided not to worry. It looked as if my freedom was only moments away. Any lack I found in his preparations could easily be made up somewhere along the journey. I wanted to be on my way.

Next, Maurice handed me a pouch heavy with coins. Again, I decided to take it on faith, and simply slipped the bag into a pocket.

"This is Mole Saint-Nicolas, at the north-western tip of Haiti proper. Your will take ship with Henriand his family. Henri is a discreet, loyal man," He guided me toward the soft sound of waves, and I could just make out masts rising up behind a low group of huts ahead. "You will be crossing to Punta de Maisi, in what was once Cuba, and then following the coast west until you reach the end of the land claimed by the Empire. Henri will then head out to sea briefly to pass between the unclaimed portions of the long island and the southern tip of Canaan. The final leg of the journey will be harrowing, but Henri and his crew have made it many times before. This a treacherous time of year, but the weather to the south seems calm enough, so you should be okay crossing the gulf. And then you will be at the mouth of the Mississippi River. New Orleans is just a brief journey upriver from there. It should pose no troubles to Henri."

As Maurice finished, we came out from between two huts and saw the wooden docks of Mole Saint-Nicolas stretching out into the water before us. A small single-masted vessel was waiting at the end of the main dock. A small group stood at the ship's side, waiting for us.

"None of them speak English, and your accent is atrocious. Try not to speak. Henri knows nothing of your identity, and the less he knows, the better for everyone. Try to keep to yourself during the journey."

The ship was tiny, more a boat, really; keeping to myself might prove a challenge, but I nodded, nonetheless. My throat was tight, and I doubted I could have spoken regardless.

As I looked out at the small craft the realization of everything that had happened to me since the *Ett Hjerte* came crashing down on me again. I wondered, not for the first time, about the versatility of the human mind. That I had been able to function at all under the immense pressures of these horrific weeks seemed hardly to be creditable. And now, with this ratty little ship bobbing at the end of the ramshackle old dock, what clarity of mind and resolve I had possessed was fast draining away.

Maurice may have told me more, but I do not remember. I barely remember being introduced to Henri, my new captain, and the two young men and one woman who would be the crew of the little ship as we made our way west.

I stood by the low railing as they pushed us off, raising the single sail, working around me to catch the warm breeze blowing out from the interior. I wasn't watching Maurice on the dock, though, or the squalid huts of Mole Saint-Nicolas. I stared fixedly at the dark shadows of the high mountains of Haiti, looming up to eclipse the bright stars of the Caribbean night sky. I watched the land slide away with maniacal focus, not paying any attention to what was going on around me, as Henri and his crew whispered back and forth, working the ship out into the little harbor and out to sea.

And as those mountains retreated into the night, as the huts grew smaller, Maurice disappeared into the darkness. Eventually, I could see nothing more of Haiti.

I wept silent tears of relief and release.

I was free.

*****

Remembering Maurice's parting words, I kept to myself as we sailed west. On our left the coast of what had once been Cuba slid silently by. For their part, Henri and his crew, sons, daughter, niece, nephews, I didn't know, they all but ignored me unless I was in the way in which case, they would gently move me, or it was meal time at which point they brought me plates of rice and stew without comment.

But even in this isolation, I was happy. The heat was invigorating rather than oppressive. The breeze was sweeter than anything I had ever smelled before. Everything looked clear and vibrant, and I knew that my soul was responding to my newfound freedom in ways both deep and subtle. In large part my mind had refused to acknowledge the seriousness of my plight, but now that I was back on course, away from my captors and their world, I felt light and almost giddy.

I didn't have a cabin, none of us did. But there were hammocks in the small hold just beneath the main deck, and I spent much of my time down there, reacquainting myself with my notes, making additions that incorporated the intriguing hints my host in the tower of *La Citadelle* had dropped.

Often, I would take out the ring and stare at its fine craftsmanship. Such an ornament would not be cheap. I wondered what might happen if I showed it to Henri or one of the others. Would they recognize it? Would they know what it meant?

I tried to imagine walking into a Haitian consulate in New Orleans, showing the ring and demanding assistance. Would they toss me out onto the street, or look at me with the hooded fear and deference I often sensed from Henri and the crew?

And what of the massive black coach that had driven me from the fortress? The fear I had seen in Mr. Black's eyes was clear in my mind. Obviously, there were factions within the ruling elite of the Empire of Haiti of which outsiders like myself knew nothing. How could I know who my mysterious benefactor served? I could show the wrong Haitian my ring and end up right back in chains.

I resolved early on in the voyage west not to show anyone the ring unless I was in desperate need. I would do everything I could from that moment on to avoid ever being under the power of another person again. I had had my taste of slavery and I wasn't about to partake of that bitter fruit again.

Eventually, we reached some invisible demarcation along the coast, leaving Haitian territory behind and entering the waters between Canaan and unclaimed Cuba. The Papal State in the new world, home to the viciously effective *Novi Mundi Inquisition*, was a mysterious realm to those of us in England. As contemptuous as their Italianate counterparts were towards the Church of England, it was said the *Novi Mundi* sects were a thousand times more opposed to the Albian equivalent.

There were also dark whispers about even more heretical behaviors in the swamps around New Orleans and the islands of Haiti that had completely abandoned my mind during my brief but harrowing time among the Haitians. These were said to be further concerns of the Pope in Rome and his Archbishop of Canaan, Grand Inquisitor Miguel de Saville y Golgotha.

Henri and the others, never loud to begin with, grew downright mute as we turned north-west, leaving the coast behind and heading out into the open waters. They were hyper-vigilant as we moved west, keeping wary eyes out all around for signs of sails on the horizon or airships overhead.

It took us less than a day to move out into the open gulf, but the oppression of fear and the sense of being watched made it seem like weeks. When the unseen coasts of Canaan and Cuba drifted off into our wakes it was with a visible relaxation from Henri and his little crew.

There was still a chance we might be seen, but we were not flying a Haitian flag, and within the gulf we could be coming from almost anywhere. The ship was a little larger than the average fishing vessels that might put out from Liberté, Washington, or Mexico, but not so much larger that it would demand immediate investigation.

We made good time, moving with a warm wind off the Caribbean at our backs, over the vivid blue waters of the gulf. The food was plentiful if plain, my companions pleasant if silent, and the weather remained clear for the entirety of our journey. It actually proved to be a pleasant respite, after my recent ordeals. And Henri and the others, despite their reticence, actually went some way to repairing my opinion of Haitians in general, or at least of these Haitians in particular.

That was, until we came in sight of land once more.

The coast of Liberté rose up off our right-hand bow one morning on the twelfth day of our journey. It was a light green smudge that soon resolved itself into a tangle of greenery and small islands, somehow both ominous and unwelcoming. I was apparently not the only one who felt this way, as the others began once more to speak in low, worried tones, casting hooded glances toward the shoreline and then back out to sea on our left. The air had grown warmer, more humid, and carried on its fitful, languid breezes an oppressive, unpleasantly organic smell.

I sensed something had changed between my companions and myself before the sun had climbed up over the single masthead. Possibly knowing that I would be able to understand French, Henri and the others began to whisper in a strange, lyrical patois that I couldn't possibly follow. They were nonchalant about it at first, casting only an occasional glance in my direction as had been their habit at the start of our voyage. But soon it became clear it was more than my newfound paranoia whispering to me that something was amiss.

There had been many small fishing vessels hovering around the horizon that morning. None of them came close, but they were there, and I could tell my companions were made even more nervous by their presence. As we approached land, we saw more of them. By the time we got close enough to drop anchor, we were being watched by four of five crews, their sails slack, their hands still.

When Henri confronted me with sheepish, sidelong glances, my imagination had worked itself up into quite a state concerning the crew's intentions. Was I being taken somewhere to be thrown into chains once again? I had checked my luggage belowdecks during our voyage, and the pack Maurice had given me had been filled with everything I might require once I made landfall; changes of clothing, bedroll, an oiled rain jacket and many other items. The wallet had not only included several thick gold coins and many silver, but a fold of Liberté livre as well. There appeared to be more than enough scrip in the wallet that I should be able to travel quite comfortably up the Mississippi without ever having to dip into the coins.

But was all of that just window dressing for a long confidence game?

When Henri stammered out his thoughts, a small but angry part of me almost wished it had been something more sinister.

Henri was afraid to head up the big river. He was going to set me on this strange shore, into that fetid, unwelcoming swamp. I was being dropped here, god alone knew how many miles of treacherous terrain between the city and myself.

My anger was intense. I toyed with the idea of threatening the old man, but his dark face was stoic, as if carved from old, stained wood. He refused to be moved by threats or pleading. The others would not meet my eyes as I looked at each in turn.

I understood. I do not mean to pretend otherwise. They were far from home, in potentially hostile waters, and I was a stranger to them. I have no doubt Maurice and my strange benefactor had intended that I be delivered all the way up the river, and they would be quite disappointed if they ever heard of what transpired there off that verdant shore, but that would do me no good in the here and now. I quickly ran out of threats or bargains. Not even a substantial pile of the coins in the little bag would budge Henri; he became more and more obstinate as I continued to press.

I surrendered, in the end. This was a simple man, out of his depth, and he had been pushed as far as he was willing to go without the eye of his master upon him. Without ceremony one of the younger men put the small dingy into the water and rowed it around to the lowest point of the railing. I climbed down into the little boat. With sure, powerful strokes the distance between the ship and the shore was crossed in what felt like the blink of an eye, and before I was even truly aware, the rowboat was on its way back, Henri and the others were already preparing to bring the ship around, and I was alone.

I watched them tack off south and east until they disappeared, then turned my back on the vast expanse of water and surveyed the hostile-seeming terrain before me. I was on a sandy beach, they had given me that much chance, at least. The land rose up from here, about five feet, to a line of low trees and tall grass emerging from a tangle of pale old wood thrown up from previous high seas.

I found a slight break in the trees, shouldered my pack, and pushed through the grass, hoping that something better than blind faith would occur to me at some point on my trek north. The small fishing boats were still there, watching me head inland, as the sea disappeared behind me around a bend in the faint path I followed.

I had no idea how far I had to travel, what might lay between myself and New Orleans, or what to expect from the people or the land I would encounter.

But as I took a deep breath of the heavy, thick air, I couldn't help but smile. A man is never more free than when he is completely and truly alone.

And my freedom was not so familiar that I could not take some comfort in that thought.

Chapter 7

Pleasure in my freedom was short lived.

The swamp was hot, sticky, and smelled like a thousand stinking animals had crawled into a mudflat and died. The mosquitos were a terror, seemingly big enough to suck me dry in a matter of hours or pick me up and carry me away. In fact, I do not believe I have ever been, in my entire life, as uncomfortable as I was in my first day in the bayous of the Mississippi.

I would travel for hours only to find myself facing an impassible stretch of water. I had seen more than one massive lizard creature, crocodiles or alligators, I knew not which, more than I would like to recount. I wasn't about to wade out into the stagnant, scum-covered channels to try and cross to the other side. And so I would backtrack, again for miserable hours, and try to find another path northward.

My first night in the swamp was, if possible, even worse than the day. The heat did not break with the setting of the sun, but if anything became even worse as my mind told me I should have found some relief with the darkness. My pack had included several modern conveniences, including a fire starter of Albian origin and several small lamps that seemed to work on some kind of stored power I could not decipher. The light thrown by the lamps, however, was soft and low, and did nothing to dispel the sense of looming danger from the pressing darkness. In fact, the only appreciable difference these lights made was to increase the number of insects swarming my position exponentially. The creatures of the swamp only grew louder with the fading of the sunset. Eventually, against my better judgement, I made a fire as best I could with dried dead wood I found on the higher tussocks, using twigs and pine needles for kindling.

The fire was a comfort despite its heat, but it was a constant chore to keep lit. I knew, as soon as I drifted off to sleep, if I could sleep, that it would die. I would wake up, if I did wake up, in complete darkness.

I once again began to doubt my own resolve, as well as my ability to see this quest through. If the trackless swamps of Liberté were defeating me so easily, what hope did I have out on the Western Marches? How would I survive in the Empire of the Summer Moon?

My plan of finding a shaman of the Comanche, or some tribes or nation, was certainly one of desperation at best. But at least it held *some* hope, if only a glimmer. But what good would that glimmer do me if I ended up trapped in the swamp for the rest of my life? The Haitian trail food in my pack would only last me so long. I had a good steel knife, thanks to my one-time captors, and an academic understanding, at least, of how to fish or trap. But I didn't like my chances if I was going to have to fend for myself for very long in this inhospitable place.

And if I couldn't even get out of a swamp, how was I going to help England regain her rightful place in the world?

I did not sleep much that night. Between the heat, the humidity, the mosquitos, the incessant sounds of the other night insects, animals, birds, and other denizens of the bog, that was no real surprise. And so, with very little sleep bolstering my mind, I was in even worse condition the next day. I made mistakes, I took paths that made no sense, requiring even more time spent backtracking and retracing my steps. This continued until not long past noon, with one bad misstep, I slid down a leaf-covered embankment of slime and mud and into the blood-warm waters of the bayou. I screamed and thrashed, imagining enormous lizards swimming silently my way beneath the opaque green of the water, until I lay on the muddy bank, gasping for breath and nearly sobbing with fear, frustration, and despair.

As soon as I caught my breath, I looked around me, got my bearings from the sun overhead, already tipping toward the west, and followed it. The Mississippi was somewhere in that direction, and once I hit the river, I would beg, borrow, or steal a boat or hire a boatman to take me north to the city.

There was no shame and only minimal risk of discovery in seeking help, I told myself over and over as I trudged purposefully westward in my sopping, clinging clothes. I wasn't going to discover anything if I died out here. And history wouldn't care how I got to New Orleans, at any rate.

And God alone knew if I would be able to drag myself out of the next cursed little rivulet I fell into.

*****

The fisherman's name was Pasquale, and he was more than happy to take my money in exchange for missing a day's working the shallows and whirlpools of the mighty river's vague boundaries. I was a little surprised when he balked at taking the livre, I offered him, only to jump at the silver penny that fell out of the little purse while I searched.

It made me wonder just how much the scraps of paper were going to be worth. Back home, the official exchange rates are cold, hard numbers, hardly seeming to shift. But on the bank of the Mississippi, with my fine new Haitian boots still squelching with bayou mud, it seemed like the situation was very different.

Pasquale kept his small boat close to the banks usually, on the inside of the many lazy turns of the Mississippi. Occasionally we would lurch across the expanse of the river to get to the inside of the next bend, and then row along that for a while.

Eventually, I started to wonder exactly how much that silver coin he took might be worth here. I knew I would have charged a prince's ransom to do the amount of work old Pasquale did to move me north.

The Creole French the old man used was almost understandable to me when he spoke slowly. However, for much of our journey together, he would natter away, seemingly unconcerned with whether or not I was following. I found myself nodding along when his tone seemed to indicate a response might fit, and otherwise spending my time sitting in the back of the little boat with the fishing equipment, packs, water, and food, watching the banks roll by. I wanted to offer my assistance, but old Pasquale only laughed, showing far fewer teeth than the normal complement, and muttered, *"Tét chaje Angle."*

From the old man's tone, I assume this was no accolade. I will admit to not researching the words, even later when time permitted.

And then, after an interminable number of hours sitting idly watching dark green jungle slide by, alternating with observing a man probably thrice my age doing more manual labor than I had done in my life, we took one more sweeping turn, and the right bank of the river opened up before us into what had, at one time, been one of the most beautiful cities in the world by all reports.

New Orleans. I will admit that, since the moment I first conceived this journey, one of the places I had most anticipated seeing had been the capitol of Liberté. It was said back home that New Orleans was a combination of Old World elegance and New World energy. It was supposed to be a vibrant, vital community where the exiles of Napoleon's *Grand Armee* were even now preparing their triumphant return to overthrow the French monarchy and take their place with the enlightened nations of the world.

I had expected brave displays of military power. I had thought to see the mixture of beautiful classical architecture combined with a vibrant commitment to a new day.

Instead, what I saw from my little rowboat on the slow, languid river was age, exhaustion, and surrender.

The white paint of the buildings, perhaps once as pristine and gleaming in the bright sunlight as it had been in my imagination, was peeling and discolored with patches of moss and mold. The streets may have been cobblestones once, but those stones were mostly covered over in mud and worse, and little effort had clearly been made to clean them.

The people I saw as we pulled up next to a low quay lining the right bank were quiet and sullen, not the rowdy, ebullient revolutionaries I had thought to find.

These men and women looked defeated. They looked tired. They looked as if the world had beaten them down and they had no intention of getting up again. It was a while before I realized that the vast majority of people in the city were much older than I. In fact, there were very few men and women my age to be found anywhere in New Orleans, I would come to understand.

No one moved to stop me, check my credentials, my business, or indeed ask my name on the docks as Pasquale tied us off and we said our swift, nonsensical goodbyes.

At least, I think he said, *'Au revoir'*, at any rate. With his accent, it was almost impossible to tell.

On the street that followed the river the people's eyes were either downcast or lost in the middle distance as they walked. I didn't know what they might be thinking or where they might be going, but this was not a happy city, I could tell.

I secured myself a room in the part of the city they called the *Vieux Quartier*. I will say this much for the inhabitants of the city: their French was much easier to understand than most of the Haitians I had met, or old Pasquale and his little fish-reeking boat.

The hotel where I secured a room was called *La Maison du Soleil Levant*, and indeed, the sign over the narrow door showed a sun rising over a low, rolling hill. As I had not seen any hills since being abandoned by Henri and his brood on the coast, I was fairly certain the image was meant to evoke some other, far off landscape.

Like much of New Orleans, this house had its mind far, far away.

The room was small and musty, the bedclothes damp. But I was free, back on my intended itinerary once more, and not a shadow of my Haitian captors remained nearby. The comfort this gave me was not to be underestimated, even as I sat on the low, soft bed and tried to come to grips with the differences between the New Orleans of my mind and the reality I had found at the end of my eternal rowboat ride.

I had thought to find allies here. Napoleon's battles with the French aristocracy were the stuff of legend. His ultimate defeat and self-imposed exile to the distant French holding were a large part of that legend.

Of course, so was the fact that he had died here, nearly forty years ago, most said of a broken heart and his own disappointment. Most in Europe had assumed his newfound nation of Liberté would explode, become a huge, dynamic threat to not only France, but Albion itself. Instead, Napoleon's every attempt to expand into the Western Marches to the north, the Comanche empire to the north west, or the Albian Duchy of Wessex to the east had failed miserably, only compounding the once-great commander's plight.

And now, buried in the last grand product of his reign, Napoleon's Tomb in the *Place d'Armes*, was just a footnote in the brutal, blood-soaked annals of this, the horrific nineteenth century.

I spent days in New Orleans, walking the muddy streets, taking in the shabby, dilapidated remnants of the once-great city. And the longer I stayed, the more it reminded me of England.

England, too, had been crushed in the moment of its greatest victory. Scholars agreed the British forces in the American colonies were only days away from total victory when the spy and traitor Benedict Arnold had sprung his trap. He had killed the apostate Washington and many of his inner circle. It should have been one of the greatest days in the history of the British Empire.

Instead, the viper had then turned on his masters. More than half the British soldiers, seduced with promises of land and glory and stories of a greater England to be created in the New World than ever could be found in the flawed and petty land of King George, had gone over to Arnold's newly announced Army of Albion.

And thus came the beginning of the end for England.

Now, to wander through the cities and towns of my homeland was to see skulking defeat and diminution at every turn. The Albian fleets, bolstered with all the resources of the New World and the tireless focus of their new overlord, had pursued the Royal Navy with a passion that had bordered on religious zealotry. Within twenty years nearly the entire empire had either been taken or had announced its own independence, knowing there was no way for the crown to intercede.

The part that rankled most was that Arnold didn't even take any of those lands. He cared nothing for establishing a far-flung dominion. He cared only for the destruction of England and the establishment of Albion as its rightful successor.

And here, in the downcast faces and dull eyes of these exiled French, I saw the same sense of cultural defeat; the same helpless, hopeless aura that has washed over the whole of England for nearly a hundred years. There seemed to be far fewer people in the city than I would have expected. Certainly, fewer than there would have been in a similar city in England, with all of her scattered sons and daughters retreating home from around the world.

But here, where I had expected streets teeming with exiled Frenchmen yearning for home, there was only a battered, defeated remnant, and most of them old.

I wanted to leave New Orleans as soon as possible. I felt like a very young man in an old man's world. Between the disappointment of finding the once-great city reduced to feeble decrepitude and the constant reminders of my own home's weakened and pathetic state, I could hardly stand to walk the streets or lay my head down on the damp pillow at night.

But what was my next step?

My travelogue and planned itinerary were clear enough: I was to head north from here, into the Western Marches of Albion. The Marches was not really a duchy, per se, but rather a half-tamed region that paid nominal fealty to ancient King Benedict in distant Winchester. In England many of the old men still called Benedict's capitol Philadelphia out of spite. But even in England, it was said that the Marches were a lawless territory where the only rule was that might makes right.

Just north of the border between Liberté and the Marches was the city of Corners. It was said to be a waystation of sorts between the more civilized regions of the New World and the half-tamed territories of the Marches and the Empire of the Summer Moon. It would be the best place to find a guide into the Comanche lands and to their capitol, Sahri.

Back in England, getting from New Orleans to Corners hadn't seemed like an insurmountable task. But then, I had expected Liberté to be a vibrant community with at least the modern conveniences of home. I could take a coach, maybe, or even a steam train north, and be in Corners in a matter of days.

Alas, as I have said, the Liberté of my expectations was a far cry from the nation I had found.

I would need to secure transport on my own; either overland transportation, a berth aboard one of the many steamships that plied the river, or, in a surreal twist of fate, somehow secure passage on one of several airships the otherwise backwards and defeated nation seemed to operate out of an airfield just north of the city.

At first, seeing them arriving and departing from afar, I had panicked. I had assumed they were Albian craft; maybe invading Liberté at long last or at the very least dropping some kind of peace keeping force into the little splinter of rebellion nestled against their border.

And indeed, I was informed many of the craft I saw out at the wide, flat facility were Albian; but they were commercial rather than military craft. Somehow, perhaps by some quirk of national inheritance given the Montgolfiers' origins, it would appear Liberté was on the forefront of airship technology.

It was a strange dichotomy to say the least, given the threadbare nature of the rest of the nation.

Still, as much as taking a ride in one of the machines was an intriguing prospect, I did not think I could abide being suspended beneath one of those huge gas balloons, remembering how the *Winglocke* had looked as it burned over the tossing waves.

No. If I was given any option, I would find another way north.

But images of my pathetic trek through the bayou plagued my dreams. The sweltering heat of day seldom gave way to anything re-sembling comfort at night, despite the advancing seasons; and the dis-comfort of the musty room, the dank bedclothes, and the oppressive heat followed me into sleep, the perfect crucible in which to conjure up nightmare versions of those horrible days.

And when I did not wake up gasping for breath in that thick, hot air, I woke up screaming, remembering the sensation of steel over my wrists and the view of the sky through barred windows or heavy burlap.

I didn't like my chances of making it north to Corners on my own, never mind to Sahri or, heaven forbid the need, beyond.

Which, however, left me in another tight spot. I may doubt my ability to travel long distances over hostile territory, but I also had nev-er had to secure assistance for such a journey, either.

Where was one to find a guide for an expedition such as the one I intended? I hardly thought it appropriate to put an advertisement in one of the city's broadsheets.

I asked at my hotel, but they only feigned confusion at my ac-cented French, and then told me that they could book passage aboard either a steamboat or an airship for a slight handling fee.

I was beginning to hate New Orleans.

I wandered the streets again, but this time watching the people more than the buildings. Over half wore some semblance of the uni-form of the *Grand Armee*, and most of them were truly ancient. Upon asking if they were all soldiers, I soon realized that a large part of the Liberté government was organized along militaristic lines. Indeed, the leader of their nascent nation was Governor General Desaix II, the son of one of the great man's closest friends.

One night, having had one too many cups of wine, I almost asked why, in a nation whose very name meant freedom, were they ruled over by a man who had only been elected years after rising to power, and never once faced any serious challenger for the position since? Luckily, even in my cups my lips knew when to stay closed.

And so I wandered among the tattered, threadbare, and fading uniforms of a once-great army, among a people born into defeat, who had never known the greatness of their forebears except in stories. And I looked for an adventurer.

There were many merchant's caravans moving between New Orleans and Corners, I discovered. Most trade with the Comanche bands moved through the Marches town. I toyed with the idea of trying to join a caravan, maybe pose as a merchant myself, or maybe a guard. But the one time I inquired, I was asked for a curriculum vitae that I was hard-pressed to fabricate on the spot, and found, further, that I was expected to provide my own weapons.

The pack provided by the Haitians had been extensively prepared, but it had not included anything any more dangerous than the long knife I had taken to wearing at my belt.

So that ruse, too, had fallen apart. I soon began to fear I would be trapped in this faded nation for eternity. Nothing much seemed to move there but the airships overhead, and those, I reaffirmed to myself, I could never ride.

One day my wanderings took me past a cemetery named, without trace of irony, Cemetery Number One. It gave perspective to this dreary city, seeing that their dead were entombed above ground, in stone vaults designed, in large part, to mimic both the houses of the living and the tombs of the ancient, revered dead.

I walked among the moss-covered structures in the murky twilight, having stumbled upon the place near sunset. And there, surrounded by death and reminders of the mortality of all things, I felt my resolve quaver once again.

I left Cemetery Number One and made directly for the river. I had found one redeeming quality of the entire city, and the best place to enjoy the small indulgences was a tiny establishment overlooking a series of waterfront docks and quays on the main roadway called *Café du Monde*. The locals called the little delicacies *beignets*, and although they were delicious wherever I found them, the little *café* on the waterfront was undeniably the best.

I settled down into a small corner table, the peeling paint on the metal furniture a dark green that hid the dirt and grime of the city well. I gently blew the powdered sugar off my first little treat and was raising it to my mouth when a low, harsh laugh sounded at my elbow. Were it any normal pastry, I might have stopped right then to ask what the joke might be, but with a *beignet* halfway to one's lips, one does not pause for anything short of a life-threatening crisis.

When I had popped the little sweet into my mouth I turned, meaning to inquire as to the humor of the situation with my mouth full of sugar and dough, manners be damned, when I pulled up short.

A woman stood by my table, a wild mane of dark hair tied into a queue hung down her back, flashing green eyes looked brazenly into mine, and an open, mocking smile played on her full lips. Her complexion was a dark *cafe au lait*, but whether from breeding or exposure to the sun I could not have said. It was healthy enough, either way, to put any English lady to shame; a clear sign that this was a woman who enjoyed the outdoors.

And indeed, in her manner of dress the same message was clearly conveyed. A tunic of many pockets was worn over a light white shirt, both tucked into rugged trousers, in turn tucked into high leather boots that must have walked a thousand miles or more. There was a worn pack over one shoulder, a long knife, longer than my own, on one hip, and a massive revolver low slung on the other. The only concession to adornment seemed to be a fine silver chain around her neck that disappeared beneath the soft fabric of her shirt.

My first thought was that I had found an adventurer.

My second was that I had *been* found by a very intimidating adventurer indeed.

Chapter 8

When I asked her what she wanted, she smiled, sat down, and took a *beignet* off my plate, popping it into her mouth.

"You've been wandering aimlessly down the streets and canals of New Orleans, shouting from the rooftops how eager you are to leave." She took my cup and dashed a swallow down, only to make a face and throw the cup back onto the table. "Tea. I should have known."

I was speechless. I opened my mouth, not even knowing what I was going to say, when she turned away and gestured for the young woman behind the counter and ordered a coffee, black.

When she turned back around to me her face was twisted as if she wanted to spit. "I don't know how you people drink that stuff. It tastes like grass soaked in warm water." She did spit, then, rather delicately all things considered, underneath our table. As she emerged, she muttered, "Albians."

I looked at her aghast and she raised both hands in a placating gesture. "Englishmen! I meant Englishmen." Then she shrugged with another sardonic smile. "Them too."

As a mug of black liquid was dropped onto the table, its pungent aroma catching in my nose, I found my tongue. "I don't know how you could drink *that*. A foul brew. How anything that smells so appealing could taste so like poison I will never know."

She laughed, a loud, hearty sound that brought us several glances from around the half-empty establishment. "*Touché*, Mr. Hawke. *Touché*."

And again my voice was gone. I stared at her, any curiosity and allure lost as the cold grip of fear began to squeeze my heart.

She saw my look and smiled. "How do I know your name?"

I nodded, closing my mouth with a snap! Her grin turned cruel. "I've been tracking you for days. I know everything about you, Mr. Hawke, and I've come to bring your quest to a quiet, unobtrusive end."

There was no smile, now. Her eyes were as hard as emeralds, her body completely still, her hands wrapped loosely around the mug of steaming liquid.

My heart was cold but sweat prickled my forehead and down my back.

I looked toward the street, mere steps away. If I tried to duck out now, beneath the threadbare rope separating the sitting area of *Café du Monde* from the muddy thoroughfare, I might just be able to lose myself in the milling trickle of vague, defeated humanity.

I shifted my weight, leaning toward the street, not daring now to look away from those cold green eyes.

And then she grinned.

The green fire of her eyes flashed into a glittering, sardonic gleam.

My fear gave way to a rising sense of indignation that burned everything else before it. I put my hands on the table and leaned forward, rising over her. I didn't know what I was going to do; she could probably destroy me in any number of ways, either physically or emotionally. But after everything I had been through, knowing the stakes and the sense of utter desperation in my gut as constant companions now for so long, the woman's mocking expression was proving too much on top of all the other indignities.

She looked up and just a touch of the humor left her eyes.

"I'm sorry. I've been watching you for days and I wanted to see how tightly you had managed to wind yourself." She leaned toward me. "Pretty tight from the way you were about to spring off without paying for your dessert, here."

She popped another *beignet* into her mouth, but I no longer cared.

I had lost the taste for them.

I did, however, take a steadying sip of tea before asking, "How do you know me?"

She shrugged, taking an unladylike gulp of coffee. "If you're wandering around the streets of New Orleans, asking every lay about and bar fly how to get into the Marches, eventually word is going to get back to Monique Dubois."

She nodded wryly at this backhanded introduction.

"Dubois? You don't sound French." Nor did she look French, with her dark complexion. I tried to settle back into my chair, but the woman had upset my calm, and the fact that the others in the *café* were shooting hooded glances at us wasn't helping any.

"I'm not. I'm a mongrel, like most of the folks you're going to run into around here. Liberté, Washington, the Marches, hell, even those folks on the other side of the border in Wessex, more or less. We're all mongrels."

She settled in and took another swig of coffee. "Sure, you've got your *Grand Armee* purists, and there are enclaves all over that try to hoard their blood lines like gold, but it's not like England here, or Mexico. My mother was from Albion, but had originally come from Ireland, I think. My father was from Liberté, but his family had been here long before Napoleon showed up. He used to say we had a little bit of everything in our back pocket. Even some Navajo, if you can believe that."

I took in her rugged dress and sure, cocky manner, and had no trouble imaging there might be some tribal blood in her past.

"No, Mr. Hawke, I'm just a woman trying to make her way in this cold, fallen world. Folks know I'm always open to a new job, and so, when the people who pay attention to such things carried me word that you were looking for help going north, Corners, maybe, or maybe even farther, and that you seemed to have the money you'd need to pay for the passage, I decided to look into things."

She eyed me up and down with a candor that I would have found disconcerting back home, but here it just reinforced my growing feeling of mild inadequacy. She smiled again, and again I felt there was more edge to the expression than maybe I deserved. "You don't look too dangerous, and so I asked around the Rising Sun, dropped a coin or two of my own, and put the rest of the pieces together without much further trouble."

"They told you my name?"

She laughed again, but this time it was a gentler sound, which put me a little more at ease until I thought I detected a hint of pity in it. "Mr. Hawke, they told me your name, they told me your room number, and for probably a groat or two more, they would have been opening your chambers up and offering me first dibs on anything of interest I found there." She shook her head. "We've got to get you out of New Orleans before the people here rob you blind. Truly, you're too good for this city."

My pride had been stung. Well, truth to tell, my pride had been pummeled savagely since the moment I had left home.

At the same time, I realized she was most probably more than capable of getting me out of Liberté and across the Marches, I also realized that I didn't want her to do so.

Now, don't misunderstand. I have always enjoyed the company of women in a proper, respectful sense. My beloved Felicity was the light of my life-

I suddenly realized how long it had been since I had even thought about Felicity. If any man had had reason to forget the comforts of home, it was me. But still, to have that good woman drop so completely from my mind, no matter the trials, was alarming.

I shook that away. I was confident there was no untoward chauvinism in the building antipathy I felt toward Ms. Dubois. My feelings for her were entirely based upon *her* attitude toward *me*.

I stood and dropped what seemed like an obscene amount of livre on the table. I had learned the amount that would satisfy the bar girl, and as I had found no other establishment that was even willing to look at the scrip, I had taken to paying at the *café* with the nearly valueless paper money.

"Thank you for your assessment, Ms. Dubois. But I believe I will continue to seek a guide without your help."

She made no effort to rise, only smiling at me again with that harsh edge. I nodded once, feeling that her lack of manners was no reason to abandon my own, and turned to walk away.

"No one's going to help you."

That brought me up short. I returned to the table, looking down at the woman as she took a sip of coffee.

"Pardon me?" I spoke stiffly.

"No one is going to help you." She glanced up at me as she put the mug down. "You sound too much like an Albian, and among the class of folk you're going to need, that's not going to help your case any."

I nodded, gnawing on my lower lip for a moment before catching myself and forcing my teeth to let go. "And why is that?"

She shrugged. "Well, firstly, a polite member of Albian society, which you sort of resemble, would have booked passage on an airship over a week ago. Even if your purse wasn't as deep as your accent seems to indicate, you were expected to jump on one of the nicer riverboats long before now."

"I don't understand." I settled back into my seat, intrigued despite myself.

"We don't get too many Albians wandering away from the airfields around here, Mr. Hawke. Especially lately, with tensions rising between New Orleans and the court at Winchester. Those that do pass through are mostly merchants who know their business, conduct it swiftly, and get on home right quick. Or an occasional Ranger patrol, given free reign within the city and between Wessex and here through one of the poorer attempts at a treaty Liberté has made, I'm afraid." She gestured toward me with the mug. "They don't haunt the city for days on end. Old Arnold and Napoleon, they weren't the best of boon companions, and even now, after the one's a decrepit breathing corpse and the other cold in his grave these long decades since, there's no love lost between Liberté and Albion."

I wanted to grin at that. I had known it, of course, but hearing it from a local made it more real, somehow, as if it carried greater weight.

The more enemies Albion had the better England's chances might be.

But she continued. "Now, of Englishman, you can imagine we get even less. Those Albians, well, the only thing they hate more than a Washingtonian is an Englishman, and the last one I ever heard about came through here maybe five or six years ago, got himself picked up by a roving patrol of Albian Rangers, dragged east, and no one ever heard of him again."

My research had found mention of the Albian Rangers, but I was more intrigued about this Englishman. "Who was he? What was he here for?"

She shrugged. "Who knows? He was in the city for a few days, then the blue coats picked him up one night and he was gone. He hadn't been here long enough to make much of an impression, and so when he was gone, wasn't none who cared enough to find out why."

I knew there were Englishman here in the New World. There was still clandestine trade with Liberté, Washington, and even the Empire of Haiti occasionally. But most of those connections were conducted through intermediaries given the eternal tensions between Albion and England.

But if I was going to be mistaken for an Albian here, and the Albians were disliked as strongly as she was saying, then perhaps travel through the more civilized portions of this region was going to be even more dangerous than I thought?

I had expected the Marches and the harsh lands of the Comanche to be the most dangerous part of my journey. Had my hatred of the Albians so blinded me to the similarities between us?

I looked up at the woman again. I needed help; I knew that. I knew that now more than ever. And I had no idea where else I could go to find it.

She must have seen the shift in my eyes, and her grin regained its cruel bite.

"You won't find anyone else, Hawke. No one is going to take a job they know I've stepped up for, and I wasn't shy letting folks know I was going to approach you." She shrugged, a luxuriant motion that reminded me of a cat. "As far as you're concerned, I'm the only game in town."

I watched her settled down, hooking her thumbs behind her gun belt, one hip cocked arrogantly to the side, wicked gleam in her green eyes.

And I knew she was right.

I was a stranger here. I had no idea what my next step should be. I had squandered what time I had had, and now, if she was telling the truth, my options were narrowed down to nothing.

And for some reason, I believed her.

I nodded and stood, following the woman toward the gap in the rope separating the sitting area from the street.

As we moved away from the table she glanced back over her shoulder. "Better drop another forty livre for the coffee."

Before I could question her on this, she was out in the street, the bar girl was watching me warily, and I dropped the two wrinkled notes with a sigh.

*****

Considering how long I had languished in New Orleans before meeting Miss Dubois, our departure from the city felt like I had been picked up by a whirlwind. She allowed me to keep my things in the hotel as we made our arrangements, although after learning how untrustworthy they were, I felt little loyalty to the staff.

We first made our way to the airfield, more to assuage my own curiosity than for any practical reason. I knew we wouldn't be journeying north by airship given how expensive such passage was and my own insistence that my feet stay firmly on the ground. Or on a sturdy ship's deck, at the very least. Still, it was fascinating to watch the operations of the airfield and see these giant machines in action.

We watched from across a narrow lake, reeds rising up all around us. There were five airships currently docked across the water. Three were the bigger cargo vessels, the gondolas suspended beneath their huge gas balloons. They were drab, grubby vessels, their utilitarian lines almost rendering even these wonderful flying machines mundane. The elaborate red, white, and blue banner of Albion was displayed prominently on the stubby fins arrayed around the rear of the whale-like balloon.

It was hard to believe they could possibly have placed boilers, furnaces, and all the other accoutrements of steam power in those flying shells. I knew it had something to do with the advanced ceramics the Albians had developed over the last decade and more, but beyond that, the best efforts of English spies had been unable to discover.

The cargo vessels were impressive enough, but it was the remaining two ships that caught my eye. The first was clearly military, similar in size, layout, and design to the doomed *Winglocke*. Its gondola and balloon were a matte black that made the blocky construction look formidable despite its lack of grace or style. The narrow hull of the gondola was studded with ports and hatches along its single deck, with a smaller, lower level probably incorporating what passed for a bridge or command deck.

The final airship, though, was a thoroughbred indeed. It had to be one of the passenger liners that we had heard so much about even in England. This was a smaller example of the type, but for all its lesser size, it surrendered nothing of the opulence and comfort it might offer its passengers.

The balloon was a rich brown with gold appointments, the gondola, perhaps thirty or forty feet long, was a creamy white with blue trim. Large windows like glowing, empty eyes, pierced the hull at irregular intervals, giving what must be fantastic views when the ship was in flight. By the churning activity swarming around the ship's moorings, it was clear they were preparing for departure.

The passenger airship was moored to a docking tower of dark stained wood and brass fittings, with a boarding level featuring wide windows and an excellent view of the other craft.

As I watched I felt the old familiar anger. That was the future there on the other side of the water. That was the future, and Albion had locked it away from my England.

In England, we were lucky to have even small balloons, and those were mainly for research or military scouting purposes. There was nothing back home like the luxurious sky cutter I was watching from the dirty reeds.

And that was all to the work of Albion.

Miss Dubois informed me that a ticket to board the floating palace would have cost me all the Haitian gold and silver in my little pouch and then some. That kind of opulence was reserved for the nobility of Albion or the wealthy entrepreneurs and merchant princes of the western nations.

And that particular ship wasn't going anywhere near where I needed to go. In the Western Marches, you might see a military ship, or, very rarely, a large cargo ship soaring by overhead, signaling some massive deal struck with the Comanche or some robber baron of the Marches. But you didn't see anything like the transport I was staring at. That was most likely headed toward Winchester, or at least one of the ducal capitals back east.

We backed away from the screen of reeds and headed home. I was in a funk. The world was rushing forward, bounding from one amazing advancement to the next, and my home was being left behind due solely to the cruel animosity of this upstart mummer's empire.

Miss Dubois made a half-hearted effort to jolly me out of my dark mood, but she wasn't one for coddling, and it showed. When she realized the depth of my commitment to my melancholy, she shrugged and left me at my hotel to seek amusement elsewhere.

Ever since our first meeting I hadn't been able to relax in my hotel. I felt the staff were more aloof now, more standoffish and quicker to take offense.

Or maybe that was simply my imagination filling in the gaps in my knowledge, knowing now that there were people here who had sold my every secret away. The fact that the price had apparently not been high only made it rankle further.

*****

The next day Miss Dubois brought me to one of the riverfront docks and we sat, eating sandwiches wrapped in waxed paper, watching the riverboats coming and going, loading and unloading at the busy marina.

These seemed much smaller than the airships, although most were larger than the gondolas alone. Many of them had seen better days and were obviously cargo ships, moving goods up and down the river and requiring little in the way of ornamentation or, indeed, fresh paint. But among these were several ships that were better maintained, running passengers rather than lumber and cotton.

Here, for the first time, I thought I detected that dynamic force I had expected from the New World. Here there was a hint of the frontier that had disappeared from England in the time of the Romans. Here, I felt we were at last rubbing up against those unknown places, those empty spots on the map that might just contain the secrets I needed.

I was looking at a gorgeous giant of a boat, all green and gold, its smokestacks splayed at the top like mighty crowns, its enormous rear-mounted paddlewheel like some magical cage holding an enormously powerful beast.

Miss Dubois nudged me with one sharp elbow and shook her head. "The *Natchez* isn't for the likes of you or me, Hawke." She used her chin to indicate a dirty white boat several slips down from the giant marvel that had captured my imagination. "*La Joyeaux* will get us where we need to be and won't attract undue attention."

I was disappointed, but not much. I had guessed we wouldn't be travelling anywhere in such obvious style. In fact, as I watched the sullen crew of the *Joyeaux* prepare her for the journey up-river, I found myself grateful we were going to be going by boat at all. As the woman's preparations had stretched on and on, I found myself getting nervous, contemplating the rigors of an overland trek.

It appeared that I would get to experience the boisterous energy of the border lands while yet enjoying the comforts of civilization at the same time - for a little bit longer, anyway.

Chapter 9

The *Joyeaux* steamed northward with the steady 'bang-bang-bang' of the drive wheel's paddle ringing out behind it. One of my gold coins secured us two cabins, although under the waterline and without windows. They were like cramped closets and provided precious few creature comforts. I found myself driven up on deck soon after we pushed off by those four narrow walls, the damp bedding, and the incessant shuddering of the outer hull.

The main deck of the steamship held a rundown *café* and casino, with various card and dice tables scattered through the center of the space while smaller tables and overstuffed, if threadbare, chairs haunted the periphery. Long, tall windows looked out over the banks of the Mississippi rolling past.

I was surprised to see quite a crowd had already begun to congregate here, but then, where else would they be? We were lucky to have gotten cabins of our own, I knew. There were a few third-class compartments below, with cots and floor space, but many of the passengers would be spending the two nights of our passage here on the deck, feigning wakefulness so as not to be ejected for sleeping in public.

Ms. Dubois had warned me when I had balked at spending the money on the cabins, of the dangers of appearing like a vagrant aboard the boat.

There was a set of wide double doors at the front of the room, and smaller doors interspersed among the windows to either side. The faint smell of must and mildew was a bit much for my sensitive stomach, and I made for the forward doors, hoping a little fresh air would mitigate my distress.

It always took me a few hours to acclimate myself to travel by water, and the steady rumbling of the *Joyeaux* was having an effect very similar to the rise and fall of the open ocean.

Out on deck I made my way to a railing that overlooked the workings of the bow and watched as the hands there put the finishing touches on neat coils of rope. The hawsers were still glistening with river water, but the men seemed happy enough as they went about their tasks, talking and laughing in a relaxed, easy manner.

"What the hell are you doing out here, Hawke?" Her voice set my spine to straightening, as it so often did. I turned to Ms. Dubois, determined to remain civil, and did my best to smile.

"I do not enjoy the first few hours of any voyage over water." I was going to say more, but she interrupted me at once.

"Weak stomach. Yeah. That follows." She tossed her auburn hair with a light laugh and headed back into the café area.

I turned back to the river, but my peace of mind had been stalled. I went back inside. Where the fresh air had failed me, perhaps conversation, no matter how contentious, would take my mind off my rebellious stomach.

Ms. Dubois had impressed upon me the importance of keeping my identity as an Englishman a secret. She assured me that if I didn't speak too long to strangers most people we met would assume I was an Albian. This bothered me more than I was going to admit. In fact, I was fairly certain she knew exactly how much it was going to bother me. But I promised to play by her rules and so, in a surfeit of caution, had avoided speaking to anyone.

All of which meant, if I wanted distraction, I was going to have to speak to her. As much as I would have rather kept to myself in that regard, or perhaps spoken to some of the other passengers, I resigned myself to the idea that we were going to be forced together for the duration of our journey.

She was sitting at one of the smaller tables by a window, a cup of her disgusting coffee steaming before her, looking out at the bank with a look of calm complacency on her even features.

For the first time, as I approached, the soft light coming through the window gleaming in her hair, I found myself reminded of my Felicity. Although they were nearly of a height, and their hair, although of very different coloring, was about the same length, there was truly very little else the women had in common. A moment's reflection, then, on why she might remind me of the woman I had asked to marry me revealed an uncomfortable realization. I believe Ms. Dubois had reminded me of Felicity not because of what they had in common, but by the vast gulf of personality and drive that separated them.

I could never imagine Felicity striking off on her own into any kind of wilderness; in England such things just weren't done. But even if they were acceptable, would Felicity Have ever wanted to head out into the trees?

Decidedly not, I realized.

But then, before this new journey, I would never have believed I'd be heading out into the mysterious beyond myself.

I shook the morbid fancies out of my head and stepped up to the table.

"Ms. Dubois, might I join you?" I had tried to keep things between us formal from our first meeting, but my sudden thoughts of Felicity left me with a vague taste of guilt and drove me to even greater efforts.

She stretched out, not looking away from the table. From the sliver of her face, I could see between the line of sunlight through the window and a fall of dark hair that she was smiling.

The guilt bit a little bit deeper still.

"I'm not going to let you so much as breath the same air as me if you keep calling me that. Call me Monique or I'll see you when we dock at Josephine."

I cleared my throat at this. Of all the things she might have asked me, I had honestly not expected this.

"Very well, Monique. May I join you?"

She tilted her head toward me and the smile widened. "Why, certainly, Nicky! Pull up a chair!"

I hesitated. "Please call me Nicholas." I tried to keep the pleading tone from my voice, but I wasn't entirely certain whether or not I had succeeded until the old edge gleamed from her smile. I had not.

"Absolutely, Nicholas. Happy to oblige." She stretched out one long leg and kicked the free chair out from underneath the table.

I looked around as I settled down, hoping to find a servant, but out here beyond the circle of gaming tables it looked as if we were on our own. I glanced at Monique's coffee and raised an eyebrow inquiringly.

She looked at me, arching her own eyebrow without comment. I refused to give her the satisfaction. I could get tea later if I still wanted it.

At the thought my stomach gave a gentle lurch and I was reminded why I had followed her here in the first place.

But now that we came to it, I wasn't at all sure what to talk about. There was no way this frontierswoman was going to know anything about my research, or the tales and rituals of the Comanche. She might be able to get me into their Empire, but she hadn't struck me as a student of the finer aspects of tribal culture.

"So, how long before we get to Corners?" We had gone over the entire itinerary before leaving New Orleans, of course, but it couldn't hurt to start there. I had always felt a vague curiosity concerning the Western Marches of Albion. We in England had a romanticized view of the region, I'm sure. But still, a place where the domestic enemies of the House of Arnold scratched out a living, plotting and planning for their eventual return and the downfall of the fiendish despots? How could that fail to fire the imagination of any Englishman?

And there I was, with every intention of crossing into the Marches myself in just a few days' time. It was enough to get a man's heart beating.

She shrugged. "Well, we should be getting to Josephine early the day after tomorrow. Small town, but most folks use it as a launching point for trips into the Marches, so there's plenty of stables there, horse trading, and outfitters. We'll be able to get what we need and be ready to go in about a day. So, we'll be heading out the day after that, and then the overland trek up to Corners could take anywhere from a week to ten days, depending on the conditions, and what we might find along the way."

I nodded, letting my mind wander over the danger and allure of the unknown. "Are we going to run into trouble?" I nodded at her holster and started as I realized the pistol that normally rode on her hip was missing.

She noticed and nodded. "The river authority frowns on passengers riding heeled. I left her back in my cupboard."

I remembered how easily subverted the staff of my hotel had been and sat up straighter as I thought of her being relieved of her firearm through this lack of concern.

She noticed, of course, and grinned again. "Don't worry. No one'll be able to find it."

I tried to settle back, but from the moment I met Monique, she had been carrying that enormous weapon around with her. At first, I was uncomfortable, to be honest. But I found now that she had taken the gun off that I had grown accustomed to it. I was less than comfortable thinking that if we had need to get out of a sticky situation, we would be doing it without that giant cannon.

She smiled again. "Don't worry, Nicholas. If things get kicked into a cocked hat, I'm not without recourse."

I nodded again, trying not to frown as she took another sip of coffee.

"So, Corners." I needed to get my mind off all of this. I had forgotten my unsettled stomach, but now my mind was occupied with even more troubling images.

Monique put the coffee back down. "Corners. What about it?"

She wasn't going to make this easy. Well, such intellectual fencing might be just what I needed to keep my mind off all my various other troubles

"You've been there?"

She snorted. "Nicholas, it would be pretty shameful of me to have taken your money if I hadn't. Are you accusing me of being a sharp?"

I didn't understand the usage of the term in context, but even so felt like I had to defend myself. "No, of course! I only meant—"

"I'm just yanking your chain, Nicky. You can't rise to every little worm I drag by your face."

I truly did not like being called Nicky, especially when she did it in that condescending tone.

"I've spent years in the Marches. I can get you wherever you need to go." She sipped at her coffee and watched the bank of the river, apparently finished with the conversation.

But I wanted to know more. It wasn't just that I wanted to know what to expect in Corners, but my curiosity about the Marches themselves had been piqued as well.

I decided to try a direct approach.

"What's it like?"

She continued to look out the window, cradling her cup in her hands, but I could tell from the thoughtful look on her face that she was thinking about my question.

I followed her gaze and was surprised to see, beyond the trees along the bank and hugging a hill in the distance, what looked like a camp with orderly rows of tents. It reminded me of nothing so much as an armed encampment.

Why would there be an armed encampment way out here, far from the normal travel routes?

"What is that?" I gestured toward the distant sight, already disappearing behind the tall willows.

She smiled and shrugged, ignoring that particular question.

"What's Corners like?" I blinked, taking a moment to remember what I had asked before I'd seen the tents. "It's strange. Bit of a mixed bag, really. Half the inhabitants are down-at-the-heels would-be pioneers, caught by their lack of preparation, knowledge, or luck. Those folks will do nearly anything for their next meal, or a place on one of the caravans heading out of town. They're a hapless lot, but harmless for the most part."

I waited for her to continue, and when she didn't, I leaned in. "And the other half?"

She smiled at that. "Well, the other half, that's where the excitement comes in, isn't it? Those are the survivors. The men and women who run Corners, who make it work as well as it does, when it does, are a breed apart. You'll find them all over the Marches. They see a need and they figure out how to fill it. They run the outfitters, the depots, the bars and brothels. They provide what others need, or think they need, as they pass on through."

She turned toward me, throwing one elbow over the back of her chair. "Corners stands primarily as a waystation for folks heading into the Empire of the Summer Moon, or the northern Marches, from the south and east, or for businessmen and drovers heading back to Albion or Liberté with their latest acquisitions. Anything folks might need for that type of journey can be procured at Corners. It's a bustling little burg when you look at in that way. A place folks can make their fortunes; or lose them, if they get dealt a bad hand."

It didn't sound like someplace I would want to stay. Her words did nothing for my sense of adventure and romance, to say the least. I felt my excitement for our journey flag and settled back in the creaking metal seat.

I don't know if Monique thought I was disappointed in this rendition of Corners' relative merits or realized the more global scope of my disappointment, but she clearly noticed the change in my demeanor.

"It's not all that bad, Nicholas. There's plenty to recommend it, for a quick stop. You probably won't be there long enough to feel any of the more negative effects. And you'll have plenty of coin left to see you on your way."

That was a touchy point in our negotiations. Monique had not yet committed to the final leg of my journey, promising so far only to get me to the border town and help connect me with the people I would need to contact to reach the Comanche capitol.

I felt I knew her well enough to say she wouldn't abandon me on the frontier, but I was also honest enough with myself to admit that I wished she had agreed to come with me all the way to Sahri.

My weak stomach was long forgotten at that point, but at what cost? The conversation had given me more to worry about, not less.

Maybe something a little less connected with my actual journey, then.

"What are the Marches like?"

She took a sip of coffee and considered my question. "What are the Marches like?" Her lip quirked, almost dismissively. "Well, they're like a lot of things, really. You're talking about a pretty broad swath of territory, stretching from the sweltering border with Liberté all the way up into the frozen norther forests. So, it's not like the Marches are like any one thing at all."

"What are the cities like. What are the people like?"

She snapped out a short laugh at that, and I wondered for a moment what I had said that was so funny.

"Cities? Nicholas, you're going to be sorely disappointed if you plan on trekking up into the Marches expecting to find cities. There's nothing up there deserving of a name quite so grand."

I knew little, to be sure. In England we heard tales of the various ... well, I guess I couldn't call them cities now. Towns? Municipalities? I didn't even know. Anyway, names like Corners and Perdition and Florian were bandied about in pubs and common houses across England. There were all sorts of stories, but they all centered around plucky rebels living lives of stalwart resolve, planning the downfall of Albion.

In retrospect, they had a lot more in common with tales of Robin Hood and Ivanhoe than they did with contemporary reports from other parts of the globe.

But that did nothing to reduce the romantic allure I felt for them.

"So, they're all like Corners, then? Squalid little dives, barely scratching out an existence in the dust?"

That seemed to take her aback a little. "Squalid? Did I give you the impression that Corners is squalid? More wealth moves through that berg than almost any city in the interior of the continent, Nicholas. Granted, much of that is in horse flesh, but there's a lot of money to be made there, both by the merchants, drovers, and such, and off them as well. No, Corners might not be fancy, but there's a lot of folks making very good coin there, even as there's all those others coming up bust."

I nodded. I could work with that. "What about the other...places? Places like Florian, Perdition?"

Now she cast a cagey look my way. "Ah, you're looking for tales from the Penny Dreadfuls, are you? Asking for the latest high adventures from the land of the *White Rain* and *He Who Kills*?"

I knew, vaguely, what '*He Who Kills*' referred to, but I had never heard of white rain before. I said as much, as she snorted.

"Nicholas, you have no idea what you're getting yourself into, do you? You know how close the Marches are to the wastes? Hell, the western half of the Marches might as well be *in* the wastes! That's thousands upon thousands upon thousands of miles of land, shattered and broken by the eruption, that still haven't made any kind of recovery even in the 60 years that have come and gone."

She was talking about the eruption of what the cartographers had called the Yellowstone Volcano. The name derived from one of the tribes that had lived in the area during the original mapping, not long after Arnold had wrested control of the colonies away from England. The eruption had devastated the central plains and broken the continent's spine. Ash had covered nearly half the land, and winters across the globe had been brutal for decades after as the entire world struggled to recover.

I knew all that. Every schoolboy knew about the Yellowstone eruption. The tribes now referred to the crater where the mountain had once stood as *He Who Kills*. There were countless papers on the name alone in the hallowed halls of English academia. But that was far from the dusty reality of northern Liberté, on the verge of traveling into the Marches, the buffer zone that had developed between Albion and the ash wastes. Beyond the purely academic, I hadn't really spent much thought on the wastes at all.

Monique shook her head. "Your eyes are going to have to open sooner or later, Nicholas. You've had them buried too long in those books of yours. You aren't going to make it in the Marches, or in the Empire, without realizing the kind of impact the *Killer* has on the entire region."

But, upon seeing my reaction to this barrage, she relented somewhat, her green eyes softening.

"It's not all bad." She said it almost grudgingly, but I had the feeling the words were coming from more kindness than she would be willing to admit. "There's plenty of beauty and wonder in the Marches. And you're right to name Florian and Perdition, in particular. Have you ever seen any pictures of Florian?"

I shook my head. I had seen a rough diagram in a book, once, but I wasn't about to mention books at the moment.

"It's amazing. The town's right on the edge of a great chasm, one of the massive fissures in the earth caused by the *Killer's* eruption. You know about the chasms?" I nodded, but she must have seen through the bluff, and so continued. "The eruption shattered that whole part of the world. Cracks ran out from the collapsing mountain and across the continent. One of them, the easternmost, goes halfway through the Marches. That's where Florian is. But there are others, and west of the mountain it was even worse. That side of the continent looks like a shattered mosaic now, with deep canyons and cracks filled with the Pacific Ocean running all the way into Washington and the Comanche Empire."

I followed her words as she drew me a picture of the Marches that far outpaced my romantic expectations. A small voice in my head wondered if she was just humoring me, providing the distraction she must have sensed I was looking for; and so I wasn't entirely sure how much of her tale I should believe. Nevertheless, I was fascinated.

"Those rifts, theoretically, could provide a transportation route all the way through the wastes and to the shattered coast in the west. There are all sorts of stories from that area that would serve your romantic inclinations." She shot me a sideways smile that had a little of its old edge back.

"But as for Florian. You should see it one day, Nicholas. A ramshackle little shantytown, yes, but there are these enormous cranes on the very edge of the chasm. They lower entire steamboats down into the water! Not big ones like this, of course, but big enough. And those boats head out into the wastes, looking for a passage through to the other side. And when they come back, they are lifted back to the top to be repaired and serviced until they're ready to go out again."

"Repaired?" I didn't know much about steamboats, admittedly, but they seemed rather sturdy to me.

Her look was growing sardonic again. "Oh, Nicholas. You have so much to learn. The shadow of the *Killer* won't cross your path, I don't think, but you should know the impact that the volcano had over this whole region anyway, just in case. How could you do so much research into this area and still be so naïve?"

That brought me up short. How could she know how much research I had done? Had she gone through my things? Had she gained more from the staff at that blasted hotel than she had admitted?

But before I could follow up with this line of thought, she was off again, and distracted me with more stories of the wild Marches.

"Travel into the wastes is terribly dangerous. There are ash falls, the twisted remnants of the tribes and earliest settlers, regions of blasted rock and flame, even smaller volcanic vents that can erupt without warning, spewing poison, boulders, and ash into the sky." Her eyes were distant again, and I had the distinct feeling she was speaking from personal experience. "There are hidden valleys that somehow remained untouched all this time. Little pockets of green tucked away in folds of the landscape. And sometimes something will leap into those little forests and set them ablaze, filling the sky with choking smoke for days on end."

She shook her head. "It's a hellish place, the wastes."

"But," now, despite myself, I was entirely caught up in her tale, my concern for privacy completely forgotten. "If it's so dangerous, why go into it at all? Why an entire industry to bring steamboats all that way and drop them down into the cracks? Just to say you made the effort?"

I knew there was a breed of person who would take risks like those she described for that very reason. I had never understood such daredevils. Personally, it was only when I was convinced there was no other way did, I feel compelled to leave everything I knew behind and pursue this desperate, drastic line of inquiry. I couldn't imagine anything that would drive me into the wastes.

But a strange spark had ignited in Monique's eyes, and I saw there just the kind of resolve I felt would provide that drive.

"When the *Killer* erupted, the pressure from the explosion ran through every open space underground for hundreds of miles in every direction." She turned to look at me, the gleam even more intense. "That included every mine that had already been dug into the gold- and silver-rich hills. That explosion blasted those metals, and more besides, out over the countryside for anyone to just pick up and dust off. Nicholas, if you were lucky, a single trip into the wastes might set you up as a lord for the rest of your life."

My own family had lost its fortunes a long time ago as the economy of England began its collapse within the chokehold of Albion's animus. But still ... if there was really gold in the wastes just waiting to be picked up, wouldn't it all be gone by now?

I asked as much, and she turned away. "You forget, Nicholas. Everything in the waste is covered in ash. In some places it's only a dusting, but in others it can be feet or even yards deep. And in many places the ash has already hardened back into stone. It's out there, especially if you find a map of the area from before the *Killer* came, but you have to work for it."

"And the riverboats from Florian?"

"Well, on top of hoping to find a route west, those rivers have been the source of much of the gold that has come out of the wastes. The gold sinks to the bottom, you see, while the ash floats on the surface and eventually washes away. Most of those boats have all sorts of ingenious diving rigs aboard. They've pulled up all sorts of treasures. For the men and women who dare the canyons, or the folks who bankroll their efforts, it can be lucrative indeed."

I let that all sink in. I had seen several maps of the Western Marches while preparing for my journey, and one of my journals even had a sketch, as best as I could manage, of the region, with the various rumored cities, or whatever I should call them, marked off. I very much doubted that my journey would take me to Florian, but I found myself suddenly wishing that I could see the town with its mighty cranes and populace of adventuring treasure hunters.

But if the wastes were so pervasive, even reaching into the Marches, which the maps in England hadn't mentioned, that made the far western township of Perdition even harder to understand.

"What about Perdition, then? If the waste is so far east, how would a city—"

She put up a hand. "I can understand you may be thinking places like Corners and Florian are cities, but Perdition? Nicholas, Perdition is like nothing in your experience."

I had to admit to myself that I knew next to nothing of Perdition, other than the name, which seemed to reek of adventure and romance when I read it in the cold, dusty Oxford library. In my more lucid moments, I could even concede that the name was downright melodramatic.

"Perdition is the gateway to the waste. Anyone desperate enough to head down the ash-covered trail leading through the big western gate, with its enormous, twisted buffalo skulls hanging from poles to either side, either knows they're taking their life into their hands, or they haven't thought it through. There is no law in Perdition. You'll be able to find anything you might need to equip a trek out into the nothing, for a price, but if you come back out again, those same souls who took your money for their cheap, threadbare equipment going in one are just as likely to take whatever gold you score when you come out again. In fact, you're as likely to die in the tunnels of Perdition as you are in the broad devastation of the waste."

"Tunnels?"

She nodded. "The wastes move further east every year. In bad years, they swallow Perdition completely. The people there live in sealed up homes and much of the town is under the earth, now, built into a series of coal mines from before the eruption."

That sounded intriguing and exotic. But the rest of her description was more alarming.

"There's no law? But there is, in places like Corners or Florian?"

Her expression turned sour and was much closer to a grimace than a smile. "Well, the Marches are technically under the aegis of Albion, remember. So anywhere they care to impose their will, they do. We'll see Rangers in Corners, I have no doubt. They usually don't get in the way of business there, legitimate *or* crooked, but if someone goes beyond the pale, they'll step in. They expect at least a modicum of outward respect for the law, at least.

"Don't forget all along the Mississippi, the eastward border of the Marches, there are Albian fortresses, guarding against any kind of rebellion that might form in the lawless regions. At the top and bottom you've got Northwatch and Southwatch, which are more fortified towns than anything else, really, but in the middle there's Alden's Tor, which is a massive walled city that would do anything out of the Middle Ages proud. And then there's Gateway, just north of the city, which is where most of the Albian merchants come through.

"But beyond the immediate territories of those cities, it's catch as catch can. There are Ranger patrols, and even some Albian army units moving around on occasional maneuvers. In Florian, there is a council of religious folks from nearly all walks of life that see that peace is maintained. In fact, it's probably the safest little oasis in the entire Marches. But then, it's named after Saint Florian, the Saint of Fire and Water, so that probably sends a message right there."

I nodded. I hadn't known the origin of the name, but I had come across mentions of the council, and the belief that Florian was a haven in a fallen, wayward region. "Is the rest of the Marche empty?"

She took what must have been the last sip of her coffee, as she looked into the cup in surprise. "No, not by a long shot. There are little settlements and communities all throughout the Marches. Each different from the next. Some are models of civility and peace, where folks work together to carve a living out of the inhospitable earth. Others are hell holes that only the most desperate, or those eager for a quick death, would wander into of their own accord. And of course, the land in between all of these is entirely lawless. There's the Kingdom, all the way up in the trees to the north, but that hardly qualifies as the Marches, really."

"The Kingdom." I hadn't heard of that. It hardly sounded like something Benedict would allow to exist for long.

"The Sacred Kingdom, is I think what they've taken to claiming as its official name." Her dismissive tone was intriguing, given the high-sounded title. "Some petty Albian noble, Melchior, fled into the far north years ago and claimed independence. Carved out this frozen little fiefdom for himself with the help of some foolish dupes that followed him into exile." Her smile widened. "They even say he has an army up there, marching around, preparing to return and face Old Ben for the throne."

That definitely didn't sound like something the despot of the Americas would allow. "Why don't the Albians crush him?" That sounded more like the Albians we were familiar with in England.

"Well, Melchior and his followers believe it's their army, but I think it has something more to do with the abject poverty of their little Kingdom and the fact that they're so far removed from anything or anyone of consequence that has so far protected them." She shrugged, moving to stand. "Still, it's probably just a matter of time before Benjamin decides they set a bad precedent and crushes them for good."

She stood, stretching like a cat, and looked around the casino. "I think I might take a turn at one of the tables." And she left. She didn't wait to see if I was following. It was such a cavalier dismissal that I hadn't even processed it before she was gone.

I thought for a moment of trying to get noticed long enough to order a cup of tea but decided against it. My stomach suddenly became aware once more of the faint shifting of the deck beneath my feet, and I moved back outside into the warm air. Maybe the feel of the breeze on my face, tepid though it was, would keep my mind off my gut.

And I had a lot to think about.

Chapter 10

I awoke to a nightmarish sound, an unearthly howling that dove into the deepest depths of human hearing and then swooped up again into the highest registers, where it held steady for a moment before sinking once more. I sat bolt upright in my little cot, the tiny closet stifling. I lashed out around me, gasping for breath.

Beneath the howl I could feel the continuous juddering growl of the mighty steam engines pushing the *Joyeaux* against the full might of the Mississippi. There was something different about the engine sounds, however; something I couldn't quite place.

The alarm, so I assumed it now to be, continued for a few minutes, and then abruptly stopped. I was dressed by then, wondering if we were about to dock, or abandon ship, or be attacked by savage river pirates. There had to be a reason they would wake everyone on the boat.

I checked my pocket watch, tucked into my waistcoat as always when in civilized climes. I have, admittedly, never been an early riser, but it was barely 7:00 in the morning, and I felt justified to think that this was a tad early for them to have sounded such an unholy din.

The passageway outside my door was empty, which I thought odd given the alarm. I knocked on Monique's door, across the hall, but she didn't answer. One deck up, on the administrative and first-class level, I encountered a pair of crewmembers preparing the lounge and service desks for the day.

The crewmembers, when asked about the alarm, looked at me strangely, muttered something about white rain, and then went back to straightening papers, fluffing pillows, and whatever else they had been busy doing. I had the thought that I should really demand answers, but it was too early. If I had had my tea, perhaps, they would have been in considerable trouble.

The next level up was the boarding and promenade deck, again nearly empty this early in the morning. Most passengers were of the carousing class, staying up late gambling, drinking, and enjoying the various entertainers the *Joyeaux* employed. They slept well past the rising of the sun. There were more workers here, but they barely spared me a glance and I decided I'd rather not try to get any more information out of them.

Besides, I was supposed to be keeping a low profile, I remembered belatedly.

The windows on this level were small and narrow, and I noticed nothing beyond them but a strange, faintly glowing white light, as if the boat was enveloped in a thick fog. I made my way up again to the casino and *café* deck.

Here, at last, I found fellow passengers. Before I could ask anyone about the alarm, however, I answered the question for myself.

The air outside the windows was a soft white, glowing faintly with diffuse, directionless light. It reminded me at once of a classic London fog at dawn. But then something strange about the texture of the air drew me closer to the window. Fog, even London fog, can be a bit grainy at times, almost as if one could see the individual water droplets suspended in the air. This fog had that quality, but in far more profusion. In fact, as I watched, it resolved itself into more of a very fine snow than fog.

When I looked down at the deck outside the window I could see, indeed, that the snowy substance was accumulating on the polished planking.

Could it *be* snow?

"Welcome to your first white rain, Nicholas." I turned abruptly to find Monique standing behind me. She looked as fresh as a daisy and held a mug out to me that I eyed suspiciously before she shoved it into my hands. "Relax. It's tea."

I looked into the mug, still not sure I trusted her with something so important, but it did, in fact, look and smell like tea. There was no cream or sweetener added, but in extremis, a man will grab onto nearly any flotsam.

A careful sip revealed that it was in fact a very passable breakfast tea.

Finally, I found myself able to address this new strangeness. I looked out again at the strange, muted world. My mind was already grinding up to speed with that first sip.

"It's ash."

She smiled, with hands wrapped around her own mug of coffee. "It is indeed."

"Does that mean the volcano is erupting?" That was an alarming thought, even though I knew the caldera of the Yellowstone volcano was nearly two thousand miles from our current position.

She dismissed this with an ambivalent wave of her hand. I tried to ignore the annoyance.

"It could be almost anything. Usually, it's a minor eruption from one of the smaller vents, or it could have been a bad combination of winds and other weather effects, picking up a drift from the ash deserts and choosing to drop it here." She looked out into the whiteness. "It's rare this far south and east, which is good. A good rain is usually enough to wash away even a heavy ash fall. Until then the area'll be a mess, but it won't be too bad. You can't go out and breath it in while it's falling, or you'll be asking for trouble."

That didn't sound particularly pleasant. "How long do they last?"

She shrugged, not taking her eyes from the window. "Could be less than an hour, could be more than three or four, if it's a bad one. It's really hard to tell when you're in the middle of it."

I noticed, again, the change in the engine sounds. "What's wrong with the engines?" I had vague thoughts of the relative weight of the ash settling on the *Joyeaux's* hull. It couldn't be that much, could it?

"The vents into the steam engines have been shuttered nearly closed to avoid the ash from clogging the airways. It'll slow us down, but it's better than the alternative." I looked curiously at her, knowing next to nothing about steamboats in general and old second-hand Albian-manufactured steamboats in particular.

"The airflow into the steam engines could stop, starving the fires of oxygen, killing the fires. No fires, no boiling. No boiling, no steam. No steam, we nose back around and drift downriver until we hit a sandbar or a snag, and then we sit there until the ashfall ends and the deck hands get out there to unclog the airflows."

I nodded, frowning. That didn't sound pleasant either.

"We're almost to Josephine, too." She almost spat the words. "This could delay us an entire day if it keeps up."

We sat down to a relatively pleasant breakfast, all things considered, and luckily, the ashfall did not last long. By noon, the air was clear, the sky was a brilliant blue, and the crew had hosed off the decks. On our little floating piece of the world, anyway, there was no sign of the ash at all. It was very different beyond the railing, however, and I found myself doubting Monique's assurances that one good rain would be enough to wash all that muddy gray away. And it was gray, now, not white. Not unlike the snows of England, the pristine silvery mantle had quickly been sullied by the soil of the earth. Things on the banks and beyond just looked tired and dirty now.

I thought off in the distance, I saw another camp, this one of course covered in ash, but I couldn't be sure, and so I kept the thought to myself. Poor devils, if it was a camp, to have to slog through all that ash on land.

But onboard our ship, the steam engines were clear, the shutters presumably fully open, and the captain was clearly trying to make up for lost time as the thud-thud-thud of the paddlewheel crashing into the waters of the Mississippi was louder and faster than it had been throughout our journey.

We made it to the small, pleasant-looking town of Josephine well before sunset, only a few hours overdue.

The town was comprised mostly of one- and two-story structures, houses and businesses clustered together around a very pretty common square, an oval field surrounded by a well-maintained earthen road. The ashfall had not been nearly so heavy here, but even the dusting they had felt had turned into a sullen gray mess. We saw folks out sweeping the wooden walks in front of their homes and businesses, and a few men up on roofs, as well.

I noticed Josephine wasn't nearly so depressed looking as New Orleans, and said as much to Monique, who snorted. "Most of the *Grand Armee's* true believers stay close to the capitol, close to what power remains to them. Once you get away from them, things are much brighter for the most part. You'll still find old timers kicking about, remembering the faded glories of times long gone, but folks out here don't tend to let them drag everyone else down with them."

As I paid closer attention to the townsfolk we passed, I realized that not only did they not have the hang-dog expressions of their

New Orleans brethren, but many of them actually bore themselves like soldiers, despite their lack of uniforms. Most were armed, often with more than one firearm apiece, and they walked with a swagger I associated more with fighters than with farmers.

They looked like they were expecting a fight, and more than ready for it; they were anticipating it.

Maybe Liberté wasn't much like England after all, then. In England, there was nowhere to go to escape the general feeling of hopelessness and malaise of defeat and the ever-present sword of Albion hanging over our heads.

Monique brought us to a respectable looking hostel where my Haitian coins provided us with two small but comfortable rooms side by side, and after a quick meal in the common room, we went our separate ways for the night.

In the morning, on fresh horses purchased from a livery stable attached to the hostel, we headed out of town on a road that stretched out to the northwest. There were no signposts, but we were close enough to the border that if you were going there, you knew where you were going. And if you weren't going there, you'd find out soon enough.

As we moved out of town I saw, again, a camp. This time there was no mistaking it, nor the martial quality of its structure and purpose. It was an armed camp, complete with a small artillery train set apart behind a sturdy wooden fence.

"Monique," I pointed over my horse's neck toward the tents and cannon. "What is that? It's the third one we've seen since leaving New Orleans!"

She shook her head. "There are currently five camps between the capitol and the border. You missed two."

She could be maddening, at times. "What *are* they?"

She shrugged. "They're camps, Nicholas. What do they look like?"

And no matter how much I pressed, she would tell me no more.

The border between Liberté and the Western Marches was undramatic. There was a guard box beside the road, but it was unmanned. Monique said she'd never seen guards posted there in all the years she'd been going back and forth between Liberté and the Marches.

The terrain didn't mark the change much, either. We had been travelling through thick forest since leaving Josephine, making good time along a path that seemed to shift smoothly between road to track and back again on a whim. And on the far side of the border, other than our way seeming to be more and more track than road, there was little difference.

We stopped for lunch in a clearing where the pathway widened out, the trees pushed back at least far enough to ease my feeling that we were constantly under threat of surprise. Monique noticed my unease, but either through an excess of concern for my pride or a complete lack of curiosity thereof, she stayed silent on the matter.

As the sun began to descend somewhere beyond our piece of forest far to the west, the light faded quickly. The shadows beneath the trees seemed to advance all around, almost as if sensing my growing unease and becoming emboldened thereby. I know I was looking over my shoulder far more often than Monique and eventually she decided to take notice after all.

"Just who do you think is following us?" Her words lacked the contempt I was expecting, and in their seriousness, I found myself more nervous than I had been moments before.

"What?" I wasn't playing dumb, but rather at a loss for words that she might take the possibility that we were being followed seriously.

"You keep looking back as if you're expecting to see someone. At first, I figured it was just your constant paranoia and the usual unease of a city boy caught out in the woods. But you've gotten so jumpy, I'm starting to feel an itch between my own shoulder blades, and I don't really like it."

I shrugged. "I don't know. Is it always so empty? The trail?"

She looked down the path over her shoulder in the direction we'd just come, and then forward again, where it disappeared into the growing gloom of a forest evening. "I've made the trip and not met a soul traveling either way." She paused, her head tilted as she continued to stare ahead. "Not often, though."

Then she turned back to me, abruptly, her face tightening. "Who would be following you?"

I thought back to all her warnings about Albians, about the Free French and their reaction toward me if they thought *I* was an Albian. And then I thought, in a flash of fear, of my strange Haitian benefactor in his tall stone tower.

Who *would* be following me?

I shrugged. "No one that I can think of. Have *you* noticed anyone?"

She twisted in her saddle again to stare at our backtrail. "I hadn't. And I was looking."

There was a hard edge to her voice that I didn't like.

"I'm fairly certain I would have noticed—"

"Good evening, Dubois."

The voice was casual, almost amused. It was rich and deep, and its accents seemed almost familiar, although at the same time exotic for reasons I couldn't quite place.

And then a chill rushed down my spine. It reminded me of someone.

It reminded me of Captain Peyton as she harangued poor Larsen on the deck of his doomed ship.

It was an Albion's voice.

I watched as Monique's face froze, and then hardened.

"Clarke." She spat the name like a poison curse, and the chill in my spine seemed to solidify into a bar of ice.

"Fine evening for a chance meeting among old friends, wouldn't you agree?" A figure rode out from the shadows before us. He was on a huge, powerful-looking horse, almost like a draft animal except that it moved with the smooth assurance of a trained athlete. The figure was silhouetted against the last vestiges of sunset, with the latticework of branches woven up behind him.

"I'm not sure I've ever called you a friend, Clarke." Monique's tone had gone lazy, casual, but her hand slide to her holster, undoing the strap that held the enormous weapon in its sheath. "And if I did, I was probably drunk."

The stranger laughed at that, an open, easy sound. "That might have been the case." He looked down the long neck of his mount as if checking the ground before him. "What's your interest in the English, Dubois? Not usually your speed."

"What's your interest in my affairs, Clarke? Although that certainly always has been your speed."

The laugh sounded a little forced this time. "Dubois, you ought to know this is official business. The Crown wants that man, and the Crown is going to have him." Although it was hard to differentiate details in the fading light, I had the impression he shifted his gaze to me. "Friend, unless you want to bring your troubles down on Ms. Dubois, you might want to think about stepping that horse of yours to the side a bit. You might also want to try to convince her this isn't her fight. No one has to die here today."

My heart had skipped a beat when the man had uttered the word 'Crown'. That could only mean one thing in this part of the world: Albion. The rest seemed melodramatic at first, but then I remembered the casual way Peyton had killed old Captain Larsen. I hadn't met many Albians, that was sure, but I had met enough of them to have decided their reputation for petty cruelty and lack of morals was well-earned.

Before I could respond, Monique had moved her horse so that she was between me and the figure. "Clarke, I'm sure you think you brought enough people with you to make this seem like a good move. But you and I both know, that's not the case. Step aside, let us pass, and you can shadow us as far as you'd like. No one's breaking any laws, no one's doing anything dangerous. You follow us, you make sure we're on the up and up, and everyone's happy."

The figure was still, now. Even the horse was like a statue. When he responded this time, his voice was flat. "It's not like your masters to involve themselves with the English, Dubois. Do they know what you're doing?"

Her back stiffened. "You know better than to play that game, Clarke. I don't have masters, and you know it."

But there was something strange about her voice, and I found myself wondering who, after all, might be behind her interest in me.

"This is all tiresome." The man reached down and took something off his saddlebow. He played with it for a moment, and a bright light flashed out as he slid the front panel of the bullseye lantern open.

The man's face, lit from below, was jagged and craggy, with one pale scar rising up through the sparse beard on his right cheek and underneath a large black patch that covered his right eye. The scar continued up his forehead and into his hairline, where an echoing lock of white hair swept back beneath a distinctive tricorn hat.

The hat of an Albian Ranger.

"English, step away from the woman." His horse, at some silent signal from its rider, took several steps forward. The lantern was held up over his head, now, sending streaks of light and shadow swinging wildly through the clearing.

The shot, when it came, was deafening. A cloud of splinters and sawdust exploded from a tree right near my head and I shied away. My horse jumped sideways as the wood pattered across its coat.

"The next will take your head off, English." I had assumed the Ranger had fired the shot, but as I looked back over at him, I saw that he was still sitting his horse, calm as you please, lantern in one hand, reigns held loosely in the other. "If this conversation stretches by so much as one more word, you both die here."

He kept calling me 'English', which was unnerving, but I realized it meant he didn't actually know who I was. But that near-miss had been terrifying. I felt as if my heart had dropped right out of my body, and my chest was now an echoing void.

I tried to see what Monique was doing, but she was busy calming her own horse who had become skittish at the shot. I felt I knew her, at least a little, by now; I knew it would be hard for her not to continue talking under the circumstances. Would the Ranger and his men kill us both over her lack of social graces?

And then there was another shot. This one sounded like a cannon and erupted right near me. But it wasn't an incoming shot, I realized almost at once. An enormous plume of white smoke reached out from Monique's pistol, now wrapped in her diminutive-seeming hand, and into the encroaching darkness.

There was a scream somewhere out there among the trees, and a solid thud as if something heavy had just fallen from a great distance. This was all followed by a continued keening sound and the thrashing of some wounded animal in the undergrowth.

"Sorry, Clarke, sounds like that wasn't as clean as I generally like. But thank you for your consistency. You've never been able to wait until a trap was fully set before firing off your mouth."

"You Papist bitch!" The Ranger, Clarke, drew his own pistol and brought it to bear, but not before that cannon of Monique's roared out again. The Albian's own shot zinged out into the darkness as he ducked behind his massive mount's neck.

Two more shots sounded, and I watched as Monique brought her own horse around in a tight circle, firing seemingly at random into the woods.

"Go!" She cried out, slapping my horse's rear with one hand. "Stay on the trail. I'll catch up!"

I was moving, crouching low in the saddle, before I could have even understood her order. But as more shots rang out behind me, I drew my horse up. Could I leave a woman behind in the midst of a battle like this?

"Go, you idiot!" Two more shots rang out, and another scream broke the forest silence.

The Ranger, looming large before me, watched as I came closer. The whites of his one eye grew large, and then narrowed. His pistol came over his horse's neck and I suddenly seemed to be riding straight toward a massive, hellish tunnel.

Then another crack of thunder behind me, and a cloud of dust erupted from the man's shoulder as, with a grunt, he flew off his horses to roll into the darkness beneath the trees. The clearing was again plunged into night as his lantern crashed into the dirt, going out with a clang.

"Go!" Monique's voice was harsh now, and other shots began to ripple through the trees as the detonations of returning fire strobed out in the night.

Her own word was punctuated by a rapid-fire snapping sound, and I looked back again, against her express orders, to see that she was holding a new weapon. This was the length of a short rifle or maybe a carbine but was thick and heavy-looking. As I watched, she twisted around in the saddle, her horse continuing to ride toward me, and unleashed a fan of lightning-like fire back down the trail. The answering fire slackened at this, and I was forced to admire the technology behind such a devastating weapon.

I knew nothing like that had ever made its way to England, at any rate.

She tore past me, reaching out to give my reigns a violent yank with one hand. At that inducement, my own horses bolted, following hers down the dark trail.

As we rode past the Ranger, I saw the man rolling in the needles and leaf mold, growling low in his throat.

Behind us, as the trees of the forest once more closed in on either side, I could just make out the rapid impacts of pursuing hoofbeats.

"Hawke, come on!" I turned back to face Monique, lowering myself in the saddle and urging my mount into a harrowing gallop in the dark.

It was only because of this, because I was focused so single-mindedly on the trail ahead, that I was able to see what happened to Monique next. Something flew out of the darkness off to the right, sweeping her from the saddle. Her horse skidded to a halt, slewing to the side with the imparted force of her departure.

There was a great deal of motion in the darkness, grunts and hard, slapping impacts. I pulled my horse up, looking quickly over my shoulder for the Rangers that had to be right behind us. I couldn't see anyone, although I thought I could hear distant shouting beneath the sounds of the fight.

I saw a glint of starlight off blued steel, and jumped down to retrieve the thick, multi-barreled longarm Monique must have dropped. I couldn't make much out in the dark, but there was a clear trigger, and I could figure out which way to point the thing, at least.

I made my way, one careful step at a time, closer to the pair still brawling in the dark.

"Stop!" I imagined my voice would be deep and commanding. I had never held such a powerful weapon before; it was almost as if I could feel strength flowing into me through the stock and handgrip.

I was shocked to hear my voice betray me, breaking like a young boy's.

I cleared my throat and shouted again. "Stop!" This time I felt I had done a more creditable job of it, but then a foot slashed out of the confusing jumble, I'm nearly certain it wasn't Monique's, and caught me in the chest. I went flying backward into a tree, hit hard, and bounced off, the ground rushing up to meet me.

The gun bounded off into the darkness.

I couldn't breathe. My back flared with pain, deep and aching. My chest screamed around the impact point. My lungs burned as the moments slid by and I was unable to suck in a breath.

Meanwhile, nearby the fighting continued. My vision was starry; I was dizzy, whether from the impact or from the lack of oxygen I couldn't tell.

"Get." The word was spat out, almost barked. It might have been Monique's voice, but it was hard to tell. I tried to rise; tried to focus on the voice.

"Get." A grunt, the sound of an impact. The voice came again, more pained than before. "Get out."

She was telling me to leave. She wanted me to leave. I wanted to leave. I wanted to stand up, find my horse, clamber on, and run off into the night. I wanted to flee this nightmare.

But that would mean leaving Monique. I couldn't do that. I wouldn't let myself be the kind of man that could do that.

I forced myself onto my stomach, slowly rising to my hands and knees, focusing on drawing one, perfect breath into my tortured lungs.

And after that, another. And then another. If I could only focus for a moment, I knew the big rifle couldn't be far.

The grunting and panting sounded weaker off to my left. Monique and her assailant were tired. There was almost no way of knowing how much longer they would last, and who would have the last bit of energy to sink a knife into the other before succumbing to exhaustion.

My fingers dug through the leaves and pine needles beneath me. I fanned my arms, searching for the weapon. The last cry from the shadows had an unmistakably feminine timbre, and I began to search even more feverishly. If she was beaten, but I had the man dead to rights when he sought to make his final move, I might still save the situation.

I might still save her.

I could not be the reason we were defeated. I might not be a trained fighter, I might have never fired a weapon outside of a duck hunt or target range, but this new world wasn't going to treat me with such cavalier disregard. I would not be the reason this woman died here in this wood.

After what seemed like an eternity, my hand came down on something hard and smooth and cold. The stubby barrel of the rifle. I scrambled to my feet, fumbling the weapon around so it was pointing in the right direction, and swung it toward the fighting.

Except that the fighting was over, and I couldn't hear anything in the darkness. Then, from a direction I would have sworn was not down our backtrail, I heard galloping hooves. I brought the big gun up, pointing toward the sound, as a ghostly orange glow began to filter through the trees.

Three big figures on tall horses came around a bend in the trail that I didn't remember negotiating in the dark. They all wore the tricorn hats and half-caped cloaks of the Albian Rangers, the blue-gray of the fabric blending eerily with the nighttime forest. The lead Ranger was holding a lantern aloft, lighting the scene.

I wanted to look back and check on Monique, but I had them now, their pistols still down while the hellish maw of her weapon was pointing right at them.

I should have shouted at them to put their weapons down. I should have given them a chance to surrender; I had them dead to rights and there are certain obligations civilized people owe each other in such circumstances.

I didn't care. I pulled the trigger.

Nothing happened.

There wasn't even a dramatic click as a hammer fell on an empty chamber. Nothing happened at all.

The men pulled up, saw me with the big weapon pointed at them, and paused, their eyes wide. But then they must have realized my difficulty, as I jerked at the trigger over and over, desperate for some result, and each of then smiled the same, malevolent smile.

"Oh, in the name of Jesus and Mary—"

From behind me, without warning, three booming explosions flared over my shoulder, lighting up the forest night.

In rapid succession the men were dashed from their mounts, the lantern flipping away. This time, through some strange quirk, the lantern didn't go out, but rather splashed oil in a wide puddle that immediately erupted into dancing flames.

"Come on, Nicholas. You're worthless." A hand grabbed the shoulder of my jacket and pulled me backward. I was still staring at the men who had been grinning only moments before, entertained by thoughts of my death.

Monique spun me violently around and pushed me toward my patient horse, relieving me of the rifle as I passed.

My mind was a numb gray blank as I was pushed up onto my mount. I have no memory of urging the horse back onto the trail, and it's quite possible that Monique lead us both in the night, not waiting for me to gather my wits.

I do remember galloping through the darkness for what seemed like forever, with all the hounds of hell roaring just behind.

Chapter 11

"Who are you?" I sat in stillness, watching as she bandaged herself by the light of a small lantern, she had produced from one of her overstuffed saddlebags.

She looked as if she had fallen into the *Joyeaux's* paddle wheel, but I was fairly certain the Ranger had gotten much the worst of the fight.

She glanced up from tying off the bandage on her forearm, gave me a flat look, and then went back to settling the soft fabric around the shallow wound.

"I'm exactly what you hired, Nicholas. I'm a woman of fortune, I live on the fringes, helping hapless souls like you into and out of the hard places out here on the edges of the world. I'm nothing more and nothing less."

She said it matter-of-factly, as if expecting to be believed, but I wasn't ready to let it go at that. "That man called you a Papist."

She snorted. "He called me a lot of things. You don't want to start with one of the harsher examples? He accused me of being a female dog, I believe." She took out a small mirror and began to examine her battered face, moving the lantern to better see. "I'm Catholic, that's true. Most people in Liberté are Catholic. Does that bother you?"

It did, a little. The Catholic church had warmed to the Church of England over the last couple of hundred years, but Albion had thrown all that into the sewer. For almost a century now, the Popes in Rome had had no time for non-Catholics, no matter how benign. They had cemented their relationships with Spain, with Mexico to a lesser degree, and with both France and Liberté as well. And, of course, all of this had culminated in Spain's ceding the peninsula of Florida to the Papacy in 1819. Publicly concerned with growing rumors of strange blasphemies in Haiti and Albion, the Pope had granted the land to the Inquisition, who renamed it Canaan. They had been using it to keep an eye on all the various goings on in the New World ever since.

If Monique was a run-of-the-mill Catholic from Liberté, it wouldn't matter much at all. But if she was some operative from Canaan, that would be a much more sinister development.

"I haven't known many Catholics." I didn't know what else to say.

She laughed, then stifled the sound. "Of course. After Bloody Mary's last hurrah ended so abruptly, there weren't many left in England. Or, at least, not many who would admit it." She shrugged, then winced at the motion. "I haven't even been to church in years, Nicholas. Honestly, Clarke was just being a fool."

"And your masters?" That had been the other thing the Ranger had said that had stuck with me. Had she been working for someone else all this time? If so, how could I trust her?

She sighed. "Nicholas, do you think I mean to kill you? Do you think I'm here to stop you from reaching the frontier? Has this all just been one lark after another, with no rationale beyond my own amusement, or the vague sense of satisfaction I might derive from stymying the strange goals of a lonely Englishman who's wandered too far from home?"

She looked up then, and her piercing green eyes flashed through the darkness. "Do you not trust me, Nicholas?"

And that was what it all came down to, I knew. Did I trust her?

She had fought for me back in the forest, that was undeniable. And she had killed men for me. I knew that too. I could still see the last three pursuers knocked off their horses, dashed into bloody piles of shredded meat with her reloaded cannon. I glanced guiltily up at her again, watching her prod at the corner of her lip, swelling and disfigured from her brawl under the trees.

If all of that had been staged for my benefit, she wouldn't have killed all those men.

And if it had not been staged for my benefit, then Monique Dubois had put her life on the line for mine. She could have died trying to get me out of that trap alive.

She could have died.

I closed my eyes and nodded. "I trust you."

"Good." She said it with finality. "You should." She looked up from her mirror. "I could have died getting you out of there."

I looked up sharply at that, but she was staring at me, a wide grin on her battered face, and I couldn't help but smile in return.

"Who was that man, Clarke? How does he know you?"

That question seemed innocuous enough, and a safer line of friendly questioning.

To be honest, now that I had, for the most part, quieted my concerns about Monique, I felt the old depression descending upon me. My hatred of Albion and the crushing sense of helplessness on a national level had driven me from my home, my friends and family and everything I knew, and thrown me out into this new, strange, violent world. And yet, rather than empowerment or validation, at every turn where I had met with agents of Albion, I had been forced to run, or worse.

I had been unable to defend myself from the *Winglocke's* sadistic captain or her crew, escaping only when *La Arbitré* had come swooping out of the approaching hurricano. Then it felt as if Monique had me fleeing New Orleans at the merest shadow of Albian Rangers, and we had hopped aboard the *Joyeaux* and headed north. And now, in the middle of the woods on the verge of civilization, Clarke and his band had sprung a trap, had tried to take me into their custody for the Lord knew what kind of abuse, and I had been pathetically unable to defend myself.

I had held one of the most advanced pieces of weaponry I had ever seen, brought it to bear against three Rangers threatening me in the night, and still I had been unable to do anything to save myself.

The edges of my vision began to tinge red as I lost myself once more in that swirling hatred and fear. They would have killed me. I had no doubt about that. They would have killed me if capturing me had proven impractical. And had it not been for Monique, a woman all but a stranger just a short while before, I would be dead now. Dead at the hands of the monsters who had already destroyed everything I held dear.

I was deaf to her response, her voice merely a vague, distant droning as my despair and fury began to swirl up behind my eyes. And so, I was completely unaware when she stopped talking, looking up at me quizzically, and then scrambling over to me, where I had begun to shake gently, my eyes unfocused as my inner mind glared across the intervening leagues at distant Winchester and my most hated enemy, King Benjamin I.

She slapped me.

I felt, in retrospect, that my life had become one long, running Romantic poem. I half expected thunder and lightning from the clear, star-flecked sky.

Instead, I came to myself and looked up to see Monique hovering over me, gauging, I thought, whether or not another slap would be necessary.

I raised one hand to ward off the possible blow, but she had apparently been satisfied with seeing the light of reason reentering my eyes and settled back on her haunches.

"Thought I'd lost you there, Nicholas." She looked around and pulled a water bottle to herself, then handed it to me. "Don't—"

I took a long pull and then nearly choked as all the fires of creation exploded in my throat, burning their way down into my chest and then igniting a bonfire beneath my heart.

I gasped, the leather bottle dropping from numb fingers. My throat closed around the blistering burn scars and I coughed and coughed and coughed.

She had poisoned me.

I heard her laughter through the curtain of pain and betrayal, and the sting of it brought me back to myself, just a little. "Why?" I was able to whisper.

"It's white lightning; rot gut. I keep it for cleaning wounds and numbing pain." She brushed a tear from her eye. It was possibly the most genuine feeling I had ever seen her exhibit, and I was only slightly perturbed that it was at my expense. "You weren't supposed to toss it all down in one fell swoop."

Liquor. Of course. I should have recognized the burning aftertaste through my pain.

She was still chuckling as I came back to myself. She was staring at the lantern, a wistful look on her face.

"I wish we could have a fire, but we can't take the chance Clarke is still out there."

Clarke. The Albian Ranger. My battered mind was reeling through the moments during my incapacitation. I had asked. She had been answering. I had also been choking, however. I thought I might be able to salvage something of her answer from my memory, but nothing came.

Sheepishly, I looked up at her. "I'm sorry. But who is Clarke?"

She stared blankly at me in the dim red light, then sighed. "You didn't hear any of that?"

I looked away. "I got lost in my own thoughts. It happens sometimes. And the past few weeks have been on the harrowing side."

She tilted her head to the side and gave me a look that I felt was more sympathetic than expected, or in fact warranted, based upon what she herself knew.

She shook her head. "Geoff Clarke. He's a captain of the Albian Rangers. We've locked horns a few times in the Marches, is all. Occasionally we've even found ourselves on the same side, briefly, to be honest. But for the most part, he's spending most of his time trying to track people down, I'm spending my time trying to get them away from him." She smiled vaguely, and in the diffuse light it gave her face a softer aspect than any I had seen since we had first met.

"He's not a bad man, although he's a true believer in Benedict, for certain." She then shot me a look from beneath lowered brow. "I'm fairly certain the two of you wouldn't get along, if it should come to that."

I wanted to spit. "No, I don't think so." Then I remembered how we had left him. "He's still alive?"

Her eyes drifted up toward the cloudless sky overhead. "God, I hope so. I aimed for his shoulder, but the rounds from my revolver are pretty wide."

I nodded, remembering the last flight of the three assailants she had killed at the end. "I saw him moving as I rode past."

She sighed. "Oh, good. I'd hate to ruin my streak. It's been years since I've killed someone I didn't mean to kill."

That seemed ominous, but I left it alone. We went back to staring at the softly swaying light in the lantern. I found myself, not for the first time, wishing I could have a cup of tea. In fact, as the cold of the evening made itself known in the silence, I thought I'd even be able to make do with a coffee, if that was all that was available.

But without a fire, we weren't going to be able to have either, and I reconciled myself to a cold, miserable night.

"So, where'd you go?" She asked casually, not looking in my direction, and my thoughts had drifted so far away from our little glen that I had no idea what she was asking.

"Hmm?" I looked up from contemplating the flame. "I'm sorry?"

"Where did you go, when you started shaking like that?" Still, she wasn't looking at me.

I felt a flush of shame stretch across my face. "Nowhere." It was short, and abrupt, and cold. And she deserved more after what she had done for me that night. "Sometimes I become ... unmoored, is how I used to describe it. When the world as it is becomes too much, the injustices too hard to bear, I begin to spiral in my mind. It usually takes something drastic to shake me out again."

"Drastic is entirely within my bailiwick." She smiled another genuine smile. "Happy I could help."

I nodded, more in acknowledgment than thanks, and went back to the flame.

"But what were you thinking when it happened this time?"

I was still in the grip of a sense of indebtedness, and so took a deep breath. "I grew up in an England in decline. We once ruled the world. It was said that the sun never set on the British Empire, our holdings were so widely scattered around the world. We had colonies and protectorates on nearly every inhabited continent."

"And then Albion."

I shook my head. "And then Benedict Arnold. Albion came later. But it's all of a piece, of course. Historically speaking, overnight it all came apart. Albion was born and declared England it's most bitter enemy. Rather than consolidate its power in the New World, or even try to take our holdings away from us, they were like a petulant child in a playground. They raped this continent for the materials needed to create a massive armada as quickly as they could, and then they began to hound the British Fleet from every sea and ocean.

"King George, in the end, even tried to make peace. The Paris Accords were meant to put an end to hostilities. I believe King George would have done almost anything, at that point, to end things. But it was all a ruse on Benedict's part. While we were distracted with the hopes of peace, his navy struck in a concerted attack around the world. It was the beginning of the end."

"The Harrying." She said the word with no inflection, but even so it burned.

"That's what the historians called it. And ever since, England has been dying a slow, pathetic, unsung death.

"Did you grow up in Liberté?"

She nodded vaguely, looking into the flame.

"Well, then you know what it's like to be raised by a defeated people; to come of age in a declining culture whose greatest achievements are behind them, the future holding only further decay and degradation."

"It's a lot to bear."

"It is."

The silence stretched on between us. I felt the burning rising once more, and tamped it down, my fists painful balls of clenched muscle in my lap.

"But you think you can fix all that."

I stared at the little flame. Did I? The historical juggernaut that had been building momentum for nearly a hundred years, grinding every obstacle in its path beneath its implacable march...did I think I could put an end to all that?

I remembered the last conversation I had had with Felicity. She had been angry, of course, with my decision to leave England on such a fool's errand, as she put it. And from that terrible row, one word, spat at me with more vehemence than I had ever seen her exhibit towards anything, continued to ring down to me through all the weeks and months that had passed: hubris.

Did I think I could fix all this?

I shrugged. "I don't know, but someone has to do something or there's no hope at all."

She went to one of her packs and drew out her thick woolen blanket. I looked at it for a moment, nonplussed, then remembered the gear she had had me purchase back in New Orleans before we embarked upon the *Joyeaux*. The blanket I pulled from my own gear was almost identical to hers, and I was much more comfortable once I had wrapped it around my shoulders.

We sat, silent and cold, staring into the single glint of orange flame as the stars spun over our heads.

I knew that this feeling of hopeless in the face of Albion was at the core of my newfound inability to find equilibrium. It was almost as if there were two voices in my head; the voice that had always been there, the curious academic who had known modest success even in the moribund world of English academia, and then the newly-awakened firebrand who had seen a lateral application for my theories, that would perhaps alter the balance of world power enough to give England a chance to claw its way out of the pit Albion had relegated us to for countless decades.

Was I growing? Was I developing? Or was I fooling myself? Was this a natural progression, or the presentation of some sickness of the mind?

Was it hubris?

"So, what is it, exactly, that you feel you will be able to do at the end of this quixotic rainbow of yours?" She wasn't looking at me; her tone was light, casual.

But I suddenly wondered again if this woman had broken into my hotel room. Had she had access to all my things, my books?

Monique Dubois had not been a friend of mine then, if she was one now. She had not even been in my hire. She had been a total stranger, with no right to bribe the maids, or desk clerks, or whoever she had suborned.

How much did she know about me and my quest?

And if she had read my books, did she find them compelling? Or was it the Haitian gold and silver in my pocket that she was interested in?

She looked at me then, eyes open and curious. "What is it you think to accomplish in the Empire of the Summer Moon? What are you going to find there that might save England?"

Had I told her that was my goal? Had she just tipped her hand?

I had never been one for intrigue and plotting. Even at university, where a school of rabid young scholars fought over the dwindling resources of a dying academic tradition, I had never partaken of the politicking or empire building.

"I don't know what I'll find." My hand, of its own accord, went to my neck and took the fine silver chain there between thumb and forefinger absently.

"What's that?" She was watching me from the shifting shadows cast by the small lantern, but her eyes seemed friendly and curious.

I pulled Merlin's stone from my shirt. "It's an artifact I found in France."

I pulled the chain up over my head and held it out to her. She let it dangle before her face, the stone spinning gently. "It's beautiful. What is it?"

I shrugged. "A stone. A key, maybe. A clue. It's very old, and features in several of our myths and legends, I believe. A similar stone has been described in several ancient texts as being the head piece of a famous man's staff, or the pummel stone of a famous sword. Each of those items have been, in the stories, attributed with fantastical powers."

One arch eyebrow rose behind the still-swinging stone as she shifted her focus back to me. "You're going to be a wizard? Or King Arthur come again?"

I took the stone back and she only smiled at me again.

I shook my head. "King Arthur isn't coming back."

I put the chain back around my neck and hunkered down.

"But you might be a wizard." She was still smiling playfully, but the old darkness was settling about me like a second blanket. I had no interest in mockery, not after everything that had happened that night. I owed Monique my life; I was ready to accept that. But I had no wish to feel the blunt end of her wit where my hopeless quest was concerned.

She turned serious, but it took me a moment before I realized her look was now appraising, rather than mocking.

"You truly believe those stories might be true?"

That was more serious evaluation than I had received, other than the strange Haitian in the fortress, since long before I had left England. I was moved to respond seriously.

"I don't know, but I have to try. There are commonalities across times and cultures; every civilization has its stories of heroes and demons, using the powers of creation itself to defend or destroy. What if there is some kernel of truth to those tales? What if, through some scientifically plausible interplay between human physiology and something else, some rare force we haven't discovered yet, such things were possible?"

She nodded, and for some reason that I could not fathom in my own churn of emotions, she seemed almost sad.

I saw the glint of silver at her own neck and jerked my chin toward her. "What about yours? What's that?"

She looked puzzled for a moment, then looked down. She pulled on the chain and what appeared to be a crucifix slid into her hand. It was a little larger than one might see in England, where ostentation in religious jewelry had never been in vogue. But it was ornate, its detailing so fine I was reminded of the ring the Haitian had given me what seemed like a lifetime ago.

There was something strange about the cross, though, as I looked at it over the space that separated us. The upright seemed longer than it should have been, and ended in a flared, curved point, almost like the blade of a scimitar.

Before I could ask about it, she slid it back into her shirt with a shrug. "It belonged to my father."

The words were casual, but the tone seemed to brook no further discussion and I was already feeling churlish for my earlier behavior so I nodded and settled back down.

It was going to be a long, cold night.

I had almost drifted off to sleep despite the energy rushing through my veins and the cold pressing in all around, when I sensed her approach. I opened my eyes, one hand rising to fend off an attack of its own accord.

She was crouched beside me, holding something in both her hands, looking down at it.

After a moment, she looked up and held it out to me.

It was a small pistol, easily held in her palm, along with a holster that incorporated a collection of hoops holding small cartridges.

"I don't want you to be in that position again. I'll show you how to use it as we head west."

I took the pistol without a word, and when I looked up again, meaning to thank her, she was already rolling back into her blanket, her back to me.

I stared at the little gun for a long time, wondering what might have convinced her to arm me after all this time.

Maybe I hadn't acquitted myself so badly against the Albians after all.

Chapter 12

It took us six more days to reach Corners. The days were not unpleasant, as the sun was high and warm, the air dry compared to the fetid swamps of New Orleans or the regions around the Mississippi. The nights were cold with the approach of winter, even that far south, but after that first night, with no sign of pursuit all the next day, Monique allowed us to have a small fire as we camped in a dell some distance from the trail.

The forests grew sparser as we moved north and west, still dominating the landscape but more distinct sections rather than one enormous wood hemming in the world all around.

Monique took her work seriously, and several times each day she would ascend to a high hill along our route, alone and dismounted, crawling the last little ways to the crown to survey not only our back-trail, but all around us, in case the surviving Rangers were attempting to swing wide around and cut us off.

She had seen nothing, for which I was duly grateful. I had not slept well that first night, and I didn't think she had either. Her bruises were fading, her dark skin able to absorb the punishment far better than my English paleness would have done.

The rest of our journey was an easy, almost leisurely ride through some of the most beautiful country I had ever seen. This might have been what England looked like, a hundred years ago, before her people were forced to mine her for every last resource, having been cut off from our far-flung holdings around the world.

It was a bitter thought and unworthy of the moment, but such had been my disposition ever since our meeting with Clarke and his Rangers.

Each night she would go over the operation of my new pistol with me. We dared not fire off any rounds, hiding as we were, but she allowed me to dry fire the weapon on several occasions until she was confident, I understood the basic operation well enough. It was tiny, my little derringer, with only four cylinders. But it would be infinitely better than once again finding myself unarmed in the midst of a battle.

At least, I told myself that at any rate. I wasn't entirely certain Monique hadn't given me the gun more out of a concern for my feelings than our actual welfare.

We were aware of Corners long before we could see anything of the town itself. A strangely striated column of smoke rose into the clear blue sky, visible from miles away, the day before Monique's most optimistic estimation of our arrival. Hundreds of chimneys, she said, made more noticeable by the complete lack of human development for miles around.

We were on a grassy plain then, the nearest forests only dark clumps of shadow dotting the horizon. But the terrain was hilly, and so we couldn't see more than a mile or so in any one direction before the natural contours hid what might be further away.

We saw vague domes of light all around us that night, flickering in the distance, illuminating the hills around them. Those were most likely caravans, Monique assured me. The men and women moving in and out of Corners on their way to business throughout the continent made for a constant flow of humanity through this part of the world. It would be stranger for us to be alone on the prairie than for us to start encountering parties as we got closer to the celebrated hub of commerce of the southern Marches.

There was a tense energy between us after that first night in the wilds. Or maybe not. Maybe it was all in my head. Monique was pleasant enough; she wasn't anymore cold or distant than she had been throughout our journey north. In fact, if I was being honest, she seemed to have warmed to me, at least a little.

Maybe it was all in my head.

Her limp cleared up over the course of that next day, and by the time she was lecturing me on chimney fires and traffic patterns through the Marches, nearly all signs of the brawl in the woods was gone save for a small dark scab at the corner of her mouth.

We hadn't discussed my theories anymore, instead passing the time with tales of the Marches and the larger-than-life personalities that inhabited this zone on the fringes of civilization, interspersed with my continuing education into petit firearms.

We hadn't suffered through any further ashfalls, either, for which I was duly thankful. I didn't relish the thought of being caught out in the open during one of those freakish storms. Everything I owned covered in fine white powder? And I was fairly certain Corners was not going to be at the forefront of the personal ablutions' movement. Other than cold baths, I figured I was going to have to get used to the vaguely unpleasant itching that was developing in various places over my body.

Thankfully, as the proverbial frog in a pot brought to a boil slowly over time is blissfully unaware of his plight, so, too, was I unaware of what I felt certain had to be a growing odiferous pungency developing around my person.

Corners was located in a broad valley surrounded by low hills. As we came up over what at first appeared to be just another rise, we found ourselves looking down at a huddle of one- and two-story buildings sprawled out across the valley floor.

The center of the town was a core of buildings more colorfully painted than the rest. A single main street drove through town, with a scattering of side streets to either side. One large building, the biggest in the whole cluster, sat in the middle at one of the intersections. It was a deep green with cream detailing; framework, balcony bannisters, and whatnot. A broad boardwalk framed the two streets, and then, where they met, the wedge of the building was flat, providing the space for double batwing doors and a big second story balcony overlooking the intersection.

The outskirts of the town were comprised of smaller buildings, shabbier and poorly painted. In fact, those closest to the edges seemed to be raw wood, with no pretensions at all towards color. Beyond these ramshackle structures were massive corrals and fenced pastures. There were several small herds of horses in various points around the fenced labyrinth, but I could easily imagine hundreds if not thousands more. At the height of the trading season, whenever that might be, it looked as if there would be more horses included in those enclosures than I had ever seen in my life.

Monique had been here before, and so I was surprised to see her sitting still upon her horse, making no move to head down into the valley. She was scanning the scene as if looking for something specific, and the more the silence stretched on, the more uncomfortable I grew.

"So...looks good...?" I tried to jar her into motion, or at least get some kind of reaction, to better gauge our situation. Instead, she gave me a flat look and then went back to looking down at Corners. She glanced to either side, scanning the surrounding hills, and I was again left with the impression that she was looking for something, perhaps expecting something.

Or someone.

"Something wrong?" I shaded my eyes with one hand and tried to see what my guide was seeing. It was a bustling town, even I could see that. In fact, it was very similar to the image of frontier towns I had built in my mind based almost solely on the various bits of sensationalist fiction I had procured in England. Sadly, given our relative position in the world, there was not much serious scholarship in England concerning Albion or the far reaches of its holdings.

My companion grunted, somehow conveying a sense of dissatisfaction and a reconciliation with that state at the same time with the one monosyllabic utterance.

"That was less than informative."

She whickered at her horse and nudged it around, heading down toward the town. "Come on."

Was that last aimed at the horse or at me? I shook my head and brought my own mount around to follow.

The streets of Corners were dirt. I imagined it would have been a mess if it had rained recently. But the dry grass of the surrounding plains promised that such a state would be rare. Indeed, the opposite held true as we rode in, anyway. There was a desiccating dryness to the air, made worse by a perpetual fog of dust suspended in the oppressive heat despite the fact that I knew winter was closing in on the northern climes.

There were many people in Corners, and they ran the gamut from wealthy factors and merchants to the rough-and-tumble hands; at the bottom of the barrel the itinerant labor, hoping to pick up enough work to pay for another day's food, or perhaps passage back to civilization.

Because this wasn't civilization, I could see that at a glance. The poorer specimens we saw had a haunted, hunted look about their gaunt faces. They appeared almost feral, glances flicking from side to side, always looking out for the main chance. While the wealthy of Corners strode the streets like kings, complete with trains of hangers-on and guards to keep the undesirables at bay.

I could well imagine that Corners was a place where a man might hope to make his fortune with hard work, a little luck, and perhaps just a touch of ruthless ambition. But those fortunes would be made on the backs of those with less ambition or less luck. This was a place where Darwin would have found his theories on full display among the most advanced of the planet's animals.

"You should go to the Gem." She hadn't turned around, and for a moment, I didn't realize she was addressing me.

"Sorry?" I felt quite dense, like the dust choking the air was clogging my mind.

Monique turned to me, her face expressionless, and jerked her head toward the big building in the center of town. "The Gem. Your best bet for passage to Sahri is probably in there."

I was being abandoned. I was being abandoned in the middle of the street of a strange, alien town.

"But—" My mind refused to make sense of what was happening.

Monique turned around, looking at me at last, and the expression on her face was painful to see.

Pity.

"I told you I couldn't commit all the way to Sahri, Nicholas. I'm sorry, but I've got other irons in the fire. There are other things I have to see to, and I can't take the time away from them to see you safely into the grasslands and back." She nodded toward the tavern now towering above us. "They'll be able to help you in there, I promise. Tell them Monique Dubois vouches for you, and no one will dare to slip you a raw deal."

I looked up at the stylized jewel on the sign hanging over the double doors. "I don't know—"

She reached out and patted my arm. A shock went through my whole body as the energy fields of our bodies connected. It was like nothing I had ever encountered in all my years of research. Like a quick bolt of miniature lightning had leapt from her into me. A quick flash of an image, Felicity sitting in my reading room back home, appeared in my mind. Not because that snap of light and heat reminded me of her, but because it didn't.

My heart raced. I couldn't let Monique leave me. I thought back to the battle under the trees when we had first came into the Marches. I wouldn't have survived five seconds that night without her. Even with my little gun now stowed deep in my pack, having her by my side had made me feel safe throughout that journey. Could I face this next leg, into an even stranger land, among even more alien people, without her?

"Please, Monique—"

She shook her head, looking me squarely in the eyes. "Nicholas, I can't. I have to find out what happened to Clarke. I have to start talking to my contacts, find out if anyone's heard news of him. Then I have to head back to New Orleans. There are people who need to know the Rangers were following us. There are people who should have known; should have warned us. The fact that they got that close means several things have failed back home. It could be a bigger problem than any you'll face on the plains."

I shook my head. There was just no way that made sense. Not to me, anyway. I wasn't going to survive without her. I knew that suddenly more surely than I knew my own name, sitting that horse in the dust and the heat.

She relented, her eyes softening, and I knew hope. Briefly.

"If you have any doubts, or if you have any questions about anyone you meet, I'll find you here later this evening. We'll go over it all then and I'll make sure you've got all your ducks in a row."

That was something, anyway. At least she was saying that I would see her again. Maybe, given enough time to think, I would be able to come up with an argument that would convince her she needed to accompany me into the Comanche lands.

Without a backwards glance, she rode off, heading in the direction of a row of warehouses and factors' offices. I watched her ride off with easy grace, that giant pistol riding on her hip, and I felt my shoulders slump.

I gave the reins to a girl working for the livery stable beside the tavern, with a small silver penny and a request that she keep an extra careful eye on him, and then hoisted my heavy saddle bags onto one shoulder and headed across the boardwalk with a hollow footstep. I paused before the doors, trying to see anything in the gloom beyond the batwing doors. My eyes were still adjusting to the sun and I couldn't see anything but vague shapes and a sense of movement within.

With a deep breath and a quick twist of my neck, I reached out with one hand and pushed my way through the swinging doors and into my first badlands saloon.

It was dark inside, and warm. There was a humidity rising from the press of bodies that the air outside lacked. The room was crowded, with a bar along the left wall hosting a score of men and women crushed together shoulder to shoulder, while the tables scattered across the floor hadn't a single empty chair that I could see.

There was a steam-powered player piano tinkling away in the back; a low stage in the beside it was empty but promised live entertainment at some time.

I didn't know what kind of entertainment might be on offer, but I doubted it would be Shakespeare.

Back home I would avoid such crowded venues like the proverbial plague. Here, unfortunately, I didn't seem to have a choice. I moved to the back of the crowd at the bar and began to make my slow way through the press of bodies. I nodded whenever anyone looked back at me, avoiding eye contact and trying to mutter apologies in a running, monotoned monologue that continued right up to the point when a big man, apparently distracted by his own problems, shoved me back with a casual negligence that would have offended me if I'd had more presence of mind.

I found myself ejected by the mob. I stood there on the outskirts of the group again and tried to find a gap in the outer ring of drinkers and talkers. There was none. I walked the perimeter several times but it felt as if each time I approached, the throng around the bar would close ranks against me. I made several more abortive attempts to push myself into the formation, but each met with no more success than the first. In the last go, a tall mahogany-skinned man with a meticulously shaped spade beard and prodigious sideburns looked down at me for a moment, shrugged, and elbowed me casually in the throat.

I found myself once again circling around the edges, massaging my throat and unable to think through my next course of action, when my hand, thrust into my pockets in a moment of dejected peevishness, found the small ring I had been given back in Haiti.

Was there a Haitian legation in Corners?

I hadn't known what kind of help the Haitians could be to me when I was first set back on my journey, other than offering me freedom from the enslavement they, themselves, had imposed. But here, in the back of beyond and on the very fringe of civilization, without any other option open to me, abandoned by my only friend, or at least companion, and being a total stranger to the continent, never mind the town, maybe it was time to pursue this new possibility?

I left the Gem and went back out into the street. In the bright light of the sun, I inspected the ring once again. The details were even more impressive there in the undiluted light. But would it be enough? I had seen men and women of just about every shade walking the streets of Corners, as well as jammed into the Gem, but none of the darker-skinned folk had had anything about them that had indicated they might be Haitian over any other origin. How was I to find an official Haitian presence in such a chaotic, unstructured place?

I walked up and down the main street, looking into windows at dry goods shops, outfitters, factors, and countless other businesses, often several combined into one storefront. However, I didn't find anything that resembled a consulate, embassy, or official mission of any nationality.

Eventually, I tired of walking up and down the main avenue. The side streets, of which there were four, all contained smaller, shabbier buildings. Some did look like businesses, of a decidedly shadier aspect, of course, but most of those buildings looked to be warehouses, stock buildings, and residences. I couldn't find anything that looked official in any capacity, including a town hall or even a sheriff's office.

It was at that point that I remembered I had left law and order behind me in Liberté, which was a troubling thought in and of itself. That place was hardly a paragon of civilization itself, and I was far, far away from even its questionable protections now.

I saw a woman in trousers and a vest approaching me, auburn hair falling over one shoulder, and my heart skipped a moment. Thank God. I had been at my wit's end!

But it wasn't Monique. Realizing that my mind, even divorced from conscious thought, had been seeking her out as I paced the high street a hundred times, was disquieting. And realizing that this woman was not the woman I was looking for just made me feel that much more alone.

I couldn't take it any longer and approached a sober-looking older gentleman with white hair and a pressed suit.

"Excuse me, sir, could you please tell me where I could find … the Haitians, sir?" I was going to say the Haitian Embassy, or consulate, or something along those lines, but remembered that I hadn't seen anything like that, and had to assume the reason for that was because there wasn't one.

But maybe lacking an official residence simply meant that the Haitian presence in Corners was to be found elsewhere, and by asking for the Haitians in general I might elicit a more helpful response.

I was in luck. It had been so long since any kind of luck had bounced my way, I had to blink once or twice as my mind came to grips with the event.

The old man looked me up and down, sizing me up for some purpose of his own, and then tilted his head back up the street. "That factor up by the big white warehouse."

He was on his way before I could thank him. I turned in the direction he had indicated and began to walk with a confidence I didn't feel. But again, luck was with me, and I saw that a large, poorly white-washed warehouse was looming up over the surrounding buildings. Beside the hulking mass was a small, similarly colored office with a simple white sign with black lettering spelling out 'Factor'.

As I approached, I noticed there was a strange discoloration in the upper right-hand corner of the sign. As I peered more closely, I saw that it was a little splotch of paint, seeming accidental or incidental, but very distinct if you're memory had recently been jogged.

A little red on top blending into a little blue beneath, with a dot of white in the middle.

A subtle, abstract recreation of the flag of the Empire of Haiti.

I opened the door and entered, immediately reminded of my brief time on the island by the distinctive smells of spicy cooking coming from a back room. Before me was a small table with four men and a woman, all with dark skin and narrow, hooded eyes, who had been playing at cards before I entered.

Now they were all staring at me as if I was a cow that had wandered into their living room.

"Can we help you?" The woman's voice was lyrical with the accents of the islands, and I found myself jarred by the sound. I probably wouldn't be able to hear that accent again without being reminded of my harrowing experiences in the southern seas.

"I was hoping I could speak to someone about getting to Sahri." I saw no reason to beat around the bush. Either these people were going to help me or they weren't, and if they weren't, I needed to get going on my next plan, whatever that might be.

The woman sneered slightly, and settled back into her chair, picking up her cards. "You're in the wrong place, *estepid*. We don't organize caravans or coaches here."

One of the men shook his head, muttering something in their corrupted French to the others, and they all laughed. Several looked at me before they were all back around the table, focused again on the next hand of cards.

"I'm sorry, but I meant that I was hoping you could assist me in finding such transportation. Not that you might get me there yourself."

In England, the social niceties that surrounded taking advantage of a polite offer that stretched from one social strata to another was a long and elaborate dance. There were calling cards to leave, gifts to procure whose cost and value needed to be carefully weighed. There was even a rigid schedule for the back and forth, before a person of higher station might deign to assist, no matter the initial offer, a person from a lower place.

I had no idea what those conventions might be in Haiti. In fact, I had no idea who the man who had given me the ring might even *be*, let alone who these people before me were to *him*. Because of that, I had decided only as I pushed open the door, I wouldn't try to emulate those old English customs, or guess at the Haitian ones. I was going to continue with the direct approach and hope for the best. My fears of the mysterious black coach that had so startled my benefactor were ever-present in my mind, but I was quite literally at my wits' end.

The woman looked at me, contempt plain on her dark face, and didn't respond at all.

Well, the next step was clear, and so I went into my pocket for the ring.

I was suddenly staring down four barrels of varying diameters, each one unwaveringly pointed at my head. Behind each dark tunnel was a pair of dark eyes equally as still.

I thrust my hands up into the air. "No!" My brain scrambled. "*Pas de pistolet!*"

That brought them up short, and several of the weapons lowered as the eyes behind them widened slightly. Not the woman's though. If anything, her outstretched arm stiffened aggressively, and her weapon shifted toward my right eye.

"I'm not armed! I need help!" I wanted to show them the ring, but I realized that going for my pocket had, in retrospect, been a bad idea in such a place and at such a time. I almost entirely missed the look of contempt on their faces when I had announced I was unarmed, however.

Monique was right. I was never going to survive the Western Marches.

"What's in your pocket?" The woman's pistol dipped to indicate my pants, but then rose again, pointed once more at my eye.

"It's a ring. I think you might recognize it."

Two of them standing behind the woman, who I saw now was implausibly tall and rail thin, exchanged a glance. I was too concerned with the barrel pointing at my brain, but I thought the look they shared might have seemed anxious.

"Get it." The woman didn't look concerned at all.

I moved with slow, deliberate motions, slid one hand into my pocket, and drew out the ring. I held it up gingerly between thumb and forefinger for them to see, turning it so the insignia would be more visible.

The two men in the back of their little group looked at each other again, and they definitely seemed nervous now.

I tried not to sag with relief as the woman finally dropped her aim. She slid the big pistol into its holster and closed the distance between us with two prodigious steps. Before I could do anything, she had taken the ring and was inspecting it by the pale light admitted through the filthy windows.

"Where did you get this?" She wasn't looking at me but at the little bit of glittering jewelry.

"A man gave it to me." I was struck, again, by how little I knew, or could even guess, about those last harrowing hours on the island.

"A man?" She did look at me now, her fine brows lowering. "Who?"

The three men watched me with round eyes. None of them had put their weapons up, but they didn't seem to be that worried about me, either.

I shrugged. "I don't know who he was. I think I was in *La Citadelle*."

The woman looked back at the men behind her. One of them shrugged, another shook his head. The third was still staring at me as if

I was some exotic animal.

The woman's eyes were lost in shadow as she turned back to me. "Was he tall or short? Thin or fat?"

"Did he have a big nose?" One of the men, looking sheepish as soon as the rest of us shifted to look at him. He shrugged to the woman and muttered under his breath. *"Eh bien c'est!"*

"He—He was about my height." I hadn't been in any condition to take special note of the man's height or weight. But then I remembered the regal, aquiline nose as the man looked out the high window at the approaching coach below.

"He has a strong nose, like a Roman."

"Gros." The man who had chimed in spat the word under his breath as if he had been vindicated.

Then I remembered the paper. After another bout of negotiation, I pulled that from a notebook and handed it over as well.

The woman gave it a sour look, then turned back to me. She nodded slightly, as if deciding something. "Wait a moment."

She gave me back the ring and the paper and turned back to the men, who huddled forward, bright eyes shifting in the half-light.

"Où est Roger?"

One of the men looked away as if embarrassed. *"Il est avec les femmes."*

She nodded, a strange, disapproving look on her face, then jerked her head toward the door. Two of the men returned the gesture and moved out, giving me a quick glance as they past.

"Sit." She waved me to a seat.

I sat.

"Do not show that ring again in the Marches." She lowered herself back into her own chair as the remaining man gathered everything up off the table, including glasses and plates, leaving no sign that the group had been gathered there only moments ago.

I nodded. I hadn't expected to show anyone the ring at all, so this seemed like a safe promise to make.

Except that in the end, I had needed to show them the ring.

My situation was getting more and more complicated.

"We will arrange for you a place on a caravan heading west. You will be safe through to Sahri, but we have no power over the Bands. Among the Comanche you will be on your own. No ring will save you."

Her dark eyes stared, unwavering, into mine. "I do not know how you came by that ring and that paper, *monsieur*. I do not know if you came by them honestly or no. For all I know, there could be an envoy dead in a ditch anywhere between this *Dieu abandonné* hell hole and Port au Prince. Even assuming you were given the ring as you say, there are Haitians who would kill you for even possessing such an item, never mind trying to leverage assistance from them with it."

I remembered the woman asking after 'Roger' a minute ago and nodded glumly. I didn't know who this Roger was, but I was getting the impression I didn't want to meet him.

The tall woman snapped her fingers at the remaining man, and he rushed to get her a gleaming pen and a thick piece of parchment. "You will go now. Randal Cole is a merchant and drover. He works out of the Empty Coffer saloon, opposite end of town to the Gem. He has a caravan leaving from Corners tomorrow morning for Sahri." She was writing with quick, violent slashes of the gold pen. "This introduction will see you into a position." She looked me up and down. "Can you drive cattle?"

I could tell from the tone of her voice that she knew the answer before I gave it. She shook her head. "I'm going to assume you can't cook, you're no good with a gun, and you shy from manual labor as well."

"I'm excellent with sums!" That's not what I thought I was going to say, but I felt as if I had spent the last few months being told over and over about all things I could *not* do.

She laughed.

I hadn't expected that.

"Do you honestly believe any businessman would allow a stranger riding out of the plains anywhere near his numbers? You are a fish out of water, sir." She looked sideways at me, then. "Where are you from?"

I remembered Monique's admonition against revealing that. "Albion." It almost stuck in my throat, but I got it out.

That hard, dark stare narrowed, and then her teeth flashed in a lopsided grin.

"Of course." She folded the paper twice and pushed it toward me. The lack of seal or signature was alarming, but again, I was a stranger here, and I wasn't about to tell this woman how to go about her business.

"I'm afraid you might find yourself digging a ditch or two over the next few days, Sir Albion. I can't do more for you, however." She stood up, but then paused. "I trust you have money enough?"

I nodded, quickly. I didn't want to seem any more needy to this woman than I already did. But even as I nodded, my brain was going over the dwindling coins in my purse. I wasn't as confident as I would have liked.

And she saw that. Her face twisted into a knot of frustration and annoyance. *"Argent."*

The man started, and then disappeared quickly through a door in the back of the room. "I wouldn't show anyone gold out here, sir. I shall provide you with enough silver to see you to Sahri, if you are frugal."

I nodded my thanks, speechless at the power of this strange little ring.

And then, before I knew it, I was being graciously ushered back out into the blazing sun.

Chapter 13

Randal Cole was not a warm man. In fact, he was about as cold as I could imagine a man might be, in this heat-blasted landscape.

I had stayed in a small, hot room in a little flophouse on the edge of town. I had given up on the Gem, which was still filled to bursting when I had returned from my adventure with the Haitians.

I had wandered around at irregular intervals deep into the evening, hoping to find Monique, or be found by her, but I had had no luck. Either she had only been trying to foist me off when she told me she'd find me, or her business had been more pressing even than she had thought.

When I finally went to bed, it was with a heavy heart and a troubled mind, .

Luckily, the old woman who owned the house provided a breakfast of toast and bacon. Of course, all she had had to drink was coffee.

I made my way to the Empty Coffer, a small, one story shack within sight of the big, bright Gem down the long, straight street. I hadn't expected the place to be crowded that early in the morning, but it was. A large crowd of men and women were gathered out front, milling around, checking the tack on their horses and the fastenings on their gear. I tied my horse to a hitching post in front of the next building down, beyond the crowd, and waded in.

I was having flashes of the day before, trying to force my way through the crowd in the Gem, but this group was a little more attentive, a bit more awake and a bit less inebriated. They moved out of my way, grunting at my smiled apologies and even, in one or two rare cases, smiling back.

I did run into the shoulder of a huge dark-skinned man in trail gear, a dark wide-brimmed hat shading his face from the morning sun, who gave me a dirty look before turning back to the group he had been regaling with some tale. The man spoke English in a strange accent that seemed to stretch each word out uncomfortably, while slurring and blurring enough of the syllables to make his meaning hard to follow. It was an unfamiliar dialect. I turned away, noting his neatly trimmed beard and sweeping sideburns, thinking that this was a man I needed to avoid if I could.

Randal Cole was holding court on the boardwalk before the Empty Coffer. He sat behind a field table, flanked on either side by huge trailriders in long dusters and wide-brimmed hats. These two gentlemen kept a gallows' eye on the crowd, making sure no one came too close.

The pistols on their hips looked almost as big as Monique's.

I waited patiently in line behind several men and women who had obvious business with the caravan forming in the street. Often, a sheaf of papers would change hands, sometimes a handshake was enough. I wasn't sure what these people were arranging, but Cole clearly worked on several layers at once.

As the woman in front of me stepped to the side and turned away, a slip of paper clutched in one desperate hand, the great man himself looked up at me, his eyes dead.

"Yeah?"

And there it was. The warmth that I would take away from my interaction with Tillman Cole for the rest of my life.

"Sir, I was hoping to secure a place in your caravan. I have—"

He waved me off with one long hand and looked out into the sun. "Don't need no more hands."

"Sir, I'm not a—." I pulled the letter from the Haitian woman from my vest pocket. "Sir, I was told to give you this."

He took the paper, unfolded it brusquely, and read it. He looked up at me, his eyes narrow and his mouth twisted in annoyance. "You got anything to recommend you for this trip? Other than this paper, I mean?"

My heart skipped. I hoped this didn't mean the woman lacked the influence she thought she had.

Then I remembered the money.

"I have silver." I took the pouch out of my pocket. I wasn't about to show how much I had before a price was struck. I hadn't forgotten that much of bargaining since leaving home.

"What kind?" The man looked skeptical, and I was a little nervous to realize I didn't know what kind I had.

"Haitian." I said it quickly, not thinking. But the look of appraisal that swept Cole's face told me I had spoken correctly.

Were the Haitians that powerful this far from their little island empire? I knew about the *Pueblo Viejo* mines from my cursory studies before leaving England, of course. No third-rate encyclopedia article concerning the Haitian Empire failed to mention their seemingly bottomless gold and silver mines. But could that power stretch this far?

I carefully fetched one coin from the bag and gave it to Cole. "How many of these?"

His look turned greedy as he turned the coin over in his hand. He gave me another look and I knew he was trying to figure out how many I might have. He wouldn't want to leave anything on the table he might sweep into his hat.

"One hundred *gourdes*."

My stomach gave a sad little flip. There was no way I had even close to a hundred coins in that little pouch. I had counted them out in my room the night before and come up with 22.

Cole snorted. "Ten of these." He held the silver coin up to shine in the sun.

Without another word I pulled nine more coins out of the pouch and placed them on the table.

They disappeared at once and he focused on the man behind me. "We leave in an hour. You're in charge of your own horse and lodgings along the way. Breakfast is after we break camp each morning, dinner is after we make it. Food will be available from the chuck wagon at midday, but we usually won't be stopping."

That bland itinerary left me with a lot of questions, but Cole was already speaking to the next man, and I was clearly gone from his mind.

I stepped aside with a nod and looked back at the mob in the street. There wasn't a friendly face in the crowd, as everyone worked at readying their own supplies. I knew my saddlebags and my pack were full, mostly with equipment Monique had prepared for me herself, including the derringer. I had tried to go through it all the night before, but I had been exhausted; I had begun to pull what I believed was a blanket from one bag, and other things had come out with it, spilling onto the floor. I had surrendered, shoving it all back as best I could, pulling the cinches tight, and flopping down onto that thin, uncomfortable bed for what I felt might have been the worst night of sleep of my life.

As I think back now, I can't help but wonder at how quickly the horrors of my time on Haiti or in the bayous south of New Orleans had faded from my memory.

I drew my horse off to the side a bit, not wanting to get caught in another tussle before we even left. I had never felt more alone in the middle of a crowd. Even at the height of the controversial turn in my career, when the entire academic establishment of England had been arrayed against my newest theories, I had had friends and family who stayed beside me. And Felicity.

Here, half a world away from everything I knew, everything I was sacrificing for, I didn't have a friend on the entire continent.

For a moment I had forgotten the nature of my relationship with Ms. Dubois, and the forceful reminder of that business arrangement still stung.

I was petting my horse's neck, my eyes lost in the middle distance, when movement on the other side of the street caught my attention. Three tall figures in gray-blue long coats with short capes attached, distinctive tricorn hats low over their foreheads, were speaking with a small clump of trail hands standing in the shade of a small shack.

Albion Rangers.

I ducked behind my horse, trying to be casual, and busied myself with the clasps and straps of one saddlebag.

"Don't worry, they don't come with us."

The voice was very near, and I jumped a bit, unaware anyone had approached me. The tones were warm and light; I was surprised, as I turned, to see a tall woman with a long blond queue draped over one shoulder standing there in neat, well-maintained trail gear, smiling gently at me.

"They don't come with us. Cole's got an arrangement with the Rangers. If they're heading out to Sahri, which they almost never do, they go on their own. But they're allowed to sniff around each caravan before we leave."

I nodded, looking back at the three Albians. They had moved to another group and were chatting with them amiably enough. They didn't seem particularly suspicious, and certainly weren't going anywhere near their weapons.

Which was a relief, because they were carrying a lot of weapons. Each of them had a massive pistol at their waist, and two had shouldered long, delicate-seeming rifles with large, bulky scopes. As they adjusted their coats in the rising heat, I saw bronze flash beneath the flaring trains. Each of them had an ornate black scabbard opposite their pistols, longer than any knife had a right to be, although shorter than the small swords of most military parade uniforms.

"They just chat folks up, mostly. It's easy to avoid them if you just move around from group to group."

She was being very kind, and it was a sad reflection on my new position in life that I immediately wondered why.

"I'm Abigail Parker." She stretched out one hand with a forwardness I was almost coming to expect from this raw part of the world, and I took it. There were callouses on her palms, and I realized yet again that this was a hard country, where you worked, one way or another, or you starved.

I introduced myself. "Nicholas Hawke." I tried to smile, but I'm afraid I didn't do too good a job of it.

She smiled and I noticed that her green eyes glinted in the sun. I remembered Monique yet again and had to force myself not to look around to see if she had come to see me off.

Of course, she had no idea I was leaving with Randal Cole's caravan, so why she would be here I couldn't have said.

"First trip out to Sahri?" She pulled on a rein and her own horse came closer so she could inspect her kit.

I nodded absently.

"What's drawing you out to the plains?" She gave me an appraising look, and I was almost sure the edge of disdain I saw there was in my imagination.

I had come up with a bit of an excuse for travelling out to the Comanche capital during the interminable night before, and I had it ready when she asked. "I'm a historian. I'm going out to collect primary sourced stories for a paper on native culture."

Her smiled widened, and it became a little harder to convince myself there was no mockery in it. "Really. A paper out of where?"

Now that stung. I hadn't thought anyone I might meet in such a place would know enough to ask that question. I knew precious little of the academic establishments of Albion, and even less of the other nations that shared the continent.

I hadn't thought it through at all, I realized.

I scrambled for a response. "Winchester College." There had to be a college in the capitol of Albion, right? And knowing the House of Arnold's penchant for British naming conventions at the strange foundation of their Anglophobia, that seemed like a safe enough guess.

And apparently I was right. Abigail Parker nodded and turned away without a moment's hesitation. Either I had guessed correctly, or we were more alike than appearance might indicate; at least in our ignorance of the Albian university system.

She swung herself up into the saddle in one smooth movement, looking down at me as she adjusted the reins in one hand. "Well, if you need any help on the trail, just come and find me. We could pass the time talking about Comanche culture." And with smile and a tip of her hat, she brought the horse around and moved off into the crowd.

I noticed a lot of movement at one end of the street and saw several large wagons emerging from a warehouse, forming a line heading down the main road, into the west.

I sighed. At least I wouldn't have to worry about bandits or Comanche raiders. We were about to embark upon what many believed was one of the most hazardous treks in the world, from the questionable civilization of Corners to the alien splendor of the plains kingdom, the Empire of the Summer Moon.

To be frank, I didn't know if I was up for the journey with this entourage, never mind alone.

Chapter 14

It wasn't yet midmorning when the caravan left the dirty little cluster of Corners behind. I had no experience with such things, but I would have said our band stretched on for nearly half a mile, all told. In the center were the five big wagons, carrying the trade goods and such intended for the Comanche in return for their horses. Arrayed along the flanks of the column, forming a vanguard to the front and a small group at the rear, were hard men and women bearing a dizzying array of weaponry. Most wore the distinctive wide-brimmed hats I was coming to associate with this part of the world, although others were wearing everything from bandanas and fedoras to a few black, glistening top hats that I swore had to be silk.

As we rode, and my mind had little else to occupy it, I tried to differentiate these hardened folks into the dedicated guards I knew any such endeavor required and the wranglers who would be responsible with steering the herd on the return journey. I theorized that the difference might be the penchant for some of these riders to festoon their mounts with ropes and whips, while another group nearly all had sheathed long guns lashed to their gear. These were not two distinct groups; there were individuals who might have both and might have neither. But for the most part, and without anything else to go by, the theory seemed sound.

At one point I noticed Abigail Parker in the distance and was startled to see she was one of the few with both a prodigious rifle and coils of rope attached to her saddle bags. She was talking and laughing with a small knot of riders, mostly long gunners by the look of them. I felt a little better, reflecting that one of the most competent-seeming members of our band had offered to help me if I needed it.

The chuckwagon was smaller than the others, riding just ahead of them and pulled by a team of four. A trail of steam or smoke issued from a small chimney in the wagon's roof, and I assumed there was an entire kitchen inside. That proved to be the case when the wide windows lining either flank of the wagon were thrown open at noon and riders began to make their way up to these, leaning in to take parcels and food from the cook and his assistants before riding off a bit to eat their lunch on the march.

I looked around me, but none of the ancillary members of the caravan, the unskilled laborers and passengers I had naturally fallen in with over the course of the day, were making for the wagon. My stomach growled alarmingly, and I tried to ascertain if our turn would come at any time soon.

"Let the trail hands eat first." A glum man who sat his horse comfortably enough, wrists crossed over the reins, muttered. "There'll be plenty, but those of us who won't be fighting if the situation arises generally let the fighters have first crack."

I nodded my thanks, rode on for several paces, then leaned over, trying not to be too loud. "About how long does that usually take, do you think?"

The man shrugged. "Caravan this size? Cole's wagon? Shouldn't be too much longer. He generally don't skimp on vittles."

That was good. Considering I had really just fallen in with this crowd by happenstance, it was nice to know I had fallen in with a good one, apparently.

And sure enough, not too long after that brief exchange, at an upspoken signal that probably had something to do with the last few youngsters in their hats and scarfs pulling away from the chuckwagon, several of the people in my impromptu group kicked their mounts into a faster gait and made for the food.

It wasn't bad. Better than I had expected, to be honest. There was a chunk of warm bread and a slab of meat and cheese, wrapped up in waxed paper, and a plain clay cup that held, of course, coffee.

I was going to have to get used to the foul brew, I guessed, if I was going to survive this new frontier.

The afternoon was uneventful, which meant boring beyond my previous understanding of the word. My horse continued to sway back and forth as the long miles rolled beneath us.

For the first time I realized I had never named my horse. I felt a slight pang of guilt at this and ended up dedicating several hours to the task.

I had settled on Bucephalus before realizing how ridiculous and grandiose that sounded. I went in an entirely different direction, then, and settled on Ben. It suited my incorrigible side. No one needed to know to which Ben it referred, and Arnold seemed like it was tempting fate a little too brazenly.

The sun swept downward before us, lighting our way long past when I might have liked to stop for the night. Out here on the wide grassy plains, with nary a hill or knoll to catch the light, I felt the day was much longer than it had any right to be.

I glumly considered what that might mean about the morning but pushed the thought away. The first day was too soon to grow this morbid.

My rear end was sore, and I began to imagine that Ben was searching out every dip in the prairie over-which he might trip, jarring me even further. I was exhausted, my throat was parched, and my clothing was drenched in sweat. The heat this far north and west was much drier than it had been in New Orleans or Port Au Prince; it really drew the moisture out of a man.

The chimney of the chuckwagon began to smoke as the lower rim of the sun touched the horizon. The hands contracted in toward the column and began to call out shouts for a halt for the night.

I slowed Ben to a stop right where we were, in the middle of the trail, and I sagged in the saddle, just glad of the stillness for a moment.

I staked Ben down to a stretch of prairie just off the main trail as Monique had taught me, leaving him to munch on the tall grass there as I made my weary way toward the chuckwagon. The cooks were efficient, handing out wooden bowls of stew and ... coffee. I had filled my canteen from a stream on one of our brief, infrequent stops during the day, but it was already nearly empty. There was a smaller wagon at the rear of our group with casks of water and other consumables, but I didn't know if they were for the likes of me and I didn't feel desperate enough to go ask.

I took my stew and stumbled back to where Ben stood, long stalks of grass waving languidly from his mouth as he chewed his own dinner.

I had nowhere to sit.

I looked all around me like a performer in a dumbshow. Of course, there was nowhere for me to sit. I hadn't set up a chair, and who would have done it for me? In fact, I realized as I stood there, I didn't have a chair to set up. I didn't know what kinds of odds and ends Monique had put into those bags, but I had blindly felt around in them long enough to know there wasn't any furniture in either of them.

With a sigh of resignation, I lowered myself to the grass, ignoring my protesting muscles, and settled onto the soft earth at last.

I spent a moment's reflection on how well Monique must have selected each of our camp sights on the ride north. I had never seemed to lack for a log or rock to sit on the entire time.

I have never been a stranger to riding. Horses were essential for transportation in England, especially with the embargo of any more modern technologies under-which we had suffered for so long. But England was a small country, in the end, and my little corner of it even smaller still. Even during the ride north from Liberté, Monique and I had never covered so much ground in such a short period of time. She had kept our pace brisk, but it had still been relatively leisurely, moving through the thick forests of northern Liberté, and the southern stretches of the Reaches.

Muscles were aching that I had never known I had. My inner thighs were on fire, my rear end sore, my sides ached, my back hurt. I was sweaty, itchy with the floating dust of the plains getting into my clothing, and all I had to drink was a last sip or two of water and coffee.

I might have been more miserable than I had ever been in my life, and that is truly saying something, given how my life had been going of late.The stew, however, was quite good.

There's nothing like misery and near-starvation as a sauce for one's dinner. Sadly, before I felt I had even enjoyed it, it was gone. And despite the biting, acrid taste, I downed the coffee as well. I brought my cup and bowl back to the cook's helpers who took them without comment, and then headed back toward Ben and my supplies.

Small, contained fires were springing up all around the growing camp. I wondered at the etiquette of joining one of those blessed little groups. I certainly wasn't going to be lighting any fires of my own.

Night was falling fast as I remembered to take the baggage and tack from my horse. Ben stood there without protesting, casting one soulful look over his shoulder at me in silent remonstrance, then went back to chewing grass.

By the time I had my gear in a small pile, similar to other piles I saw forming up around me as close as I could tell, it was getting quite dark. I stood again, hands on hips, and looked about me, trying to gauge what my next course of action should be. Tents were rising up around me and I cursed myself anew.

Did I have a tent? Even if I did, how was I going to raise it? How could I have overlooked something as simple and essential as shelter?

I looked around for a familiar face, hoping to see Abigail Parker, perhaps, or maybe the glum man I had spoken to briefly at lunchtime. But in the shifting light and shadows of the rising fires and the fading glow of sunset, I didn't see anyone I recognized.

I went down on one knee and opened a saddlebag, knowing that I was now racing against the dying light of day. I pulled out long stretches of fabric, found several metal poles nested together in a side compartment of the bag, and balls of twine.

There was no way I was going to be able to set this tent up in the dark, alone.

I cursed myself that I had not paid closer attention to Monique's raising our tents as we traveled from Josephine to Corners. I had watched her every night, thinking I was being attentive, but I realized now that I didn't remember a single step in the process.

"Need some help there, partner?" The voice was incredibly deep and resonant. I was reminded, for a moment, of the tall Haitian with the aquiline nose, but then this new accent pushed into my brain. The drawling vowels, the clipped, blurred consonants.

I stood, turning, and found myself looking up at the enormous man with the sideburns and the spade beard that I had inadvertently bumped into that morning.

"Looking a little lost, there, tenderfoot." His teeth gleamed in a broad smile, and I saw that he had several friends, men and women in similar gear, standing behind him, all of them grinning.

I looked down at the pile of fabric I thought might be my tent and wrestled for a moment with my bruised and battered pride.

My pride won.

"No, I'm doing quite well, thank you. Just getting a blanket. The night is clear and warm. I thought I'd sleep beneath the stars."

In fact, as I spoke, I did see several people around laying out blankets and bedrolls without tents. Of course, most of them were near the fires that had already been lit, but not all.

The man with the beard laughed. "Certainly. Well, if you need any help, just ask for Clay." He leaned in closer to me and I could smell spirits on his breath. "Be happy to give you a hand."

That seemed strange, but I nodded my thanks and began to turn away, when Clay moved past me, seeming to incidentally hit me with his shoulder. It was like being hit with a swinging log, and I spun to the ground, falling down amidst my gear.

His friends laughing and clapping each other on the back as they walked past me, the big man, Clay, moved on as if nothing had happened at all.

I sat up, sighed, and did the best I could to gather my things around me. It was almost completely dark, now, and there was absolutely no way I was going to be able to do anything with this bundle of strange fabric and other material. I felt through the lot until I encountered something that felt like it might be a blanket, wrapped myself up in it, and rolled onto my back in utter exhaustion.

Above me, the glittering trail of the Milky Way stretched across the sky, with wisps of high cloud drifting between us from time to time. A sliver of moon rose off to the side, bathing the landscape around me in a gilt silver glow, and I was suddenly struck by the natural beauty of this land once again.

It served as a slight salve to my troubles and despite everything, I drifted gently off to sleep.

*****

I woke up stiff and sore, all of the wonder that had followed me into slumber evaporating with the hot morning sun. The bright orb was just peaking over the horizon behind us, and already it seemed the world was painfully bright and getting warmer by the moment.

As I rose with a pained grunt, I noticed that many people were already up and about, their little camps packed away. The smell of bacon was strong in the air. Apparently, it was true: Randal Cole didn't skimp on the vittles.

I looked down at my feet, at the ruins of my gear strewn around my little patch of grass and sighed. I had slept with the crumpled fabric of my tent beneath me, the bulk of my thin bedroll on top of me, and the unmistakable geometric designs of my nice wool blanket within easy arms reach, folded, off to my left.

I shoved everything into the gaping saddlebag as best I could before wandering over to the chuckwagon, not wanting to leave behind evidence of my incompetence. When I returned to Ben's side, however, I found Abigail Parker, already mounted, hands crossed comfortable over her saddle horn, looking at me with a lopsided grin.

"Had a little trouble last night, did you?" She tilted her chin toward the pile of bags, cloth of tent and blanket still peeking out of one of them.

I shrugged, my mouth full of bread and bacon. When I had swallowed, I tried to conjure up a smile of my own. "I encountered a shortfall or two in my practical trail knowledge, yes."

She laughed. "Well, tonight, how about I help you set this stuff up before it gets too dark, so I can show you how it's done?"

"That would be inordinately kind of you, thank you." I lowered my eyes, humbled by her offer, but even more so by the flood of gratitude the simple gesture caused.

I was warmed further by her willingness to ride with me as the caravan set out soon after. We spoke for hours, and I followed her voice, the only truly friendly voice I had heard in days, with fascination. There was something about her accent that made her speech that much more compelling, but even without that, her stories of the plains would have kept me rivetted.

Not long before noon she explained that we were in a stretch of civilized prairie which bandits and raiders from both sides of the border generally avoided.

When I asked what made this seemingly undistinguished stretch of grasslands different, she nodded towards a thin column of smoke I hadn't noticed before. In the distance I could just make out the smudge of buildings rising out of the grass, but it was too far away to make out any details.

"A settlement?" Even that shouldn't have had such a taming influence on the infamous ruffians of the Marches, I thought. But Abigail shook her head.

"Celestials." She said the word in a whisper, casting a glance back at the distant town.

That confused me. "Chinese? Japanese? Why would that matter to bandits?"

She shook her head again. "They're not regular settlers, Nicholas." A strange little jolt of energy seemed to skip across my heart as she said my name, and I tamped it down. What was I, some awkward schoolboy, to keep latching onto these women who showed me the slightest kindness? And what of Felicity? I shook those thoughts out of my head in favor of the current interest, focusing again on Abigail's words.

"They came here to work on the railroads, laying track and whatnot. Cheap labor from China, while Albion focused on...other things." She looked away for a moment, and I panicked. Had she realized I was English? Was she showing some kind of sensitivity to my probable reaction to this reference to Albion's perennial fixation with my nation's destruction?

Or, more likely, she had her own uncomfortable connections with the monsters of Albion, I thought.

I hadn't seen much sign of railroads here in the Marches, or even down in Liberté, and I said as much.

She nodded. "No, once the airships started to see more common usage, laying rail out here in the hinterlands made a lot less sense. They've still got an extensive network within Albion proper, but out here in the marches, when they need to get somewhere fast or move large amounts of folks or material, they use airships, now."

That made sense. "There aren't any tracks out here?" In England, lacking a great deal of the modern technology that made airships and the more advanced steam-powered machines so efficient, rail lines were still the most common form of transportation all over.

She shrugged. "There are a few routes finished up. There's a big bridge at Alden's Tor, in the middle of the Mississippi. That reaches out to Florian. It's how they get most of those steamboats they put into the gorge there. And there's an unfinished sideline heading up north, toward the Kingdom, and south, toward Corners."

I thought I was following now. "And the Chinese workers were abandoned when the work stopped?"

She thought about that for a moment and shrugged. "Abandoned or walked away themselves. I don't know anything about China, but out here a man or a woman can rise as high as their luck and their willingness to work will take them. Some have filtered out through the other communities, but most form up their own little towns, like that one, and they keep to themselves."

I watched as the distant town slid past, fading away behind us. "What's it called?"

She shrugged dismissively. "Don't know. Probably some Celestial name, if I had to guess."

I couldn't help but think there was something odd about her casual attitude toward these Celestials. Was it that it seemed forced? It felt as if there might be more about these reclusive immigrants she wasn't saying. We rode on in silence. Abigail's lack of curiosity concerning the Chinese was a little alarming, but shouldn't have surprised me, in retrospect. I wasn't moving among the salons of London, after all, but riding the high plains toward the legendary Empire of the Summer Moon in the company of a real drover's caravan. I was, again, far out of my depth.

The Chinese had figured prominently in my research as I planned out my journey. Much of the information I had found pointing to the link between ancient civilizations and the pattern of events and stories I was interested in had shown the Chinese to be very close to those very ancient roots. In fact, when trying to decide where I might go for guidance, China had been on my short list, along with New South Wales and Cape Town. I had ultimately decided to venture into the lands of the American native nations because I thought it would be easier and they would be the closest to the sources of these tales.

Maybe, if Sahri proved a dead end in my search, I should return to one of these nameless Celestial townships and see what I might find?

Abigail stayed with me through our traveler's lunch, but then moved off to take a shift with one of the flanking groups. I was left alone as we moved ever onward, into the west.

That night, as the chuckwagon's smoke rose up to meet the setting sun once again, she appeared by my elbow, grin firmly affixed, and leapt down off her horse. Without a word she reached up and unfastened my saddlebags and began to take out the contents, pilling them up neatly in the grass.

Watching her set up the tent was like watching a miracle worker, and I wasn't entirely certain I would be able to do it myself if the need arose, but as I helped her neaten up the area around the little shelter, I was hopeful that maybe I wouldn't have to do it alone.

As we worked, she had brushed up against me several times, seemingly by accident, and I was shocked at how quickly my heart was racing. This was ludicrous. And yet her smile was so beguiling, and her easy talk so disarming, that I felt right at home with her . I am ashamed to say I didn't give Felicity a second thought.

Abigail had gone off to see after her own things and I was just looking at my snug little camp with a sense of justified satisfaction, when Clay, the big dark-skinned man and his friends rode up.

"Looks like you got yourself sorted, eh, English?" The words were dropped casually as the little band rode by, but I felt my stomach tighten. The cruel chuckles fading away as they continued on didn't help.

Why would the man say something like that? How would he know I was English? Was he working with the Rangers? Would he sell me out to them if he was? Were there any Rangers in Sahri?

I was still standing there, lost in fear and doubt, when Abigail returned. She saw the look on my face and jumped down, going straight to me. "Is everything okay? What happened?" She looked around the little camp to see if anything was amiss, but of course it was all fine. The problem was in my head.

"Nothing." I muttered. "It's nothing." I saw that her horse still carried all her gear, and my brows furrowed. "You haven't pitched your tent yet?" It was getting dark. Soon, I would have had a hard time differentiating between one stranger around me and the next.

"Would you mind if I set up here beside you?" She smiled again, and the tension in my chest changed its tone.

"That would be fine." I winced, remembering Felicity's dislike for that ambiguous, milquetoast word. "I would like that."

Her smiled widened. "Excellent."

Sooner than I would have thought possible, even after watching her put up my own tent, Abigail had hers set up just a short distance away. We settled down in front of a small fire she had built between the two.

We sat across from each other and were laughing deep into the night. It was a marvel, how quickly my aches and pains faded in her presence.

When it was time to turn in, we slipped into our respective tents. I didn't know about her, but I felt a strange reluctance. I could have spent the entire night talking under the stars.

*****

"Hey, English, you got a second?" The deep voice jarred me out of a very pleasant dream, and I bolted upright, nearly collapsing my tent around my head.

"What?" I was hardly awake, the soft wool of sleep still wrapped around my consciousness, and I couldn't place the voice, or even make much sense of the words.

"Come out here, you coffee boiler. We got business with you." I couldn't detect any anger in the voice, but I was starting to fear that the accent, and the gravely depth of the voice, were unmistakable.

"Clay?" I combed my fingers through my hair and pushed my way out of the tent. Sure enough, the tall black drover was standing there with several of his friends. We had been on the trail for four days, and he had become a regular trial each time Abigail had been away. Somehow, even before I had placed the voice, I knew who it was going to be.

What I was not prepared for was the sight of Abigail Parker, being held awkwardly by one arm, beside him. She looked angry, all the softness of her face gone, and glared at me through burning, narrowed eyes.

She had two of my journals in her free hand.

"English, these books your'n?" The big man reached around and plucked the books out of her hand and waved them in front of me.

I was all out to sea. What was going on?

"Yes, but—"

"Come on, you little bunko-artist. You want to tell him, or shall we?" He gave Abigail a gentle shake, and she turned her glare on him.

"We caught her going through your bags by the light of your dying fire. Wouldn't have thought twice about it, 'cept we saw you guarding that particular bag quite carefully earlier in the day, thought there might be something interestin' in there for any concerned party might come along."

"Didn't figure it'd be books." That was spat by one of Clay's compatriots.

The big man smiled his flashing smile. "No, we didn't. Didn't figure this little fast trick for a flannel-mouthed chiseler, either, though, so there's that." He glanced aside at her. "Been watching you for a fair bit, missy. This route ain't that common, and those that ride it been doin' so for a long time, most of us. Didn't recognize you, and that's more'n a mite strange."

Before Clay could finish, Abigail twisted around in his grip and elbowed him, hard, in the ribs. The man flinched away just a little, his smile never wavering, and let her go.

With one last scowl, the woman was on her horse and galloping off into the darkness. The others watched her disappear.

"You gotta watch prairie trash like that, English." The big man looked back down at me, hands rested comfortable on his belt, one thumb hooked behind his big gun. "She was out for something from the get-go. We saw her helping you set up, going over your plunder with just a bit more care than the situation warranted."

I was still staring out into the night, a strange, hollow ache in my chest and a sinking feeling in my gut. Who had she been? What had she been looking for? Why, of everything she must have seen without my even noticing, had she taken my journals?

"Don't feel bad, English. We've all been bilked by a pretty face a time or two, right?" He looked around, and everyone was nodding.

"Some not even that pretty." One man elbowed one of the women in the group, who returned the gesture with enough force to cause a grunt of pain.

"Thank you." I wasn't so far gone in my newfound misery as to forget my basic manners.

"No need, English." Clay shook his head. "On the trail, folks follow a few rules. There aren't many of them, but they're important. We're all workin' together 'till we get back to civilization. If you can't trust your trail mates, you'll quickly come to no good when the rains come."

"Please, call me Nicholas." I turned to look up at the man. "And sincerely, thank you. They might not be very valuable out here, but the books are very important to me."

The man grinned wider but shook his head. "We've all been there, English."

I sighed, but let it go. "What's going to happen to her?"

He shrugged, turning off into the darkness. "She'll be gone by the time the sun's up. She wouldn't want to stick around for the lashing Cole'd give her when he hears."

And I was alone again. I looked at Abigail Parker's tent, then my own, and the red embers between, and then crawled back into my little shelter.

I didn't get any more sleep that night.

Chapter 15

The rest of the trek was lonely and hard. I made it a point not to talk to anyone; not that it would have been an issue; no one was interested in talking with me. I received a cold, formal apology from Randal Cole, who seemed more annoyed at the need than sorry for what had happened.

Clay and his friends kept their distance as well, as did the small band of passengers with which I travelled.

There was no further sign of Abigail Parker. I assumed she had left the caravan in the night, although I didn't know how safe it was to travel this territory alone.

Something told me, however, that she'd probably be okay.

I cursed myself regularly throughout the rest of the journey. It wasn't normally like me, to allow myself to be swayed by a pretty face or a kind word. And yet she had completely fooled me, clearly. And a fool I had been.

What else might she have seen as she put that cursed tent up? Who was she? Was she working for someone?

I tried to go through our time together. Did she have an accent? Was she Albian? I felt my heart stutter in my chest at the thought. If any Albian knew my true purpose here, or even suspected, they wouldn't bully me or torture me; they would kill me out of hand, whether they believed I had a prayer or not. My friends and family would never know what happened to me. Felicity would never know what happened to me.

I would disappear forever, and no one who cared for me at all would know where or why.

I went over every moment I had spent with Abigail Parker. I tried to remember back to the conversations we had had, for any clue of her true identity or purpose. Was she just an opportunist, as the other trail hands believed? Was she just looking for some poor fool to dupe, make a quick score and run?

That just didn't make any sense, unfortunately. If she was just trying to make some quick silver, why take my journals?

Which then, over and over again, brought me to the most terrifying question of all: had she had a chance to read anything out of them before she had been caught?

If she was working for Albion, or any other organization in this part of the world, those journals would read like the ravings of a madman;. the final result of my research that I never dwelled on for too long. If I *was* able to somehow unlock those ancient secrets, to reintroduce those primal forces into this modern age, I meant to upend the very natural order of the world.

My plan was to use that power, whatever it proved to be, to break Albion's death-grip on England. Whether to strengthen my homeland or to weaken Albion, I didn't know. For all the research I had conducted, nothing could give me any insight into what form these powers I sought might take. Despite the consistencies in the ancient stories, there was still a wide gamut of possibilities. No matter what, though, I hoped, no, I *knew* that I could breathe new life into my home with them.

But then those powers would be unleashed. I was not fool enough to think that I would be able to keep them secret forever. Human nature being what it was, these new realities would expand outward, and a new equilibrium would be established in the world. I didn't care what that new balance might look like so long as I was able to knock Albion from atop its pedestal before it happened.

To any normal person, feet firmly planted in the mundane world, those conclusions, read by the flickering light of a trail fire, could only indicate the writer's complete loss to sanity.

But if that woman had found those conclusions in the journals, if she had garnered even an inkling of my purpose and she could convince some other agency of the truth of my words, those powers might be unleashed before I could use them to serve my own ends.

If, against the odds, this woman had discovered my secrets, seen to their potential, and was able to convince anyone it was *not* complete bunk, it was more than my life at risk, now; it was my hopes for England. My dreams for my homeland's future.

And I had endangered it all by dropping my guard for a pretty smile and a flashing eye.

I will admit that I knew the deepest of dark despairs, then. The anchors of my life had been shaken by this new wrinkle in events. I doubted not only the sanity of my quest, as I had since the beginning, truth to tell, but the foundations of my life back home. What did it say about my love for Felicity if I could so easily cast my eye somewhere else?

I had never lost myself so willingly to Monique. I didn't know what that meant, but I knew in my heart that it was true. Monique was attractive, she was a strong, independent, intelligent woman. She wore the same strange men's garb as Abigail Parker, that left so little to the imagination. And yet I had managed to keep my head on straight with her.

Each time these thoughts circled back, I was left with a foul taste in my mouth and the desire to spit the poison that was strangling me into the grass. But it was a poison of the mind, not the body, and that was not so easy to expel.

The final days of our journey felt like forever. At night I was able to manage to get the tent together, for the most part. It almost never collapsed in the night, and I was almost always able to sleep through, when sleep would come, without poking my head out of the flap at every little noise.

On the fourth day after the incident the caravan crested a rise, and, in the distance, I saw a party of mounted figures watching us from a nearby hill. I couldn't make out much in the way of detail, but I thought they were dressed in tans or duns, with far more flesh showing than most of the people I had traveled with into the west.

I wondered if they were a scouting party or perhaps border guards for the Comanche. Had we passed into the Empire of the Summer Moon? The landscape looked pretty much as it had since the first day or so out of Corners. Rolling hills of waving grass stretched out to the horizon all around us, with small clumps of dark forest scattered here or there. The only real difference, if there was one, might be that the hills were even more gentle now, the land evening out into a flat plain before us.

I would have asked someone, if there was anyone to ask. But after everything that had happened, it seemed everyone nearby was as reticent around me as I was around them.

Once more, I was alone in a crowd.

The journey was uneventful, even as my mind devolved into chaotic darkness. I paid little attention to the day to day affair of the caravan, taking my meals off on my own, just Ben and I and no one else, and pitching my tent as far from the others as I thought was safe.

Eventually one day we saw a column of thin smoke on the horizon. It reminded me a bit of Corners or even the Celestial compound, but more diffuse, covering a much wider swath of the skyline. There was a renewed energy around me as the long dark smudge continued to resolve itself over the course of the day into a massive collection of buildings that had to be a city.

However, as I stared at the shadow, something nagged at the back of my mind. There was something strange about the buildings emerging from the general jumble. The city of Sahri, or Tuhubitah Sahri, to give it its full name, easily covered a footprint similar in size to New Orleans or other large cities I had seen. It was nothing like London, or Winchester from the reports, but a city clear enough. It was situated atop one of the gentler hills, slightly elevated above the surrounding territory.

But nearly all of the buildings were only one or two stories. Most were topped with strange, crown-like protuberances. I didn't know what to make of these until we had gotten close enough to see the individual structures better. Almost every building was unfinished, with top floors of timber framing and nothing else.

As we came even closer, the strangeness of the other buildings, too, became clearer. We could see far too much sky through them. It was as if every building was graced with a plethora of windows. At first, I was in awe, to think of how much glass this would demand. Where was the glass coming from? The city of Sahri must surely be a glorious place of beauty and light.

Of course, this wasn't the case. My sense of wonder was short lived as I realized that most of sky I was seeing was not coming through wide, glittering windows, but rather massive unfinished holes in the walls.

The city of Sahri was incomplete in almost every way.

The streets, as we came among the first outer buildings, were grasslands, not even dirt. The buildings we passed were empty shells, gaping doorless frames and glassless windows watched us pass in silence. It looked as if each building had been hastily thrown up, framed and walled in timber or mud, and then left to slowly settle back as nature reclaimed them for her own.

It was the strangest place I had ever seen.

Toward the center of the city, we saw more substantial buildings, with actual doors, glass in the windows of some, and even tall walls arrayed around the more finished specimens. Other buildings were just as incomplete as the ones we had already passed, but there were structures built inside them, like shacks built into the empty shells of bigger ruins.

One structure we passed on our way into the heart of the city was massive, a huge, sprawling compound with a variety of red flags flying from an eclectic collection of poles and staves. Each flag was subtly different, but they all seemed to show a primitive rendition of an animal, possibly a buffalo or a bull. The gates to the compound were guarded by bronze-skinned young men and women with long, silken black hair who watched us with uncaring eyes as we passed.

A smaller compound came up on the opposite side of the street soon after, the unmistakable symbol of Albion flying over the three-story tower at the center of the complex: a wheel of eight blue swords on white bars, all over a red field. Just the sight of the flags was nearly enough to bring up my breakfast.

A man rode out from the Albian trade mission and met Randal Cole in the middle of the street. The men clasped forearms in the Albian tradition and then sat easily in the middle of the grassy sward, talking as the rest of the caravan sat and watched. I was parched, hoping against a steadily depleting hope that I might be able to find somewhere that could serve a decent cup of tea and trying not to be embittered further while we were forced to wait for an Albian.

The fact that my conveyance to Sahri was a caravan whose ultimate purpose was to provide my sworn enemy with the best horseflesh on the continent had been a strange companion throughout my dark, silent journey. There were times when I had found the irony heartening in the depth of my frustration and anguish, but an equal amount of time it was just another thorn in my already sore side.

Eventually, the two concluded whatever business they had been conducting, and we continued on our way. One side effect of the pause, whether it had been intended or not, was that the heavy wagons had caught up to us, and for the last leg of our journey, the caravan was a compact formation, the center of ever-increasing attention from the people of Sahri.

And that was another strangeness in this otherwise already bizarre experience; nearly all of the people we were seeing, the vast majority of those watching us from the half-completed buildings, the more-finished compounds and houses, and even those standing in the streets, were of apparent European descent. The pale faces watching us plod by far outnumbered the bronze-skinned folks intrigued by our passage.

If this was the capitol of the Comanche nation, should it not have been filled with Comanche?

There were also far fewer people than I would have expected. Even as we entered the large central square, only a small crowd, mostly composed of children, had gathered to watch the events unfold.

There were three more large compounds around this square, each flying red banners like the buffalo flags we had seen earlier. One showed a dizzying array of stylized trees, their sky-reaching branches echoed by equally extensive root systems below. Another set were of a graceful horned animal. The third, and by far the largest complex in evidence, flew the strangest flags of all. Most featured a white triangle on a red background, with some kind of cloud or a smaller inverted triangle attached to the tip. In many of these it looked almost as if a pair of angry eyes glared out from the uppermost shape. The tallest-placed banners, however, featured a red sun rising in the center of a red sky, with five red beams extending out from it, all delineated by a white circle as a backdrop. I could not ascertain if there was any significance in the placement of those rays, their size, or disposition.

I wondered why this compound, of all we had seen, seemed to include two different kinds of banners. Did it house two different tribes or clans? Did one design denote the clan, and another some imminent member in residence?

There were many possible precedents in my own history that I thought might bear, but without anyone to ask I could only speculate on the strange display.

As I had been looking at all the banners, however, the wide gates of the biggest complex had opened and an entourage emerged, riding on beautiful steeds towards Cole and the head of our column. The big wagons were brought forth, and many of the trader's old hands began to unload them, laying out trade goods in ordered piles on the grass of the square.

If this city was so full of Europeans and so lacking in the native Comanche, had my quest failed before it ever began? I was seeking out the wise men and women of the tribes. I needed to find the spiritual center of their culture, and had thought that this capitol, home to the greatest and most powerful native nation on the continent, had to be the best place to look.

But instead, I found this strange city of half-finished buildings full of white men and women seemingly hanging on at the very edge of the vast empty plains that marked the true power of the Comanche.

I had to get away from the caravan and begin to collect answers for myself.

As Randal Cole was still busy with the Comanche, I went in search of one of his lieutenants that might be able to discharge me from the company. I suppose I could have just ridden away, but I didn't want to alienate these people in case I needed to join them on the return journey should my hopes be dashed.

As it happened, the only person I recognized from Cole's inner circle, at least I thought he was a member of that group, was the big dark-skinned man, Clay. I approached him, my hat in my hand, and thanked him again for the service he performed, saving my possessions from Abigail Parker and her strange interest.

The man smiled that cruel smile and nodded. He said nothing, but after waiting a moment more, I turned with a slight bow and walked away. As I mounted Ben, I saw him give me a jaunty, flippant wave, that smile still firmly in place, and suppressed the desire to throw the fig at him. I needed to remember, I might need these people again, no matter how much they irked me.

I tried a smile myself, nodded one last time, and turning Ben in a random direction. I left the square in hopes of finding someone, anyone, who would answer my questions.

Chapter 16

My worst fears were quickly realized as I rode through the empty-seeming streets of Sahri: there was almost no one in the city. And nearly everyone I *did* see was white. There were even more dark, African faces, whether Haitian or Albian or Washingtonian, than the bronze of the native tribesmen.

I was getting desperate, looking for anything that even remotely resembled a pub, restaurant, or hostel, when finally, I saw a crudely hand-lettered sign over one sad-looking structure whose mud walls had been finished with unpainted wood. The windows still stared blindly, with no glass reflecting the hot sun overhead, but what little breeze there was stirred rough curtains that at least gave some semblance of decoration to the outside of the establishment.

The sign read, as best I could make out from the faded white paint, 'The Horse's Head'. There was a blob of white paint even more faded than the letters that might have been some sad artist's rendering of such an object, but it was almost impossible to tell.

I tied Ben to a post outside and almost left my gear behind before remembering where I was and what the stakes were. I slid the saddlebags off the horse's back, thanked him quietly under my breath with a pat, and went to push the door in, to see what the Horse's Head had to offer.

The door nearly fell off its leather hinges and I tumbled into the warm darkness within in a most unceremonious heap.

I expected to hear an immediate eruption of laughter, as I would have earned from nearly any such establishment I had ever entered, from Corners to Cornwall. Instead, there was an uncanny silence, followed by a muffled, high-pitched, "I'm sorry, are you alright?"

I looked up into a bespectacled face, wrinkled with age, dark from the sun, with a tousled crop of white hair waving wildly above. The man's eyes looked huge behind the glasses, but there was no doubting the sincerity in them.

There was also no doubting the man's accent.

"You're Scottish." I was almost certain. Somewhere in Britain, definitely, but I would have put a substantial sum on his being from somewhat north of the wall, as they say.

The man smiled wistfully as he helped me to my feet. "Edinburgh, in fact. Born and raised." He bent to retrieve my luggage, lifting it with a grunt and handing it right to me. "I do apologize for the door. You learn to expect certain things once you've been here for a while, and you tend to take them for granted eventually. Newcomers can be caught out on occasion. I'm afraid it's easy to let your standards slip, here on the ragged edge of civilization."

Then he endeared himself to me forever with his next utterance.

"Would you like some tea?"

*****

Angus MacDonald, as it turned out, had lived in Sahri for just over two decades. He had come via Corners very nearly, as far as he could remember, the year I had been born. He had come seeking adventure but had stayed through a combination of inertia and fear. It is not easy to motivate oneself to undertake a treacherous journey when certain death lies in so many directions.

In fact, Gus, as he preferred to be called, painted a pretty bleak picture for anyone from the United Kingdom who might be seeking a means of escaping the Empire of the Summer Moon. To the north were the lawless stretches of the Western Marches, worse by far than the more tamed region around Corners. To the north and west were the endless ash deserts of the waste. South was Washington, where the descendants of the American rebels held Englishmen in nearly as dark a light as the Albians who had displaced them.

In short, an Englishman in Sahri was surrounded by folks who didn't think too highly of him. If it was possible to eek out a living here among the Comanche, it was by far safer to stay put.

I was onto my second cup of tea, my first having been thrown down my throat in unseemly haste. I was determined to savor the second, wrapping my hands around the warmth of the cup despite the heat of the day. Gus MacDonald was a wonderful speaker, as were so many of his countrymen, and I could have listened to him for days. It had been so long since I had heard a voice from home, the mere hundreds of leagues that separated Edinburgh from London were as nothing compared to the seemingly endless journey that had brought me to this little rundown corner of the world.

"You have landed in an odd city, Mr. MacDonald." I turned to lean one elbow against his well-polished bar, looking through the gauze-thin burlap of the curtains at the strangeness of Sahri.

"You don't know the half of it, Mr. Hawke." It might have seemed formal, to anyone not from the cold, bleak island we both called home, but there was a certain undeniable comfort in the old formulas, and I was happy to indulge in them. "This is by far the strangest place I've ever even heard of!"

I looked around at the construction of his little pub, noting the slapdash nature of the framing and the worn-down wattle-and-daub walls. "It's like a city within a city." I smiled a bit, and amended, "Or more like a town within a city, actually."

He laughed at that and nodded. "It is indeed. Or, rather, it's like a city built by people who had only a vague sense of what makes a city in the first place and have never visited one in their lives."

"One has to imagine there's a story behind all that somewhere." The scholar in me was intrigued by everything I had seen of Sahri, and even more so as I had not yet ascertained what it might mean for my quest.

The old man nodded again. "Certainly, certainly. Would you like another cup? I'm the only one who drinks it around here, and I've got plenty stashed away."

I shook my head, not wanting to relinquish my cup until I had sipped it to the bitter leaves. "But I would love to hear about Sahri."

I had already told Mr. MacDonald that I was a scholar researching ancient lore and he had taken me at my word. The sting of my conscience wasn't even great as that, essentially, was indeed what I was doing; the end purpose to which I intended to put that research notwithstanding.

"Well, as I've heard it told, Sahri was built, just as it appears, to be a city where no city was meant to be." He tilted his head to indicate the window. "You'll notice there's no natural transportation route out this way? No rivers, no real roads to speak of. It's a city in the middle of a vast plain, with nothing but rolling hills for hundreds and hundreds of miles in every direction."

I had noticed that and said so.

"Well, years and years ago, nearly four decades now, I think, the Comanche decided it was time they were taken more seriously by the other nations of the continent. Traders and merchants were always seeking them out, tramping all over the prairies, looking for the nomadic bands and wreaking havoc with their herds, their prey animals, and all. It was getting harder and harder to arrange for the size of transfer in horse trading that the growing nations of North America were demanding of the best breeders in the world. So, the Five Bands, as they call themselves, came together and decided they needed some kind of outpost that might serve to contain the contamination of their trading partners while at the same time offering some legitimacy, in the currency of the European cultures, to their Empire.

"And so Sahri was born. They whipped the entire place up in less than a year, laying down the streets, throwing together the shells of buildings, even putting in wells and setting aside some land for cultivation for foreign visitors." He looked amused, but there was also a strange taste of pride in his words. "The Comanche bands don't really go in for buildings and such, for the most part. They live out on the plains, in camps, sleeping in tents and whatnot under the stars."

After my recent experiences with the caravan, I shuddered at the thought of living like that all your life. Still, what one was accustomed to, I guessed.

"It was left for anyone looking to do business with the Comanche, who might want to set up a permanent base of operations in Sahri, to claim whatever shells they wanted and adapt them anyway they wished. The bands don't really ascribe to the concept of personal ownership of land. So, if you wanted to set up a legation, or a consulate, or whatnot, you just trekked out over the plains, picked an unclaimed building, and made it your own!"

If you were happy to live so far from actual civilization it didn't seem like too terrible a way to get up in the world. But, quick on the heels of that thought, was the realization of just how far from civilization we really were.

"Is that what you did? Came out here to start a pub?" I waved a hand at the casual construction around us.

The old man laughed. "Oh, heavens, no! I was a much younger man, then. I was just following the road ... or the lack of road, in any case. I ended up in Sahri, liked the feel of the place, and found a niche here. Old Jedidiah Ogilvy ran the place back then. She was a corker. I poured and cleaned for her for a few years, and eventually she just up and joined a caravan heading out of town. She hadn't established the place either, of course. It's sort of a net, catches the itinerant, keeps them for a spell, and then sees them on their way again."

I smiled, taking a last sip of tea before holding out my cup for more. "And are you feeling the call of the open plains? Any plans to leave all of this wealth and glory behind anytime soon?"

He smiled a sad smile. "No, I figure they'll bury me out on the plain one day. I've no one to get back to, no home that will miss me, no reason at all to go back, in fact."

That struck me as both sad and alarming, as I thought of what I, myself, had to lose.

"No, the Comanche aren't bad landlords, as such folks go. They keep to themselves, mostly, and as I've got my own beers brewing, and a still out back, most of my clientele are of European descent."

I mentioned my surprise at finding that the Comanche capitol city held so few Comanche, and he laughed out loud.

"Yes, well that's really the root of the joke, isn't it? In fact, it's right there in the name: Tuhubita Sahri. It actually means black dog, in Comanche. Supposed to be the height of insulting mockery, apparently. None of the bands really take the place too seriously. They want a place to conveniently go when they need to trade for something, which at the same time will keep the white man off the plains and easily contained. They don't much care for cities as a general rule, and so it falls to those of us who call the place home to maintain it. "

"And yet those compounds on the square? Those seemed like permanent places, full of tribesmen?"

He nodded, smiling broadly. "Well, they're not above a little hubris, now, are they? Each of the Five Bands wants visitors to see them as in the ascendant, of course. There are those three compounds, which I believe are currently held by the *Root-eaters* and the *Antelopes*, and of course, *Those Who Turn Back* have been at the top of the ladder for years now, I don't imagine that's changed much since I was last down that way?"

I shrugged. "The banners were trees, triangles, and some horned animal, so I would gather *Antelopes*?"

He nodded. "They're also rather casual with their heraldry. Nothing is formalized and each family or clan is free to make their own flags. The names are ancient and don't really reflect much of the modern bands or their proclivities." He held up one hand. "Well, aside from *Those Who Turn Back*, I think. They're pretty strange, compared to the run of their kind. It's not a triangle, either, by the way. It's a volcano; *The One Who Kills*. They've got a strange affinity for the wastes, and they're very cagey about why."

That struck a chord. Maybe *Those Who Turn Back* would be a good place to start my searches here.

"There are Five Bands in all?" I remembered the buffalo sign which would make for four.

"The Buffalo-eaters and the Honey-eaters." He bustled around preparing a new pot of tea.

"And the leaders of these bands are not generally in residence here?" I was still trying to understand the structure of this strange place, and it was escaping me.

"Oh, no, not usually. Each will have some representatives in the city, certainly. And if a major caravan is expected you'll see more powerful members of the band leadership here." He looked at me owlishly then, as if a puzzle was coming together before his eyes.

He pointed at me with one thin finger. "You've come with Randal Cole."

I nodded. There wasn't much reason to deny the charge. If I hadn't come with the caravan, I would have had to wander in on my own, and I knew I hardly presented a man capable of that particular feat.

He smiled. "Then you'll have come from Corners? How're things out that way? Haven't been back in over a decade."

I shrugged, not feeling that I was really an authority on how Corners might or might not be doing. "Seemed well enough."

He chuckled. "It's no London, to be sure. But your standards tend to slip after you've been lost in the back of beyond long enough."

I shifted around to lean on the bar with both forearms, the cup of fresh tea in both hands. "Mr. MacDonald, if someone wanted to get to know *Those Who Turn Back* better, how might that be accomplished?"

That got a strange look from the old publican. "Well, I'm not entirely sure why anyone would want to do that, Mr. Hawke."

There was an edge to my name I didn't quite like the sound of.

"Like I said, I'm looking for old stories." I kept my voice as casual as I could. "You make it sound like *Those Who Turn Back* have the most interesting stories to tell."

He stared at me for several heartbeats. I felt that I was being measured up, and I was hoping that I wasn't coming out the worse for the experience. Meeting such a gregarious source of information was fortuitous. Not to mention how nice it was to speak to a person with the familiar accents of home.

He shrugged after a moment more, and his smile returned, although it might have been a shade less bright.

"Well, the *Turners*, as I call them, are the only band to have a formal presence in the city. It's why they've been on the ascendant for so long. In fact, with Cole's caravan having been expected for a while, you should probably find Chief Piawahoo in residence in the big compound. He'll have most of his wise council with him, I'd imagine. Just the chaps you'd want to talk to about the old tales."

I leaned ever closer, hardly willing to believe my ears. "Would they see me, do you think? A ... white man?"

That seemed to give him pause, and he rubbed his chin in thought. "D'you know, I've no idea? No one I've ever known has been interested in that mumbo jumbo malarkey. Not sure anyone's ever tried to get close to any of it."

I sat back on the shaky stool and absently sipped at the fresh tea. If I could speak to the elders of this mysterious band, I thought, I just might be able to learn something more about any connection they might have with my own old tales.

I knew this was a long shot. I had always known it was likely going to be very difficult to break into such a tight, ancient circle of trust. I was pursuing what had to be their most powerful, ancient secrets. There was every chance, I knew, that I would fail. But I had to try.

I touched Merlin's stone around my neck. My only real hope was that with the stone I might be able to show them I knew a great deal already. I didn't, of course, but I was hoping they wouldn't look too closely at that.

It was a thin hope, but it was all I had.

First, I needed to see if they would even talk to me.

Gus had continued. "They have all sorts of names for those folk; wise men, medicine men, elders. And they're not just menfolk, either. They've got plenty of women in those councils, too."

I almost asked if he had ever seen anyone with something like Merlin's stone, but then I remembered the old man saying he hardly had any contact with the tribesmen. What he knew was probably hearsay or rumor and needed to be taken with a grain or two of salt lest I walk into an untenable position and ruin what little chance I had with some brash misstep.

Gus MacDonald was happy to offer me a little cot in a room out back for a relatively small fee, and after I took a quick turn around the city, I resolved to make it an early night. The Horse's Head was full when I returned, with the glorious sunset still blazing just over the western horizon, and I was tempted to settle in for a drink or two with some of the patrons. There were even a few hands from the caravan that I recognized.

But those familiar faces were closed when they saw me, and I decided I'd rather not talk to any more strangers for one day. Besides, it had been a week since I had slept in a bed, and even the ratty little cot was calling to me with a nearly irresistible siren's song that I could hear clearly over the hum of conversation in the pub.

It was ratty and might have been one of the most uncomfortable beds I had ever slept on.

But it was a bed, and that made all the difference.

Chapter 17

The dry heat of the plain was less than pleasant as I awoke, but I was getting accustomed to it. Out on the endless prairie there had always been the morning breeze riffling through the grass all around, a cool sound even as the burning sun began to sear off the evening's chill.

But in the city of Sahri, the pleasant sounds and sensations of the wind were replaced with all the myriad stenches of humanity pressed tightly together into a confined space. The smell of the warm grass was barely a side note to the noisome cacophony.

I gathered up my possessions, not trusting even the kind-seeming Scotsman with my treasures, and brought Ben out of the empty, half-finished building next door that served the pub as a stable after a quick breakfast of oats and a blissful last cup of tea. I vowed that, whether I was successful or not, I would be stopping by for another cup or two before I headed back toward civilization.

The streets were nearly empty, and I was again struck by the abandoned feeling of the city. Even a large caravan like Cole's had completely disappeared into this twisting warren of strange, half-baked architecture. If the streets had been dirt or cobbles, I would have thought I was in one of Europe's worst slums. But instead, I was riding down the center of a green sward in the middle of one of the most powerful capitals in the New World.

I saw occasional Europeans, speaking in a dizzying array of accents and languages. There were even small parties of Comanche, keeping mostly to themselves or standing and gaping in obvious curiosity at the pale men and women moving past.

The central plaza, or field, I supposed was the better word, was easy to find, as the random-seeming layout of the city streets was belayed by the fact that they all led to that main square.

And there I saw the first impact of our caravan. There were blankets scattered across the clearing, and the largest crowd of Comanche I had yet seen wandered among them, looking at the goods scattered across each. It looked like a Portabella Road market on a Sunday, complete with food vendors and little children running around causing mischief.

Now, at last, it looked like a tribal community.

There was no money changing hands that I could see, and none of the caravan hands were standing by the blankets. The trade goods were just lying there, unguarded, apparently for anyone to pick over.

I led Ben along the outskirts of the area, watching, fascinated, as the people plucked items from foodstuffs to luxury goods off the scattered swatches of fabric, disappearing, for the most part, into the city. I assumed most would then filter back out onto the plains beyond.

It was while I walked one of my latter circuits of the square, my stalwart mount following placidly behind me, that I became aware I was being followed.

He was a small ebony-skinned man, dapper in his European dress, vest and tie, jacket held casually over one shoulder. He feigned interest in a blanket full of books and papers, not looking up as I watched him, but there was no doubt in my mind that he was keeping tabs on me out of the corner of his eye.

He had been shadowing me throughout that latest circuit as well, I realized.

My heart began racing. What was this, now? My first thought was the Haitians and the strange connection that had developed between myself and the strange, reclusive island empire. But then, the man could just as easily be an Albian Ranger.

One of the first things Benedict the traitor had done upon establishing his strange, bloodthirsty kingdom was to fundamentally change the nature of slavery. Nearly every slave held in the former colonies had been freed overnight and given full legal status as citizens of his new kingdom. But slavery had not been abolished. Instead, Benedict had instituted a kind of indentured servitude more along the lines of the classical concept. Vanquished foes could be enslaved, or individuals could cover their debts by offering themselves up to the institution, and yet at the same time, every slave had the ability, with diligence and prudence, to purchase their freedom back once more.

So the man watching me casually from across the square could be almost anyone.

And then he looked up, our eyes met, and he gave me a strange, open smile.

His teeth were completely gold.

I stopped in my tracks. I had no idea what I would do if he approached me. Was he hunting me? Was he aware of my inability to defend myself? What if he came for me right now, in the open, before all of these people?

I remembered my derringer too late, stowed away in the bottom of a pack. I should have taken it out the moment the caravan had broken up.

I was completely defenseless through my own foolishness.

Who kept the peace in this strange, chaotic city? Would the Comanche stop the man if he came at me now? Would there be some intervention by my fellow white men?

I realized, all in a moment, how dangerous this place was and how dangerous it was to lose sight of the differences between the city of Sahri and the more conventional cities of my experience. There was no authority I might plead my case to here if I found myself the subject of violent attentions.

My gaze swept the area, looking desperately for any sign of possible escape. The big complex with the banners of the *Turners* and the universal banners of the Empire of the Summer Moon was only another half-turn around the square from my position. Without thinking about it I began to make my way in that direction. I tried to remain casual in my movements, but I knew I was moving too quickly for that to have been really effective. A small voice in my mind began to scream at me to jump onto Ben's back and make a desperate gallop for the compound, but I refused.

I cast one quick look over my shoulder and the little man with the gold teeth was still standing where I had first seen him, still watching me with that open grin, his hands now casually placed on his hips. There was a small pistol riding high on his belt, but he didn't appear to be threatening me in any way with the placement of his hands.

I almost stopped then. I almost went back, feeling once again the illusory safety of a crowd, to demand of the man who he might be to me, and what he meant, smiling at me in such a fashion without introducing himself.

But a small voice in my mind refused to let go so easily of these most recent lessons. I had little recourse here, should an armed man decide that my presence was impeding him in some way. I couldn't brace the man in the open air, brazenly expecting some nameless ancient authority to protect me. I had truly left the culture I had known all my life behind. I would have to remember that.

We stepped out of the crowded plaza and into the relative peace and quiet of the *Turner* compound. There were two guards flanking the gate, a heavily muscled pair, a man and a woman, but other than looking at me through slitted, suspicious eyes, they did not hinder my entrance.

Inside, the compound was a courtyard that had been designed by someone who had not cared much to learn what a proper courtyard should look like. Before me was the largest building I had seen in the city, three stories tall and stretching away in extensive wings to either side. To the left was a long, low building, open-fronted, with space inside for scores of horses. There were many already in residence, and I was reminded again of old Angus MacDonald's words that these people had more of a presence in Sahri than the other bands.

To the right was another long low building, but this one had been partitioned into sections and had leather curtains hanging before each compartment. It looked like nothing so much as a stable that had been repurposed to house people; overflow guests from the main building, perhaps; or maybe visitors from less-favored clans or families.

There were several small groups of people standing in the courtyard, speaking quietly to each other in a relaxed, easy manner. Although several of the groups looked to be predominantly older folks wrapped in all manner of fabrics and skins that reminded me of nothing so much as the chitons and togas of ancient Greece and Rome, there were plenty of others here much younger, wearing everything from traditional warrior garb of tight doeskin trousers and loose vests to denim and cotton. These youngsters were, almost everyone, carrying all manner of weaponry, with ornate black- and silver-finished firearms featuring prominently among them. These weapons looked to be quite impressive specimens, and yet, unfamiliar as I was with such things, I could not have said why aside from their ornamentation and size. There was no sense of the hustle and bustle of a political hub among any of these groups; it felt nothing like the House of Commons, or even Windsor Castle.

What it looked like, really, other than the armament, was nothing so much as the common area of a college or university.

And other than the costumes worn by the people chatting, of course. I led Ben to an empty stall in the stable, and when no one objected, I brought him inside. I didn't want to leave my gear and books behind, but it would have hardly made the right impression, trying to force my way into a meeting with a head of state, even among such strange surroundings, with heavy saddlebags thrown over my shoulder. I did, however, load up my ruck with the most important books and journals.

I fished out the pistol with its heavy holster and dropped that into a pocket.

And of course, I had Merlin's stone around my neck, under my shirt.

I made my way toward the big central building, nodding politely to this person or that as they all came to realize a stranger was moving in their midst. By the time I made it to the flap over the wide main door, all conversation in the courtyard had ceased and they were all staring at me as I made my way into the building with a sheepish, low wave.

Inside, I was mildly shocked to see contemporary furnishings. Either someone had trekked an entire suite of tables, chairs, sideboards, and other items over the prairie, or a very skilled craftsman had come here to serve in the strange splendor of this exotic place.

The wooden floor was covered in a dizzying variety of rugs, furs and hides, and sitting in many of the fancy chairs were older Comanche, differentiated by the deep wrinkles in their bronze faces and the white laced through their long dark hair. These reminded me, continuing the stream of thought from the courtyard, of any number of professors or lecturers I had encountered during my education and afterward, when I had joined them as an academic researcher myself.

One group in particular, two women and one man, stopped their conversation and turned in their chairs to watch me approach. There were younger people hovering around the edges of the big room, each of them carrying more of those elaborate guns, but everything came to a halt as I stopped before the trio in the center.

They said nothing as I stood before them, only looking up at me with ancient, rheumy eyes. One of the women did smile, which I took as some small encouragement.

"Good morning." I have always been annoyed when watching people shouting at members of another culture who might not speak the same language, as if the volume at which one speaks might force meaning through the language barrier.

Sadly, I found myself speaking loudly to these elders. I tried to convince myself it had more to do with the fact that they were old than that they were from such an alien culture, but I fear the truth is somewhat less flattering.

At a momentary loss, I bowed. I'm not at all certain why I did this, but I did.

It seemed to amuse them.

"I was hoping to speak to..." My voice trailed off as I realized I forgot what the leader of *Those Who Turn Back* was called. Chief... something. That wasn't going to be enough to get me past these gatekeepers, I knew, or the younger, more physically intimidating guards around the edges of the room.

"I was hoping to speak to your chief." It was the best I could do, and it was better than standing there gaping like a landed fish.

The three elders stared at me, blinking owlishly without making further comment. All movement and conversation in the big chamber had stopped, and everyone was watching me. Clearly, they were going to make me earn this.

I grasped for some possible approach. The chief's name had been some long conglomeration of unfamiliar syllables I could hardly put together now. Keeping things generic hadn't helped.

What did I have to offer as a key into this closed society? I was clearly an outsider here, my very skin declared that I didn't belong. What kind of reception might any of these people be able to expect if they barged onto the scene before Buckingham Palace, demanding to speak to the Queen? They wouldn't have made it *this* far.

But, if they had something that might prove some connection to the sovereign of the United Kingdom, maybe...

I drew out Merlin's stone and pulled the silver chain over my head. Holding it gingerly before me, I let it sway slightly in the air before me, gleaming in the sunlight streaming through from adjoining rooms.

The man looked sharply at the woman in the central chair, who only gazed impassively at the stone. The other woman, the one who had smiled, also glanced at her companion, but with slightly more decorum, and then shifted her gaze back to me, her smile gone.

The old woman staring at the stone, without a change in her old mahogany face or gleaming black eyes, shook her head once, sending her long, white-streaked hair shimmering.

At that vague signal the room emptied at once. Without a spoken word, all the younger people filed from the chamber, and even the other two elders stood, none-too-firm on their feet, and shuffled off. The woman who had smiled cast one last look back at me before turning away, shaking her head, and walking, stoop-shouldered, through a side door.

In a moment, I was alone with the last woman. How could they leave me alone with an old woman? What if I meant some mischief? How could they know she would be safe?

Unless they felt I could be no danger. Unless, for some reason, they thought this woman could protect herself from any kind of foreign agitators.

And then I saw it, nestled among the other decorations and items of jewelry hanging about her neck. There, in an elaborate silver cage that put the Haitian setting to shame, was a stone that looked eerily familiar, despite differences in color and sheen. Where Merlin's stone was a deep blue beneath the black finish, the old Comanche woman's stone was a brighter aqua, what I believed they called turquoise.

The woman brought no attention to her own stone, but it was the first hint of validation I had found in years. My heart began to race, and chills ran across my scalp and down my back despite the warmth. for the first time in a very long time, I knew hope.

She nodded peacefully toward the stone I was still holding out. "That is quite a pretty bauble." Her voice was dry and cracked like old leather. The wrinkles of her face writhed into a smile that somehow failed to convey more meaning than a slight shift of the landscape.

I lowered my arm, gesturing with it to her own jewelry. "I noticed you have a similar piece." I forced the words out, thick with emotion.

The smile deepened, somehow, looking almost as if it might swallow her face, and a responding twinkle in her dark eyes seemed to indicate a more genuine emotion. She stroked her own stone briefly with one stick-like finger, nodding amiably.

"Like recognizes like, does it not?" Her gaze drifted off me and into the middle distance over my left shoulder. As the moment stretched on with no further comment from the old woman, I began to wonder if she had suffered some sort of fit.

And then her eyes snapped back into focus, boring into my mind, and all trace of her smile was gone. "The reverse, of course, is also true. You are no initiate, boy. You wave that stone around like some kind of talisman, and yet you have no understanding of what it is. You are like a child with a gun, unloaded though it may be."

That stung, not least because it was entirely true. But there was also a flood of relief at her words so strong I could hardly contain myself.

I was no initiate. But the corollary of that was that there *were* initiates. There *was* a secret here to learn. And this woman knew it. I was certain, now.

"Please." I fell to my knees onto the soft pile of carpets and furs. I was shocked at my own debasement, but I could let nothing stop my progress now, leastways my own pride. "Please, ma'am. I am not an initiate, that is true. But I have looked for so long. I have come so far. I am worthy, I promise you. Please." The woman swam before me, and I was mildly chagrined to realize that my eyes were filling with tears.

She glared down at me, her head shaking slightly from side to side. Was she saying no, or was it a mild palsy of age?

"It is not for me, or for any of the true people, to judge your worth." She stood, shaking on her old legs. "You will find no help here among the Comanche, I wager. But we are a free people, and none of us speak for any of the others, especially among the wise." She reached behind her and picked up a short staff, then rapped the chair she had been sitting in loudly, twice.

The other elders did not return, but a small force of young people, a variety of weapons at their hips, entered, lining the walls once more.

"You will not meet Chief Piawahoo. You have no place here among We Who Turn Back. But your stone, at least, may see you to a meeting of the wise, once. It will earn you nothing more, mark you, but the wise will hear you once, if never again."

The warriors began to move toward us, and I rose quickly, backing toward the main doors, my head on a swivel. But I couldn't leave, not yet. The woman had told me I could speak with the wise, but even if those were the people I needed to meet, she hadn't told me anything about *how* to meet them.

"Please, wait." I stopped on the threshold, but the well-armed younger tribe folk continued to press me toward the door. "How will I speak to you? I *am* speaking to you!"

"You have spoken to me." She corrected imperiously. "You will not speak to me again. When the time comes for you to meet the others, you will know. This evening, you will be approached."

She turned away and was soon hidden by the warriors now moving toward me more aggressively now. Although none of them drew a weapon, several were caressing pistol butts emerging from intricately worked holsters, or rifles slung casually over their shoulders.

I found myself back out in the courtyard under the warming sun and stopped to assess my situation. My heart was still pounding, my cheeks still wet with tears, and I had very little idea what I should do next, but I shook that off. I was close. I was so close. And suddenly, now, my goal was a concrete reality. There *were* secrets to learn, and these were very much the people who could teach me.

When I backed out of the big building, the men and women in the courtyard watched me curiously, as if waiting for something interesting to occur. When it was apparent that any excitement involving me had already occurred inside, they went back to their own conversations and ignored me. There seemed to be little urgency from the Comanche *Turners* to force me back out into the city center, and so I drifted into the shade of the stables to think about my next actions.

Somehow these wise ones were going to find me over the next several hours and presumably tell me where to go next. Should I go back to the Horse's Head? A cup of tea sounded perfect at that point. Or should I continue to poke around Sahri, see what I could see?

Or should I stay near the *Turner* compound? Could I take a chance that they might not be able to find me when the time came? What motivation did they have to come and find me at all? Perhaps, if I made it hard for them, they would lose what little motivation they had.

I couldn't take that chance.

But I couldn't very well stand in the square all day. It was not even midday. A peek out the gate showed that most of the goods had been taken away; there were only a few blankets left, and those seemed to hold bulk foodstuffs, nothing interesting for any latecomers, apparently.

The Horse's Head wasn't too far away from the square, and I decided that I would rather stay close than take a chance.

I recovered Ben from the stables. He seemed none the worse for his short sojourn among the Comanche animals, and my packs appeared undisturbed. I led him toward the square. As we walked out the front gate, I immediately recalled the small man with the golden smile, and I jerked in remembered fear. I swirled around, my head swinging from side to side, scanning the area where I had last seen him.

None of the blankets or crowds in that corner of the big clearing were still there. In fact, no one was there at all, including the man with the golden grin.

I straightened, shrugging the tension out of my shoulders, and turned to Ben. I had walked here earlier, but I didn't feel like walking now. I hauled myself up into the saddle and turned him back in the direction of MacDonald's public house.

Chapter 18

I didn't bother to ask MacDonald's permission when I returned, but instead brought Ben into the makeshift stable myself and situated him with some of the bailed grass kept there for the purpose and a small, dried apple I found in a bucket by the door. Then, eager for that tea, I made for the rear door, thinking to sneak in, claim one of the smaller tables in the back and establish myself for the afternoon, hoping these wise folks could find me.

I pushed back the hanging and slipped inside. A strange smell, like a combination of exotic spices, struck me. It wasn't entirely unpleasant, but at the same time it was alien and had a strange, slightly disorienting effect. I pulled up short, the flap still held in one hand. And out of the gloom a man approached quickly, his head down, a tight grin pressing his lips together.

"G'day, Nicholas." The words were pleasant enough, and I nodded as he passed, holding the leather drop aside for him as he exited.

And then I realized what had just happened, and who the man had been.

How did the little black man know my name? I felt certain I would have recognized someone with such a brilliant smile in the caravan. And I remembered the Haitians in the warehouse all grinning at me, ivory teeth all. So, who was this man?

And how did he know me?

I stood in the doorway, watching the man walk through the alleyway between the two incomplete buildings and disappear around a corner without a backward glance.

My heart tripping painfully in my chest once more, I ducked into the pub, went straight to the bar, and suppressed the desire to reach across and spin the old man forcefully around by the shoulder.

When he turned, a vague, friendly smile on his face, he froze upon seeing my expression.

"What's wrong, Mr. Hawke? You look as if someone's walked over your grave!" He leaned in close. "Did something happen with the *Turners*?" His gaze skittered toward the door through which I had just emerged, as if fearful that some massive bronze-skinned warrior might come crashing through at any moment.

I shook my head. "No, that's fine. Who was that man?" I jerked my thumb over my shoulder, indicating the same door. "The man with the...with the teeth?"

He looked puzzled, settling back down from his momentary concern. Again, I was reminded of the differences between the cities of home and this new, frightening place. Gus was worried that I might have brought the Comanche down upon him, and rightfully so. If I did something to anger our hosts and then brought their fury back with me, what possible recourse would he have?

But that was hardly a flash in my mind, now. That probably said something about my state of mind concerning this new frontier, but I had more pressing concerns, with this strange gold-smiled man dogging my steps through this alien place.

"Who was he?" I leaned over the bar, ignoring the open curiosity in the faces of the few other patrons scattered among the tables.

Old Gus looked again at the door, then back to me. "Who?"

I had only brushed the mysteries of the Comanche, and already my mind was slipping into a frightening state, more open to strange thoughts. Could my pursuer have possibly been in this small establishment and the old proprietor not know it?

I threw my hand at the door, desperately wanting to interject some concrete reality into the situation. "The man who left just now! He walked right past me as I came in! Who was he?"

The old man's face relaxed into a vaguely nervous smile. "Oh, that gentleman!" I might have been slightly embarrassed by the sudden flush of relief I felt at those words, but that would have been the man I was a week ago, or perhaps a day ago. The man I was that day had learned how pathetically unimportant my pride was turning out to be.

I was happy to learn the man was no phantom, but my joy was short-lived, as Gus had very little else to add.

"I didn't notice anything strange about his mouth, I'm afraid. Although he did have a way of speaking, sort of tight-lipped, now that I think about it. He came in a little while ago, had a glass of shine, talked a bit about this and that, and then he was gone." He shrugged. "I couldn't even honestly tell you what we spoke of it was so trifling. Had a bit of a melancholy air to him, to be honest; something about the eyes. Seemed a good enough gent, though."

That seemed an odd statement, regarding a small, dapper, formally dressed man with a smile of gold, but I let it pass. "Did he mention me at all?"

None of the rest of this had given the old man pause, but that did. "You? Why would he have mentioned you? Do *you* know the man?"

I waved that away. "No. I saw him in the square this morning on my way to the compound. He smiled to me as if we were old friends, but I've never met him before in my life."

And then he called me by my name in the door just now, I wanted to say. But I kept that thought to myself and instead asked for a cup of tea.

While Gus went about setting a kettle on the small potbellied stove behind the bar, seemingly having given up on the curiosity of the man with the golden smile, I tried to bring my racing heart and labored breathing under control.

The stranger might have been in the caravan, mightn't he? I certainly hadn't met everyone in the big group over the course of the journey, and if the man had kept his mouth shut, what hint might I have had of that salient feature?

Or he might be a friend of Monique's sent to keep an eye on me. That gave me a momentary blush of relief, even thinking of that capable woman in the depths of this confusion and chaos. But if he was acquainted with her, would he not have mentioned that? Why be so mysterious?

And that brought me back again to the Haitians. I knew I couldn't judge a man by the color of his skin. There were men of African descent in nearly every corner of this continent, and only a vanishingly small percentage of them were Haitian. But the man in the tower who had plucked me from that slaver's block had said he would be keeping an eye on my whereabouts.

Was the small, gold-smiled man one of those eyes?

In the end, I knew, there was no way for me to tell. I would have to keep a look out for the man, assume nothing, but I couldn't let his ambiguous behavior deter me from my goals, not now that I was so close to achieving them.

Gus placed a cup of tea on the bar before me and I saw he had made himself one as well. I thanked him and took a careful sip, invigorated by the familiar smell. As I dragged deeply of the moist steam, I thought back to that strange gust of dry scent at the door and lowered my cup. I sniffed carefully at the close air of the pub but could detect no trace of the spicy odor now.

Just one more strangeness in a life that had been turned on its head, I decided. And, thinking of strangeness, my quest came rushing back into my mind. I had all day, it seemed, but was determined to waste none of it.

I cast a look around the room, but there were no Comanche present. I turned back to the old man and leaned closer. He had lived among these people for decades. Perhaps he might know something of the path I was hoping to join that night.

"We hear lots of strange stories concerning the Empire of the Summer Moon back in England." I tried to keep my voice casual, afraid to tip my hand and reveal myself to be a maroon, if this man was a skeptic. "Have you seen anything like that?"

Gus smiled, and this time I was sure it was entirely genuine. "You mean like mystical spirits and whatnot? No, I can't say as I've noticed anything like that. There's always been some confusion as to how the Empire could defend itself against its neighbors when they've all got the best weapons money can buy, and the bands were still using bows and arrows and rocks on sticks, but you can't discount the power of a cavalry charge throughout history, and I think a solid case could be made that the Comanche are the best mounted warriors in a very long time.

"Old Benedict might have rooted them out, if he'd turned all of his power in their direction early on, but he was too focused on the British Isles, as you know. The politics of the plains were allowed to shake themselves out relatively undisturbed, with the Washingtonians stinging from the big betrayal and defeat, the French in Liberté reliving the glory days of their youth, and the folks of the Marches happy to have any kind of authority to turn to. By the time Albion decided to focus west again, the Empire was established. It would have taken a full-on military commitment to get them out."

That sounded about right, although I'd have to say, it did seem a bit implausible, even given the political chaos of the era, that the Comanche could dominate such a wide swath of land for so long without an industrial base of their own.

Perhaps the competition for the plains wasn't so great? And the area did hug the desolation to the north. Even with the endless rolling hills of grassland, maybe there wasn't enough here to make warfare worthwhile?

Although it all made sense, for the most part, it was also disheartening. I would have thought, having lived among them for so many years, even a skeptical Scotsman might have noticed something strange. Maybe it was all in the imagination. I felt the waning energy in my chest despite the warmth of the tea.

"Somehow, they've amassed quite a collection of guns, too, despite not having any real industry to fall back on. And every one of those weapons is a work of art wrought in black and gold and silver that would make a Haitian pirate blush. And, of course, you can't discount the uncanny accuracy of their more primitive weapons, either. The best Comanche warriors, with sufficient incentive, can drive one of their arrows straight through armor on a good day." He shrugged. "There's tales, too, that the land's not so hospitable to white folks. Torrential rainfalls can sweep away an entire settlement without a trace if their luck's bad."

That brought my head back up. I tried to imagine what metaphysical abilities I had theorized concerning the ancient legends would look like to a modern observer. Strange weather phenomenon, particularly adept warriors able to perform feats that might beggar the imagination?

There was enough here to hang my hopes on, at least.

I thanked old Gus and took a fresh cup of tea to a back table, pulling my journals out of my ruck and stacking them neatly on the scarred old wood. I needed to get into the right mindset to make detached, clinical observations. If I was going to be able to separate myth from reality, I would need all my faculties in order.

*****

I took a light lunch and then made a quick circuit of the block to aid my digestion before falling back once more to that little corner table and my books. The similarities I had noticed in the old stories so long ago had been one of the first clues that led me onto my current path, and I had begun to make lists of classifications of these occurrences. Once more I bent my mind to that task, trying to imagine what kind of scientific structure might be imposed upon powers that could cause such events.

I posited a kind of influence over the weather, obviously, which might include lightning and thunder generation, but that might also be something else. Perhaps manipulation of energy?

I thought that one category had to be enhancing normal human abilities to superhuman levels, whether it be strength, or stamina, or intelligence. Now, what if the power enhanced those abilities, but not necessarily of the person who possessed that power? What if there were some correlation between the enlightened the old woman had spoken of and the performance of their followers? Might there be some kind of catalytic effect, maybe, to some of these abilities?

And then I listened to myself, and I heaved a sigh. Powers. Abilities. My most vociferous critics back home, those academics and scholars who accused me of living in fairy tales and of denying the hard realities of the adult world, would have had a fair day with the thoughts that were now running through my mind if they had been here to read them.

I was honest enough with myself that I could admit such a direct correspondence between my theories, amorphous as they were, and an ability to impact the physical world in defense of my homeland, was almost laughable. Science hardly ever worked that way, allowing you to see the fruits of your inquiry so directly with such an immediate, lateral application to real-world problems.

But I had to have some structure upon which to hang my findings, did I not? If I was allowed to observe anything metaphysical at this strange gathering of the wise, how might I understand what I was seeing, if not within some framework that I would have to create myself?

I settled back in the seat. I had no idea what I was getting myself into, but I thought, no matter how much I wanted to find something out here that might bring Albion to her knees, I needed to approach this night with full scientific skepticism.

I didn't know what I was going to see, or what I was going to be shown, if anything. But if I went in with stars in my eyes like some soft-brained mooncalf, I would have only myself to blame when the night spat me out in the morning none-the-wiser.

That day may well have been the longest of my life. The pocket watch I had brought all the way from England was a perfectly service-able piece, but that day I would have sworn it wasn't working at all.

I decided to have a light dinner in the pub, and Gus obliged, providing a small plate of steamed greens and a little chunk of meat ... probably horse ... from a nearby tavern. I found myself unable to eat, however, as the anticipation continued to build in my stomach.

Eventually, as the sun began to slant in from the west, I found I could no longer stomach his excellent tea, either.

Darkness continued to descend outside, and my nerves began to unravel as I fretted that perhaps I had been forgotten. Or perhaps the old *Turner* woman had been vetoed in her curiosity, and the wise ones had decided not to send for me after all.

I was growing more and more frantic, and was nearly ready to leave and head toward the *Turner* compound myself in the last gray light of twilight, when the curtain was pushed aside and a furtive look-ing fellow slunk in. I almost leapt out of my seat before drawing my flaring impatience back under control.

Just because this young man was apparently a member of a Co-manche band did not mean he was the messenger for which I had been waiting.

I observed him from the shadowed corner table. He was young, which I had not expected. I had been thinking another elder would come for me, although that made little sense in retrospect. Of course, they would summon me through a servant, someone more inclined to run about the city on errands for the old wise ones.

But if I had been asked to describe a possible messenger of the wisest elders the bands had to offer; I would not have described this young man. His black hair was long and lanky, hanging down over his shoulders in gleaming strands. He was dressed in native garb, doe-skin trousers and a vest, but his vest was festooned with pockets, with all sorts of items sticking out of them. He peered into the shadows with eyes that seemed to struggle with the gloom, his youthful face scrunched up with the effort.

There were several items hanging around his neck, but I could see at a glance that there was no stone like mine there.

Eventually, I could wait no longer. The man's gaze had passed over me several times without acknowledgment, and I wanted this to be over, one way or the other, as soon as I could see to it. I stood, waiting for the head on the long, bobbing neck to pivot back in my direction, and then gave him a sharp wave. The man reared back slightly as if I had threatened to throw something at him, and then he smiled a wide, almost manic grin.

I counted at least three collisions with chairs and tables in route to my position, but eventually the young man was standing before me, and I lowered myself back into my chair. I shook my head at Gus, who was about to approach, eager to have one of the Comanche in his establishment. The old Scot frowned before returning to his place behind the bar.

"You're him?" The boy's accent was heavy, almost guttural. I was reminded of several German speakers I had met while traveling through Europe on my research.

I couldn't have said if I was 'him' or not, but I nodded. "I am he."

I gathered up my books and slipped them into my bag. Standing, I shrugged the strap of the bag over my shoulder and gestured for the door. "Shall we?"

The young man, who smelled vaguely of spoiled onions, nodded in a slightly jerky manner. "Absolutely!" He looked at the teacup on the table longingly, but I pushed down my instinctive response to offer him a cup before we left.

If the night went well, maybe I would stand him for a cup after. And if not, I wouldn't be so inclined to spend much time with him at all.

Out under the emerging stars, the young man nodded again. "I'm to bring you immediately, señor." That seemed odd, but my mind was hurtling toward destiny, and I was paying less and less attention to the trivialities around me. "The elders will be meeting before the moon rises. If we haven't arrived by then, we will not be admitted. I recommend—"

"Then let's go!" I wanted to shake him. I looked around the street, but he didn't seem to have ridden a horse. "Do we need mounts? If we do not arrive on time, I'll know the reason why."

I have always tried to be kind to servants and others of the working class. I have never understood the innate sense of superiority that some of my peers occasionally evince in similar circumstances. However, as this young man and his seemingly lackadaisical approach to his tasks were standing between me and the realization of all my hopes and dreams, I felt a little civility could be done away with.

Again, his head wobbling back and forth on that long neck, my guide stammered out a response. "No, señor. But we should move quickly."

So, we wouldn't be going that far, then. I'll admit I had very little idea when the moon might rise this time of year, but I couldn't imagine we had that much time. Unless it had taken the young man longer to find me than anticipated...

"How did you find me?" We were striding purposefully down the grassy way, hollow, empty buildings to either side. "I made no secret of my whereabouts, but I didn't notice anyone following me."

The boy shrugged, panting a little with the exertion of our march. "I was told where to go, señor. I do not know how they knew where you would be."

I nodded to myself. That made sense. And then, if these people were going to have a hard time tracking down the palest person on the continent sitting still in a pub all day long, then would they really have had anything to offer me by way of insight?

Perhaps I should feel more confident in this encounter *because* they knew where to find me.

We passed the occasional European going about their own business in one direction or another. Even a tribesman or two crossed our paths. None of them took undue notice of us, and I saw no sign of the dark little gold-mouthed man who had haunted the edges of my thoughts all day. We continued on without a pause, my young guide making each turn quickly, clearly knowing his path.

It struck me that this young man, even if he wasn't one of the elect, or even a particularly highly-placed servant, might be a good man to know. "My name is Nicholas, by the way." By that time, even I was starting to feel the impact of our quickened pace.

I didn't know if the bobbing of that ungainly head was a nod of acknowledgement or the natural operation of our swift walk on that long neck of his. But he did respond, throwing over his shoulder, "Chitsiru."

A hardly prepossessing name, but then, he was hardly a prepossessing boy. "You work with the council of the wise ones, do you?"

It struck me that I still had no idea what to call this organization that had summoned me. Were they a formal group, like parliament or court? Was it an informal gathering of those who have achieved a certain level of enlightenment? And if that was the case, who then decided the relative merits of each person's claims to illumination?

"I do." So, although I doubted 'council of the wise' was their official designation, apparently they were at least a semi-organized group, and this young man was a member, some level, anyway; a junior member, certainly, I would hope, but surely he would know more than old Gus MacDonald.

A thought leapt into my mind, fully formed, and I blurted out, "are you of the enlightened?"

I might have been mistaken, but I believe his feet skipped a pace and he almost tripped on the smooth, even ground. He quickly righted his gait, but there could be almost no mistaking that stumble. I had struck some kind of chord, surely.

"I am." This time he did not turn back as he spoke, his shoulders rising with a deep breath. Whether he was bracing himself out of wounded pride or fear of exposure I couldn't tell. But if he *was* an initiate into whatever secrets I was now brushing against, it would surely be to my benefit to cultivate this relationship farther.

"Do you have a stone?" This was almost an afterthought, and certainly not something I anticipated causing any kind of distress in my guide. But this time he did stagger, and whirl on me with such force I was afraid he was going to attack.

"What?" He was breathing heavily, but he had seemed to be having a hard time with our pace all along, so it might have been that. But his face was twisted with an emotion I could hardly identify. The street was dark now, only light spilling from the occasional occupied building providing any illumination.

"Ah—" I grasped for a response that might defuse the suddenly tense situation. "A stone. Do you have a stone?"

He looked at me through slitted eyes. "Of course not." He looked like he wanted to say more, but then turned with a start and continued on his way. "We must hurry. You can't be late."

I jogged to catch up with him, feeling the distracting pain of a stitch developing in my side. "I'm sorry." I was not happy I had upset him, of course, but his reaction was heartening on two separate scores, nonetheless. Firstly, clearly there was some relevance to the stones. I had suspected, especially after my brief morning meeting in the *Turner* compound. But even more to the point, I now knew that the stones were a controlled resource, most likely very rare. This young Chitsiru was initiated in their use, or at least into the mysteries of their power, I believed, yet he did not possess one.

On the other hand, the old *Turner* woman had displayed her stone prominently on her chest. Clearly, they were not so dear as to be kept entirely hidden from view.

The young man was hurt, but he still seemed to be leading us with the same unfailing sense of direction with which we had begun our little trek. However, he was upset, I felt, and I didn't want any further trouble.

"I am sorry." I skipped along, trying to catch up. "I meant no disrespect."

He came skidding to a stop, and I pulled up next to him. My head went from our current direction of travel to his face and back again, and I had to stop myself from begging him to continue on his way. I owed him a moment's restraint, at least.

"You have one." It was not a question, but a bald, direct statement.

I had revealed the stone in the compound and obviously the word had spread. I saw no reason to deny it now.

"I do." I almost took it out, but something stopped me.

A hungry look had entered Chitsiru's eyes. "Can I see it?"

The reluctance grew, and again I glanced quickly down the street. I didn't want to seem rude, but at the same time, if I was not admitted to this council because we had dawdled in the street, I'm not sure I would have been able to contain my anger.

With an exasperated sigh I pulled the chain out of my shirt. I did not slip it over my head, but dangled it briefly, long enough for him to see it, to note the unnatural blue sheen beneath the polished black surface, and then I dropped it back beneath my shirt again.

As soon as his eyes had focused on Merlin's stone, a hungry glint had ignited behind his gaze, and I was glad I had hidden it once again. "We need to continue on."

He shook himself, as if a man coming out of a deep sleep, but the shadows never left his eyes, even as he nodded and turned wordlessly to continue our journey through the nighttime city.

As we continued through the dark, field-like streets, the buildings around us took on a more run-down, almost melted appearance. Here, clearly, no attempt had been made at upkeep, and the structures were slumping in their wooden frames, abandoned and empty. There were no lights, my companion a mere ghost beside me, and it occurred to me that I hadn't seen another person for quite a while.

"Is it far?" I tried to keep my voice calm, not wanting to reveal the slightest weakness to my sour-smelling guide.

"No." Chitsiru's voice was clipped as the single syllable dropped into the silence. Clearly, I had offended him again. Probably by not letting him see the stone any longer?

Soon the walls around us were mere outlines, none more than a foot or two high, and stretching out before us in the darkness was the vast plain of the Empire of the Summer Moon. Out of that darkness appeared two more Comanche, these on horseback, holding the reins of two additional mounts who stood serenely, gazing at us as we approached.

One of the two warriors barked something in their incomprehensible language to my guide.

Chitsiru shrank back at the tone and muttered a quick response. His reply seemed almost plaintive, but without knowing the meaning of the words, that was only a guess.

The warrior who had spoken, a woman, turned to me. "Mount." There was no malice in the word, but there didn't seem to be any way I could refuse, either. I was at their mercy if I wanted to see these wise ones, and any doubts or misgivings I might have were as nothing in the face of the approaching culmination of everything I had been dreaming for so long.

I mounted, the horse calm and patient as I fumbled in my nervousness. I was surprised when the woman retained the reins, however. Clearly, I was not going to be leading my own mount on this journey. That seemed foreboding.

I looked up at the sky, trying to ascertain how imminent moonrise might be.

Behind me, Chitsiru clambered onto his own mount, no more adroit than I had been, and I thought I caught a glimpse of contempt exchanged between the two warriors.

We headed out into the darkness, the woman leading my horse at the front of our little band, Chitsiru beside me, and the male warrior behind us all. We were going down a gentle slope, and it might have been pleasant if it hadn't been for the uncomfortable speed and the fact that I had no control at all over my mount.

My mind wandered as we rode. I found myself thinking back to the popular Penny Dreadful gothic romances back home, myself cast as the hapless young victim being led to his doom. Those luckless young bucks never seemed to twig to the situation until it was too late; and what was it that always tipped the murderers' hand in the end? The fact that they let the victim see their faces, or where they were headed.

If they meant to keep the boys alive, they would have blindfolded them, or put a bag over their heads.

And I knew no hero was waiting in the wings to come and save the day.

I came to that memory with a sudden chill as I looked out over the near-invisible roll of the nearby hills. My heart began to beat faster with the realization. Was this a one-way journey for me? Was I being separated from the easterners and the Europeans in Sahri to be quietly killed out here in the grasses?

Were they going to kill me for my stone?

That thought had a frighteningly plausible ring to it.

I tried to remain calm while I thought my way through this new fear.

Could I pull the reins of my horse from the woman's hands? Maybe.

Could I outrun Comanche warriors on the plains? Never.

But they might not wish me ill. I repeated that in the echoing vaults of my mind several times. It wasn't as if there was conventional law and order in Sahri. Any of the lords of the grasslands could have gunned me down in the street at any time without a single thought, I knew.

If they had wanted me dead, there was no need for such a grand display.

Except, this way, they could have my stone with no one in the city being any the wiser.

And it was this nightmarish cyclone of fears that was tearing through my mind as we topped a shallow rise and a low, small valley spread out before us. All thought ceased.

Stretched out all across this bowl, invisible from the city whose glow could still be seen in the sky behind us, was a vast camp. Tents of all sizes and shapes stretched away across the valley, sprinkled with small, well-maintained fires around which clustered groups of dark silhouettes, standing and sitting.

From out of the darkness to either side walked more warriors, these bearing massive black and gold rifles casually across their forearms. They nodded to the woman and her warrior companion and looked at me with open curiosity. No words were spoken; they must have been expecting us.

After a momentary pause, we continued on our way down into the camp. Any doubts I might have entertained were soon dispelled as I realized there were no children or elderly in evidence. The men and women standing to watch us pass were all of fighting age, hardened warriors whose eyes were clear and bold. Many bore the ebon and gold weapons, and I noticed, for the first time, the strange sheen many of them bore, as if they were carved, polished stone wrapped in goldwork, rather than the ironmongery of the weapons I was familiar with.

I was in an armed camp, preparing for war.

Chapter 19

Who were the Comanche preparing to fight?

I remembered the oldsters on the streets of New Orleans, the lack of younger adults I had marked as I wandered that city, lost and alone, before Monique had found me. I remembered the camps we had seen in the distance from the decks of the *Joyeaux*, and hooded glances of the armed men and women in Josephine.

I remembered the strange words of Clarke in the borderland forest.

There *was* a war coming.

Between Liberté and the Comanche?

Were the Comanche and the Free French allied against a third party?

Could it be they were aiming to strike against Albion itself?

My heart, quite forgetting the fearful reality of the moment, began to beat even harder against my breastbone, but with hope. If the Comanche were going to war against Albion, perhaps I could join them. If they would show me how to unlock the powers of my own stone, they might then let me ride with them.

I wouldn't have to return home, try to find some linear application of the strange powers I was hoping to discover, some way to bring about the weakening or destruction of my foes from halfway across the world.

This night may not just be the culmination of my quest, it might launch the final attack on Albion itself.

My spirit was soaring as we rode up to a low palisade of thin sticks at the far edge of the camp. This would not prove much of a barrier against a determined foe in battle, reminding me more of a cottage fence or animal enclosure. It was large though, sweeping away into the distance on either side, and within all was darkness and shadow. A small fire burned in the center of the dark ring, and I could see shadows moving about in the gloomy half-light.

To either side of a gate in the palisade stood two of the largest Comanche warriors I had ever seen. I assumed they were Comanche, however, as I noticed subtle differences in their dress and appearance. Were there non-Comanche among the lords of the plains?

The woman led my horse to the gate and dismounted smoothly. Her companion hopped off his horse behind us, and Chitsiru slid to the ground beside me. With similar lack of grace, I dropped onto the grass as well, trying to pierce the gloom within the dark circle. The wise ones had to be out there, didn't they? Could that distant fire be the final destination of my hunt? Years of searching to end here, beneath the open skies of this young continent, weeks away from anything I might call civilization?

"Cro." I didn't know the word, and hadn't heard it before, but as the woman holding my mount's reins said it, the larger of the guards at the gate nodded, so I assumed it was his name.

One of the gate guards took the reins of the horses as the other, Cro, opened the grass door, gesturing us through with a serious expression on his noble face.

The man's dress was not very different from the other Comanche warriors I had seen, save that he wore nearly as many adornments around his neck as the wise ones at the *Turner* camp. And at his hip was a massive knife with a cruelly curved blade that looked out of place here on the plains. I thought I saw a gleaming gem embedded in the polished leather handle of the weapon, but in the shifting light I couldn't be sure.

The woman grabbed my elbow firmly but without malice and guided me through. Behind me, our other companion from the city took Cro's place with a nod, and that man escorted Chitsiru through the gate.

As we approached, I saw distinct figures emerging from the confusing blur of darkness, dancing flames, and shifting shadows. Most of the figures were seated around the low, red fire, while several more stood at one end, clearly addressing the assembly. Farther on I saw three large teepees and a low thatched round house, but they were all empty and dark.

This, then, was the Comanche council of the wise.

And they were old, I saw as we came up to the circle. Most of the men and women wore their hair long in the plains fashion, flashing white in the darkness, with only a hinted streak here or there of black. Dark eyes glinted in the firelight as they regarded my approach, and the three men standing before the circle stopped speaking, moving to sit back in their places without taking their eyes off us.

The woman guided me around the circle, all those old eyes tracking our course and brought me to where the trio had been standing. She indicated with a quick press of my shoulder that I should stay there and stepped back.

I saw that Chitsiru had held back, his hungry eyes hidden by the shadows of his cheekbones.

I stood there, alone and at a complete loss, as the circle of ancient sages stared at me in silence.

Was I supposed to speak? What was I supposed to say? I imagined their silence rising before me as the final barrier to my goal and remembered again the dismissal of the *Turner* elder as she deemed me unworthy of her own consideration.

The silence stretched on into a torturous, ringing void and my mind froze completely.

Gradually, I saw that the men and women of the circle seemed to be glowing with a silver light that had not been there when I had arrived. White outlines appeared around their heads, their shoulders, the distant fencing that I could not have seen only moments ago.

My heart stopped at this manifestation of a power I could not understand.

And then I saw it out of the corner of my eye. A massive white disk rose majestically behind me into the sky.

Moonrise had arrived.

"You bear a stone." My attention whipped back to the circle of elders, but I could not tell which had spoken.

I nodded without words, pulling Merlin's stone from my shirt, lifting the silver chain from around my neck and holding it out for them to see.

"I do."

"You do not understand its significance." Another voice, subtly different from the first, but rising from the group in anonymity.

I looked at Merlin's stone dangling from my grip, and I shook my head. "I think I do."

I had to earn my place among them, I realized. I had to show them that I was worthy of their attention and respect. Only then might they entrust me with their own secrets.

This was not unlike a doctoral thesis, I realized.

A newfound confidence built within me as my framing of the experience shifted subtly.

"This stone belonged to a great man of my nation's past. He assisted one of the most beloved leaders of the ancient world to unite my people against countless threats after we had been abandoned by the most powerful empire the world has ever seen."

There was some guess work in that, but I was confident enough in the classical texts that placed Arturus, last Dux Britanniarum and his advisor Ambrosius as figures of history during the Roman withdrawal. There were far more stories of Arthur and Merlin with their more familiar names, of course, but I had always been of the opinion that they were more recent tales built upon those ancient foundations.

One of the old crones in the circle nodded, and I watched the bright moonlight glint off the collar of jewelry and adornments that hung about her neck. "Knowing one possible provenance of a stone proves nothing of your deeper understanding."

It was time to make a leap of faith.

"I know its power can call wonders into being. I know it has the ability to change the world." My desperation, never far from the surface of my thoughts, came rushing to the fore now. "Please." I fell to one knee in the wet grass. "Please. I know this stone can unlock mysteries that have been unknown in my own land for over a thousand years. We have lost our connection with these parts of our past; we have lost our way. Please show me the path to enlightenment. Please show me how to use the stone, to help my homeland in its most desperate hour."

Again, these people had brought me to tears, and again, I didn't care.

The ring of sparkling eyes regarded me in total silence. I raised my own glance to see Chitsiru. My thin, ill-favored guide was not watching me, but my stone. His head swung slightly, unconsciously, side to side with the slight swaying of Merlin's stone within its silver cage.

"You know nothing of what you ask." An old man, this time, snarling out of the silver-gilt night. "The stone grants you nothing but what is inside you." He spat, looking me up and down with hard, rheumy eyes. "And you are hollow. I can see that even through the veil of years."

Several white-haired heads around the circle bobbed in agreement. I saw many of the faces closing against me, only a few still seeming open to further discussion.

"Please." I repeated the word, desperation robbing me of my eloquence. "Please, I can be worthy. You are my last hope. The last hope of an entire people."

"Europeans." Another old man spat. The wrinkles of his face nearly enveloped his eyes, only two white sparks of fire glaring out of the shadows. "You sorely overestimate our concern for Europeans."

I shook my head. "My people mean you no harm! We are powerless—"

An ancient woman cackled at that. "Your people. Your own designations mean nothing to us, Englishman." She whipped one withered arm off to the east. "England, Albion, you are all the same to us; thieves, murderers, and animals."

A man rose unsteadily to his feet. "Why would we give you anything, Englishman? What claim do you have on us?"

I shook my head again, standing myself, my hands before me as if warding off a stalking enemy. "No! I make no claim! I come here begging for insight! I need your help. I have only glimpsed the truth through a thick fog. I know nothing, I admit it!"

The tears were not of joy, now, but of desperation.

"You will have an eternal friend in England, if I can bring this power back to my home and turn Albion aside! We—"

"We have tasted the friendship of England." Another old man rose, and his tone, sad and distant, was worse than the anger of all the others. "It is nothing to us. We have hundreds of years of injustice to make right, Englishman. What purpose would that serve, to give you the power we ourselves have only now decided to unleash?"

As he said those words, his hand rose to rest on the handle of a pistol that sat in an ornate holster at his hip. Another of the black and gold pieces I had seen so many of the tribal warriors carrying.

Were they connected somehow with the stones?

"The stone can give you nothing you do not already possess, regardless." The man continued, clearly willing to give me more than the others.

In my desperation, I was willing to accept any information that was offered.

In my foolishness, I believed I would be given a chance to put that information to use.

"The path to that enlightenment is a deadly one, many perish along the way, and the trail is different for every supplicant. A price must be paid, as well, and that price is different each time the path is walked. None can tell what you might be asked to give, nor if you will survive."

My head shook back and forth so violently my neck ached. "I will give anything!"

My foolishness knew no bounds, and my understanding of what the old man was saying, as I look back at that pivotal moment, was laughable.

He shook his own head sadly. "There is no need."

"That path is not for you." One of the women rose, her stick-thin arms folded.

"Do you think we would see the ancient power of the earth melded with your destructive, deceitful culture?" She laughed, and the sound chilled me to the bone as I finally felt the tenor of the people around me.

They would give me nothing.

Then why bring me here?

The first man to stand held his arm out toward me, palm turned up to the stars. I looked at that empty palm, confused, and then shied away as a ball of bright blue flame erupted on the dark flesh. Behind that fire, the man's eyes regarded me sadly, azure dots dancing there.

One by one, the wise council of the Empire of the Summer Moon rose, and each lifted a hand toward me. One steamed with cold, another disappeared in a ball of shadow that engulfed it. One man's eyes flashed solid white, the beams of light almost painful to look upon; a woman summoned the ghostly image of a giant, savage-jawed cat that crouched between her and the low fire.

Eventually, each of the elders was standing, some fantastical manifestation called into being before them, all of them staring at me with calm, unwavering eyes.

And then their hands lowered, and the wonders flared into darkness again.

"We grant you this, Englishman, before the end." Most of them lowered themselves back down to the grass, save for the first man to stand.

He continued to speak. "We cannot have this power combined with yours. Your people have wandered too far from the path of the Great Spirit and Mother Earth." He shrugged, not unkindly. "Your past is lost to you and cannot be recovered. Your people will not sustain even the merest spark of what you have just seen."

"You are unworthy." An old woman snapped out spitefully.

The old man glanced at her reprovingly, shaking his head. "Worth does not enter into this, we all know that, to our chagrin." He looked at me again. "Belief is all, and your people believe in nothing."

He raised a hand and summoned the warrior with the massive knife forward. "Before the end, we would give you one last gift. Your foes will be brought low. Albion lives on borrowed time, and her pride is her undoing. Already, her enemies prepare themselves."

His eyes turned regretful, almost, as he turned away. "Go, knowing that. Even if you are not here to see, Albion will fall."

I didn't understand. God help me, even after all of that, my mind was still lost amidst the wonders I had just witnessed. Everything I had posited, everything I had hoped without an ounce of concrete proof beyond the stone I had carried all the way from France, was true. The ancient stories were real. There was magic in the world, for lack of a better term. I had seen it, though my sight had been blurred with tears.

Even if I would not be here to see?

The noble guard stepped forward, drawing his strange blade, as the old man continued.

"We will bear your stone with us at the end, and it will fuel the final assault on Winchester and the House of Arnold."

The knife rose, its blade beginning to glow a searing white, and I understood at last.

Chapter 20

The ornate weapon came up, blade a sliver of the sun, bathing the entire circle in clean white light. The man's eyes reflected diamonds from their darkness, and I thought I saw a note of pity there.

The woman, my guide from Sahri, had raised her pistol, as well, and I saw with the confusing clarity of terror that there was no muzzle in the barrel. There was no gaping maw as I had come to expect when such a weapon was pointed right at my face. Instead, there was a blank flat surface.

What kind of gun was that?

Then, with a flash of realization and a sudden, fierce desire to live, I moved.

I shoved the stone into a pocket as my other hand plunged into my ruck and withdrew Monique's little pistol.

I cannot fully explain what happened next as my memory is a blur of images, moments of clarity interspersed with nightmare flashes that cannot be real.

I must assume my guards were completely caught off guard by my actions. I was a cowed academic in their eyes; a weak effete that did not merit their sharpest attention.

The woman folded around the wound that blossomed in her stomach, I choose to assume she lived to rue her assessment.

The roar of the gun's discharge startled me, just as Monique told me it should, and the entire circle froze as if we had all become some macabre painting, focused around the warrior woman clutching at her wound.

Some kind of animal instinct took over, and the world became a stuttering swirl of images that even now I can barely recall or translate. I saw the circle spin around me, the darkness beyond their arrayed tents swelling with a shuddering, shaking speed.

A fence. The palisade. Grass and thin wooden rods. Pain and frustration, clawing desperation, a crashing sound, a falling sensation, pinwheeling arms, the darkness of the open plains.

I ran.

As I ran, a cacophony of destruction erupted all around me. Lightning coursed across the land to either side despite the glittering stars in the cloudless sky. The ground behind me erupted in a series of detonations that nearly shook me off my feet. I heard the roar of a giant hunting animal, staccato crashing of guns. My left arm burned, my sleeve smoldering at the passage of some great heat. Moments later, my right leg was locked in agonizing cold, frost crackling along my pant-leg as I continued to run.

My lungs burning, my arms pumping at my sides, my legs churning beneath me. I stumbled over a dip in the prairie. I fell, rolling onto a shoulder, tumbling down a hill. I sprang up again, breath shallow, chest tight, eyes focused on the silver-limned grasses in the distance.

The rapid beat of many hooves behind me. I was trying to out-run a nation born to the saddle; warriors the likes of which the earth has not seen since the Mongol's Golden Horde.

I was on an empty plain. Nothing but waving grass and small clumps of trees for countless miles in every direction, save for the farce of a city on the edge of the grasslands. Ideal terrain for a rider to catch a man.

The hoofbeats grew louder. They may not have come to match my hammering heartbeats, but that is my memory.

I was a dead man. To be killed for no crime of my own, but the actions of people as far removed from me as I was from the Haitians, the Free French, or the Celestials.

My breath, coming in ragged, desperate gulps, was further hampered by despairing sobs that wracked my entire body, tears streaming down my cheeks.

The hoofbeats were like thunder, and I knew the end was upon me.

A crushing weight crashed into me from behind, knocking me off balance and sending me reeling into the soft grass. I was heading down a steep incline, and with the added impetus of the blow I reeled down the hill, losing all sense of direction, my throat closed in terror and exhaustion. Arms wrapped around me, legs as well, and a half-familiar scent occluded the warm smell of grass in my nostrils.

Sour, rotten onions.

A high-pitched voice grated out a single, harsh command I could not understand, and the hoofbeats, already far above, veered away, fading off into the distance as we fell.

We rolled to a stop at the bottom of the hill, in a shallow ravine as best I could tell from the dirt walls that now rose up before and behind me.

A skinny arm was clutched over my throat, and a thin-fingered hand was clapped over my mouth. I could not have breathed had I wanted to, but the hand silenced me as surely as a gag, had I been capable of making more than a faint, childish mewling.

"Silence." A harsh whisper in my ear; Chitsiru, of course.

I nodded, trying to show him I understood, and as he loosened his grip, I tried desperately to stifle the shallow, tortured gasps for breath.

My body shook uncontrollably, and the young Comanche pushed himself away, putting his back to the low wall of dirt and glancing up the hill.

I rolled onto my hands and knees, my gorge rising, and I clenched my teeth shut against the acid burning its way up my throat.

Beneath the harsh pounding of my heart in my ears and the roaring of my tortured breathing, I could just make out distant hoofbeats above.

An impact hit me in the collarbone, something gathered up my shirt and the strap of my ruck, and I was thrown violently into the soft dirt of the ravine wall. Again, Chitsiru's bony forearm was across my throat, my shoulder blades pressed desperately against the cold soil.

Voices spoke far above us as the horses drew up to the top of the hill and paused.

A burning white light flared into the little valley as if a sliver of daylight had been unleashed into the night, and I remembered the guard's terrifying blade. The beam swept up and down the fold in the landscape, penetrating nearly every shadow save for the strip of night within the gulley in which we hid.

As quickly as it had appeared, the light snapped off, plunging our little world into a darkness that seemed even more profound for the absence of the light. Above, the sound of hoofbeats resumed, speeding up and quickly fading into the distance.

*****

I lay still, my breath slowly returning to some semblance of its normal pace and depth. Neither of us moved for some interminable time, and the moon, which had hug the horizon when my nightmare began, was already swooping toward the far horizon when I slowly came back to myself.

I turned, meaning to thank Chitsiru for saving my life, when I stopped, finding him staring at my right hand, a strange calculus clear in his eyes.

Somehow, against all plausible expectation, I was still holding my pistol.

And Chitsiru was staring at it.

Why?

I looked down at the gun. I had fired it just that once, I thought. Although I couldn't really be certain. Suddenly it felt like it would be a bad idea to break the pistol open to check for live charges. I looked up at the young man who had saved my life, against all reasoning and every argument for his own safety.

He must know he was a fugitive now as well. Everything that had happened around the council fire was a nonsensical blur, but I could fathom that much, at least.

Why would he have thrown everything away for my sake?

Why was he still staring at the gun?

It was then that I noticed the small, ornate knife he clutched in one hand. The blade was chased silver, the handle some dark, polished substance, bone or onyx, possibly. It was hardly a prepossessing weapon, and yet seemed to possess more of a presence in my world than its size might warrant.

I straightened against the wall, painfully aware of the cresting hill above us. I shuffled sideways, opening some distance between us, sure to keep my little weapon clearly visible, glancing occasionally at his knife.

"Thank you." I whispered the words, forcing them through gritted teeth. If I could normalize the situation between us, I felt I had to try.

Chitsiru shook himself and then raised his eyes to mine. He looked as if he was waking up from a deep sleep, then nodded.

"We can't leave here tonight, but we don't dare move during the day." That made sense but brought to mind an entire course of questions I had not thought of until that moment.

How could escape even be possible? I was now lost in the middle of the western plains. I was being hunted by the greatest mounted warriors in the world in their own territory. I was days of grueling travel from anything remotely resembling civilization save for their own strange capitol.

"We should head north." He spoke as if he had read my thoughts. Although, in retrospect, there weren't many things I could have been considering, in that moment. "The frontier is only a few days ride; Perdition only a week or so beyond."

I began to nod weakly. Then I remembered my journals.

"I need to go back to Sahri."

Chitsiru looked as if my hair had burst into flames. The mixture of horror and disbelief would have been almost comical in other circumstances. Here and now, however, it only served to remind me of what he, himself, had already sacrificed.

"We cannot." He shook his head so violently I was afraid it might fly off his shoulders. "I cannot. *You* cannot!"

I sagged once more against the dirt. "I have no choice. After this," I waved weakly to indicate our current circumstances. "After this, I have to start all over."

My entire body was in excruciating pain. My heart ached; my head was ringing. My mouth was as dry as a desert. Even the thought of starting over was enough to bring tears to my eyes, except that apparently my body lacked the moisture to produce them.

"I have to." I wasn't begging. I was stating an absolute fact. I might have said "The sun will rise in the morning" with the same conviction.

And he must have sensed that.

"We cannot emerge until after sunset. And then, we will only have a few hours in which to travel before the moon is too high for our safety, and we will have to find refuge. And we will have to take a very circuitous route, to avoid being seen. It may take us more than one night to reach Sahri this way, but this close to the city, we have no choice.

"The man with the blade is Cro, chief hunter and warrior of They Who Turn Away." A haunted look shadowed Chitsiru's face. "He will stop at nothing to retake us both, now. Our only hope is to get as far away from the Five Bands as we can."

Sunk deeply in my own despair, I could not see the full depths of the young Comanche's misery.

I had only a little water and no food. I had left almost everything at the Horse's Head, thinking, foolishly, now, that I would only be gone a little while.

I was too tired to argue, too heartsick to fight. I just nodded, curling deeper into my misery at the bottom of the gully.

As I brought my arm up, I realized I was still holding Monique's little gun, and I looked at my companion again, the bright knife still tight in his hand.

I didn't dare fall asleep, I realized.

"You sleep first. I'll keep watch." I tried to play it off as casually as my abused body and mind would allow. From his immediate response, I thought we were more alike in that than I might wish.

"Alright." He didn't fight, didn't argue. He settled lower against the wall, slipped the knife away among the pockets of his vest, and closed his eyes, thin arms wrapped around his bird's chest.

Soon, his breathing had settled into a regular, deep rhythm, and his body slackened in sleep. If he was feigning, he was a better actor than I would ever be.

As the sky lightened in the east, I tucked myself more tightly against the wall and settled down for a long, painfully day.

I must have fallen asleep in moments.

Chapter 21

I woke up to see the last, blood-red light fading in the west. Chitsiru sat nearby, staring at me hungrily, but no closer than he had been the night before.

His little blade was nowhere in evidence.

He had not killed me in my sleep, nor taken my stone and run off.

Whatever he wanted from me, it was more than simply to steal the stone, then.

Or perhaps there was some personal code of honor or something interfering with him just taking what he wanted.

Either way, I had to address it before we took another step together.

"Why did you—"

"We must leave." He cut me off, rising from his crouch and dusting off his britches.

I tried to rise, grunting as the pain came crushing back. "No. Please—"

"We have no time." He looked up the hill, and I flinched at the idea of climbing back up that steep slope. "We need to cover as much distance as we can before moonrise."

I shook my head. "No. Why?" I planted my feet, resolute.

He looked at me, his eyes narrowing, then sighed and looked away. "I can help you."

I nodded. "You already have. I will be forever in your debt. But *why* did you help me?"

He shook his head. "Not in this. I can help you unlock the stone."

That brought me up short. "You can?"

He nodded, withdrawing the blade and showing me, as if that should mean something. "I have undergone the rituals. I can recreate them, I believe."

That didn't make any sense to me, from what I understood of the Comanche and the wise council. "If you've gone through the ritual, why don't you have a stone?"

His face tightened. "There are not enough. Many have undergone the rituals without possessing a stone. Most of the stones in the Empire have been broken for ... for other purposes."

"You can break a stone?" There was so much I didn't know.

He nodded again, glancing down at his knife. "You can." This time his gaze flicked to my pocket, and something clicked in my mind.

I recoiled at the mere thought of damaging Merlin's stone. Then I started, realizing what my young guide was thinking. "You want me to break my stone."

He looked at me again, his face steely. "I do. I will unlock these secrets for you, if you will break your stone and share it with me."

"I don't know how to do that."

"I will show you when the time comes."

My head shook back and forth with the thought. To break Merlin's legacy? The stone that had saved my nation so long ago, and been borne by so many English heroes? I couldn't.

Could I?

And yet, without Chitsiru to guide me, how else might I even hope to unlock the powers the elders had revealed? I lived on borrowed time for as long as I remained in the Empire of the Summer Moon; of this I was certain. And I was further certain that no one within the Bands, or their guest tribes, would make the offer he was making now.

In fact, even factoring in the unthinkable desecration of my stone, his offer sounded too good to be true. But then, why, if the stone had been his goal all along, wouldn't he have done that in the night? My battered body probably never would have woken up, and he'd be long gone by now, the complete stone in his possession.

"Why?" I reached out and turned him to face me. "Why not just take it?"

He pulled away. "I will not." He looked horrified. "I will take you through the ordeal, and in return, you will give me a shard of your stone. You will do this no matter the depth of your powers, be they great or weak."

And once again the scope of my ignorance was made manifest. "What does that mean?" I didn't want to pull him around again, to risk him closing off from me in anger, so I moved stiffly around to confront him. "What do you mean, the depth of my powers?"

"We must walk." He gestured down the gully, away from the faint crimson glow in the sky. "We can talk, softly, as we move." Again, the little knife disappeared.

I nodded, trying my best to follow. After a few steps, as my body seemed to grudgingly shake itself out into some semblance of order, I repeated my question.

Chitsiru shrugged. "It is as the elders told you. Even going through the ordeal will not guarantee you power." There was a bitter undertone to his voice, but it was too dark for me to see his face. "There are some few who do not even survive."

That part of the elder council's spiteful lesson came back to me. "Some who make the attempt die. How many?"

He shrugged again. "Ten in a hundred? Fifteen?" He spat into the grass. "If they are chosen, but found unworthy, it is best that they are removed from the true people."

Those odds were worth it, of course, although even a fifteen percent chance at death was more than I had imagined in my foolish fantasies.

I remembered, vaguely, the nightmarish array of visions and abilities I had witnessed around the council fire. "Were the wise ones showing me their powers before they ordered me killed? Is that what I was seeing?" Even then I feared it might have been some kind of hallucination.

"They were." He quickened his pace, and I struggled to keep up. "Old Sahmah meant it as a final gift, I think." He shrugged, I think, from his tone. "All of the elders of the council are powerful in that way, in addition to their wisdom."

"But going through the ordeal is no guarantee I will be able to unlock that much power from the stones."

I could have sworn he snarled at that. "The stones have no power by themselves. They grant the power to those who are chosen. The ability comes from you and you alone. The stones merely provide you with a connection with the Great Spirit and Mother Earth, offering you a small portion of their power."

I nodded, struggling to keep up despite the pain and exhaustion. So, the stone was not the source of the abilities, but rather, like water damned behind a mill, provided the energy to unlock something within each person? Did the energy fields of my earlier discoveries interact with that power, then? Was that the connection I had sensed? Did they amplify that energy, somehow?

But then, if those abilities were in everyone, or at least in eighty-five to ninety percent of the populace, why was it nascent? And was it in such a high percentage of every population? What if, as the elders said, in Europe we were so lost to this connection to the earth, or whatever the true source of these phenomena was our connection with whatever the source of this power was, that the chance of success was even lower? And what if the cost of failure, rather than some other inherent weakness in the supplicant, was death?

Might I have a far greater chance than fifteen percent of dying for my dream?

I would try it no matter what, I knew. I could not turn aside now, having seen the evidence of all my theories made manifest.

Although I did not relish the thought of death.

"I agree." I said the words quickly, before I could change my mind. I am certain I imagined the resentful tug of the stone in my pocket.

He looked back, his eyes reflecting the starlight overhead. "You agree?"

"Take me through the ritual, the ordeal, whatever, and I agree to share the stone with you."

Another thought stopped me.

"Will breaking the stone weaken it?"

There was a new energy in his voice as he responded. "In two? Not appreciably." The light now glinted from his yellowed teeth. "If there power within you, it will still manifest with such a stone."

We walked in silence for a while before I found myself asking again, without realizing I was going to. "*Why* didn't you just steal the stone?"

He continued on without replying for several paces, and I thought maybe he hadn't heard me. Or maybe he was ignoring me.

Or maybe he didn't want to answer.

Then he did. "There is a strong component of belief in the power of the stones. I do not know if taking a stone from an unwilling man will affect my faith in its workings, but I dare not take that chance. All of this would have been for nothing if that happened."

Another minute or more passed before I asked the next question that had occurred to me. "I have heard that the Comanche concept of personal property is ... fluid."

He didn't speak, and time dragged as we trudged along, before he looked at me with flat eyes. Whether I had gained his ire through my assumptions about his people or my question concerning his motives, his eyes told me nothing.

"If I am to possess a stone, I would rather not take any chances with its efficacy. Should I try and fail with one, defeated by my own mind, I could lose my way with all."

The more he spoke on the subject, the duller his voice became. But I was too enraptured with these newfound wonders spooling out before me to pay this further mind.

I tried to process all he had said. Did *I* believe strongly enough? Very much so, after the council had tried to kill me in so many curious and unique ways. But there was still a part of me that kept its distance from that faith; the part that continued to wonder if there might not have been some kind of hallucinogenic in the council fire, perhaps.

And if I didn't believe, was *that* what caused one to fail the ordeal, maybe even die in the process?

And then, as I slogged on behind the latest companion and guide fate had seen fit to send me, another implication of his words occurred to me.

"What if it happens that you see a chance to gain my stone by some other means, before you lead me through the ordeal?"

He turned again, and I thought the heaviness in his voice had faded, just a little. "Well," he said, his voice almost light, "that will be an interesting day, will it not?"

*****

I was starving, but the fear had never left me, and nothing would have convinced me to stop, even if we had had any food. We drank from the occasional rill running at the bottom of the ravines to which we clung like desperate rats and otherwise continued the long, desperate crawl around the outskirts of the city.

After about an hour of this, my mind a constant whirlwind of images from the events around the council fire, I thought I was ready to ask another question.

"How many people, once they go through the ritual, can use the power they unleash in such a direct, violent manner?" I didn't think one man, no matter how destructive his attacks, was going to convince Albion to abandon its endless harrying of my homeland. That was going to take something far more dramatic, if it was going to happen at all.

But, having witnessed those bolts of energy, the lightning, the heat, and the freezing cold myself, all seeming to come crashing at me from the circle of elders, I wondered just how much such offensive capacity the Comanche and their allies could unleash.

The bitter twist to Chitsiru's words grew tighter. "Not many may manifest their power so forcefully without additional assistance."

That was something of a relief in our current predicament, but far less comforting given my long-term goals. "Those powers are rare? Is the wise council chosen for such ability?"

I was certain it was no longer in my imagination. Chitsiru was angry. "Most of those pursuing you were not from the council fire. Those were warriors."

That brought me up short. I had assumed only the wise would be inducted into the elite status of stone wielders. But then I remembered that Chitsiru himself had apparently undergone the trial, and he was younger than I. "How many of your people endure the ritual?"

He did not answer for a long time, and the realization dawned on me that all this was a deep betrayal of his people. A further betrayal, considering what he had already done for me.

When he responded at last, his voice was dull. "Every Comanche warrior undergoes the trial. Those of other tribes may aspire to do so as well, through proven commitment and dedication to the Bands and their goals."

I had thought I'd seen non-Comanche in the war camp and, as I thought back, in the city as well. "Other tribes?"

This, apparently, he was more willing to discuss. "When He Who Kills awoke and broke the world, many tribes lay in the path of his destruction. Only through the grace of the Great Spirit and the love of Mother Earth were the Five Bands spared the brunt of his wrath. When the earth had stilled and the clouds of ash settled, the truth of the new world was revealed to us. The elders of the Comanche let the remnants of the other tribes who had been in the Killer's path know that they would be welcome." He stumbled over something in the darkness, and then continued. "Most of the guest tribes do not venture near Sahri, keeping to the plains and the low hills to the north and west."

"Wait." Despite my curiosity concerning these various nations all sharing the territory of the Empire of the Summer Moon, his earlier words came crashing back to me. "All of the warriors undergo the trial?"

Again, Chitsiru was silent. His next muttered response was less than enlightening, and after that, I could get no more out of him. "A violent mind can be augmented through the use of a broken stone. There are means by which their destructive inclinations may be harnessed for the purposes of the Bands."

I tried to ask him more, but he remained silent.

What had he meant? What kind of augmentation was possible, through the stones? Was he hoping to gain some of that power for himself once my own stone was broken? What means were available to harvest those who would not be able to manifest such destructive power on their own?

And then an image of the strange, ornate weapons born by so many of the warriors came back to me. Could those black and gold objects, with their stoppered muzzles and gilded flanks, be the means by which the Comanche unleashed these powers within their warriors?

The advantage they saw in this course of action must be great indeed, for them to risk ten to fifteen percent of their fighting strength to unlock the potential. It would make sense, if the guns were something like the magic wands and staffs of the old fairy tales, allowing those warriors attuned to the stones to channel their destructive impulses, as Chitsiwru had said ... that might explain how the Comanche had maintained their independence and their power in the face of the rising nations that surrounded them.

That might also explain why Chitsiru had said the Comanche were short on stones. If they were breaking these rare gems to create their fantastical guns ... I tried to remember how many of those weapons I had seen.

Many.

And I had no idea how rare the stones were. I had certainly never encountered another in all my research, and it had taken me years to track down Merlin's stone in that little French chapel. Maybe here, in the New World, the stones were more plentiful?

Were there other cultures, then, who might have unlocked their mysteries?

That was unsettling. I had taken up this quest thinking to awaken an ancient power, unseen in Europe and beyond for over a thousand years. But what did I truly know about this power, or about this new continent that I had so vainly thought to march into and bend to my will?

I couldn't worry about that. I had to keep my eyes on the goal and consider the wider ramifications to the fields of history and ethnology when my work was done and England safe.

But even in the silence of my own mind, those words rang hollow. I had seen wonders, to be sure. Or at least, I had seen something none of my earlier life had prepared me to understand.

But could even this power truly render England safe again?

*****

We took a circuitous route, indeed, back toward the city. Although we did not quite reach it on that first night, we could see the soft lights of Sahri above the horizon of the distant hills, and I knew it would only take an hour or so the next night and I would have my gear, my journals, and Ben.

That was, if old Gus hadn't sold it all. Had the old man known what I had been heading toward when I left his public house the other night? But that was sheer paranoia, of course. The old Scot was no more a Comanche stooge than I was.

But what about the devil with the golden smile? How did he fit into all of this? Chitsiru had denied knowing anything about the man when I asked. But I realized that, even motivated by the self-interest of the stones, I shouldn't really trust him any farther than I must.

We stopped before moonrise and I watched the ivory orb, only slightly smaller than the night before, rise over the distant hills, bathing the landscape in silver light.

By that light we could see roving bands of Comanche patrols, and I knew they would never let me go. Not only did they know I had a stone, they most likely lacked Chitsiru's fear about taking it from an unwilling man. They could never let a European, as they said, leave the plains knowing what I now knew about their own capabilities and intentions..

   The more I reflected on everything I had seen since arriving in New Orleans the more I realized that the true power of the Comanche, from their strange weapons to the weather to the mysteries I had seen opened before me at the council fire, was in large part thanks to the stones I had come so far to find.

   The idea that the enemies who surrounded them would gain this power would, of course, be abhorrent to them.

   They had no reason to trust me. They didn't know me, and history was fraught with instances of the same betrayals and treacheries that had been perpetrated upon the tribes of the Americas for hundreds of years.

   I was just another in a long line of Europeans to them. People just like me had done terrible things here. The secrets I now knew, from their intentions of war to the powers of the earth they had awakened, could well threaten their very existence.

   Would I have felt any different if I had found myself standing in judgement before a nascent Benedict the Betrayer eighty years ago?

   I was honest enough with myself to say I would not.

   And even more so, I was honest enough with myself to admit that this new world had more allure for me than I had ever thought possible. Maybe not tired old Liberté, but the Western Marches? The Empire of the Summer Moon, even? I had heard several tales of the broken coast, far to the west, with its pirates and island kingdoms that had harkened back to the adventure stories of my youth.

   I felt a pull to the west I had never felt before. Was it strong enough to cause me to abandon my quest? To abandon my beloved England and all the people I knew and loved in life? To leave them to the slow death to which Albion had doomed them?

   Of course not, I decided at last in the silence of the bright night. But the answer had not come as quickly as I would have thought.

*****

   We returned to Sahri in the pitch dark of the next night. The sunset had faded completely in the west and the moon was nothing more than a glint of silver on the horizon. We approached from the east, having traveled all the way around the city to avoid detection.

Chitsiru might not have been any kind of great Comanche warrior, but he was an excellent guide on that dark journey.

We kept to the abandoned streets as much as we could, skirting around the edges of the city until we moved in, straight toward the Horse's Head. We sat in the empty shell of a building across the street, watching the comings and goings of the European clientele until Chitsiru was satisfied no one was watching. He then gestured for me to go in through the broken building next door and I nodded.

Ben gave a low whicker of recognition as I slunk into the makeshift stable, and I felt a little jolt of warmth for the old man that the horse was still there. The warmth became a flood when I saw that Ben's stall had had its straw replaced and fresh water was in the trough.

It had been over two days since I had eaten, with only gully-water to drink. That thought led me to the food I knew Gus would have cooking, and then, of course, to the last tea I might taste in a very long time.

I pushed back the curtain separating the outbuilding from the pub and glanced into the room. There were several tables full of patrons, but no sign of the dapper little man with the golden teeth. Angus MacDonald was behind the bar, a contented half-smile on his face, a steaming mug by one elbow.

I knew I shouldn't indulge, not with Chitsiru waiting across the street and all the Comanche Empire searching for us. But as Gus smiled widely upon my entrance, and his insistence of making me a cup, I found my resolve crumbling. In the end, I stayed for a cup, but had him make several sandwiches and wrap them in waxed paper. I collected my things while the old Scot made tea in two long stoneware bottles for the road.

I told him not to mention he had seen me, and he laughed.

"You think the Comanche even talk to us?" He waved my concerns away. "They'll find you on their own, or they won't. They're a rather fatalistic lot, to be sure. You look out for yourself, and I've no doubt you'll make it home in one piece, a resourceful fellow like yourself."

It had appeared the other white folk in the place had taken no special notice of me, and as I slipped out the back, having left one of my last gold coins behind for Gus to find, I felt fairly confident that we would be able to sneak back out of the city and turn north without trouble.

Chitsiru was nowhere to be found when I guided Ben through the slumped rubble at the back of our hunter's blind across the street, but before I could even think of what I might do without him, he led another horse into the alleyway out back and gestured for us to move on without a word. I could see that he had saddlebags stuffed with supplies himself, but still offered him one of Gus's sandwiches. He waved it away and I shrugged.

Gus made a damned fine sandwich, and I was just as happy not to have to share.

We led our horses through several broken houses before emerging into an avenue that paralleled the avenue of the Horse's Head a couple streets closer to the edge of town. I wouldn't have even thought to move right through the empty buildings, but it made sense as I followed Chitsiru through the dark maze of ruins.

But as we came out into the street, a figure detached itself from the shadows further down and stood in the middle of the grassy sward, hands on hips and gold teeth gleaming in the starlight.

"Bonjour, encore, Nicholas."

Chapter 22

Chitsiru shot me a look over his shoulder that I knew, despite the darkness, could not be complimentary.

I stood straighter, ignoring my guide. "Do we know each other?"

The man laughed a deep, easy laugh. "No, but we share an interesting acquaintance, and I believe you find yourself now in a bit of *las peine, ai-je raison?*"

Creole, just close enough to my classical French for me to follow his meaning.

And the last piece of the puzzle slipped into place.

"You're Haitian."

Poor Chitsiru looked perplexed, and I knew we needed to be on our way. But there was a chance, if this man was in league with my friend from *La Citadelle*, that he might be able to help.

The man nodded and walked closer. "If you might have something to show me, I might have something to show you." He rotated one shoulder, shifting a heavy pack there.

I scrounged in my pocket for the ring and withdrew it, holding it out in the dim starlight. "This?"

The man came up to me and held out his hand. Again, I caught a whiff of spices and this time, beneath them, something unpleasantly sweet.

I felt a natural distrust for the golden-smiled stranger, but the Haitians in Corners had saved me, certainly, and it seemed we had shaken our pursuers for the moment, at least. I felt I could spare a moment, at least. I casually reached my left hand into the pocket where I had taken to keeping the derringer during our return across the plains. I wrapped my fingers around the grip.

Just in case.

The man took the ring and barely gave it a second glance. "Thank you." He shrugged off his pack and lowered it to the grass between us. "And the *Houngan* thanks you, as well." That was confusing. Was it a name? A title? Could it be the man in the tower? The stranger bent over the pack and reached inside. "It is a shame, is it not? When kings and princes cannot be trusted to know their place?"

He stood again, a wickedly curved knife, its blade as black as midnight, in one deft hand.

"Now, if you will only let me know why his majesty saved you from the block, and what mission you perform for him now, I promise, your deaths will be swift and painless."

I pulled my fist out of my pocket and aimed the little gun at the middle of the man's chest. "Not another step, friend."

I thought I was getting the hang of this frontier nonsense. Trust no one and you would not be disappointed.

But the other man continued to advance, his golden smile only widening.

When I shot the woman in the council circle it had been an instant reflex. I had had no time to contemplate the consequences of pulling the trigger. I found now, watching this man with his strange smell and his ghoulish, golden grin, that such thoughts can only slow the reflexes.

Beside me, apparently stunned, Chitsiru only watched with wide eyes. Behind us, the horses shied away as if catching the scent of a predator.

It was as if time had frozen for all of us on that dark, isolated street save the strange little Haitian.

Then the starlight sparked briefly off the edge of the black knife and I pulled the trigger.

The detonation of the round came crashing back at us from the surrounding walls as the gun bucked violently against my hand. The round caught the Haitian just beneath the sternum. He staggered, looked down at the spreading stain there, and the sickly-sweet smell was redoubled. Then he looked up again, grin even wider, and took another step.

I shot him again, and then again. The fourth time I pulled the trigger there was only a hollow click as the hammer hit a spent casing. Apparently, I *had* only fired one shot at the council fire. And apparently, I had lacked the presence of mind to reload the gun through the long hours between then and our encounter on the street.

But three shots were enough, as the Haitian folded up around the spreading stains, falling onto his side without a sound.

Without checking on the body, I stepped back to Ben's side and mounted without a second thought.

It must have been a good instinct, because I saw Chitsiru rise onto his own horse beside me. Together, we turned away from the corpse in the grass, intent on getting as far from the site of the gun-shots as possible.

We ran heedlessly down the grassy streets, then. He took the lead after a moment, and I was content to follow. I realized, as we tore through the last few buildings on the edge of the city, that I had left the Haitian ring behind, but I wasn't about to turn around now, not with the wide plains opening up before us.

We galloped clear of the last buildings at full speed, my cheek pressed to Ben's neck as he bolted across the open grass, making for the deeper darkness to the north.

The recklessness of our flight compounded the recklessness of my firing three shots in the street, but I didn't see what choice I had had then, and I didn't see what choice we had as we fled.

The Haitian had taken a bullet to the gut and it hadn't fazed him. What could that mean? Was he lost to some exotic drug? Some kind of zealot for the cause? Who was the *Houngan*?

Through the confusion of my thoughts, I heard something that caused my heart to drop before my mind could assign meaning to the sound.

Hoofbeats. Horses at a pounding gallop behind us.

Pursuing us.

Hunting us.

Chitsiru didn't even look back, only hunkered down in his sad-dle and kicked viciously at his mount's barrel, shouting desperately into the beast's ear.

I shook Ben's reins, screaming at him to run, but then looked back, knowing what I would see: a line of Comanche riders bearing down on us, their exotic weapons coming up to spit death across the plains.

My first thought was utter confusion. The pursuers wore far too much clothing to be Comanche. Far too much for most Europeans, in fact. Cloaks and half-capes unfurled behind each rider as they leaned into their mounts' furious gait, heads lowered. I could barely make out faces beneath the strange hats they wore.

Beneath the strange, tricorn hats they wore.

Albian Rangers.

I spat a curse. This was insane. How could the Rangers have found me out here on the plains, so far from the forests of northern Liberté?

It didn't matter. What mattered was that they had found me. And they were coming on fast.

A shot rang out over the plains. In all that vast space it was almost lost, seemingly insignificant among the endless rolling hills and high dome of stars overhead. But I knew that one of those fat bullets striking their mark would put an end to any of us, riders or mounts, no matter how comparatively small the round might be.

The lights of Sahri were disappearing behind us, but I doubted we would be able to recreate our miraculous escape the night of the council fire.

The city's glow was almost lost on the horizon, and still the Rangers pursued, the distance between us closing slowly. I wondered if Chitsiru could have escaped them had he been willing to leave me or my stone behind.

Perhaps not. As I said, he was not the best Comanche I had ever met. But I should not speak ill of the man, as he stayed beside me as we fled.

And then a crackling blast echoed across the plain, thunder, following a bolt of lightning that seemed to stream across the ground, beneath the clear sky.

Another group of riders, coming up from the east, was closing on us. These, I thought, staring through squinting, tear-blurred eyes, were Comanche. Probably a search party, out looking for Chitsiru and me.

And they had found us.

The Rangers turned their attention to this new threat, and the two groups began to exchange fire. The enormous pistols of the Rangers boomed out, flashing with red-tinged bursts of flame. The returning shots from the closing Comanche sounded slightly different, more like actual thunder, but otherwise they seemed like conventional shots.

Until another bolt of lightning seared across my vision, taking one Ranger in the chest; throwing him from his horse and into a tumbling, smoking ruin on the grass.

Far from deterring the others, they seemed to redouble their fire, and two Comanche fell.

After a few more moments of this, Comanche turned and ran back into the darkness. The Rangers, who had never changed the direction of their charge, bent toward us with renewed purpose.

They didn't fire, though. Not again. Instead, they chased after us, up hills and down, closing the distance moment by moment, until at last their mounts were breathing the same air as ours, all of them heaving like bellows.

One Ranger dropped his reins and leapt from the back of his horse to hit Chitsiru full in the side, sweeping him from the saddle. The two fell in a tight roll, the Albian coming up on top, knee planted in the Comanche's back, a blade glinting in the light of the rising moon.

And with the rising of the moon, I knew it was only a matter of time before more Comanche parties would find us.

Sadly, it probably wouldn't matter to us when that happened.

Chitsiru was lost in the night as Ben continued his heroic run, trying to outpace the Albian pursuit. But soon enough I, too, was swept from my mount to go bouncing painfully across the ground. Several of the injuries from the night of the council fire screamed, as cuts reopened, and tortured muscles were wrenched once again.

I came to a stop in a heap and found myself, at last, looking up into the face of my captor. The man was replacing the small hat and straightening out his eye patch.

His black eyepatch.

It was Geoff Clarke, the Ranger captain who had almost caught us in the borderlands between Liberté and the Marches.

His gaunt face smiled down at me, and I thought I saw a glimmer of appreciation there, for a hunt well-run, perhaps.

"You're not an easy man to run to ground, Mr. Hawke."

I was bone-weary, and my soul felt utterly depleted. I didn't even care how he knew my name. Everyone in this damned place seemed to know my name.

They dragged Chitsiru up and dumped him into the grass beside me. Poor, loyal Chitsiru, I thought. More the fool me.

"Now, we'll be having company here before long, English, so let's make this quick, shall we?" The Rangers were standing in an arc behind their commander. They glared at me, no doubt blaming me for the losses they had already suffered that night. "This time there's no papist bitch here to save you.."

I shook my head to clear it. Had the man asked me any questions yet? Did I know why he had hunted me across half a continent? *Had* he hunted me? How could he have known I was in Sahri?

"My superiors need to know why you are here, English. And I don't have the time nor the inclination to be patient." He stepped closer and his booted toe came down quickly on the fingers of my left hand where they were still splayed in the grass. He ground them into the dirt, and I grunted with the sudden, startling pain.

"Why are you here?"

The blast that killed the first Albian horse was deafening. The poor beast's carcass flew into the air, spinning, sending a shower of bloody viscera across the grass before tumbling to a halt, steaming in the cool night air.

The Rangers had hunkered down at the thunderous detonation, looking in all directions for whatever might have caused such destruction.

I knew, though. I remembered from that night.

The Comanche had hidden these abilities from their neighbors for decades, possibly for centuries. They would only use them now under very specific circumstances.

They did not intend for any of us to survive the encounter.

Two Rangers leapt toward the dead animal, rolling over its body to take cover behind its bulk, their massive pistols raised, looking for targets.

Clarke and the others crouched low, their cloaks flaring out around them, the blue-gray blending into the grasses. They all had weapons drawn, from the big handguns to some spindly-looking long arms. They began to fire in one direction, due west, and I turned from my position, on my knees in the grass, to see a much larger band of Comanche approaching.

At their head rode a huge warrior, a gleaming white blade brandished overhead.

"Give me the stone!"

That broke through the terror and confusion, and I turned to Chitsiru, glaring at me with wide, wild eyes, his hand outstretched like a wretched claw.

"Give it to me! I can use it!"

Here we were, trapped on the plains between two terrible threats: our situation no less dire than Odysseus staring down Scylla and Charybdis. Like the great wanderer, was my fate, too, to be decided by my trust in friends?

I hoped I'd have better luck than him.

I nodded and took out Merlin's stone. I stretched out my arm, the stone dangling between us, and then stopped.

With gunfire and hellfire erupting all around, Chitsiru had eyes only for the stone. Greed flared there. His face was tight, every fiber of his being straining toward this lodestone of his desire.

I gave it to him.

As his hands closed around the stone he seemed to come back to himself. He looked at me, and I was struck by the haunted light I saw on his face as he curled his arm to his side, Merlin's stone crushed in a death grip.

He looked at me, something animal and tragic on his face. He shook his head once, mouthing the words, "I'm sorry."

And he was on one of the Albian's horses, charging into a night flaring and flashing with all the fury of a battle among the gods.

Somehow, defying logic and sense, Chitsiru's path wove through all of that destruction and he faded swiftly into the night.

I snarled. "No!" I stood and was suddenly flying through the air. One of the Rangers had spun and lashed out with one foot, catching me in the chest and throwing me violently onto my back. Air exploded from my abused lungs and I rolled in the dirt, cradling my chest in agony.

The figure came crouching over to me. "Stay down, you idiot."

And I recognized the voice.

Why did I recognize that voice?

She looked down at me then, and her contemptuous smile cut me deeper than a knife.

Abigail Parker.

"Hello, again, Nicholas." Before I could reply, if I could have replied, she was spinning away, that cursed cloak sweeping around her, and one of those strange rifles rose in her hands with the speed and surety of long training. The weapon barked, coughing a gout of fire and smoke, and a distant horseman went down.

A flare of light blasted out of the darkness and a bitter cold swept over me. Rimes of frost glittered in the grass and one of the Rangers, a man who had stood to reload his rifle, was struck by a beam of absolute cold.

With half a scream the man froze, ice forming across his uniform, across his flesh, across his eyes. And then, with another pulse of power down that strange beam, the statue of a man shattered into countless jagged splinters.

I could not understand the Rangers then; why would they not throw down their weapons in terror? They could not know what they were facing. There was no way they knew about the arcane powers of the Comanche. But they continued to fight, even as the distance closed and the remaining warriors clashed with the remaining Rangers in personal combat.

Cro's white-hot blade left blinding scars of light in the darkness, passing through flesh and bone as if they were shadow. The man's face was calm, almost regretful, as he sent two Rangers dropping to the grass.

I rose stiffly to my feet, wandering aimlessly through the brutal fighting, my hand clutching my useless, empty pistol, my mind echoing with loss.

And in the middle of all that chaos, violence and death, lost to utter despair, I was snatched from the earth with such ferocity that I nearly lost consciousness.

The world bounced around me, my body screamed with the pain; a scream my lungs lacked the breath to voice.

I had the impression of a horse and rider close behind me but my vantage was too high. I was standing, wasn't I? Hadn't I been standing, my feet planted firmly on the earth? I was looking at the wild eyes of a horse in full gallop on a level with my own. How was I so high in the air?

Then I saw the rider's face, tucked close to the horse's neck. Beneath a battered, wide-brimmed hat two dark eyes flared with anger.

It was Tillman Clay.

"Hey!" From the melee all around, that familiar voice called out again. "He fancies *me*, now, you know!" The figures lost in the battle were receding from my sight, but I could make out the malign grin on Abigail Parker's blood-streaked face as she shouted, not at me, but at another rider following close behind Clay.

That rider turned in the saddle, producing a gargantuan pistol and sliding into line despite her pounding gait. A pistol I I recognized.

The explosion of the shot was like mountains crashing together.

Abigail Parker was thrown backwards by the impact of the blast, her body limp and still.

Monique turned back, not looking at me at all, her eyes focused on the distant, dark horizon.

Clay muttered one word through a grim smirk, teeth clenched against the effort of his ride.

He was just close enough for me to hear it.

"Bitch."

Chapter 23

It was a nightmare ride that lasted well beyond the dawn. The rumble and flash of the battle between the Rangers and the Comanche had faded behind us and was nothing but distant thunder and heat lightning when we stopped just long enough for me to get more comfortably situated behind my rescuer.

My rescuer, Tillman Clay.

The big dark-skinned man smiled amiably enough, his eyes a little wild with the energy and excitement of the flight, I think. But Monique wouldn't let me talk as we stopped, gesturing for me to hop up behind the big Washingtonian so we could continue on our way.

There were countless Comanche bands out searching for me, I knew, and so I complied. There would be time enough for talk when we were safely beyond the borders of the Empire of the Summer Moon.

I was utterly frantic, but fear of death can focus even the wildest heart. I needed to talk to her, to tell her what had happened.

We needed to pursue Chitsiru! The bastard had stolen the stone, and without that, all hope was lost.

And with Ben left behind on the plain, I no longer had my journals, either. Not that they mattered any longer.

Without Merlin's stone, my quest was at any end.

I now knew, with the certitude of my own eyes, that even my wildest theories were true, and yet that power was now forever out of my reach.

But if I didn't recover the stone, it had all been for nothing.

As we pounded across the grasslands, my despair rose up to choke off hope.

Chitsiru might not have been the best rider among the Comanche, but he had showed himself much better than I had thought.

And I didn't know which direction he had run, either. It occurred to me, for a moment, that he had to be heading north like us, with similar reasons. But north was vast on this strange continent, and every mile we pounded across could mean we were farther away from him, and my stone.

Without the stone I might as well have died on the high plains. There was no purpose to any of this without it. I was good for nothing.

England would continue its inevitable slide toward death, and everyone I loved would live out their lives in wretched hopelessness.

At least they would be spared the thoughts that tormented me on that long, endless ride. There *had been* hope. There had been a possible salvation. I had seen it.

And I had lost it.

Even the surprise that met us with the rising sun was not enough to break through my despair. Ben must have followed us out of the battle and across the plains. He came up to us as we stood by my rescuers' horses during a rest break beneath the warming sun.

I almost smiled to see him, and Monique allowed me to shift from Tillman's horse to my own, but even Ben's survival and the recovery of my journals was not enough to lift me from the valley of my sinking anguish.

Far better to have loved and lost than to have never loved at all, the poets say.

The poets lie.

*****

I could tell Monique felt I should be far more grateful, and I tried to summon up a smile for her as we stopped at noon the day after the battle by a small stream for some water and much-needed food.

It was jerky. Beef, probably.

Horse, maybe.

I didn't care. I forced several strips down, gulping water from a skin in equal measure and lapsed back into pathetic silence.

They had saved my life. I knew that. There would have been no way to escape out on the plain with the Albian Rangers and the Comanche both vying for my head. I had had no hope.

When Chitsiru had taken the stone, I had thought he might be able to save us both. It had been a wager made in the heat of battle, the screams of the dead and dying all around. If I had come all this way to stake England's future on the stone, should I not be willing to stake my own, immediate safety on it as well?

But, of course, in the end it had not been the stone that failed me.

It had been Chitsiru.

And the stone was gone.

Monique was staring at me as she sat, chewing absently on a strip of jerky. Clay was resting with his back against a chunk of rock, a look of calm peace on his dark face as he raised it toward the hot sun.

"How did you find me?" I tried again to smile, but found I was unequal to the task. I tilted my head toward Tillman Clay. "Was he working for you the whole time?"

Her glance shifted toward the big wrangler and then back to me again, a slight smile hovering at the corner of her mouth as Clay gave a slight snort.

"Tillman wasn't working for me. Tillman is working for me *now*, but he wasn't when you first met." She shrugged. "I was busy tracking something down in Corners, but I knew you were heading out with Cole's caravan. When I came looking for you, I ran into Tillman. We've worked together before. He helped me track you down in Sahri, but you'd already disappeared."

"Quite a light show off to the west a few nights back." The big man yawned, teeth flashing. "Night you vanished? Figured you'd be comin' back this way sooner'r later."

Monique nodded. "We staked our claim on one of the less run-down outer buildings on the east side of the city, figuring you'd swing around to avoid pursuit if you were coming back. What was it, heat lightning?"

I tried to conjure up some response, but then saw the grin, and shook my head.

"No, if you made it through that, you were going to be coming back for your horse, and for your damned books."

"How did you know my books were still in Sahri?" I perked up a little at that. "Did you go through my things?"

The incident with Abigail Parker on the trail to the Empire of the Summer Moon still stung. I didn't like thinking Monique had gone through my packs any more than the—

"Abigail Parker. You know Abigail Parker?" I shook my head, looking away. "Knew."

Monique spat into the grass off to her side. "I'm assuming you're referring to Abby Poole. That Ranger that got mouthy last night? Yeah, we go way back. She's been riding with Clarke for years."

Monique's face twisted into a bitter mask. "Clarke kept me busy in Corners, kept me distracted, or I would have noticed her plain as day riding with Cole. And I don't expect we've seen the last of her, either."

That made no sense. Monique's enormous pistol had blasted the woman off her feet and into the darkness. Certainly, a shot like that would have been fatal. "You shot her..." I pointed to the enormous gun in its holster at her side. "You shot her with that."

Monique sighed, and Tillman laughed again. "I was bearing special shells, trying to avoid an incident with the Comanche. I think you'll find she's got a damned ugly bruise somewhere around center of mass, and she's probably not breathing too well right now. But she'll return to haunt our backtrail before too long."

Why would Monique care about the Comanche any more than she had cared for the Rangers in the frontier forest?

But before I could ask, she distracted me with her next question.

"How do you know Abby?"

I paused. My acquaintance with Abigail, as I continued to think of her, was still a subject of much chagrin and frustration. I was not proud of the way I had acted, nor of how quickly I had lowered my guard in the face of what I now realized had been her determined efforts of enticement. She had distracted me, and then she had almost made off with my research.

The Rangers, who must have been shadowing the caravan the whole time, would have taken me in Sahri, and that would have been the end of my quest.

Except that here we were, only a couple days later, and my quest had ended anyway.

It also explained how Clarke had known my name.

And it didn't matter, because unless we found Chitsiru in that vast expanse, my search was over.

I sighed, feeling my shoulders slump as what little fire had lit in my chest guttered and went out.

"They got your pretty stone, eh?" She seemed genuinely sorry, and somehow, I thought that hurt even more than sarcasm.

I nodded but could say no more.

"That Comanche you were with? The one from the *Turner* compound?"

My attention piqued at that, just a little. "How long have you been following me?"

Tillman Clay snorted again and stood, his body rolling out of its slouched position as if he was rising from the dead. "No one followed you that day, English. But there's only one white man went through the gate that day, or any day in the last month or more. You ain't been that hard to keep track of. Ain't like you been tryin' to keep yourself hid." He turned from resaddling his horse, dark eyes glittering with sudden suspicion beneath the brim of his battered hat. "You ain't been thinkin' you been hidin', have you?"

"We better get going." Monique rose as well, bending to pick up her own saddle. "We've got to get off the prairie before another Comanche war party finds our trail."

"War party?" I hadn't said anything about the camp I had seen out on the plains.

Monique nodded as she cinched her saddle into place. "That second bunch of Comanche that hit the rangers wasn't a scouting party like the first. They were loaded for bear, and they came in hot. There's something brewing out beyond Sahri, and there's no telling how many warriors they could call on right now."

Tillman swung into his saddle and spat a wad of tobacco into the grass. "'Less'n you can tell us, there, English?"

Monique looked down at me from her own saddle as I struggled to get the tack onto Ben. "What happened to you out on the grass, Nicholas?"

So, I told them, at least what I could remember. Most of it wasn't clear even then and had only grown dimmer with time. I told them of the light and the thunder, and my desperate run across the plains, and of Chitsiru's rescue. I tried to be dispassionate on that score but spat the words as I mentioned him.

"He took your stone." Monique nodded.

I shook my head. "I gave it to him. I gave it to him, and he ran."

And now there was nothing left. But was there even a reason for me to go home? What was there in England for me? Scorn and condemnation? I had failed everyone and everything I cared about.

Maybe I should just head west. Maybe I could establish myself as a pirate somewhere among the islands and poisoned inlets of the broken coast.

I left out most of the revelations Chitsiru had shared with me during our time together, but everything else I laid bare. It was easily the most violent, difficult stretch of hours in my entire life, including everything I had gone through since the *Ett Hjerte* had crossed the Atlantic.

"And that doesn't even include the Haitian." Amidst all the other strangeness, I had nearly forgotten the small, dapper man with the golden smile who had accosted us in the street.

As my stomach wrenched into a painful knot, I realized that I had not forgotten the memory so much as suppressed it.

I had killed a man.

"Haitian? Monique leaned forward, her eyes suddenly intense, all sense of pity gone. "What Haitian?"

I was caught off guard by the intensity of the question but rallied gamely enough. "A small Haitian I think tracked me to Sahri." I looked at Monique and Tillman, then thought about Clarke and his Rangers. "I seem to have been relatively easy to track, in retrospect."

Monique leaned down to take me by one shoulder, her eyes burning. "Did he find you? What happened when he found you?" She seemed to be looking me over as if inspecting me once again for injuries.

My body had been battered and abused since the council fire, as she was well-aware. But she apparently did not find what she was afraid she might, and so rocked back a bit, letting me answer.

"He met us on the street just before we were out of the city." I could see his golden smile again, hear the tone of his warm, buzzing voice.

I could almost smell that strange spicy mixture covering up the sickly-sweet aroma again.

"I killed him." I jumped to the end of the tale, not wanting to revisit any more of that encounter.

"Killed him? Killed him how?" She still had one hand on my shoulder and shook me gently as she asked. "You saw him die?"

I shrugged. "With the derringer you gave me. I shot him three times."

That seemed to reassure her, and she settled back.

"Where?" Tillman's deep voice broke into whatever it was that had risen up between us.

"What?" I shook my head and looked up at the big drover. Ben stood placidly beside me, the saddle half-cinched on his back.

"Where did you shoot him?" his face lacked the imminent concern Monique had shown, but there was still a weight to his gaze that seemed at odds with his casual demeanor.

"In the street." My shoulders slumped. Right in the middle of the street. I had shot him down in the middle of that street like a dog.

"Not what I meant, you soaplock." He leaned down and I had the sudden feeling he wanted to hit me. "Where did you hit him when you shot at him?"

I stammered my response, shrugging again. "The gut? I hit him in the stomach."

Clay leaned back and spat into the grass. "The belly." He turned to Monique. "If you're right, that wouldn't do it."

I looked at Monique, confused. She shook her head. "No. And I *am* right." She looked back at me. "You shot him three times?"

I thought back to the encounter. I had fired three shots. I knew that, because I had only had three shots left, and the gun had been empty as we rode away. I knew I hit him with the first shot, and I knew I hit him with the last, the impact that had set him crumpling into the street. I might have hit him with the second shot as well, but who knew?

"I think I did. Two or three times, at least."

"All in the gut." Clay, again, unsatisfied.

"Yes. All in the stomach."

Clay looked at Monique. "That wouldn't do it. We need to get out of here."

She nodded absentmindedly. "We do." She gestured at the saddle. "You need to get that tight, Nicholas. We need to leave."

I was new to all this, I knew that. But I resented the way I was being treated by these two veterans of this strange world. "He was dead. I watched him fall."

That seemed to amuse Clay, but Monique simply nodded, her tone grating. "I'm sure he fell, Nicholas, but we need to be going. He's not dead, and he'll be after you with even more persistence than Clarke or the Comanche."

Her tone was so cold, so flat, that I suppressed the further denials that rose in my mind. I cinched the last straps on Ben's saddle and clawed my way up onto my perch. I settled down, and then nodded to the others. "Let's go, then."

Clay snapped his reins and sent his big roan northward, moving quickly into a ground-devouring gallop, and I was forced to urge Ben faster than I would have normally pushed him to keep up.

As we continued our headlong flight toward the nearest edge of Comanche territory, I tried to puzzle out what there might have been about the man with the golden smile that had shaken Clay and Monique so much. It was hard to tell with the big trail hand, and I had a hard time imagining Monique scared of anything, but they had both been off kilter since my mention of the man with the golden smile.

He was dead. The man had been shot three times in the chest and belly. They said a belly wound was a long, slow, painful death, but irreversible. Those fat slugs must have made mincemeat of the man's innards. He might have survived for a few hours after the shooting, but not much longer.

I wondered what could possibly have happened in their lives that would cause Clay and Monique to doubt my word in this. And that line of inquiry, silently tumbling through my fevered mind, then led me to wonder who they might be to each other. What kind of history did the strange woman from Liberté and the Washingtonian brute share? And what kind of experiences lurked in that shared past that made them doubt that a man who had been shot three times in the gut might possibly not only survive, but thrive, eager for vengeance?

I knew I had shot him three times. I was certain that second slug had staggered him back.

Three times should be enough to kill any man.

I had hit him three times.

Hadn't I?

*****

We had been riding again for more than a day. We probably would have been riding still if Clay's horse hadn't hurt its leg in the dark. We were huddled together at the bottom of a shallow ravine that reminded me of the sanctuary I had shared with Chitsiru after the council fire.

Clay lit a fire in the lee of a large boulder, and I enjoyed my first hot meal in days. I even took a tin cup of coffee without complaint, hugging it to my chest as it cooled.

The fire was banked, coals glowing a dull red, as the stars wheeled overhead, and I contemplated trying to sleep.

I knew it wasn't going to happen.

The stone was a key to everything I could have wanted and more. What I had seen here on this endless grass-covered plain was the salvation of England and the doom of Albion. Things that the 'learned men and women' of the world would never allow within their philosophy were real now, I knew.

Or, at least, I thought I knew.

The altercation between the Rangers and the Comanche warriors outside of Sahri had revealed a great deal of the mysterious power of the stones. Even if there had been some sort of substance in the council fire that might have colored my perception, it would have long passed from my body by the time Chitsiru and I had made our way into the city and out again.

There was very much something more to these Comanche than anyone in Europe would ever remember.

"Maybe this was for the best, Nicholas." Monique's voice was soft, and when I looked over at her, she wasn't watching me, but staring into the dying fire. "The forces wielded by the Comanche are unnatural. Nothing good can come of trucking with such powers."

I couldn't believe my ears. She knew why I was here. She knew what had lured me halfway around the world and dragged me out onto this isolated plain. She knew what was at stake, and what theories had brought me so far.

"England—"

Tillman Clay snorted that deep, dismissive laugh of his, and I looked briefly in his direction.

But he wasn't looking at me. He was looking at Monique, and his face was a mask of scorn.

"Didn't take too long, girl." He was chewing on something. Jerky, maybe, or that vile chaw "Sure you want to go down this road? Don't think it's on the approved trail."

"Enough." She snapped at him, and he smiled, resting back against the stone. "You ask any border sheriff in Washington if the Comanche would agree that nothing good comes from their hoodoo."

"Savages." The word was vile, but there was no venom in her voice. "They worship trees and rocks, Clay. Are you going to set your moral compass on such people?"

This time, the big trail hand laughed out loud. "Fallen from what, Dubois? They don't follow your God, most of them. They haven't fallen from anything they would recognize. And I assure you, your judgement on them carries no water at all as far as they're concerned."

She shook her head and looked back at me. "What they think doesn't matter. Do you truly believe you do yourself any good, in your soul, turning to such dark powers, no matter the perceived need?"

I was confused. "Why would you bring me this far if you didn't approve?" I felt the anger building, and I didn't care. "And who the hell are you to give or withhold your approval of anything?"

I stood, looking around for Ben and my gear. "I don't need your approval, Monique. I thank you for all you have done for me—"

"Wasn't her yanked you off the grass." Clay's words were said with a cruel smile, and I ignored him.

"But I don't need you anymore. I don't need either of you."

I stormed toward the horses but stopped before I had covered half the distance. I had no idea what direction I should be going. North, I knew, but other than a vague sense that I should follow the brightest star, I had no idea how to find that trail.

Everything I had said was true, although ungrateful in the extreme. But it didn't matter, anyway. There was nothing spurring me on now.

Without them, I had no hope of finding Chitsiru.

The anger and the energy spilled from me, and my entire body slumped as I stood in the shadows. My pursuit was done, and there was no need for me to be churlish when there was no more path for me to follow.

Something told me Monique was not going to help me find the fleeing Comanche.

Monique seemed to sense my thoughts. She didn't move from the fire, but leaned toward me, the light from the coals bringing out a vibrant red in her hair.

"It's gone, anyway, Nicholas." She turned on her hip and rose to come to me, touching my shoulder. "We need to get you somewhere safe where you can recover. The stone is gone, regardless of all the rest of this. I'm sorry if my words distressed you."

"It's not, you know." There was a strange light in Clay's eyes as he watched us in the shadows. I couldn't tell who, exactly, he was looking at, but his next words made that clear.

"The Comanche hasn't got many places he can go."

I remembered something Chitsiru had said, and a burst of energy rushed through my body.

"Perdition."

Clay nodded. "Perdition. He'll be there, and it ain't so big we won't be able to find him. We should be able to get your stone back in no time."

I couldn't quite understand the poisonous look Monique shot the big man, but I didn't care.

"Yes." For the first time since that terrifying battle on the plains, I knew hope again. "Yes, he'll be in Perdition! He'll be in Perdition, and we can catch him!"

"Clay—" There was violence behind Monique's hard mask, and fire in her gaze as she stared at the tall man. But the drover just shrugged.

"You people have to let us make our own mistakes, Monique."

I was so lost in the swirl of my own resurgent hope, I missed that. Only later would I remember those words.

Only later, when it was far too late.

"The man's got a dream. He's following it. Do you love Albion so much you would deter him from following this quest of his?"

She spat off to the side as if her mouth had flooded with poison, and her anger was enough to penetrate even the thick cloud of optimism that had shrouded my mind.

"I have no love of Albion, as you know. You're setting him on a path—"

This time, as he responded, I was taken aback by the softness of Clay's tone, almost as if he was consoling her.

"I'm not settin' him on any path, Monique." He tilted his head toward me without looking away from her angry face. "He's been on this path for longer than either of us have known him. And he has a right to see its end, no matter the price."

I took the calm, matter-of-fact tone as reassurance of my own realization, and again, was nearly blinded by visions of catching Chitsiru, regaining Merlin's stone, and forcing him to guide me through the mysterious ordeal.

In addition to these heart-warming thoughts, I had never before considered Tillman Clay a friend. He had been a bully, an upstart, and a scold over the course of our acquaintance, but never before had he been so supportive or helpful.

The two responses, in strange combination, must have over-whelmed my sense, then. It is the only excuse I can think to offer for my utter lack of concern for Monique's words that night.

"But his soul—"

Again, I missed it.

"Is his own."

Silence fell around us, the sound of insects out on the plains only punctuating the lack of speech.

Monique's face did not relax. She did not slacken her tight muscles or break their locked stare.

But with almost casual disdain, Clay *did* look away, setting once more against the rock and tipping his hat down low over his eyes.

"Either way, we gotta get going at first light. Don't want any of the tide o' strangeness sweeping up behind us catching us out here in the open. The Marches is another two day's ride, at least. No matter where you plannin' on going next, our next step better be out'a here, and worry about the rest at some later date."

Monique's gaze slid from the big caravanner to me, and then away. Without another word or glance, she prepared herself for sleep.

"First watch is yours, Englishman." And she rolled herself into a blanket and grew very still.

I stood there, beside Ben who continued to contentedly munch away on rich grass, completely at a loss as to how this had happened.

But truth be told, it didn't matter much. It didn't matter at all.

Chitsiru, the little thief, was making for Perdition. He had no-where else to go.

And we would be there as well.

And the stone would be mine again.

The power would be mine to wield.

And Albion would bleed.

Chapter 24

Sunrise caught us already on the move, and for the first time in days, I didn't mind. In fact, I was so eager to catch up to Chitsiru that I couldn't focus on anything more.

Tillman Clay was as silent as he had ever been, after that night by the red fire. He acted no more my friend on the last leg of our journey to Perdition than he had been during the whole of the caravan to Sahri. This was a little confusing, as he had been so supportive against Monique's rising challenges that night.

But, as I have noted, my mind was not at its most astute as we made our hurried way across the plains.

Even after crossing the unremarked line between the Empire and the Marches, the threat of the Comanche loomed large in my companions' minds. And the Albian Rangers, no doubt following close on our heels as well if they had survived their encounter north of the capitol, were as much of a threat. In fact, having been dogging my steps since the forests of Liberté, they might have loomed even larger in my own fears. Had I been paying any attention.

Monique, for her part, had grown increasingly more aloof after that night. Days of hard riding made it difficult to talk, but even during our brief stops, day or night, she kept her distance.

I attributed this to her disappointment in Clay, as far as I thought of it at all. Most of my waking moments, those not spent in the saddle, urging Ben to his best speed, I was pouring over my journals, trying to tease out some hint as to what the ordeal might be, or how I might better prepare myself.

I tried to ascertain how I might know the risks, as well, but even knowing that there was a ritual barrier between me and these legendary powers, there was little to be gleaned by the vague stories of the past.

Chitsiru would have no choice but to guide me through it all when we caught him. My pistol was loaded once again, and I knew now that nothing would stop me from gaining the wisdom I sought. The rest would sort itself out after I underwent the ordeal, I had no doubt.

We were only a day or so out of Perdition when Monique came to me after we made our evening halt. Tillman Clay was off doing some chore of his own and we were alone. I was seated with my back against the dead, dry bole of a scrub tree, flipping through my most recent journal, going over the notes I had scribbled out since our ride up the Mississippi on the *Joyeaux*.

We were alone, and it is a testament to the sluggishness of my thoughts that the significance of this salient fact did not loom larger in my mind.

"Perdition is not a place for the weak."

She said this in an almost off-hand manner, as she slid the saddle off her horse and brushed down the animal's coat. I looked up at her from my position on the ground, half confused by the statement and half annoyed that her first words to me in days should be a further effort to dissuade me from my path.

"We haven't got a choice, though, right?" From the sketched maps in my journals, I knew there wasn't a settlement of any significant size anywhere along the border where the Marches jogged west, thrusting to the north of the Empire of the Summer Moon toward the desolation of *The One Who Kills*.

"It would be a long, rough journey, but we could be back in Corners in a couple weeks." She got out a canteen and took a long swallow of water. "Florian would be even closer, if we can cross the Rift, or about the same distance if we go around."

Florian. The mysterious town on the edge of the huge crack in the continent, filled with tainted water, flowing into the desolation.

Monique had painted a very romantic image of the place on our journey north. I thought I could almost picture the vast cranes, rising and lowering steam ships into the gorge.

Could one board such a ship in Florian and sail straight across the wastes to the broken coast in the west?

It was an intriguing question, one that had occurred to me more than once since first learning about the town. I would very much like to see that coast one day, and ride one of those ships into the ash wastes and beyond.

But that journey, if it was ever meant to be, would be taken once I had passed through my present crisis. I would be another man, then. Perhaps with the power of the stones at my call and Albion's threat a bitter memory, the lure of the west would be something I might heed.

Or perhaps, with that kind of power coursing through my veins, such petty curiosities would pass from me completely.

I was keenly interested to know the man I would be on the other side of this ordeal, but there were countless steps between here and there, and every one of them needed to be taken, in the proper order, before I could let myself be distracted.

"Tillman says we need to go to Perdition, anyway." It was the old, plaintive tone I had always hated, and doubly so when it crept into my voice in front of Monique for some reason, but I didn't care. "He said—"

"Clay only worries about Clay." The anger was back, and I held up one hand to stave off any further attack, but she continued. "Don't hang your hat on the friendship of a drover, Nicholas. Half the time Clay doesn't know why he does what he does. His loyalty lasts as long as your coin, and then he's gone."

"At least it's a measure everyone can agree on." The big man himself was back, walking right into the little camp and dropping a pack by his other things. He didn't seem to have taken any offense at all from Monique's words. "That's more than I can say for some others."

"He's just as likely to die in Perdition as he is to find that damned savage."

I reflected that she seemed to only use such charged language when she was extremely upset but thought no more on it as I looked to Clay to refute her statement.

I was disappointed.

"That's true." The drover spat a wad of dark juice into the grass. "But it's a choice he has to make. You don't get to make it for him. I don't get to make it for him."

"Are you going to save him if some wreck of a human tries to kill him during his first night in town?" She spoke through gritted teeth, but all I took from this was a desire for Clay to come back at her with even more strength.

"I will if he pays me." The man's teeth flashed white in the dark. "How about it, Hawke, you gonna pay me? I'm thinking I've seen the last of Monique's coin, given the last few days."

I still had Haitian coin with me, although not nearly as much as I had started out with.

But how much would a man like Clay command? I had little doubt the situation would work against me in any negotiation.

"You're paid up through Perdition, Clay." Monique straightened, and I was mildly confused at her tone, considering her recent stance or our heading to that questionable destination.

Again, that bright grin. "I am. And I'll stand by you both right into town. Then I'm off to find a drink, a meal, a bath, and a woman, in whatever order the good Lord sees fit to provide." He looked over at me. "Unless I've got reason not to."

I fished around in my pocket and came up with a silver Haitian coin. "Would this keep you around?"

Before I was aware, he had approached, Clay stepped back, the small metal circle flashing in his hands. "It will if he's got a couple friends to keep him company. Or, barring that, I'll stick around at least until we get your stone back."

Monique's eyes narrowed. "You weren't going anywhere."

And once more, that smile. "Well, you have me there, ma'am. I would like to see it for myself, before our paths diverge."

He flipped the coin back to me, but in the dark, distracted as I was, I missed it with my clumsy grab and knocked it farther out into the shadows, beyond the feeble glow of our small fire.

"Perdition is a god-forsaken place, and no mistake." The deep, rumbling voice followed me out into the darkness as Clay and Monique settled down on opposite sides of the fire, clearly content in letting me scramble for the coin on my own. "It's a den of nightmares and hellish visions on the very edge of the Wastes. We'll see more human misery within the first thirty steps into town than you've seen in your entire life, Master Hawke. But I'll see you and your stone reunited before I leave you to the tender mercies of the demons who call that place their home." He settled his head onto one of his packs, battered hat once more sliding over his face. "Then you can decide if a few silvers are worth trying to go it alone."

I didn't end up finding that coin, which left a foul taste in my mouth as I settled down in the darkness beyond the fire's glow out of a perverse sense of misplaced pride.

Something told me I was going to regret losing it when I paid the man his three.

Because something else told me I was definitely going to be paying.

*****

The world around us began to change around noon the next day. The horizon ahead seemed to take on a strange, soft glow I hadn't noticed before. It was subtle enough I hadn't realized it was happening until it was definitely there, and then I couldn't remember when, over the past several hours, it hadn't been there.

My throat was scratchy, as well, and no amount of water soothed the irritation.

"It's gonna be a bad one." Clay jerked his chin toward the horizon. "The Killer's spoor comes farther and farther out every year."

Monique looked with a nod. "Time was you'd never get a storm this far south." She reached down without looking and slipped a water skin from its place by her saddle horn. Closing her eyes, she took a deep draught. Then she looked over at me.

"You need to drink." Monique spoke between sips. "It won't feel like it's helping, but it'll be better than the alternative."

I looked at her with horror even as I scrambled to take out my own flask again. "What's the alternative?"

Clay laughed. "You got lungers over in England, Hawke?"

I cleared my throat, trying to suppress an involuntary cough. "Consumption? Yes, we have that. Many miners—"

He laughed again, harder. "Consumption." He spat into the grass; grass I noticed, for the first time, was much shorter and sparser than it had been. "Black lung from the Killer's a sight bit uglier than consumption." He pulled his kerchief up over his nose and his dark eyes glittered with malicious humor.

I looked at Monique, who had not yet raised her own bandana, although I did see that it was tied around her neck. She gave the big man a sour look. "You won't need anything over your mouth for hours yet."

Which, of course, indicated that eventually I would need something over my mouth.

Or I could end up a 'lunger'.

Worse than consumption.

I twisted in the saddle and began to rifle through my pack until I pulled out a neatly folded kerchief of my own. Without a word I tied it around my neck, then fended off the desire to pull it up over my mouth.

I wasn't going to give the man the satisfaction.

The terrain around us was turning silvery, and the clouds of dust rising from the horses' hooves were brighter than they had been. I knew what it was by then, of course, but it didn't change the crawling sensation that it sent down my spine.

I remembered the ash fall that had struck the *Joyeaux*. The momentary beauty of the scene had quickly turned ugly as the implications made themselves known. And as we rode north, leaving a trail of dirty brown behind us through the gradually thickening ash, I saw the logical end result of those storms over time.

We had left the Empire of the Summer Moon behind us four days ago, but the effects of the wastes, looming to the west like a terrible scar across the continent, were only now making their presence known.

Monique finally pulled her bandana up nearly to her eyes but by then I had been breathing through mine for over an hour.

How could people live like this?

Seriously, what could possibly lure someone to set down roots in such a blighted place?

I had not seen a living tree in hours, and the ever-present grass had faded away not long after. We were traveling through a white world that reminded me nothing so much as a Happy Christmas card illustration. All sound was deadened, nothing moved as far as the eye could see but an occasional swirl of dust in the distance.

"If you think this looks bad," Clay's voice was muffled, but his eyes crinkled in mirth at the corners as he watched me over his bandana. "You should take a day trip into the *real* waste, once we settle down."

I looked out again over the devastated landscape all around and tried to imagine how it could possibly be worse.

My curiosity about traveling west from Florian waned precipitously.

At least, muffled by our kerchiefs as we were, casual conversation was curtailed.

There were no more attempts to dissuade me from finding Chitsiru and my stone, and I was left, in the silence of my mind, to imagine my next moves as we plodded through the dead, silent world.

*****

I am certain there are more inhospitable places on earth, but I have never had the misfortune to experience them myself, and I will never go out of my way to seek them out now.

The storm struck right around sunset, and the swirling white fog that rose up all around, wind blowing it in strange, beguiling shapes, wiped the world away. The only reason I could keep my bearing, other than the shifting shadows of the others in the ash, was the strange red glow of sunset buried somewhere far away to the west.

We made camp in the muffled, stifling silence of the ash fall. It was nearly impossible to keep a fire burning, and we retreated into our small tents without much talk, our voices stifled by the bandanas. I do not remember falling asleep, listening to the never-ending hiss of ash sliding along the length of my canvas shelter.

The first full day, and our horses began to struggle. I have had many opportunities to thank God for the companions he has sent me over the course of my life, but none was nearly so poignant as crossing that last stretch of ground between the edges of the Western Reaches and the township of Perdition. If it had not been for Monique Dubois and Tillman Clay, both Ben and myself would have been dead on that second day.

There was a kind of kerchief, either specifically designed for the equine head or ingeniously tied to fit over it, that made it possible for our mounts to breath in the increasingly thick air. Ben's lungs labored like enormous bellows and he was staggering in his steps by the time Clay stopped us with a raised fist and swung down off his own horse. I wasn't certain what he was doing, squinting through my burning eyes at him wrapping the fabric around Ben's muzzle, but as I watched, the animal's breathing began to settle down and soon he was standing easy once again.

It was when the big drover looked up at me, one thumb raised in either a question or a signal that he was done, that I noticed, with tears streaming down my dust-streaked cheeks, that I couldn't actually see his eyes at all.

He was wearing a pair of strange spectacles with wide, dark lenses sealed along the edges with leather gaskets that sat up against his flesh, obviously providing a seal.

My own tortured eyes tightened, and I turned to look at Monique, sitting her horse nearby, and I wanted to snarl as I realized that she, too, was protected from the ashfall, having donned some kind of bug-faced mask that would keep the ash out of her eyes.

Apparently, their care for me and their preparation for this hellish journey had not extended to bringing any kind of such protection for me.

Thus, in addition to difficulty breathing, the constant abrasive susurration of the ash wind over my coat and hat, I was treated to the troubling experience of my visual world narrowing, moment by moment, until I could barely make out Ben's bobbing head before me, my companions wraithlike shadows hovering beyond. The rest of the world was nothing but a washed-out blur of directionless light.

The taste of burning was thick in my throat despite my tight bandana. It made talking nearly impossible and any conversation was limited to the absolute necessity of keeping each other alive.

I had not thought to ask how long an ash storm like this might last, and by the time the question occurred to me, it was too late.

That ceaseless hiss was enough to drive a man mad, as it became almost the only sound in the entire world. The sound of my horse's hooves was muffled by the ash, both the powder falling all around us and the accumulating layer on the ground. Occasional dull flashes of white light would erupt above us, some kind of lightning, I have to assume. The accompanying thunder was flat and distant, making me feel more isolated and alone than total silence might have done.

After some time, which I arbitrarily had decided must be noon on the third day of the storm, the air around us seemed to lighten. It was almost impossible to judge the passing of time in that empty hell, and if you had told me we had been journeying for a week, or a month, or a lifetime, I do not know that I would have argued the point. Even the brightness of the sun finally washing through the thinning ashfall wasn't enough to alleviate the anguish that had settled into my mind. It was as if my spirit had been crushed by the constant whisper of the falling ash and a little sun wasn't going to bring it back any time soon.

But then, as if a gray-white curtain was parting before us, the distant landscape could be seen again. Shapes began to swim out of the formless glow; distant hills at first, and then closer, darker shapes that resolved into the buildings of a town.

A town unlike any I had seen before.

Perdition.

Chapter 25

The buildings of Perdition were strange. Each structure looked soft and rounded, as if made of mud that had not been allowed to dry properly. The roofs were domed, most likely to keep the ash from accumulating and crushing them after a storm or two. Each of these strange, rounded roofs was studded with what looked like chimneys, each topped with a bulbous shape of its own. They looked more organic than architectural, but I could not for the life of me guess at their purpose from any distance.

A network of low structures like halls connected many of the buildings, while others were isolated in the gray haze of the ashfall. I had never seen anything like it in all my travels. Even drawings I had seen of African huts or the elaborate tents of some of the plains nations of America could not come close to these alien constructions.

The denizens of Perdition were venturing out into the sunlight even as the drifting ash faded off to the north. The figures I could see through the streaming blur of my still-flowing tears looked fat and ungainly, and it was only when we had closed the distance between us that I realized they were all wearing voluminous oiled-leather greatcoats and what looked like nothing so much as long-tailed fishermen's hats. Most faces were hidden beneath these hats, or hoods beneath those, or covered completely in large-eyed masks of a dizzying array of styles and appearances.

"Well, they bounce back quick as always." Clay hawked and spat a gray gobbet into the drifts beside the trail. I looked to see that he had pulled down his bandana and pushed his spectacles up onto his ash-streaked forehead.

Monique had bared her face as well, and I was surprised to see her taking short, measured breaths rather than the great gulps of air

I was looking forward to enjoying myself as I pulled my neckerchief down.

Seeing her refrain, I paused, and she nodded. "The ash isn't gone yet, just the pieces you can see." She lowered the eyewear again, and then pulled up her kerchief. "More harm's been done by folks who thought the worst was past than by fools who never knew what was coming in the first place. The worst of the ash is the fine stuff you can't sense. Best keep covered up until we can get inside."

Clay nodded, and I saw that he was buttoned up again as well.

I followed them toward the largest building in town, a round structure that looked more like a medieval keep than a frontier tavern. The domed roof of this building would have done a small cathedral proud, and the chimneys made the whole thing look like an image from a child's story book.

As we approached, a man came staggering out of one of the small connecting halls, many of which led to the same building. Our mounts seemed agitated and shied away as the man, cursing a blue streak, pulled a tiny horse out into the light.

"Damn your eyes, you filthy animal!" He snarled; his violent, harried expression clear on his uncovered face. "I swear, you balk on me again I'll—"

There was a staggering eruption of sound that shattered the ash-muffled stillness, and a flash of red-tinged fire far too close beside me for my own comfort. I shied away from the report, giving Clay a startled glance.

The big man was holding one of his big pistols in a hand that made the weapon seem dainty by comparison. A column of white smoke drifted from the barrel and the cylinder of cartridges that swelled the thing's sleek lines.

The man with the tiny horse was more than startled. He was thrown back into the darkness of the hall with a grunt and lay there in the shadows, unmoving.

"That was hardly necessary." Monique's mild rebuke was scarcely what I had expected. She seemed no more than mildly annoyed with the big man, as if he had just used a harsh word at church or belched at the dinner table.

Clay grunted and brought his mount up close to the hall. "You see a chance you take it, for that kind of cash."

He hopped down and moved toward the body, holstering his gun and drawing a huge, gleaming knife.

"Elton Fiche, was it?" She watched, unconcerned, as he went about some business with the newly generated corpse. I stared, horrified at this new reminder that I had left the civilized world far behind me. What was I to make of this sudden violence of my one companion, or the nerve jarring nonchalance of the other?

"That or his brother." Tillman Clay stood, wrapping something in a red handkerchief he had pulled from a pocket of his jacket. The parcel was about the size of a small sausage, and he slipped it negligently back into his coat. "Elton's worth a bit more, but Elis'd be worth it too. Never could tell either of 'em apart."

I stared at them both, then to the boots in the dust, pointed at the sky, then back to Clay and Monique.

"Bounty?" My voice was a whisper, either from the days of ashfall or the shock of the moment I could not tell.

Clay nodded with a dark grin as he hoisted himself back up into his saddle. "That and an object lesson, English. This ain't London. Hell, it ain't even Corners."

Monique gave him an annoyed look and then turned her eyes on me. "He's got a point, Nicholas. Most places, there's something, whether it's the actual law or some sense of custom or shared humanity that would protect you. Even in Sahri, folks would think twice about coming at you in broad daylight. Here? There's nothing between you and the next man's bullet but your own native wits."

"But yeah, the bounty made the lesson a little sweeter, for sure." Clay snapped his reins and made for the big building ahead. "I can cash this in back home for some bucks, but even at Corners there'll be agents who'll pay me a decent cut of the list price for a Fiche." He grinned again and spat. "Either of 'em."

"Won't the authorities..." I had heard everything they had said, but as I cast a look back over my shoulder at those still boots, I couldn't help but feel they must be wrong. "Won't someone want to know what happened?" There was a soft, pathetic whinny from the darkness, and I remembered the strange, tiny horse. "And what about his horse?"

Clay grunted. "Well, firstly, it couldn't have been his horse. He prob'ly stole it. The Fiches aren't sticklers for personal property, their's or anyone else's. Secondly, unless his brother's here too, and my luck ain't that good, there's not a soul in Perdition who'd care a wit about either Fiche unless he'd contracted to do some work for 'em, and if that's the case, I'll pick up that contract too."

I shook my head, still numb from the sudden, casual violence. "But the body—"

"Nicholas, no one here cares." The mild sense of pity I had gotten from Monique a moment ago was gone, replaced with annoyance. "Someone'll have to take care of the body, but out here, that's not so hard. They'll drag him out a couple hundred yards into the wasteland and the animals will be happy to have him."

I was familiar with the evolving concepts of morality and virtue that had been sweeping Europe for the last several decades, but I couldn't envision a culture that could condone such wonton killing and expect to continue in anything resembling a peaceful existence.

Unless the philosophers might say that Perdition was not its own culture, but perhaps an isolated byproduct of one? Or of several? The place might work as a release valve for all the surrounding cultures, in fact.

That might make sense, even to the most modern, advanced sensibilities. A place with no moral compass, allowing adjacent cultures to live by even slightly more civilized dictates.

It made a certain amount of sense, actually.

And meant that I could count on nothing rational at all, here.

I went cold as my mind reached the conclusion Monique and Tillman Clay had been trying to drum into my head all this time.

I swallowed, wished for some water, wished then for something stronger than water, and blinked away a strange, chilling fog in my vision.

A man in a grimy overcoat emerged from the large double doors of the big building to collect the reins of our horses and lead them through wide barn doors set into another corridor hall to the left. I was hesitant to let them take Ben, his bags filled with my things, but Monique just nodded reassuringly when I hesitated, and with a sour twist to my lips, I watched my horse disappear into the darkness.

"You really think he came here?" Thoughts of Merlin's stone had never been far from my mind since the battle on the plains, and the closer we got to Perdition, the more those thoughts churned violently. Even the realization of my own mortality could not have kept the thoughts suppressed for long.

Chitsiru the thief. Chitsiru the betrayer. Chitsiru the man who had in a moment of desperation turned all my hopes and ambitions to dirt.

Could he be here, in this strange, quiet town where people were allowed to shoot each other with impunity?

"He's here." Clay stepped through the doors into a small, dark room, and turned to arch one eyebrow at us before we followed him inside. "Everyone ends up in the Warren eventually."

The chamber acted as a sort of filtering system for the building's interior. The doors closed behind us, and there was several moments before the more ornate doors before us swung silently open. In that time, there was a strange whirring hum at the edge of my hearing that I could not place. Clay and Monique began to take off their coats, scarves, and head gear, and I did likewise. A box to our right was open, and Clay deposited his dust-covered clothing into it without a thought. Monique followed suit, patting some last errant ash dust off her pants. After a moment, I dropped my own coat into the box, followed by the gear they had given me to help me survive the ash. When we were all clean, the strange sound looming larger in my mind, the doors opened just as I was about to ask about it, and my companions went inside without waiting for me.

I followed, and my unspoken question was answered for me almost at once.

The room we entered was large, laid out much as I had seen saloons and public houses arrayed before me all my life. The ceiling was high, well over twenty feet, and a balcony looked down at us from a second floor. There were doors all along that level, behind the intricate wrought iron railing and the milling bodies of the house's guests. Several men and women of what I had to assume was negotiable virtue lounged along the railing, watching the throng below with calculating eyes.

And above it all, suspended from a carved and contoured white ceiling, were enormous fans. The blades moved slowly as I watched, propelled by a dizzying array of belts and gears that tied them all together.

It must have been similar fans I heard in the antechamber. It all made sense as I watched. The place was clearly designed to handle the constant pressure of the ash storms outside. It was quite cleverly done, I realized as I watched the huge blades spin. The belt apparatus disappeared into the wall at several points, and I assumed there were steam engines or something similar somewhere in the building, providing the power.

The room was bright, lit with some kind of oil lamps, I thought, hanging from the walls and setting two huge chandeliers, each hanging below the level of the fans, to gleam with warm, shimmering light.

This then, was the Warren. A saloon like no other.

The buzz of conversation that had met our entrance stilled as the crowd took us in, but then ramped up again almost at once as we were deemed no great distraction from the current run of entertainments on offer.

Clay moved toward an empty table without consulting Monique or me. It didn't seem to bother her, so I made the conscious decision not to let it bother me.

An unseen signal must have passed between the dark-skinned drover and the woman behind the bar, as three glasses and a dark green bottle were dropped onto our table before I had had time to choose a seat.

I noticed, as I sat, that although the men and women in the tavern were making a great show of disinterest in our arrival, many a covert glance was cast our way. The man who dropped the bottle leaned down to Clay.

"Was it you did for Fiche?"

Clay nodded, then put up a finger that stopped the man from leaving. "Which one was it, Elton or Eli?"

The man smirked. "Elton. Eli's too smart to come up this far." He bent down again. "You just wanted the one? I'll get the other for you before we drag him off, for a little taste of the cut."

Clay sneered at the man. "It just takes the one. And if you or any of these other gophers try to catch my wind south with the other one, you know ain't no one down there going to believe you did it, and I will be right on your heels."

The man's grin faded at that, and his face turned a strange shade of green. He shook his head with a nervous, jerky motion, then backed out into the crowd, heading back to the bar.

"Everyone wants to be a hero." He spat as he pulled the cork from the bottle and poured himself more than three fingers of a bright clear liquid. He didn't offer to pour for either of us as he clanked the bottle back down on the table and tossed the entire drink back in one motion. "Everyone wants a piece."

"Maybe you should go get the other one, just to take the possibility of a claim jumper off the table." Monique didn't seem fazed by Clay's lack of manners as she moved to pour herself a more conservative drink, then looked to me for further guidance.

I couldn't nod quickly enough.

"I never take both." Clay shrugged. "It's become something of a trademark. First jumper tried to claim one of my bounties, I took her out as she was leaving town with my gold in her pocket. Ain't never been a second."

I knew they must be speaking about bounty hunting, and although I found the topic intriguing, given the number of times I felt I had been hunted since leaving England, I couldn't focus just then. We were surrounded by the folk of Perdition, and the idea that Chitsiru might be in that very room with me, maybe even wearing Merlin's stone around his neck, was more than I could bear with anything resembling equanimity.

The people around us seemed to represent every station on the gamut of rich to poor, and ever shade of personality from elegant to gaudy. I was intrigued, again, at the concept of a society that might support such a wide variety within what had to be a relatively small population.

Not to mention the dead man even now lying on his back in the ash outside.

"How are we going to find Chitsiru?" I took a sip and almost spat it all over the table. I don't know what I had expected, but the burning heat that scoured its way down my throat was not it.

Clay smirked, but didn't offer further comment, for which I was duly grateful.

When I had recovered from that sip, I gestured around the Warren with my glass. "This is quite an interesting place."

Monique shrugged. "They've come up with some curious innovations to deal with the environment, that's for sure."

I shook my head. "That's not all, though. Why are they even here? Why would anyone want to live in this waste? Never mind with all of this." I gestured again to the grandiosity of the room, the strange dichotomy of the rich and poor, the stylish and the vulgar.

Clay regarded me across the rim of his raised glass. "What do you know about the Killer?"

That took me aback. What did the enormous volcano crouching in the midst of the waste have to do with Perdition? "I know the basics. I've studied other such eruptions. Vesuvius, Santorini. Why?"

"When the volcano erupted, it had several interesting effects on the landscape." The man's dark smirk tightened even further. "Aside from shattering the continent and killing countless souls, of course."

Monique put her glass down with a sharp report, giving the big man a sour look. "Strip the ghost stories from the telling, and it's short and sweet, Nicholas. The force of the eruption swept across the world here, and the convulsions sent a wave of fire underground, filling every mine and tunnel with hell."

Clay poured himself another drink and nodded. "imagine every mine for days in every direction belching its golden, silver guts out all over the landscape."

Then I remembered. Monique had told me this story on the *Joyeaux*. I still found the image of a land strewn with gold and silver to be more than a little intriguing.

Then I remembered the last few days, and I shuddered.

"Exactly. It's all out there somewhere, lying around for the taking. But it's buried under tons of ash."

Monique sipped her drink. "Using survey maps and posted claims, many people were able to figure out where the biggest deposits might be; they went into the waste. A lot of them never came back."

"The taste you've just got doesn't even give you an inkling of the waste, English."

She nodded. "Most never came back, but of those few who did, many came back richer than kings."

I looked around the room again, took in the men and women at the height of fashion, and those who looked like they were wearing their last rags, all rubbing elbows beneath those immense chandeliers.

"Could you stop calling me that?" I forced myself to look him in the eye, ignoring the images of the dead man in the ash that rose unbidden in my mind. "At least while we're back among people?"

He looked at me for a moment in silence, then nodded once, with a shrug. Then he continued as if I hadn't spoken.

"Yesiree." Clay chuckled. "So now Perdition's home to those who've made it, those who dream of making it, those who bankroll the dreams and delusions of fools, and those who prey on all the rest." He waved around with his empty hand. "And the Warren's where they all come together."

I sighed but nodded. Monique's explanation all those weeks ago made more sense, now. The desperate or the self-deluded would come here, and they'd need all manner of equipment and guidance. Anyone who came out might well come with untold gold dripping from their saddle bags. There would always be those who would cater to men and women who had managed a sudden windfall like that.

"You'll find just about anything an up-and-coming big bug might want to buy, fresh out of the wastes, here." Clay tilted hit head to indicate one group of well-dressed loud mouths at a nearby table. "There's fashions from Winchester and Paris, liquor from Italy and Spain. There's almost anything you could imagine, all for about four times what it might go for a hundred miles east."

I shook my head. "How are we going to find Chitsiru?"

Mention of the boy sent a shadow over Monique's face that I didn't like, but Clay spoke before she could take a breath. "Perdition's like one big burrow, Hawke. If the halls don't' connect two buildings, there's tunnels that do. In fact, the whole town is built on top of an old coal mine. That's what the little horses are for. The place eats a prodigious heap of coal every day, powering all their fans and vents and doodads."

I had wondered about that. About how they might possibly keep enough fires and engines going to justify all those chimneys without a tree within leagues. Coal would answer, I supposed.

"He'll be here, and there are only so many places to hide. It's not like he can be camped out in the woods outside of town." His grin turned vicious again. "There ain't no woods."

"We'll find out where he is in short order, Nicholas. We'll have him before the sun comes up. And then you'll have some choices to make."

Chapter 26

I managed to nurse my first drink until I had finished it without completely embarrassing myself, trickling a little of the burning fluid down my abused throat at a time. After that, they seemed to go down much more easily. By the end, my exhaustion, coupled with the drink no doubt, was weighing heavily upon me indeed. What passed for sleep out on the plains, with ash whispering all around us, had not been restful. My quest, after years of searching and a harrowing journey halfway across the world, was nearly at an end. If Monique and Clay were right, we would find Chitsiru here. And if Chitsiru was here, he would have the stone. I would force him to bring me through his rituals, and the world would open before me.

England might soon be free.

I didn't remember any discussion of rooms, the negotiation of fees or even climbing the sweeping stairs to the elaborate balcony. In fact, I remembered nothing until I woke up, my head spinning in a strange, muddled sort of way.

A very small, attenuated voice in the back of that maelstrom of pain and confusion and drink whispered that we must not have found him before the sun came up.

My skull was pounding arrhythmically, summoning me up out of warm, sweet oblivion. It took me a moment to realize the banging was not in my head alone. It was accompanied, or perhaps caused by, an echoing battering against a door somewhere off to my right.

I sat up, found myself on a very comfortable bed with nice, heavy bedclothes sliding down into my lap.

I was fully clothed, but someone had deposited me into a very comfortable bed.

My next confused thought was that it must have cost a small fortune.

The thought after was a mildly curious musing on who had paid that price.

Something told me my companions must have gone through my pockets and taken the coins from my last reserves of silver.

Then I remembered that the clattering was not in my head, but that someone must be banging on the door to this very room.

There was an oil lamp on a small bedside table. Wincing with the effort, I reached over and turned the wick up. I gasped at the stabbing pain in my eyes as the brightness lashed, but took several deep breaths to steady myself and swung my legs over the side of the bed.

My shoes had been taken off, so there was at least that nod to common decency.

I concentrated on the solid-looking door before me and realized there were words rumbling up behind the pounding.

My name. Over and over, in various tones and timbres, all of them deeper than I would expect from Monique.

Clay.

I pushed myself up off the bed. My body was informing me it could not possibly be morning yet, but as there were no windows in the room, it could have been the drink giving me the lie l found my shoes by the door and bent down with a grunt to force them onto my feet. They were not, of course, the fashionable footwear of my time in England, but the low, sturdy boots I had been given back in Haiti

Eventually, I made it to the door, mumbling something that might have been an apology, might have been a curse, and opened it.

Clay was standing there, resting one shoulder against the wall and smiling roguishly at one of the women haunting the balcony. From the sour look on her face, she was realizing he was more of a casual admirer than an interested customer.

"Wha—" It was the best I could come up with as the sensory assault of the still-rollicking common room of the Warren crashed against my tortured senses.

Clearly, my body had been right. It could hardly be morning with the establishment still so active.

"Up and at'em, sunshine." Clay's teeth glowed in his dark tangle of beard as he gave me a resounding thump on the back. "Monique's found your wayward lamb, but we have to move quickly. Looks like he's trying to sell your rock."

*****

Clay led me to the curving staircase, past annoyed and disappointed workers. From the higher vantage I could see gaming tables along the sides of the room, everything from cards to dice to even a couple strange spinning devices that looked quite intriguing in their mechanical sophistication. But I was still having a hard time focusing, and so stuck close to my companion's broad back, spending most of my remaining mental acuity on descending the stairs in one piece.

"He's trying to sell it." Clay yelled over his shoulder. His voice was like an avalanche, roaring down over all the other sounds that cackled in my ear, but I nodded, happy to be able to make any sense of it at all.

Wait.

"What?" I shouted myself, not caring about the looks I received from the patrons around us.

"He's trying to sell your stone." Clay shrugged. "From what Monique's saying, he would have gotten away with it too, probably been long gone. But the interest is high, even here. And he's gotten greedy. He didn't take the first offer, from Bharton, the man who owns all this." He gestured with one hand at the saloon around us, but by the tone in his voice I assumed he meant more than just the Warren. "Most folks want to sell something of any value quick here, they sell to Bharton, he takes care of the rest. But not your boy. I gather that rock of yours really is something special, and he knows it."

For that to be true, Chitsiru must have revealed some of the story behind the Comanche stones, then. He might have even provided a demonstration of his powers, whatever they might be.

If the wrong people found out about those powers and their connection to the Empire of the Summer Moon, it posed a greater danger to my wild scheme than even his stealing the stone in the first place.

"Where are we going?"

Clay was pushing toward a low door in a dark, empty corner of the crowded space. "Down. The deal's supposed to be taking place at a small broker's shop on the edge of town. Monique's gotten herself an invite, but we have to be there before the whole thing starts or we'll be dealing with more than just your friend."

As my mind began to spin back up to something like its normal speed, I grew more panicky. I remembered Chitsiru's fevered stare, whenever he had caught glimpse of Merlin's stone. He was going to sell it, now?

That didn't seem right at all.

Maybe he was getting desperate, this far from home, without friends or allies? Maybe the frantic longing I had seen writ plainly across his face had not been enough to dissuade him from the fortune he could well secure with the stone's sale.

I couldn't be sure, but that didn't seem right.

The door led into a dark, confined room with a gaping hole in the floor. A rickety-looking stairway descended into that hole, and nothing but darkness seemed to be coming back out.

"Down into the tunnels, master. It's the only way." He smiled, eyes glowing in the darkness, and went down.

The stairs went much deeper than I had expected, but there were low, soft lights set into the walls of the shaft, giving just enough light to see Clay's huge bulk as he sank into the gloom. At the bottom, the tunnel was rough-hewn stone, stretching forward and behind into darkness punctuated by more of the small golden lights.

"This is how most folks in Perdition get around during a storm." The man's voice was low, echoing off the surrounding rock disconcertingly. "Think of these tunnels as the streets of a town and you won't go far wrong."

We passed occasional doors that I gathered led back up to buildings above. Other openings, without doors, led into blackness; coal shafts, I assumed, maybe leading to seams that had played out long ago. There was a dank, moist taste to the air that seemed strange, given the arid, ash-swept waste above.

A strange pressure built in my ears, accompanied by a sensation that was hard to describe. Almost a sound without sound, was the best I could manage. A hissing, whispering sound, but much lower than the hideous mutterings of the ash against my tent walls. This seemed bigger, somehow, while at the same time not nearly as loud.

At first, I attributed it to my abused mind. But the sensation did not fade with my rising consciousness, and eventually I had to ask.

"The river." Was the only reply. Further inquiries failed to provide additional insight. So, river it was, I decided, and tried to banish the haunting presence from my mind. Some subterranean waterway, at least, might explain the moisture in the air.

We saw no one else in the tunnel as we moved, and I commented on that to my guide. If this had been a street above in a more normal town, I would have expected to see some lost reveler stumbling about.

I stumbled, myself, even as the thought occurred to me; a humbling moment.

"Think of this as more a back-alley, I guess." Clay grunted. "I took us out the back of the saloon, heading to the broker along a smaller passage. The bigger, wider tunnels look more like streets, and that's where you'll find your night wanderers right around now."

I thought I heard a scraping sound behind us, but there was so much scraping within my own skull I dismissed the thought. It, too, could have been the river, I supposed.

Thinking of the river, I realized that the sound that was not a sound had faded somewhat, as had the wet taste of the air. In fact, I thought I caught an almost spicy smell now, and wondered if there might be spice merchants in Perdition. It made sense, considering all the other things successful prospectors might be expected to buy up above. But how sophisticated could these people's palates be? I'd been here less than a day, and all I could taste was ash.

Given that, I realized, spices might be in even higher demand than elsewhere.

The tunnel narrowed as we followed its turning, twisting path. There were fewer and fewer doors and passages as we stalked through the dimness, until a long stretch of stone wall was passing by on either side without break; We finally emerged into a small chamber with a very strong-looking door at the far end. It was wood, stained with age, banded in iron, with an intimidating lock set in the right-hand edge.

There was no signage or indication of what might lay on the other side, but Clay seemed satisfied, so I just stood by him while he rapped sharply with his wide knuckles.

An armored window slid open high on the door and a wrinkled face peered out at us. I caught the impression of wild white hair above and below the eyes and remembered old Scandinavian tales of elves and dwarves from my childhood.

"What?" Never had I head so much suspicion and contempt loaded into a single syllable, and I had made a study of distrust and disdain since my arrival on this continent.

"We're with Monique." Clay's voice was low and rumbled off the stone walls around us like thunder. "She'll have mentioned us, I believe."

The man blinked his rheumy blue eyes and then nodded. The window slid shut with a click and there was a dull thud, the sounds of mechanisms turning and clacking vibrated within the door, and then it slid open. A short, wildly hairy man in a dark waistcoat and pressed pants stood before us. His shirt beneath the waistcoat was immaculately white, and he settled a small set of round spectacles onto the bulbous nose that protruded from his thicket of beard and mustache.

"Of course, please, come in." He gestured for us to pass him into the next chamber, then closed the door behind us. He whirled a large metal wheel set into the wooden surface, and the clicks and clanks reversed themselves. I could see the door sitting deeper into its frame with the sounds.

"We'll be upstairs." The short man muttered and gestured with one clawed hand as he scurried past us. The stairwell here was better lit, but at least as deep as the shaft beneath the saloon. At the top we came to what looked like a small storage room, then out through a narrow door into a much more comfortable sitting room with rugs scattered over the floor, elegant yet comfortable chairs, tables of polished dark wood and a sideboard well-stocked with bottles that made my head begin to throb anew just to look at them.

Monique was standing by the sideboard, looking through a leather-bound book when we came in. She set the book down, but the smile I had expected to see on her face did not materialize. She was all business. I was reminded of the woman I had first met in New Orleans, the intervening weeks fading away.

The room was dark, faintly lit by several oil lamps placed around the chamber. There were, indeed, no windows, and I realized I hadn't seen one since our arrival. It made sense, when I thought about trying to keep the ash from infiltrating their homes and businesses.

"Took you long enough." She spat at Clay, all but ignoring me.

"Couldn't get him out of bed." The big man shrugged and moved to the sideboard, helping himself to a glass and a bottle of amber liquid. My stomach churned as I watched him with morbid fascination.

There was something different about Monique that struck through even the haze of my muddled mind and the slowly rising burn of my anticipation. She had changed since I last remembered seeing her in the saloon. She no longer wore her practical trail gear, but was dressed in severe black clothing that looked almost like a uniform. Tight fitting pants emerged from a long frock-coat more reminiscent of the Albian Ranger gear than anything else I'd seen since my arrival, and my mind, already juggling too many thoughts, emotions, and challenges, started with sudden, unreasoning fear.

Could she be a Ranger?

"Ma'm, if I could go?" The little broker was cowering in the corner, as far from Tillman Clay as he could get, while refusing to look directly at Monique.

"That doesn't make any sense, Master Amery, does it." Her voice was hard, and I watched as he flinched as if struck. "You need to open the door and invite our quarry in or he will run, and our agreement will be void." Her words seemed to hint at a threat that sent the man even deeper into despair. He nodded wretchedly and pressed himself deeper into the corner.

She turned her gallows' gaze on me, and it took a conscious effort to stop myself from cringing, too. "Your Comanche friend is supposed to be here soon to try to sell the stone. Mr. Amery here has been kind enough to contact the other interested parties and tell them the transaction required an extra day of preparation. We should be undisturbed for our night's work."

Our night's work should have been recovering my stone and then convincing Chitsiru, with whatever means necessary, to take me through the ritual of attunement.

Something in her voice told me that was not the work to which she referred.

"My stone—" I felt the sudden, crushing certainty she did not intend for me to keep Merlin's stone. All her objections came back to me in full force, and I felt my hands begin to shake.

Something gleamed at Monique's throat as she moved around a table lamp. That strange crucifix I had seen before. She was now wearing it openly over a black cravat.

"Nicholas, when we have the man and the stone, we will talk." She was approaching me with what I think she assumed would be a reassuring smile on her face, but her resemblance to a stalking lioness doomed the effort.

"I appreciate everything you've done for me, Monique. God knows I wouldn't be here, most probably wouldn't even be alive, if it wasn't for you, and Tillman as well." I tried to bring the big drover into the conversation, but he just grunted and turned to examine the other bottles on the sideboard. I couldn't leave it there, though. "I intend to go through with this, once Chitsiru arrives. I've come too far to turn back now."

An emotion I could not identify flicked across her jade green eyes. Anger? Frustration? Pity?

I couldn't trust my own ability to read her, I realized.

"Nicholas, when I've explained everything, you might feel differently. But now is not the time—"

Something stirred in my chest. Something that had been building, biding its time for years, something that had been riled up by every
offhand comment she had made along the trail, something that had
been born in a dusty old library I could barely remember, and that had
chosen this moment to emerge, fully formed, into the flickering lamp
light.

"I will not feel differently!" The words now feel like those of a
child I remember them, but then, in that moment of pain and despair,
they were the most heartfelt I had ever spoken. "That stone is mine!
I have earned it! And whatever powers it might possess are mine as
well! There is too much at stake in this for anyone, even you, to gainsay
me now!"

I had no trouble reading the look that swept briefly across her
face then. She was angry.

I watched as she stalked toward me, eyes narrowing, one hand
rising as if to push me back against the wall.

And there was a knock at the door.

The broker jumped as if he'd been pinched. Even Clay's head
jerked away from the bottles.

My head jerked as if a cannon had just been fired through the
wall.

Monique stared into my eyes for a moment longer, having halt-
ed her approach, and she closed them with a sigh.

"Master Amery, I believe there is someone at the door?"

After a lengthy hesitation, during which whoever was outside
the door knocked several more times in an ever-increasing tempo, the
little man tried to navigate his way across the room while staying as far
from all three of us as he could.

"Gentlemen, I think we should retire to the shadows?" Monique turned to look at the door, sliding into a dark corner behind a
high-backed seat.

I looked at Clay who had put down his drink without any seeming urgency and rested one elbow against the sideboard while reaching
out with a hand to turn down the wick of the lamp there. The receding
light quickly left him nearly invisible with his dark skin and clothes.

I looked from side to side for somewhere to hide, panic-stricken
that Chitsiru would see me and flee into the night once again, while
at the same time the hot energy building beneath my heart made it
almost impossible to think of hiding.

As I watched with dawning horror, realizing that my chance of ducking behind a chair or into a shadow had fled, the little man made it to the door, reached out with one shaking hand, and it swung open.

A figure dashed inside with a furtive glance over its shoulder, a dust-laden cloak swirling with the panicked movement.

The room was filled with an uneven gasping of breath.

The figure turned to slam the door shut behind it, not waiting for the broker. "Please, hide me. They're coming!"

The smell of rotten onions came to me faintly over the scented oils of the lamps.

With an unsure hand the cowl of the cloak was pushed back to reveal long, matted tangles of black hair and wide, staring dark eyes that darted around the room, seeing nothing.

Chitsiru had arrived.

Chapter 27

Chitsiru's eyes widened even more as the broker gave a strangled squeak and dove into a side room without a backward glance.

The Comanche's head tilted at the sudden flight, eyes narrowed slightly with suspicion; the fear in them guttering just a little, and he turned back into the room.

I cannot explain what happened next, only to say that I was possessed by my basest, most animal instincts. Everything I had sacrificed, everything I had lost, everything I had done to fulfill my self-appointed quest, had been undone by this man. I would never have called him a friend, nonetheless his actions during that frenzied violence outside of Sahri had stung like the bitterest betrayal.

I launched myself across the elegant little room with a scream of pure hatred and rage.

I had a vague impression of Monique reaching out to me, her face stretched into a surprised mask. On the other side, I thought I saw Clay smile vaguely as he stood to his full, impressive height.

I didn't care about either of them in that moment. I had eyes only for the cringing man in the ash-covered clothing, cowering pathetically before me, his eyes two pools of shimmering night.

I launched myself the last few feet and crashed into him, my hands closing around his throat. We toppled backwards into the foyer of the little building, a cloud of ash rising around us as I landed atop him with another animalistic scream.

I was shouting incoherently into his paling face, but I could not tell you what I might have screamed. I can guess, of course, but I have no actual memory of the words.

I remembered the satisfying sound of his skull hitting the floor over and over as I pulled him toward me and then dashed him down again to the cadence of whatever epithets were spilling from my twisted lips.

His hands scrambled weakly at the claws that held him fast, that slammed him back down over and over, not allowing him to take a breath, let alone speak a word. There was blood, I remember, and a vague sense that I was breaking something vital to my mission. But there is a time in every child's life when the destruction of something is more intriguing than the consequences that will result from the breaking, no matter how dire they might be.

I was a grown man trapped in that moment.

It was Clay, eventually, who pulled me off the limp form. I was still screaming incoherently, but the big man yanked me to my feet and let go with one almighty slap that cracked my head back and brought a sudden and violent halt to the flow of nonsense.

"I think you said you needed him?" I looked around, coming slowly to my senses, a very large portion of my mind still crying out for violence.

Clay was smiling down at me as if he was almost … proud?

A soft, pathetic sound was emerging from the crumpled pile of fabric and bones at my feet.

Chitsiru was still alive.

I regained enough of my faculties to sigh with relief. I felt no remorse over the violence I had just committed on this pathetic man, but dead, if had been smart enough to secret the stone somewhere before coming, would have been a further hindrance to my quest.

When I glanced back at Monique, she was glaring at Tillman Clay as if he had bitterly disappointed her.

I decided to ignore that look, for now.

I nodded my thanks to the big man, who released me with an answering tilt of his head and stepped back slowly, hands outstretched to ensure himself that I wouldn't topple over.

I swayed for a moment but kept my feet. Looking down at Chitsiru's crumpled form, a small ration of my sanity returned. My vision was still red-tinged and jagged, my breath coming in harsh, rasping gasps; my fists were still clenched into painful knots of muscle and bone.

But I refrained from taking out my rage any further on that pathetic form.

"Get up." I rasped, and I was disturbed by the sound of my own voice. "Get up and give it to me."

Chitsiru pushed himself up onto his hands and knees, his entire body still shaking. His shoulders were bowed, his head low, and there was no spirit left in his frame.

He was broken. Even the fear that had motivated him as he entered had fled.

I watched, the sound of my own knuckles popping loud in my ears, as he reached into the cloak and withdrew a small object that he then slid over his head and held out, eyes remaining on the ground.

It was Merlin's stone, still in its cage of Haitian silver.

I grabbed it so quickly the chain sliced his fingers, but I didn't care. I inspected the stone and felt an instant comfort in its unnatural sheen and the play of colors between the layers of its strange glow.

I glared down at him again, my anger only slightly abated. "You will assist me in the ritual. You will assist me now, here, and there will be no more hesitation."

Chitsiru, still looking down, nodded slowly. But even as the rush of victory flooded my core, a single cold syllable snapped out behind me and stopped me in my tracks.

"No."

It was Monique, of course.

I looked back at her, my own shoulders hunched and protective. She was still in the shadows, standing straight and tall with her auburn hair seeming to flare out around her like a halo. The necklace almost glowed with reflected light, but there was no such reflection in her eyes. All I saw there was a frightening combination of sadness and determination.

"No one is going to be performing any rituals. This farce is over, Nicholas, I won't humor you any farther." She held out hand, palm upward, and I saw that she was wearing fine black leather gloves. "Give me the stone and we can get out of here."

I couldn't believe her words. I shook my head, dumb with disbelief and aggravation. I turned back to Chitsiru. "What do you need? Do you have everything? Can we begin now?"

Again, he nodded. His voice was a harsh, shattered whisper when he spoke. "There are many rituals. I do not have the materials for the traditional Comanche ceremony, but there are others." He looked up, and his eyes were haunted, his shoulders slumped in despair. "They are said to be more dangerous; hardly ideal. There are elders who will not allow them to be conducted, and entire nations who do not sanction their use. But I know several. Let us get this over with so I can be done with all of you."

I nodded. Every other concern fled from my mind. "Let's." I sank down in front of him, grabbing him by the shoulders and staring into his haunted eyes, ignoring the rising bruises I myself had placed there.

This man was about to betray his people, I realized. Everything he knew, everything he believed, said he should not help me. Why *was* he helping me? He had had the stone and lost it. What was there to compel him further?

But it didn't appear that I needed to compel him. Chitsiru was broken and wanted only for all of this to be over.

I could understand that.

"Nicholas, you can't do this." Monique's voice was closer. She had approached while I was focused on the collapsed man before me.

"You can't stop me." I was barely aware of her looming up behind me. The stone burned in my hand, Chitsiru's averted gaze was almost my entire world.

"Nicholas, stop." There was no warmth in that voice now; no friendship or concern. It was as welcoming as the crack of a whip.

"You can't stop me!" I repeated, spitting over my shoulder before turning back to Chitsiru.

"Actually, I can." The deep click of the big hammer being drawn back on her pistol echoed through my world.

I felt the cold metal of the gun's barrel pressed lightly to my right ear. "Nicholas, you need to stand up. I can't let you do this."

Chitsiru was focusing on her with terrified eyes, his body vibrating with tiny, constant tremors.

The metal at my ear seemed to grow even colder. She did not press it painfully to my flesh, nor did she apply any more pressure than she had first used. But the looming presence of that enormous weapon had a gravity all its own and demanded my complete attention.

All thoughts of the stone and the ritual fled.

"Monique, don't do this." Clay spoke with a calming tone, as if trying to gentle a nervous horse. "You can't be serious. What harm could this cause? The man's made his own decision."

The pistol pressed a little harder against my ear then, and I could picture her turning to the big cowboy. "Tillman, I think we're done here. You can go. Nicholas, please stand up and turn around. I need the stone."

This made no sense. She had been trying to dissuade me from pursuing the Comanche ritual for days, of course. She'd made no pretext otherwise. But what possible claim to Merlin's stone could *she* make? Why did *she* want it?

I stood, slowly, terribly conscious of the gun pressed to my head. Chitsiru watched me rise, not moving from his place on the floor. I turned, not knowing what to expect when I faced Monique.

I did not expect tears.

"I'm sorry, Nicholas. Someday you'll realize this was the only way." She lowered the gun, for which I was duly grateful. But I made no move to hand over the stone.

When she realized I wasn't moving, she frowned. "Give me the stone, Nicholas."

I shook my head, but that was the extent of my courage; I was unable to speak.

Monique's eyes narrowed, her lip developed the slightest curl of frustration, and her hand began to rise.

The building shook as a thunderous impact resounded from somewhere beneath us.

Dust cascaded down from the ceiling overhead, and the bottles on the sideboard clinked and chuckled to themselves.

"What the hell?" Clay snarled, looking behind him at the door that led back down into the tunnels.

"What was that?" The little broker peered into the room, his eyes even wider than they had been. "What's happening?"

Monique grunted, lowering the gun and moving toward the back door. "Someone's knocking downstairs, I think."

The old man shook his head convulsively. "No one's ever knocked like that."

Another rumbling shook the house, this time with even more violence. The accompanying sound echoed through the building as if coming from deep within the earth. The dust continued to cascade down, and the bottled rattling together jumped on the smooth, polished top of the sideboard.

"Clay, you care to do the honors?" Monique's arm was braced straight, the pistol aimed down into the floor.

The drover snorted. "I thought we were done here. I thought I could go." He didn't move to leave, but he didn't move closer to the back door, either.

She glared venomously at him, and then glanced at me. "Stay here."

She moved toward the door but was obviously torn. She couldn't have believed I was going to stay once she left the room?

She wasn't. She stopped at the door and sighed. She glanced again at Clay. "I don't suppose you'd accept an apology?"

"Sorry, darlin', it's a seller's market. And I ain't goin' into the cellar." He smiled, looking back out into the foyer. "I think we should all just leave, take up this conversation again in another location. Say, the Warren?"

The quake that shook the building next felt as if an explosion had been detonated below. That wasn't someone knocking forcefully on the iron-shod door. Someone down below was trying to break it down.

"What is happening?" The old man's whine broke the sudden, shaking silence.

Monique and Clay exchanged a look that terrified me. Whatever was causing the trouble between them, they were both willing to forget it in the face of that cyclopean hammering.

Monique nodded, and again I was distracted by the glitter of silver at her neck. "I think we could talk somewhere else."

"Wait, you can't just leave!" The little broker looked like he was about to weep.

Monique moved away from the door, gun rising to point at the unassuming wood. "You're more than welcome to join us at the Warren, Master Amery. I don't think you want to be here when—"

The next and final blow was more than the sound of an impact and a frightening shake. Something snapped below in the old mine shaft with the splintering crack of a main mast coming down in a storm. The building shuddered violently, and several bottles overturned, one shattering on the floor.

None of us moved.

Chitsiru's breath was a high, thin wheezing, and he was the first to stir, pushing himself with his feet until his back was up against the wall of the foyer, eyes fixed, wide and white, on the back door.

"I think we need to go, now." Clay moved toward the front entrance and yanked the cowering medicine man away by the collar of his cloak. "I think we should all go now."

I nodded, moving quickly for the foyer as well. Looking back, I watched as Monique slid toward us, sidling backwards, her raised pistol now on the door. A door that seemed far thinner now than when I had entered it just a few minutes before.

Amery looked like a man trapped between nightmares, watching the three of us in the foyer, then Monique sliding through the freshly fallen dust, and then the back door.

And then Monique stopped.

She had to have been the first to hear it, but there was no disguising the sound of heavy footsteps on the stairs leading down into the old mines, audible to the rest of us moments later.

The steps weren't slow and deliberately menacing, but neither were they hurried in any way. Whoever was climbing the steps was in no great rush, but they weren't dillydallying either.

"Nicholas Hawke, I hope I haven't missed you."

The words were mocking, the faint, lilting accent hauntingly familiar.

Familiar to me from the dark and empty grass street of Sahri, the night Chitsiru and I had returned to fetch Ben and my things.

The accent was Haitian.

And I had thought the speaker dead at my hand.

I felt myself shaking before the door swung open. Monique had looked back at me with a question clear in her eyes, but I was frozen in place, unable to look away from the door, unable to move any closer to escape into the night and the dubious safety of the ash-covered streets of Perdition.

The footsteps reached the landing outside and paused. My focus narrowed down to the doorknob. Was it shaking? Had it just been grasped by someone on the other side? What was about to happen to us all?

I screamed as Monique's gun shattered the still, terrifying silence. A massive hole appeared in the center of the door.

She fired twice more, two more holes flashing into existence, one far to the left of the first, the other far to the right.

Silence returned and stretched on interminably as we all stood, still as statues, watching the door.

And then the door shattered, sending splinters flying over us all. It fell into the room in four or five pieces beyond the sawdust and smaller fragments.

A small figure stood in the doorway, hands clenched at his sides, a tight golden smile on his dark face. The faint scent of spices filled the room, and I wanted to vomit.

"Well, that was hardly hospitable."

This time it was Clay's pistol that barked, filling the nerve-jarring silence with noise and light.

Dust jumped from the man's coat as two bullets hit him square in the chest.

And he wasn't fazed in the lease.

"Inquisitor." The man's strange eyes flicked over Monique and, had I not been stunned by the sheer firepower that had just been unleashed in my vicinity, not to mention the clear lack of its efficacy, I might have made more of notice of the word.

"Revenant." Clay spat.

What was happening? My mind was numb. I had shot this man three times myself; the first human I had ever turned a weapon upon in anger. Monique's enormous pistol had barked out its challenge three times through the door. When I had first seen the figure standing there, I assumed she had missed. Maybe I had missed as well, back in Sahri? Maybe the moment had played tricks upon my eyes. But there was no doubt about Clay's marksmanship. I had seen both shots strike the man right in his dapper vest.

And he was still grinning at me.

Directly at me.

"I was wondering how much longer it would be before I'd smell your kind again." Monique stepped back to stand in front of me, while Clay had stepped forward without my realizing it, to join her, shoulder to shoulder. "You're a long way from home, friend."

The man laughed, but there was no joy in the sound, no humor. "The *Houngan's* reach is long, madam, as I'm sure you are aware."

She nodded, while her hands flew through well-remembered movements to refill three of the chambers of her gun. "So, not even pretending you're here on the auspices of His August and Imperial Majesty? Has the *Houngan* emerged from the shadows at last?"

The man's smile never wavered. I noticed it never touched his eyes, either however. They remained dull and cloudy. "You might want to ask your friend there, cowering in the back, what Jacques-Victor may be about. He was bandying his name all over Corners. I merely want the stone, with the little man by the door as a happy bonus, and I'll be satisfied."

It was Monique's turn to spit. "Your satisfaction is not my concern, fiend." She snapped the cylinder of her pistol back with a loud crack. Another gun, smaller than the first, appeared in her other hand. "In fact, I aim to see you out of this world before sunrise. And you *won't* be returning again!"

The golden-smiled Haitian never wavered, never even seemed to move, but suddenly there were three glittering fragments of light flying through the air toward us.

"Duck!" Clay spun and pushed me down, grunting as he staggered forward on top of me. I thought I heard two impacts somewhere above me, but I couldn't be sure in the confusion of my tumble backwards.

I did hear several gunshots, two distinct timbres, and figured Monique was firing both pistols at the figure in the doorway.

"Why, Inquisitor, your kind are usually better prepared." The mirth in the man's voice was cold and cruel. I heard a brief cry of pain and saw Monique, her black clothing streaming behind her, leap for a chair.

"Clay, get him out. You'll have your pay!" She was breathing heavily, but then I think we all were at that point.

All of us save the strange Haitian.

"But—" Clay's voice contained a pained note I was too distracted to recognize.

"You need to go. Don't worry about this. I'll take care of it." Her voice was vague, distracted, and punctuated with several more gunshots.

At each report, a pathetic cry would squeak out by the door. I was wondering if it might be Chitsiru, and was turning in that direction to check, when a something seized upon my collar and hoisted me into the air by main force. I found myself propelled toward the door, which approached with dizzying speed, and then there was a crash, and I was through.

I flew through a soft, whispering fog and slid to a stop on my back in a pile of warm ash. A moment later Chitsiru skidded out past me, Clay's huge form eclipsing the warm light of the parlor beyond as he reached back for the broker.

As the two men came dashing out the door, Amery staggered with a cry, his arms flailing in aimless circles, and he collapsed into the ash in a sill heap.

Something on the man's back, long and thin, gleamed silver in the light from the open doorway.

"Damnit!" Clay muttered the curse under his breath as he moved toward me, hunched over almost double, favoring his left side.

"Get up, you bastard." I might have taken offense to that, but the man ran right by me, leaving me to rise on my own, and dragged Chitsiru to his feet.

"We need to get to our horses by the Warren." He glanced over his shoulder and then hunkered down against the falling ash. "And of course, the weather couldn't hold."

Had I not been beside myself with fear, confusion, and resentment, I might have been afraid of the soft, warm particles floating down around us. Monique and Clay had spent enough of their time regaling me with how dangerous the stuff was to breathe in.

But at the moment, some things seemed more dangerous than others.

"What about Monique? That man ... that *thing* ... what is he?"

Clay didn't look at me as he pushed Chitsiru's uncomplaining form along through the strange, whispering darkness. "Revenant. Haitian. Bad medicine."

I was familiar with the word. Some kind of ghost, I thought, known in folklore for returning to a place important in its life. I wanted to scoff at the very idea. But then, I had just witnessed the thing take more bullets than I cared to think.

And I was still holding a stone I firmly believed to have once belonged to Merlin the Magician in my hand at that very moment, that I was hoping to turn against Albion after a torturous ritual—

I was hardly one to be denying folklore.

Behind us, there were several more gunshots, sounding dull and distant in the heavy ashfall. Then, like a rising sun, a bright light flared to life behind us.

It seemed to eat the darkness and the ash alike, jumping and swirling like a living thing released from some eternal confinement.

The broker's little rounded house was on fire.

"Good girl. Run!" Clay hunkered down and pushed Chitsiru harder. As they passed me I noticed the shaft of a silver knife protruding from the big man's shoulder.

"He got you!" I made the observation before my mind could fully run through what it was seeing. I wasn't telling him anything he didn't already know.

Clay snarled, turning to grab me and pull me along, when he stopped, looking back, his face eerily lit by the burning building.

"Oh, damn your eyes." He muttered, his shoulders slumping.

I whirled, expecting to see the Haitian running toward us. Instead I saw a party of riders emerging from the swirling ash. In that darkness, my eyes squeezed nearly shut and tearing uncontrollably, I could make out no details aside from the tricorn hats each rider wore above inhuman-looking ash masks.

And fluttering half-capes, waving behind them like flags.

"Oh, no." It was Chitsiru's broken voice. "They found me."

Chapter 28

The Albian Rangers. I didn't know why Chitsiru would have a particular fear of the agents of Albion, but I knew they spelled certain doom for my own prospects if they caught me again.

"Damn, damn, damn." Clay kept repeating the word in a numb monotone even as he turned again and pushed Chitsiru and I deeper into the storm.

There were cries behind us, but I could not make out the words. I cast several desperate glances behind me, watching as the Rangers skirted the burning building.

Monique had not emerged from Amery's, I realized then. Monique was in the building that was burning down even as the Rangers whipped their mounts past it.

Clay pushed us both into a darker, shadowed alley, and I realized we were up against one of the low wooden passageways that connected the various structures of the town together. The big man's hands flew over the wood, searching blindly for something.

If I had thought it through, I would have tried to help, but by the time I realized he must be looking for a handle, a dim light appeared, a rectangle outlining a wide double door, and we were moving through it, out of the ashfall and into the dark, warm interior of a stable area.

Clay drew the door shut behind us, slamming a heavy bar home to lock it tight.

We didn't wait for the Rangers to arrive, but were once more pushed along, this time down the passageway, horse stalls to either side, their inhabitants whickering at us as we passed. The big man was looking up, regarding numbers etched into the cross beam above each stall entrance. I was glad he seemed to remember where our horses might be, because I couldn't even remember arriving.

Monique was gone. She was in that burning round tower. That thing had gotten her. And if it had gotten her, it meant it was still going to be coming after me.

What did it want from me? The stone, obviously, now. But why? Who was the *Houngan*? What kind of strange political intrigue back in the Empire of Haiti had I fallen into? Could that man in the keep really have been the Emperor? Why would he want to help me? And who among the Haitians would want to stop him from helping me?

The stone.

If the man with the golden teeth wanted the stone, that must have been why my savior among the Haitians had released me. He wanted me to do something with the stone. But what?

Chitsiru stumbled and I reached out to keep him moving.

Monique was gone. I kept coming back to that. The woman who had seen me safely through countless dangers and trials since I had wandered lost and alone on the streets of New Orleans was gone.

And then I stopped. A single word jumped, burning, into the forefront of my mind.

"Why did that man call Monique 'Inquisitor'?"

Clay looked back at me, face twisted with exasperation. "Does it matter now? We need to get you onto a horse and out the north side of this passage before the Rangers break through that door or decide to ride around. That's all over now, anyway." He looked back again and paused when he saw I hadn't moved. "Look, Hawke, don't sell Monique short, okay? I'm fairly sure no single revenant has her marker, whatever that looked like out there. But it's not just that thing, or the Rangers I need to get you two away from, see? Monique means well, but she serves more than one master. And she means to stop you from doing whatever is you want to do with that stone of yours."

"You don't know anything about this. Why do you care?" I shook my head, holding the stone so tightly I thought the edges might draw blood. "Why do you care about any of this?"

He laughed a quick, empty bark. "I don't care, you halfwit. But in Washington, a man's free to pursue his dreams. I don't believe anyone should be able to tell you what you can or can't do, as long as you're not harming me or mine, and your heart's in the right place." He gave me a smile then that I thought might even actually be genuine. "And besides, if this all works out, it goes poorly for Albion, yeah?"

I nodded, still suspicious.

"Well, then, you can't possibly doubt that a Washingtonian has any more cause to love Albion than does an Englishmen. They betrayed us just as surely as they betrayed you. You all might have had more to lose, but we lost everything."

There was an angry glint in his eye now that I didn't like, until I realized it wasn't aimed at me.

I nodded again, deciding that I must be satisfied with that.

He took me by the shoulder. "Good. Now, let's get you two mounted up. You head west, as fast as you can go. You can do this ritual of yours out in the wastes?" He looked piercingly at Chitsiru, who just nodded miserably. "Okay, then you do that. Ride hard as you can until dawn. Keep an eye out on your back trail, and when the sun's up, and you're sure you're alone, go ahead and do your worst."

Then the full meaning of his words occurred to me.

"You're not coming."

He looked away, almost as if he was embarrassed. "I'm not getting paid enough for all this, Hawke. Revenants, Rangers, going against Canaan and whatnot?" He shook his head. "No. I've got my own to look out for, and ain't no one's going to be around to do that if I get myself shot up in another man's war."

He coughed once, nodding toward the next set of stalls. "No, sir. I'm cashing in my chips right here. You'll be okay, though. I'll lead the Rangers off on a merry chance eastward. By the time they realize we're not together anymore, you'll have your chance. They'll be mad as hell, but they won't do nothing. They ain't got a warrant out on me, and those kinds might have a peculiar sense of honor, but what kind they got, they gott, and they stick to it."

He didn't say anything more, just stomped over to the next stall, his horse whickering a welcome inside, and began to saddle the animal.

Soon enough, the horses were all kitted out, Chitsiru leading Monique's horse. Clay said she wouldn't mind, and if she did, maybe she shouldn't have been so high and mighty.

We led the horses to another set of wide barn doors in the passage and Clay held up a hand for silence. He slid one side open just enough to peek outside. It was still pitch dark, the hiss of heavy ashfall whispering its hated refrain. The sky off to our right was just a touch brighter than the rest of the heavens overhead, but the light was a faded gray, not the brilliant colors of a promised sunrise in less blighted lands.

Clay and I were huddled up in dust gear again, our own clothing, washed and cleaned, folded neatly in the stalls. Chitsiru was still in his long cloak, a spare kerchief from Clay's saddlebag wrapped over his face.

We looked at each other as the gray light continued to build behind him.

And then the pounding of hoofs broke the stillness, and my heart dropped once again.

I expected Clay to slap my horse's rump and send us off with one of his interminable, ululating shouts, but instead he stood there, surrounded by the falling ash, hesitant in the face of this new, approaching threat.

I watched the big man's head swivel back and forth, peering through his thick ash spectacles into the swirling haze as the thunder of the Albian Rangers grew louder, bouncing back at us out of the darkness, defying any attempt to ascertain the direction of their approach.

As the hoofbeats swelled, Clay spun toward me and pushed me back toward the shelter of the passage hall behind us.

"Get back inside! Shut and bar the door. Head downward." He reached out and grabbed Chitsiru, pushing him toward me. "Lose yourself in the tunnels. Someone will come find you." He shoved each of us and we staggered through the doorway. "Keep going down!"

He stared out into the churning half-light, at Clay, staring at me through dark, inhuman lenses, back at Ben, looking over his shoulder with vague curiosity, and then the gray, grainy dawn beyond.

Then the door was slammed shut in my face.

I scrambled around in the hay on the floor and finally found the heavy bar for the door, slamming it home and turning to look left and right down the wide, low hall with its array of stables stretching into the distance.

I had no idea which way to go. Something seemed to be pulling me to the left, I thought the saloon might be in that direction.

But did I want to head toward the saloon? Wouldn't that be full of people?

But might that be better? Would the Rangers do anything untoward with witnesses gathered round?

Then I remembered Clay shooting down the bounty in cold blood.

I was wandering lost and alone in a strange world that followed none of the rules I had known all my life.

There was no promise of safety within the walls of the saloon any more than anywhere else in this strange, stifling place.

I pulled Chitsiru to the right, hoping that was away from the Warren. We might be safer with the strangers gathered within the saloon, or we might not. But if we remained isolated and alone and avoided the Rangers until Clay or someone else came to help, we would be better off for sure.

Chitsiru allowed himself to be pulled along, no more invested in our future than he had been since I had dropped him to the parlor floor in the broker's house.

There was a splintering, crashing impact behind us before we had taken a dozen steps. Whatever Clay was doing out in the ash, it hadn't diverted all the Rangers. Someone was trying to batter through the thick door.

I pushed Chitsiru faster, peering into the shadows, looking for some passage downward.

We had turned a corner, leaving the door and the pounding far behind, when I saw a dark passage between two stalls yawning to our left. I gave Chitsiru a shove and followed him into the darkness. There was no stairway, but a rickety old ladder thrust up out of a pitch-black shaft.

Chitsiru showed the first signs of initiative then, pushing away from the edge, his head shaking violently back and forth. He kept muttering a single, monosyllabic word under his breath that I thought must be the Comanche equivalent of no.

Or maybe hell no.

At that moment a rending crash rolled down the hall toward us, and I shook my own head.

"Hell yes." I spat and pushed him up against the ladder. The thin, foul-smelling young man fought me for a moment longer, sobbed, and then grasped the splintered rungs with desperate strength. After a few more moments of heartless prodding, he began his shaky descent.

As we made our way down, myself occasionally having to push on Chitsiru's head with my booted foot to prod him along, the sounds of soft cursing and frantic footsteps above us faded away. Below us, accompanying occasional gusts of warm, dry air, another sound was building. It was a strange, artificial sound accompanied by a distant, infernal roaring.

Eventually, after what felt like a lifetime of jerky, incremental descent, the man below me gave a soft cry and fell off to the side. As this wasn't accompanied by a horrifying, fading screech, I assumed we had reached the bottom and Chitsiru had collapsed with relief.

If we were at the bottom, we couldn't just sit on our petty victories. Anyone following us down into the mines, and they *would* follow us down eventually, would stumble over us without trouble if we stayed there.

We were in a fairly large chamber blasted from the living rock beneath Perdition. It was some sort of supply room, judging by the stacks of barrels and crates around us. Small oil lamps set in the walls glowed softly, casting no more light than was required to give the vague dimensions of the space and hints at the shapes of the piled objects around us.

A whicker behind me sent me whirling, clawing for the little pistol I had nearly forgotten over the course of the night's strains. It was, of course, a small set of stables housing several tiny horses akin to the one we had seen upon our arrival ... could it have only been a few hours before? The little animals barely came up to my hips and would be no use as mounts. The grinding, mechanical sounds, underlaid with that distant angry roar, were closer, coming from the deeper darkness of what must have been a passageway off to one side.

For the moment we were alone, with no one to help us; no one to follow. Somewhere above the Albion Rangers were closing in. Tillman Clay might be trying to help us somehow or he might have already headed back out to the encroaching ash wastes around Perdition.

Or he might be dead.

Monique and the Haitian Clay had called a revenant might—

I stopped that line of thinking before it could paralyze me with fear or the crushing despair, I could feel lurking around the edges of my awareness.

We were alone, for good or ill, and it was for me to decide what was to be done next.

A realization dawned bright enough that I almost winced, but I contented myself with a grim smile instead.

For less than a heartbeat I considered how to urge Chitsiru to his feet, then with a shrug dragged him up and pushed him in the direction of the deeper darkness.

"Wha—" He screeched as I gave him a shove, but he quieted almost immediately, most likely at the surprising echo of his own hapless voice.

Outside of our supply chamber was a corridor, rough-hewn stone walls marching off in either direction, each as likely as the other. The machine sounds seemed to be rumbling toward us from both directions, so I just picked one at random, left, and dragged my luckless companion along.

We would lose ourselves in the warren of old mining tunnels, and then we would see what we would see.

The sounds ahead got louder and for a few paces I took comfort in this, thinking that any errant sound we might make would be lost in the cacophony, our pursuers none the wiser. But then, with each step we took, as I strained to divine any special meaning from the grinding, hissing, roar, I realized that it would hide those pursuers just as surely, and the fear and chill returned despite the building heat.

Our corridor did not follow a straight path, but rather wound around, back and forth, as the old miners had followed a seam of coal deeper into the earth. When at last we rounded a corner to find the source of the sound, I realized I should have known what to expect long before.

Had Clay not told me the entire town was powered by massive steam engines? And would those steam engines not, most likely, be found beneath the town, where the power they generated could be distributed upward to wherever it might be needed?

The chamber we entered was enormous, as it would have to be. The engines were massive. They dwarfed the huge machines that had driven the *Joyeaux* or even the *Ett Hjerte* which had carried me across the Atlantic Ocean.

There were four, their pistons driving with a deafening hiss as the roar of the furnaces echoed off the far stone of the distant walls. Pipes disappeared up into the darkness overhead, and I thought I could make out black shafts up in the ceiling by the light of the lamps and the dull, angry red glow of the house-sized burners.

And beneath it all, running through the chamber below in a stone canal that would have made the Roman's proud, was the source of the bass note that carried the symphony of near-painful noise along. It was a river, captured somehow far overhead, probably from beyond the ash waste. This river had slipped beneath the surface somewhere far away, and then been channeled here by Man, the water both powering large metal waterwheels as well as being channeled into various container tanks for use by the steam engines.

The sound was deafening, but without any branches along our path, anyone tracking us would find us easily enough.

I looked around, letting Chitsiru collapse beside me. The steam engines were plenty large enough to hide behind, being, as they were, as near enough to twenty feet tall each as not to matter.

I spared a moment to wonder how the ravening appetites of the burners were fed without a crew of coalmen working tirelessly in the dark cave but knew there had to be some Albian trick to the machinery, and dismissed the thought with a savage, jealous snarl.

I grabbed my companion by his collar and dragged him along for a step or two, croaking all the way, until he was able to stagger to his feet and stumble after me into the shadows. We crossed a narrow bridge over the dark, swirling waters of the subterranean river. I tried to ignore what it might mean to fall into such a flow. I continued to pull him with me until we were behind the far machine, between it and the back wall of the cavern.

The heat was hellish; a sheen of sweat slicked Chitsiru's pallid face. As we stopped, hidden now from the mouth of the vast cavern, a dawning realization brought the light of fear and pain back into his dull eyes.

I could see in those darting black orbs what he had just realized. He knew what was going to happen next; he knew the bargain we had struck so far away and so long ago was about to come due. His next actions would betray his people, everything he believed in, everything he held sacred and dear in life.

And I would be damned if I was going to give him a choice in the matter.

Chapter 29

I realized I still had the little pistol in my hand, and rather than let the gesture go to waste, or seem indecisive in my actions, I raised it to point at the Chitsiru's chest.

"The ritual."

I hoped he wouldn't call my bluff. Not that I would have hesitated to kill in that moment. The world had wrung every last drop of human kindness from my heart. Fate's conspiracy against me, against my people and my homeland, had never seemed more plausible than in that furnace of a cave, surrounded by the infernal advancements of my enemy, betrayed and abandoned by every person who had seemed a friend in this half of the world.

But if I were to kill Chitsiru here it would mean cutting myself off from my last best hope. It would end here one way or the other, and for me to murder this man would be for me to admit defeat and consign not only myself, but England herself to oblivion.

Sweat and fat tears tracked lines through the grime and dust on the man's cheeks. He refused to look me in the eye, and I waved the pistol in his face, hoping I seemed threatening.

My voice, at least, must have carried the proper message. It shook with the passion of the moment.

"This is the time, Chitsiru. This is the place." I lowered the pistol but kept it within sight. I didn't want him to forget the weight of his next decisions. "Lead me through this ritual, or we're going to have a problem."

"You have a problem, Nicholas."

I had not thought to hear that voice again. I whirled, relief warring with fear.

It was Monique, standing behind us, the shimmering bulk of the nearest furnace close enough she could have reached out and seared herself on the metal. Her clothing was torn and scorched, her hair in wild disarray, but she was alive, she looked well enough, and she was pointing her huge cannon at my head.

Chitsiru cried out and shied away, huddling at the base of the nearest cave wall, hands over his head as if this might save him from such a formidable weapon.

But Monique had no care for the medicine man. She had eyes only for me.

I thought again how unlike Felicity she was. Her cold green eyes were hard with conviction, the set of her mouth as firm as the earth itself. Her outthrust arm did not waver, and the eternal depth of the pistol's barrel seemed to gape at me like the mouth of hell.

"Give me the stone, Nicholas. You have no idea what you are about to do; what it will cost you. You have no idea what it will cost us all." Her words were steady, reasonable, but they carried with them no sign of doubt or weakness.

I shook my head. "I can't. I won't. You heard Clay—"

"Tillman's not here, Nicholas. He doesn't understand. This has nothing to do with earthly freedom, or the childish vendetta you both feel for Albion. Albion doesn't matter in this at all. The stakes are higher than you can possibly imagine, and your immortal soul is not the least item on the scales."

I had to laugh at that. "My soul? What the hell do I care about my soul? What are you even talking about?"

I remembered the Haitian's words in the broker's parlor.

"Inquisitor."

Her head tilted so slightly I wasn't sure it even happened. "The stone must be delivered to Golgotha Keep. The Archbishop will see that it is secured against further interference. We cannot allow the gateway this would open to be disturbed."

I felt my burning brow furrow at her words, then my eyes widened at their deeper meaning. "You know what this is?" I held Merlin's stone up in my left hand. "You know what these are? You knew they existed, and what they can do?"

"They are Satan's tools on earth, Nicholas. They are bait in an ancient trap that has led too many men and women straight to hell. And with each new iteration of this old dance, countless thousands of innocents are dragged down as well."

Her eyes took on a desperate cast of their own. "Please, Nicholas. You don't know how dangerous those things can be. More and more are being found each year. When they were confined mainly to the Empire of the Summer Moon, we could let it go, monitor their use without resorting to all-out war to eradicate their poison. The Comanche and their brethren are fallen creatures, anyway, doomed to damnation for their pagan ways. But if Europeans discover their power, if the abilities unleashed by the unholy pact can be shaped by minds already open to science and study, there will be no telling where that might end." She took a step toward me. "It could mean the end of everything we know, and a thousand-year reign of darkness on the Earth."

That seemed wildly unlikely; her fear seemed to be rooted in the superstitions of the Church and not actual knowledge of the stones. But she did know *of* them; even more important, she seemed to have confirmed what Chitsiru had said about their usage, and their relationship to one attuned to their power.

I retreated, moving in a wide circle to keep away from the furnace, trying to keep the cooler stone of the chamber's wall by my side.

"Monique, I don't have a choice. This is my only chance. England's only chance." I brought my left hand behind my back as if that might somehow protect me; protect the stone from her determined gaze. "You have to let me do this. I won't turn back now."

She followed me, moving with the lithe grace of a stalking hunter. She shook her head. "I can't." It was nearly impossible to tell if those were tears coursing down her own cheeks; we were all sweating terribly.

I felt cold stone press against my back and realized I had circled myself into an alcove. Stone behind me, stone to either side, and no way out as Monique stopped in front of me, the ruddy glow of the furnaces casting red highlights through her hair.

"I'm sorry, Nicholas." Her gun rose again, and the note of finality in her voice was unmistakable.

I realized, then, that they *were* tears.

There was little consolation in that realization.

And then Monique jerked forward, stumbling to one knee, and the hand cannon went off with a deafening roar that cut through even the din of that place. A buzzing whine told me either the shot or a ricochet had come closer to my head than I would ever want, and I fell aside, hands over my ears in a futile attempt to protect myself from the noise, the bullet, or the woman's wrath; I wasn't sure which.

But there were no further shots. And there were no further words, either.

I peeked out from behind my raised arm to see Monique sprawled among the gravel and detritus of the cavern floor. She was still, unmoving, her hair spilled around her head like molten bronze.

Behind her, Chitsiru stood with a chunk of stone held loosely in one hand. Even as I watched, it dropped from his numb fingers, his body swaying with the sheer force of will it must have taken to pull himself out of the pit of his despair to take action.

I could not tell if Monique was alive or dead, and that terrified me. But not so much as the idea that she might get up again. She had planned to kill me. I had no doubt at all, and only the Comanche's sudden bout of bravery had saved my life.

I knew, too, that the power of the stones must be formidable indeed. If the Inquisition in the New World was so terrified of them that they would go to such lengths, there could be no doubt.

And she had said stones. She had known not only that there was one, but that there were many. I knew that already, of course, but hearing the words from her had carried even more weight than the evidence of my own eyes.

I rose, staggered over to Chitsiru, and grabbed him by the shoulders.

"Now!"

I had thought we might need to continue our flight, run from Monique in case she was only stunned, only to rise moments later and put a bullet through my eye.

Then I thought maybe I should shoot her where she lay, stunned or dead or feigning either. If England was, in fact, on the line, should I not be willing to go through any exigency to see to its safety?

But I could not. I would not.

I switched the stone into my right hand, holding its chain between my flesh and the pistol grip of the little weapon Monique herself had given me, and I bent down to pick up her own, far more formidable firearm. Its weight was immense, and I grunted as I stood.

Chitsiru backed away as I moved toward the bridge, and I decided not to disabuse him of his fear. I needed him moving. Moving and scared was better than just scared, no matter what he was afraid of.

At the bridge I looked back once. Monique had not moved. In the uncertain light I couldn't see if she was breathing or not. I hoped she was.

I threw her gun into the oily waters of the river and then pointed mine at Chitsiru again, forcing him backwards and to the far wall. He moved with broken indifference again, now; as if confronting Monique, even from behind, had been the high-water mark of his courage, and there was nothing left now.

If it was going to be done, it had to de done now. Before someone else found us, before another interruption. If the Albians or the Haitian stumbled upon us, I had no doubt they wouldn't have hesitated as Monique had.

I pursued Chitsiru until his back was against the far stone wall, again hidden from the chamber door.

"Now." I put the barrel of the derringer against his slick forehead. "Right now."

Chapter 30

The words meant nothing to me; meaningless syllables that refused to stay fixed in my mind for more than the space of time it took to utter them. Chitsiru needed to repeat them to me after each phrase, like a call and repeat round at a Christmas pageant.

He had said the meaning of the words was unimportant, that it was the effect the sounds, and the focus required to repeat them, had on my mind that needed He had tried to make some last-minute case against the effort, saying that these less-safe rituals favored by the outland nations within the Comanche empire were meant to be performed beneath the open sky and far from running water.

But I dismissed these as facile superstitions. There was a science at work here. I knew that. I had studied it. I understood the energy fields each living creature emanated, and I knew that the stones were merely keys to unlocking the power those fields might grant a focused, disciplined mind.

That last was more conjecture than fact, but I had run out of time to refine my theories any further.

Again, we ran through the harsh sounds of the ritual. I could discern no effect on my mind at all, only a rising exasperation. If this didn't work, if he was unable to grant me this final, desperate wish, I was going to throw him into the river and not look back.

We continued the recitation for what seemed like hours. The hand clutching my stone throbbed. Chitsiru had carved strange, outlandish symbols into the flesh of the palm there, pressing the stone into the rich, dark blood. He had used the small silver knife he had taken from the council of elders. I had seen, before the blade descended into my flesh, that there was a small sliver of stone in the handle, not unlike Cro's fighting knife. Again, he said the meaning of the symbols was less important than the connection between my blood and the stone, and the presence of the chip of stone within the handle of the little blade.

Important or not, the words burned, carrying with them a strange sense of violation I had never experienced before. Eventually, however, that strangeness wore off, leaving only the tedium of the throbbing pain and the continuous, senseless utterings.

My mind began to wander.

I saw Felicity again as if I were already back home. She was disappointed in me, of course. She was so often disappointed with me, especially in those last few years when my research and my theories had taken me so often away from home.

I saw my parents and all of their eminent friends, all staring at me with disdain and contempt. The strange boy so full of promise, who had gone all that way, had claimed to have such grand schemes and hopes, and it had all come to nothing.

I wanted to scream at them, to explain everything I had gone through, everything I had done, and been forced to do. I wanted to tell my parents everything I had seen of this New World, and all of the enemies Albion had created here in her very own back yard.

But they didn't care.

Chitsiru's words burned through me, carrying with them all the shame and anger of my failure.

I was nothing.

I was less than nothing; I was a stain on the honor of my family and my nation.

It was good that it would all end here, in this insufferably burning cavern so very far away from home.

The shame was like a fire in my heart.

And then the fire spread. Fanned by the words that coursed through my mind of their own accord, still meaningless, still mere jagged sound, but now excruciating in my throat, in my heart, in my blood.

The pain from my abused hand faded into the flare of the greater anguish.

I might have screamed then, I don't know. I don't remember. It would have made sense for me to scream, I am certain of that much, at least.

Somewhere far from the swirling fire and pain and disappointment and failure, I felt a distant shock to my knees.

I had fallen, I realized, without truly being conscious of the fact. I was kneeling in the rough gravel of the cavern floor.

It should have hurt. Most certainly would have destroyed the knees of my trousers, and gouged deep cuts into my flesh.

But this was all lost in the whirlwind of fire that had consumed my world.

The words echoed all around me now. The sounds of the furnaces, the river, the machinery that surrounded us was all drowned out. There was only the sound of the litany Chitsiru had drummed into my mind, dancing through my consciousness like a woman with blades for feet.

And still I said them.

Something dribbled over my lips.

Spittle, I hoped.

Blood, I feared.

What had Chitsiru said were my chances of survival? Fifteen in a hundred? Worse? And that had been the familiar ritual, conducted by people close with the earth. This mongrel version, passed down through the nations most affected by the Killer, were said to be far more dangerous.

And I knew there was no way to be farther from the earth than I.

All was pain, then. My world was fire. Fire of shame, fire of failure. Fire of helplessness.

I had been a fool to think I could do this. It had been hubris the likes of which the world had not seen in millennia.

I was going to die, and England was going to die with me. Everyone I knew, everyone I loved, was doomed, and they didn't even know it yet.

I had failed them.

They did know it. They were staring at me, disappointment glaring from their eyes. They watched as I writhed on the cavern floor, hopeless and helpless.

My heart was hammering against my breastbone, threatening to break through and join the fires that burned all around me.

The words.

The words were echoing the furious racing of my heart.

Or my heart was beating to the rhythm of those strange, alien, hurtful words.

My blood was on fire. My flesh was on fire.

I was being consumed, and no one of consequence would ever know what had happened, how close I had come. I was one of the weak, the pathetic, those who could not pass through the ritual and live.

Or maybe I could stop. Maybe I could cease the recitation that meant only my tortured death. Maybe if I stopped saying these hateful words, it would all end.

Maybe I could survive.

The glaring eyes of my parents, of my fiancé and my friends, loomed larger behind the wall of flames that engulfed me now. The contempt I saw there pained me more than the fire blazing within my chest and snaking through my limbs with tendrils of agony.

I tried to stop. God help me and save me from my own cowardice.

I tried to stop saying the words.

And my mouth continued to move. My throat continued to work despite having been seemingly stripped of every last scrap of flesh. My jaw moved of its own accord. My lungs labored to push air through the fire.

I did not stop.

I could feel tears course down my cheeks in a distant, foreign reality where skin still wrapped my tormented flesh.

I couldn't have screamed had I given into the bone-deep impulse. I knew it now. This was the energy field of my body being turned against me, undoing my being from the very essence of who I was.

Chitsiru had won, in the end. He had protected the sacred mysteries of his people and relegated me, the unbelieving foreigner, to damnation in the process.

I forced my eyes to open. It was the most difficult thing I had ever done. I glared at him, moving fearfully away from me into the shadows, through the shimmering haze of pure, unadulterated pain that radiated from the core of my soul.

I looked into his eyes, and I saw there what could only be a shimmer of triumph skulking behind the terror.

This was all by the man's design.

Movement behind him caught my attention despite the world-engulfing sensation of my burning.

A figure stepped out from behind the last boiler.

Waves of ruddy heat washing up behind the figure silhouetted its stained half-cape and the tricorn hat sitting at a crooked angle.

One hand, hanging casually at the figure's side, held a pistol even bigger and heavier than the weapon I had dropped into the river.

One eye flared out from the silhouette's shadow in triumph.

A screeching voice broke behind me. Chitsiru. He was screaming words at me now, fists balled up in impotent rage, spittle flying with each syllable, eyes nearly bursting from their sockets, as if desperate to finish.

Even within the prison of my tortured body, with all the sounds of my own damnation and death roaring in my ears, I could hear the explosive detonation as that enormous pistol fired.

The sound, the pain, the fire, and the rage rose to a crescendo, shaking the foundations of the world.

And then there was nothing.

Chapter 31

I came back to myself with a shuddering cough that seemed to rise from the soles of my feet. My body convulsed with my lung's desperate attempt to expel whatever had so offended it.

And with that convulsion, with the arching of my back and the clenching of my shoulders, my body screamed in anguish.

And I almost laughed. The sound was more of a tortured gasping wheeze, but the intention was the same.

I was alive.

I had survived whatever betrayal Chitsiru had intended.

As I remembered those last nightmarish moments of the ritual, I remembered the appearance of the Albian. There were enemies close at hand. Mortal enemies nearby who meant nothing but harm to me and mine, and I was as helpless as a newborn calf.

I struggled to rise and collapsed down onto my hands and knees, retching with the continued effort to breathe.

If the Rangers were in here with me, they would find me easy prey.

I do not know how long I stayed there, caught between rising and collapsing, taking careful, measured sips of air to test my protesting lungs.

It felt like an eternity.

There were new messages arriving in my mind as time stretched on, however. My knees were throbbing, and somehow that seemed right and proper.

My right hand was on fire, but this was a distant, pulsing burn rather than the torment of the hellfire through-which I had only just passed.

My hand.

My hand was injured.

I scrambled to my feet, clutching my ravaged hand tightly. Through the pain I could make out no sensation within the balled fist, I pried open my eyes, gummed closed by the combination of tears of pain and the dust and detritus of the cavern.

I could not see.

Had I gone blind? Had that been the ultimate price of my hubris? Was that going to be the lasting legacy of all my vaunted ambitions?

The pain was still coming, crashing over me in a tidal rhythm that seemed somehow to echo something larger looming over the cavern. That agony, somehow at once shared and isolating, made the darkness all the worse.

Something had killed the furnaces all around.

The silence encroached upon my slowly awakening mind. The roar of the furnaces, the grinding of the gears and the hiss of steam and water were gone.

I was in utter darkness, only the sound of the river, off to my right sliding inevitably down its stony course gave my world dimension and orientation.

I clasped my left hand over my burning right, feeling for something, anything, that might be hanging there.

There was nothing.

I pried open my right hand, desperately feeling for the stone with my left.

Nothing.

I fell once more to my hands and knees, scrambling in the jagged debris with both hands despite the utter lack of sensation in my right.

Tears coursed down my cheeks, my breath once more coming in ragged gasps.

All of this madness, and if I lost the stone, it had all truly been for nothing.

My left hand grazed against something smooth and cool. Something incongruous in that dark, hot hole.

My breath caught in my throat and I returned to that spot, heedless of the twinges from my knees. My right hand now clutched claw-like to my chest, useless.

My left found the inconsistent smoothness again. Something as fine as a spider's web brushed my fingertips and I clutched it. It came up heavier than it should have been.

The silver chain. It had to be. The silver chain with my stone hanging from the one end.

I cradled my right hand beneath my left and a dull sense of weight through my wrist told me something had landed there amidst the tormented flesh, sticky with blood.

I closed my stiff fingers around the stone and my tears were renewed, but this time with relief.

The litany of failures and setbacks that had brought me to that moment was phenomenal, but I had the stone once again and all would be well.

But only for that moment.

I stood, grunting with the effort. My back was bowed, my shoulders slumped, both my hands, now, the left cradling the injured right, were held to my chest as if clutching the last precious article of my life.

And they might well have been.

I had lost everything. From the betrayals and misdirection, the attacks and insults, I was left in that hot, moist cavern alone in the dark with my stone.

Heat rose again in my chest, but it was the merest echo of the roaring flames that had consumed me during the ritual. It was the fire of hatred, stoked anew by the surety of my failure.

I had come here, so far from Bromley, so far from my home, to learn about this stone, to decipher its secrets, the secrets of the ancients, and to unlock them for the betterment of my England.

I had come here to seize the future from the clutches of the demons of Albion and give my beloved home a chance one more.

And all of that had been stolen from me.

The heat I felt rising in my chest was the merest echo of the burning of the ritual, but it called that torment to my mind, and that only fed the anger even more.

I wanted to scream, but my voice was gone. Another casualty of this horrific ordeal?

But even as I hissed my fury into the darkness, I became aware of the strangest thing.

I could see the world around me again. The cavern walls were dim and indistinct, the boiler off to the side vague. Everything was limned in a ghostly blue glow whose shade and texture were strangely familiar.

The hissing of my failed scream faded into silence as I looked around me. The world continued to resolve itself.

My eyes adjusting to the darkness? But even then, there would have had to have been light coming from somewhere for my eyes to see anything at all.

There was no denying, I could see. More and more details emerged out of the darkness. A slumped shape before me, collapsed against the dark stones of the wall, had to be Chitsiru, and my anger burned even hotter.

But then I saw that he was looking at me, staring at me with wide, dull eyes.

He was dead. There was no doubt in my mind. And the glistening wetness, the jagged wrongness of the lines and contours of his chest, told me how. The Ranger's shot must have taken his heart and spread his blood across the wall behind.

I looked behind me, and there was the figure of the Ranger, his own cloak draped across his still body. He had been thrown against the boiler and fallen back to the hard, unforgiving ground. Stunned or dead I could not tell, but the sight of him sent the burning in my chest to new, triumphant heights.

The blue of the light enriched the azure wool of the man's cloak despite the layer of dust and ash.

My hands tingled.

It was not an unpleasant sensation but was utterly alien all the same. I looked down, and I gasped.

A ghostly blue flame wreathed my hands.

I held them up to my eyes, the light sending shifting shadows sliding all around me.

I opened first my left hand, then my right, to gaze down upon my stone, burning with a cool, dancing azure flame that tickled my flesh but nothing more.

The throbbing of my anger and my pain was still present, but now it was tamped down by the rising chorus of sheerest joy as I held the stone aloft.

I focused on the fire and it dimmed. I concentrated, and it rose again, higher than before. It danced to my will as I bent my mind to its ethereal shape.

I was the master of the stone.

I turned toward the Ranger, wondering exactly what else I might be able to do with my newfound power. Might I set the man on fire with actual flame? Could I cause him to dance and writhe to my whim?

Power arced from the stone, striking the boiler that loomed above me, grounding into scorched points along the cavern wall, and dancing along the outlines of my tormentor's still form.

I squeezed harder, heedless of the pain, and the lightning flashes lashing out from the gentle flames blazed with the strength of my hatred.

I gritted my teeth in triumph, focusing my will upon the prone form.

A soft moan rose up behind me and I whirled again, holding the stone higher still, worried, now, that I still might have no way to defend my newfound power.

Something moved in the shadows behind the silenced boiler, something pale and unsteady, rising from the ground.

The figure moaned again, and my eyes flicked to where Chitsiru still lay, regarding me with his dead eyes.

The shape took a step toward me, then another. My own pain and anger seemed to rise and fall with the rhythm of this stranger's unsteady whimpers.

I wished I still had my derringer, but I doubted I could have hit the boiler, never mind the figure beside it, with my injured right hand or my inept left.

The stone, almost as if responding to my doubts, flared anew, lashing out with bright whips of energy that snaps and hissed into the world around me.

I was truly something new, I realized. I was something that the Old World had not seen in a thousand years.

I wielded the power of nature as a tool or a weapon. I was changing the world around me with a thought.

Those ancient men and women would have called me a wizard, a sorcerer, a witch. And for the price of the energy I now wielded, I would have let them call me all that and more.

That was when I realized the intensity of the flame in my hand had now illuminated this new figure standing, gaping at me.

The man was nude. That was my first thought. How had a nude man found his way into this catacomb without my knowing it?

The hair on his head was wild, a dirty blond that soaked up the azure flavor of my flame and gave it back with bright golden highlights. Dark eyes stared at me in wonder and terror, his right hand, looking stiff and awkward, was held to his mouth as if to stifle any further cries of pain.

The man's nose was a blade above that clutching hand, sharp and aristocratic.

Dark blue eyes that glinted from my sapphire flames stared back at me with dawning horror. The light of my fire danced there in that darkness.

I gasped.

I stepped back, shocked.

I knew those eyes.

I knew that hair. I knew that nose.

I knew that stiff, injured hand.

The man standing before me, as naked as his birthday, was bleeding from several wounds, including ravaged knees that looked like they should have buckled long ago.

That right hand still curled before that familiar mouth, dripped blood.

No doubt from its ravaged palm, desecrated with pagan symbols sliced into the flesh.

I heard a gasp behind me, a muttered curse, and a scramble in the rubble of the floor; footsteps echoed across the chamber, over the bridge and out through the single entrance.

I couldn't bring myself to care.

I was staring into dark blue eyes the mirror of my own.

For those were my eyes. That was my hair, my nose. Those injuries were the self-same injuries that even now sent waves of agony through my own body.

That was me, standing there, staring at me.

That man was me.

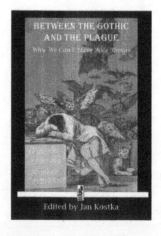

The City of the Old Gods

The Swords of El Cid

By

Robert E. Waters